NO COMPROMISE

"Get away from me." Her voice was a breathless whisper.

Curving an arm around her waist, he pulled her even closer. "Do you really want me to go away?" he asked, peering down at her through his lashes.

Their gazes met, fusing, each cataloging the gamut of emotions crossing the other's face, as they shared an intense awareness of each other. There was no denying the sensual magnetism pulling them together.

Jolene felt herself succumbing to his clean, masculine scent, the raw, unleashed power in the arm around her waist, and the shimmering gold undertones in his deeply tanned olive skin. The blood roared in her veins like molten lava, eliciting a giddying sense of physical arousal.

Michael stared down at the woman pressed to his chest, glorying in the crush of her breasts. He saw the rapidly beating pulse in her delicate throat, its pulsing matching the throbbing in his groin. He wanted her, wanted to make love to her on the grass, under the tree, with nature's glory as their silent audience.

Lowering his head, he took her mouth, gently, his tongue parting her lips. He swallowed her groan of delight as her arms came up and circled his neck. Curving one hand under her chin, he held her, making her his willing captive.

You're falling in love with her, a silent voice crooned to him. He didn't know how or why, but he wanted Jolene Walker in his life.

Books by Rochelle Alers

HAPPILY EVER AFTER
*HIDEAWAY
''First Fruits'' in HOLIDAY CHEER
HOME SWEET HOME
''Hearts of Gold'' in LOVE LETTERS
*HIDDEN AGENDA
*VOWS
*HEAVEN SENT
SUMMER MAGIC
**HARVEST MOON
**JUST BEFORE DAWN
**PRIVATE PASSIONS
***NO COMPROMISE

*Hideaway Legacy First Generation
**Hideaway Daughters and Sisters Trilogy
***Hideaway Sons and Brothers Trilogy

Published by BET/Arabesque Books

NO COMPROMISE

Rochelle Alers

BET Publications, LLC
http://www.bet.com
http://www.arabesquebooks.com

ARABESQUE BOOKS are published by

BET Publications, LLC
c/o BET BOOKS
One BET Plaza
1900 W Place NE
Washington, DC 20018-1211

All Kensington Titles, Imprints, and Distributed Lines are available at special quantity discounts for bulk purchases for sales promotions, premiums, fund-raising, and educational or institutional use. Special book excerpts or customized printings can also be created to fit specific needs. For details, write or phone the office of the Kensington special sales manager: Kensington Publishing Corp., 850 Third Avenue, New York, NY 10022, attn: Special Sales Department, Phone: 1-800-221-2647.

BET Books is a trademark of Black Entertainment Television, Inc. ARABESQUE, the ARABESQUE logo, and the BET BOOKS logo are trademarks and registered trademarks.

First Printing: February 2002
10 9 8 7 6 5 4 3 2 1

Printed in the United States of America

To Gwendolyn Osborne—aka Word Diva—
served up especially for you!

In the same way also, these people have visions which make them sin against their own bodies; they despise God's authority and insult the glorious being above. Not even the chief angel Michael did this. In his quarrel with the Devil, when they argued about who would have the body of Moses, Michael did not dare condemn the Devil with insulting words, but said, "The Lord rebuke you!"

—Jude 8–9

Good News Bible
(Today's English Version)

THE HIDEAWAY LEGACY

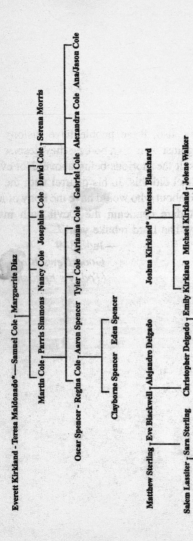

Everett Kirkland - Teresa Maldonado* — Samuel Cole ⊤ Marguerite Díaz

Martin Cole ⊤ Parris Simmons Nancy Cole Josephine Cole David Cole ⊤ Serena Morris

Gabriel Cole Alexandra Cole Ana/Jason Cole

Oscar Spencer - Regina Cole Aaron Spencer Tyler Cole Arianna Cole

Clayborne Spencer Eden Spencer

Matthew Sterling ⊤ Eve Blackwell Alejandro Delgado

Salem Lassiter ⊤ Sara Sterling Christopher Delgado Emily Kirkland ⊤ Michael Kirkland Jolene Walker

Joshua Kirkland* ⊤ Vanessa Blanchard

Isaiah Lassiter Eve/Nona Lassiter Alejandro Delgado II Esperanza Delgado Teresa Kirkland

*Illegitimate birth

Part One

The Courtship

One

"I can't believe you're actually leaving, sir."

United States Army Captain Michael Blanchard Kirkland glanced over his shoulder when he heard the familiar voice; his grim expression softened as he stared at his assistant standing at attention in the doorway of the small space he shared with another military aide. A slight smile tilted the corners of his firm mouth.

"At ease, Franklin." He turned back to filling the canvas bag on his desk. "You've got a serious case of denial."

Second Lieutenant Kyle Franklin stepped into the office and closed the door. His dark gaze lingered on the tall, perfectly proportioned physique of Michael Kirkland in civilian clothes. He'd seen his superior officer out of uniform many times over the past year, but only outside the Pentagon. The realization that Captain Kirkland was to begin an official leave of absence saddened him, because he'd enjoyed serving as his assistant.

"I just hoped you'd change your mind, sir."

Michael pushed a small leather-bound planner into the bag and zipped it. He was finished. Now, all he had to do was walk out of the world's largest office building, retrieve his car, drive to the 14th Street Bridge, cross the Potomac River, and make it to his residence in Georgetown and freedom.

He'd spent the past four years waging an undeclared cold war with General Harry Cooper—a war that could only end without a winner. General Cooper wanted from him what he was unable to give any man: his passion. That he reserved for women only.

At first he thought he'd imagined the two-star general's subtle interest in his private life, but as one year became two, three, and then eventually four, he knew that the older career officer would never approve his request to return to his former post as a highly trained military intelligence officer. And, because Coop, as most of his staff referred to him, had become more aggressive with his sexual advances, Michael had requested and was finally granted an official six-month leave.

Coop was livid once his aide had gone over his head to solicit the approval, but there was little he could do to contest it after the request was authorized by the head of the Joint Chiefs of Staff.

Lieutenant Franklin did not understand that he had to leave before he was court-martialed. And if General Cooper had made an attempt to physically touch him, he would've forfeited his life; what Michael had to decide was whether he would dispatch Coop quickly, silently, and mercifully, or make him suffer until he begged to die.

However, Captain Michael Kirkland had no intention of spending the rest of his life in a military prison, so he'd opted to temporarily walk away from a way of life that had become as essential to him as breathing. He loved every phase of the military—from the tactical maneuvers to the special training operations—as much as he loathed Harry Cooper for forcing him to retreat to civilian life, much like a coward deserting his post.

Reaching for a lightweight khaki jacket hanging from a coat tree, he slipped his arms into the sleeves, then, without a backward glance, walked out of the office and out of the Pentagon.

Quickening his pace, he made his way to the parking lot and his assigned parking space. Pressing a button on a keyless remote device, he opened a door to a late-model SUV and placed the bag behind the driver's seat before slipping behind the wheel; minutes later he left the boundaries of the Pentagon behind. Late-afternoon traffic moved quickly, and half an hour later he unlocked the door to the converted carriage house he'd purchased three years before. It was now his permanent and legal residence. It had become a sanctuary—a place where he shut out military deceit and simulations, but as he crossed the foyer and walked into the yawning space that had been set up as a living-dining room, it suddenly felt like it was a prison without bars. He had six months, one hundred eighty days, to decide whether he would continue his military career or become a civilian.

At thirty-two, he was still young enough to consider another career. His credentials were impeccable: He'd graduated with honors from the U.S. Military Academy at West Point, and during his tenure in Washington he'd returned to college and earned a law degree.

Running a slender hand over his coarse, black, close-cropped hair, Michael closed his eyes and inhaled deeply before slowly letting out his breath. He repeated the act a half dozen times, feeling some of his tension and anxiety easing. He opened his eyes and the clear green orbs shimmered with confidence under a sweep of incredibly long, thick black lashes. He wouldn't think of his future—not now.

A clock on the mantel of a massive fireplace chimed the quarter hour. It was five forty-five. He'd promised he would attend a surprise birthday celebration for his friend's mother. The engraved invitation indicated cocktails would be served promptly at seven.

Climbing a winding wrought-iron staircase that led to a loft containing a trio of bedrooms, he pulled the hem of his shirt from the waistband of his slacks. A slight smile curved his mouth. A social gathering was what he needed to take his mind off his uncertain future. It had been months since he'd accepted a social invitation, and he knew the McDonald soiree would only be a temporary diversion; but he was willing to accept anything at this time.

He would take the time given him, and before his leave ended he would determine where life would direct him.

The telephone rang, startling Jolene Walker. She'd been so absorbed in writing the first draft of a grant proposal that she'd shut out everything around her. It rang again, the flashing light indicating the call had come in on her private line. Glancing at the small brass clock on her desk, she noted the time, frowning. It was 4:30. How had the afternoon slipped away so quickly?

Picking up the receiver before the third ring, she said softly, "Jolene Walker."

"Jolene, it's Stuart."

Vertical lines appeared between her large, expressive dark eyes. She'd registered a tremor in his voice. "What's the matter?"

"I'm calling from the emergency room at Johns Hopkins."

Her pulse skipped a beat. "What happened?"

"It's Keisha. She fell out of a tree at her grandmother's and broke her wrist. Trina called me at work, hysterical. I had to come. I'm sorry about tonight. I've decided to spend the night in Baltimore. I don't want to leave Keisha right now." His words were running together.

"Don't apologize, Stuart. Your daughter needs you." What she didn't say was that Keisha's mother probably needed him, too. "And please don't worry about tonight."

A heavy sigh of relief came through the earpiece. "Thanks, Jolene. You've just taken a lot of pressure off me."

"Stuart?"

"Yes?"

"May I make a suggestion?"

"Sure. What?"

"I think you and Trina should consider a reconciliation."

A profound pause followed. "I . . . we've talked about it a few times."

"Talk some more," she suggested in a soothing tone.

"Maybe I can get her to agree to come with me to see you for marital counseling."

"I can't be your therapist. It wouldn't be ethical."

"Why not?"

"We're seeing each other."

"That's true. But remember, Jolene, we're not sleeping together."

"It doesn't matter. You and I have a personal association. If you're serious, then I can always recommend another counselor."

"I'll talk to Trina and see what she says. I've got to go. The orthopedist just walked in."

The call ended with a dial tone. He'd hung up abruptly. Raising her eyebrows, Jolene held the receiver for several seconds, then replaced the receiver in its cradle. Now she was faced with her own personal dilemma. She needed a date for a catered dinner party.

Drumming her fingertips on a stack of papers, she closed her eyes. She could call and cancel, but quickly dispelled the notion. Claire McDonald was board chairperson of the organization that employed Jolene as its executive director. Not attending Claire's birthday celebration, even if it was a surprise, would be tantamount to treason.

She opened her eyes. It was two and a half hours before the affair, too late to call anyone to fill in for Stuart—not that she had a list of names of men who were beating down her door to date her. That time had passed.

After she'd ended her marriage to Cheney Clarke, there had been a number of single, African-American men in the nation's capital and surrounding environs who'd openly admitted they'd been waiting until her divorce was finalized; men who were more than aware that her marriage had been doomed even before it began. But this was now, five years later, and she didn't have a date for tonight. She had only agreed to go out with Stuart Richardson because it was mutually agreeable. He did not want to get too involved, and neither did she.

Pulling her lower lip between her teeth, she knew she had to think of a solution—quickly. As a social worker, she had pat answers for everyone but herself. Shaking her head, she reached for the telephone and punched in a number, waiting for a familiar voice.

"Sutton residence."

A smile parted her lips once she heard the greeting. "I have a problem, Paige."

A throaty feminine laugh came through the wire. "If you have a problem, then the world must be coming to an end."

"I'm not kidding," Jolene said. The three words came out between clenched teeth. "I don't have a date for tonight."

"I thought you were coming with Stuart."

"His daughter had an accident."

"Was it serious?"

"She broke her wrist."

"That is serious. You're still coming, aren't you?"

"That's why I'm calling. I—"

"I *know* you're not going to miss my mother's party just because you don't have a date," Paige said, interrupting her.

"It was you who insisted upon having couples."

"And I will have couples. Last night when I went over the guest list with my socially deficient brother, he informed me that he'd invited a guy he met when he attended graduate school in Japan."

"Is this guy coming unescorted?"

"That's what he told Damon."

Jolene let out her breath in an audible sigh. At least she wouldn't have to sit at a table by herself. Paige's invitation indicated a dinner party featuring a French theme: bistro tables with two chairs at each were to be set up on the Suttons' expansive outdoor patio, with a medley of French dishes, desserts, wines, and champagnes to be served.

"What does he look like?"

"I don't know. But we'll find out soon enough."

"I'm certain we will." There was a hint of laughter in Jolene's voice. "I'll see you at seven."

Ending the call, she put her desk in order. As the director of an agency offering comprehensive services to substance-abusing, battered women, she had dedicated her life to the clients who sought to reclaim their lives through sobriety and empowerment. Her dedication to her career was complete and absolute. She'd sacrificed her own short-lived marriage, spent most of her savings, and continued to forfeit a conventional social life in order to make the Sanctuary an ongoing success.

Her platonic relationship with Stuart was straightforward and undemanding. He was still in love with his ex-wife, and Jolene had no desire to remarry. They shared dinner, an occasional movie or concert, ending each date with a chaste kiss and a promise to do it again.

She'd given Paige her word she would attend the surprise dinner party because she'd declined two prior events hosted by her best friend. A knowing smile curved her lush mouth. Paige was definitely her mother's daughter. She, too, had become a D.C. social maven.

Claire McDonald née Nelson and her husband, Walter, were descendants of two of the oldest and most prominent Washington, D.C., African-American families. And the prerequisites for becoming a Nelson or a McDonald had been established more than a century ago: marry well, marry educated, and marry light—the lighter the better. There were a few members from both families who were so fair in coloring that some had passed over into the white race. However, most conformed to the established family rules— except Paige. She had fallen in love with a dark-skinned man who, at the time, was a detective with the Chicago Police Department.

Claire had barely recovered from her daughter's insubordination when she'd had to cope with the announcement that her son, Damon, had proposed marriage to Melissa Kyoto. Damon had met Melissa after she'd come to the States to pursue a medical career. His love affair with all things Japanese had extended to an affair of the heart. It was said that a collective groan of despair was released from young, single D.C. African-American women everywhere once Damon's engagement made the society section of the *Washington Post*.

Gathering her handbag and leather tote, Jolene wondered if Damon's friend was Japanese. She'd never dated any man outside of her own race, but there was always the first time. After all, she mused, it was only for one night.

Two

Jolene walked to the door of the office bearing her name and position, flicked a wall switch, turning off an overhead light, and then closed the door softly behind her.

An eerie silence greeted her. She was the last one in the building. All of the support and clinical staff had left for the weekend. The Sanctuary operated out of a spacious converted two-story, two-family dwelling on a quiet street several blocks from the Dupont Circle Metro station. It blended in well with the neighborhood's many bookstores, cozy cafés, elegant restaurants, art galleries, and funky bars. She doubted whether many neighborhood residents or business people were aware that the treatment program offered women who came through its doors a safe haven and a few hours of respite from whatever awaited them once they returned to their own homes.

Pressing several buttons on a panel near the rear door, she activated the silent alarm system and closed the self-locking door. She made her way to the staff parking lot, and a minute later started up her seven-year-old Toyota. An intermittent grinding sound reminded her that she had to look for a new car. The timing belt was severely worn. Her mechanic had warned her that the vehicle was in its death throes, yet she hadn't taken time to follow up on his suggestion.

This weekend, she told herself. It had to be soon because she doubted the car would last another week.

She let out an audible sigh as she backed out of the parking lot. Her life was resuming a semblance of order. At the beginning of the summer she'd returned to the gym to work out, cut her hair—which provided her with an additional quarter of an hour each morning—stopped skipping meals, and agreed to date again. Stuart Richardson was the perfect choice; he'd become an escort rather than a boyfriend. This arrangement fit perfectly into her plans, because there was no room in her busy schedule for romance or an intense relationship.

Ignoring the noise coming from under the hood of the Celica, she avoided the curious gazes of other drivers and passersby, and the startled expressions of those sitting on benches around the fountain. Barring a traffic jam, she could expect to arrive at her apartment in a newly renovated three-story Georgetown brownstone within ten minutes.

A red light stopped her progress and a young man on a moped eased up beside her, his teeth showing white against his smooth dark brown skin. "Hey, beautiful. I've got an extra helmet and room for one more," he crooned, winking and offering a seductive grin. "Your hoopty don't sound too swift."

Jolene forced back a smile, shaking her head. "No, thank you."

"Just thought I'd ask," he countered.

"Damn," she whispered under her breath when he sped away, weaving in and out of two lanes of traffic.

The light changed and she took her foot off the brake, easing it onto the gas pedal, hoping to lessen the ear-shattering rattle. Even a guy on a motorized scooter believed his mode of transportation was better than her car. In a way she had to admit it was. At least his bike didn't contribute to the city's noise pollution. She managed to go about ten feet before stopping for another red light. Rush-hour traffic had slowed to a crawl.

She'd balked at getting rid of the car because it had once belonged to Jeanine. It represented the last tangible link to her identical twin. Beautiful Jeanine Moore, who'd died too young. Vivacious Jeanine, who'd lived too fast, existing on the edge, testing the limits, and in the end lost everything she'd ever wanted at the hands of an abusive husband.

Blinking back tears, Jolene stared through the windshield. A cacophony of car horns jolted her out of her reverie. The light had changed again. It was early August, and a Friday afternoon in Washington, D.C. Government workers were pouring out of the Dupont Circle Metro station; cars with out-of-town plates, filled with tourists, added to the traffic nightmare. Most drove at less than fifteen miles an hour, craning their necks to get a glimpse of the places of interest detailed in their guidebooks, while the heat and oppressive humidity—which were as much a part of the city's summer personality as was the Capitol building, White House, or the Washington Monument—added to the orderly chaos of her adopted home.

Jolene finally left the circle, and the bumper-to-bumper traffic eased before disappearing like a puff of magical smoke. She entered the city limits of Georgetown, maneuvering along a quiet tree-lined street and parking in front of her building. Glancing at her watch, she noted the time. She would take a leisurely bath before readying herself to attend the surprise birthday celebration for Claire McDonald. She did not have to rush; the Suttons lived six blocks away in a well-preserved Federal-style residence on two acres of landscaped property that had become the envy of their neighbors.

Slipping out of the Toyota, she gathered her bags, closing the door with a solid slam. She walked up the steps to the brownstone and opened the front door, stopping in the vestibule to pick up her mail before continuing up three flights of stairs to a spacious two-bedroom apartment. She liked living on the top floor. It provided her with ultimate privacy, she didn't have to contend with someone stomping over her head, and climbing the staircase was the perfect complement for her twice-a-week workout sessions at the local gym.

Shifting her tote and handbag, she turned a key in the lock, pushing open the apartment door. Afternoon shadows pouring through floor-to-ceiling windows bathed everything in a warm, golden glow. Closing the door with her shoulder, Jolene dropped her keys and mail on a small table in the entryway. The tote slid to the highly polished parquet floor beside the table. Her handbag found its place on a straight-back chair, and she slipped off her sandals and placed them beside the tote. Relieving herself of her shoes concluded her daily homecoming ritual.

Walking in bare feet across the cool wood floor was comforting and refreshing as she made her way into the bathroom. She had to select a dress for the evening's festivities. A slight smile tilted the corners of her mouth. *A blind date!* She was thirty years old and she was going to have her first blind date. A shiver of anticipation shimmered through her. She looked forward to the evening with an excitement usually reserved for high-school girls going to their senior prom.

Reaching for a glass jar filled with crystal bath salts, Jolene turned on the faucets in the antique claw-foot tub, adjusted the water temperature, and then poured a handful of crystals under the running water. The space was quickly filled with the calming scent of lavender. She stripped off her clothes, leaving them on a padded corner bench. Before returning to the tub, she pressed a button on the small radio on a nearby shelf, then stepped into the tepid water and sat down. Her lids came down as she closed her eyes, willing her mind blank.

Within minutes she forgot the victimized women who sought refuge at the Sanctuary. She forgot last night's telephone call from her mother that had informed her that Lamar Moore was scheduled for parole at the end of September. What she couldn't and refused to forget was Lamar Moore's involvement in Jeanine's suicide. He hadn't pushed her sister off the balcony of her high-rise apartment building, but Jolene held him responsible because he'd violated a court order of protection to stay away from his estranged wife.

Lamar had sobbed out his innocence as he'd been led out of the courtroom after his sentencing hearing. His protests had not affected Jolene—not until he'd turned and glared at her through his tears. She'd recognized hatred and something else. The something else was death. Their gazes had locked for several seconds before he'd issued a soft threat, the words chilling her, not permitting her to move or breathe. And she would remember them to her grave: *"I didn't kill the bitch, but I promise when I get out I'm going to kill you!"*

His threat had echoed in her head for weeks; she'd lay awake at night, crying and reaching for Cheney. But Cheney wasn't there to hold her, to protect her, so she'd cried alone, completely vulnerable. Her loathing of Lamar Moore had waned over the years, replaced by an invisible fear that he would eventually carry out his threat against her life, and the fear had changed her completely.

She'd decided to live permanently in D.C., and had begun an intensive regimen of self-defense courses. The only thing she refused to do was learn to use a handgun.

The soothing sounds of a familiar song came through the radio's speakers, and she hummed along, concentrating solely on the lyrics. It took about ten minutes, but after a while she even forgot Lamar's deadly threat.

Twilight wrapped itself around the sprawling patio like a diaphanous veil, as a sprinkling of stars emerged in the darkening navy blue night sky. Dozens of flickering oil candles, strategically positioned lanterns and floodlights, a dozen bistro tables with seating for two, and the soft sound of taped music filled the rear of the Sutton property; muted conversations were swallowed up against the backdrop of the familiar strains of a classic Miles Davis jazz composition.

Michael Kirkland accepted a glass of wine from the bartender, turned, and then saw her. He stepped away from the portable bar and froze. Nothing moved, not even his eyes. He hadn't realized he'd been holding his breath until he felt the tightness burning his lungs, forcing him to exhale.

The wineglass in his left hand remained untouched as he watched the tall, slender, sable-skinned woman curve a bare arm around Paige Sutton's neck while pressing her cheek to her hostess's soft, scented one.

She's stunning! he mused.

The woman smiling at Damon's sister was tall, dark, and shockingly beautiful. Natural arching black eyebrows set off a pair of large slanting eyes that crinkled in a most beguiling smile as she spoke quietly with her hostess. Her coloring was a startling contrast to Paige's pale skin. Her eyes were also dark, much darker than her flawless mahogany complexion.

She turned her head slightly, permitting him an unobstructed view of her face. It was a perfect oval. Her cheekbones were high, her nose delicate. However, it was her mouth—full and arrogant, an arrogance that gave it the look of a perpetual pout—that garnered his rapt attention. The burgundy color on her lush lips highlighted and complemented her rich brown complexion.

His lazy, penetrating gaze lingered on the raven black hair cut close to her well-shaped head before shifting to the area below her neckline. The de rigueur sleeveless *little black dress* claimed a square neckline that hinted of a soft swell of breasts each time she inhaled; the crepe de chine fabric skimmed her curvy body, ending at her knees.

His gaze drifted downward to her long bare legs. Her calves were well developed, ankles slender. They reminded him of a dancer's legs. A hint of a smile barely touched his firm mouth when he noted the burgundy color on her groomed toes in a pair of black sling-strap, high-heeled silk-covered sandals.

Sweet heaven! Even her feet were beautiful.

Michael Kirkland was cognizant of every component of his personality, making him who he was, and what he admired most was beauty: a country's topography and natural wonders, its history, language, its arts, and women—especially its women. He'd traveled the world, losing track of the number of countries he'd visited in his lifetime; but the woman talking to Damon's sister was the most exquisite female he'd ever seen.

Was she the woman Paige said had come unescorted? Was she to be his date and dining partner for the evening?

Raising his glass, he took a sip of the cool wine, his gaze

never wavering. He knew it was impolite to stare, but at that moment he couldn't help himself. Unconsciously he willed her to turn around and meet his admiring gaze.

Paige's soft gray eyes narrowed attractively as she smiled at Jolene. "You look fabulous with short hair." She ran a hand through a wealth of unruly reddish-brown curls falling over her forehead. "I'm thinking about cutting this mop very short, but I don't have your face."

Jolene stared at her best friend. Paige McDonald-Sutton was more attractive than pretty. Her bone structure was too pronounced, her face too angular. Her eyes were her best feature. They were a cool, clear gray. She was a more feminine version of her father, while Damon had inherited his mother's striking beauty. Paige was of medium height, and her slightly rounded body was artfully concealed under a black linen tunic with a pair of matching slacks. She was three months pregnant.

She and Paige had met as undergraduates at the University of Chicago. Paige was a pre-med major while Jolene's concentration was social work. Paige had spent more time sleeping at the Walkers' modest ranch-style home in a Chicago suburb than she had in her dorm room. Their close relationship had ended once Jolene had graduated and moved to New York to pursue a graduate degree in social work while Paige had entered the college's school of dentistry for a specialty in oral surgery. After completing her residency and internship in Chicago, Paige had returned to Washington, D.C., with a degree and a husband.

Jolene had reconnected with her friend after accepting a position as a school-based social worker at a Washington, D.C., high school. Three months after she'd officially became a D.C. resident, she'd met, fallen in love with, and married Cheney Clarke. The brilliant, charming legal consultant had appeared to have everything she'd wanted in a husband and partner—everything except sensitivity and generosity. He'd refused to share her with anyone or anything, and that included her family; their marriage didn't survive a year because whenever Jeanine had called, she'd come. Cheney had stubbornly refused to understand why Jeanine was unable to leave an abusive husband. He'd finally issued an ultimatum: him or Jeanine.

Jolene had refused to abandon her sister, and in the end everyone became a loser. Jeanine Walker-Moore lost her life at twenty-five, Lamar Moore was sentenced to serve five years in an Illinois state prison, the elder Walkers lost a daughter, she lost her twin and only sibling, and her marriage ended when Cheney filed for a divorce, citing irreconcilable differences.

"Why don't you wait until after the baby's born to have your hair restyled?" Jolene suggested. "I'll treat you to a day spa for a complete beauty makeover."

Paige laughed, the soft sound of her voice carrying easily in the warm night. "You're on, girlfriend." She wound her bare arm through Jolene's. "Let's see if I can find your date." Her gaze swept over the assembled guests. Aside from Jolene, her brother and future sister-in-law, and Damon's friend, all of the guests were her parents' close friends and business associates.

Leaning closer, Jolene whispered, "Don't tell me he's the one with the corporation up front and the comb-over do?"

Paige recognized the short, portly, partially balding man standing at the bar. He was a special assistant with the FBI. "Not quite. Your date is the complete opposite of him."

"Are you saying he's the frog after the princess kisses him?"

"I don't think he was ever a frog, Jolene." She took several steps. "He was standing right here before you came in."

"Where's your brother?"

"Damon went to pick up my parents. They think he and Melissa are taking them out to dinner. Let me ask Kevin if he's seen him. Meanwhile, why don't you get a drink from the bar?"

Jolene walked over to the bar and ordered a sparkling water with a twist of lemon. While the bartender prepared her beverage, she studied the small group who'd come to the buffet birthday celebration. She recognized a diplomatic attaché from the Japanese consulate, and his wife. She'd met Mr. and Mrs. Reiko Ezawa at a prior McDonald soiree. She inclined her head in acknowledgment when the elegant attaché bowed politely.

Her gaze shifted to a tall man dressed in an expertly tailored dark suit with a double-breasted, single-buttoned jacket, standing several feet behind the Japanese couple. Even though the patio was brightly lit, his face was shadowed. She had the uncanny feeling that he was staring directly at her. She shivered noticeably, the curling hair rising slightly on the nape of her neck. At that moment she wanted to look away, but couldn't. It was only when the bartender handed her her drink that she was released from the spell.

Her attention was redirected when Kevin walked out onto the patio with Paige. They were a striking couple. Forty-year-old Kevin Sutton was ten years his wife's senior. Tall, dark, and extremely good-looking, Kevin completely ignored Paige's family's critical assessment of his less-than-prominent ancestry. Claire McDonald's stance had softened noticeably once Paige had announced that she was going to have a child; after all, the baby would claim the bloodlines of the Nelsons and the McDonalds. Kevin, a detective assigned to the homicide unit of the D.C. Police Department, was still quite formal with his in-laws, but hinted he would offer an olive branch after the birth of his son or daughter.

Kevin smiled at Jolene, lowering his head to press a kiss to her cheek. "I'm glad you came. Paige wanted me to introduce you to everyone. I believe there may be several people here tonight you do not know."

Jolene wanted to meet the man with the mysterious energy. She went through the motions of shaking hands and repeating polite phrases with the small group of eighteen. All were dressed in what she thought of as after-five casual chic. Their understated haute couture had not come off department-store racks. It was obvious that most frequented the specialty shops along Connecticut Avenue and the array of sophisticated boutiques in the Georgetown Court.

Several waiters meandered around the patio, carrying trays, offering appetizers of traditional French foie gras with celery and walnuts, salmon tartar with smoked salmon served with a red onion caper sauce, *tellines à l'arlésienne*—sautéed garlic clams—and moules farcies—gratinéed mussels on the half shell.

Again, she felt the short hair rise on her nape. Shifting, she made an attempt to turn around and was thwarted by a solid object. She moved to her left, but couldn't escape. A large clay planter blocked her way.

"Don't turn around," crooned a deep male voice close to her ear. There was a slight trace of a Southwest intonation in the command. The timbre of the voice reminded her of Avery Brooks.

It was he! She knew instinctively it was the man who'd stood in the shadows staring at her. He was her date!

"Who are you?" She didn't recognize her own voice. It had dropped an octave, quivering slightly as if she were out of breath.

"I was going to ask you the same question." His warm breath caressed the left side of her neck, feathering over a bare shoulder.

He moved closer, the heat from his body searing her flesh through the delicate fabric concealing her nakedness from him and the world. She hadn't realized he was so tall. She stood over six feet in her heels, and he towered above her by at least another three inches.

"You could've found out who I am if you hadn't run away when Kevin made his introductions," she countered.

Michael stared at the soft glossy curls covering her head, pushing his hands into the pockets of his trousers. At that moment he did not trust himself *not* to touch her.

"I didn't run away. It's just that I prefer making my own introductions."

He'd just revealed a lot about himself. He was used to being in control. She wanted to turn around to see the face that matched the deep baritone voice, but she was enjoying their subtle cat-and-mouse game. It had been a long time—too long—since she'd flirted with a man.

"Why?" she asked.

"When I see something I like, I don't like a go-between."

Her professionally waxed eyebrows shifted slightly. "You like what you see?"

"Very much."

He was direct—very direct and very different from most men she'd met over the years. "Are you always so narcissistic?"

"Narcissistic? I think not. I'm just candid."

It was time for her to take control of the game. It was time for it to end.

"Well, Mr. Candid, will you show yourself, or are we going to continue to play twenty questions?"

She held her breath as the stranger shifted his position until he stood in front of her, less than a foot away. A slight smile touched her lush mouth. She was right. He was tall—very, very tall, at least six-three, maybe six-four. Her breath caught in her chest, her smile wavering and disappearing completely the instant her gaze came to rest on his face.

Three

She extended her hand, the motion stiff, mechanical, arm jerking as if a puppeteer had pulled a marionette's string. "Jolene Walker."

Her fingers were enveloped in a warm, protective grip; a hint of a smile played at the corners of her admirer's mouth when he stared down at her.

"Michael Kirkland, Miss Walker. It is *Miss* Walker?"

Tilting her chin slightly, she gave him a direct stare. "Yes, Mr. Kirkland."

She schooled her expression not to reveal her stunned entrancement as she studied Michael Kirkland's perfect symmetrical features. They were as delicate as a woman's—high cheekbones blending into a lean jaw and a strong chin. His firm mouth, neither too full nor too thin, was undeniably masculine, and the raven black, short-cropped hair falling in layered precision against his scalp reminded her of a seal's coat. However, it was his eyes that mesmerized her. They appeared a clear leaf-green, framed by long black lashes, shimmering like precious jewels in his sun-browned face.

Extracting her fingers, she effected a courteous smile. "Nice meeting you, Michael."

He inclined his head. "My pleasure. I was told that we would share a table tonight."

"That is also my understanding." She wanted to look away, but couldn't. There was something in his entrancing, questioning gaze that was hypnotic. She arched her right eyebrow. "Is something the matter?"

Lowering his head, Michael stared at the toes of his highly polished slip-ons. He was smiling when he glanced up at her again. "I was just wondering why a woman who looks like you do couldn't get a date for tonight."

Vertical lines appeared between her large eyes. "Who told you I couldn't get a date?"

"Paige mentioned that you couldn't find a date."

Her chest rose and fell heavily, drawing his gaze to linger on the spot below her throat. Did he believe she was such a loser that she couldn't find a man to accompany her to a dinner party?

"I had a date."

Michael watched the rapidly beating pulse in her throat. Jolene Walker wasn't as calm as she appeared. When he'd stood in the shadows watching her, she'd reminded him of a black diamond: dark, beautiful, but cold to the touch. Apparently there was some warmth beneath the poised exterior.

"He stood you up?"

Her lips thinned noticeably. How was he—a stranger— so perceptive? "No, he didn't. He had a family emergency. What about yourself?" she asked, deciding to turn the tables on him. "Why didn't you bring a date?"

He took a step forward, bringing him only inches from her. It was then that she recognized his cologne. It was the masculine counterpart to hers: Thierry Mugler's Angel. She found it hard to draw a normal breath. Michael Kirkland was too close, his presence too powerful.

"I didn't bring a date because right now I'm not seeing anyone." And he wasn't seeing or sleeping with a woman— hadn't been in months. He hadn't needed any distractions. Not when his future was so uncertain. He'd needed all of his energy and concentration, and most women he'd dealt with in the past required a lot of time and attention—attention he was unable to give them.

"All work and no play makes for a very dull existence."

He forced a half smile. "I don't know about being dull, but I can assure you that when I play, I play very, very hard." *And I also play for keeps,* he added silently. "How hard do you play, Jolene?"

She folded a hand on her slim hip. "Not as hard as I should."

"Why not?"

"Because for me it's been all work and very little play."

"We're going to have to do something about that."

Again, her eyebrows rose in a questioning expression. "How?"

Lowering his lids, Michael stared at Jolene's startling beauty, deciding he liked her. He found her lovely, intelligent, and quick with a retort. He would be hard pressed to intimidate her.

He'd met so many insecure women that he believed he'd become jaded. Some of them wanted to please so badly that they usually compromised themselves. His mother and sister complained that he was too selective, and that he would end up a frustrated old bachelor. He was quick to remind his mother that his father had been thirty-eight when he'd married her. Vanessa Kirkland usually gave him a look that indicated *end of discussion.*

"I'll have to show you."

She shook her head. "Sorry, Michael, but I'll pass."

Crossing his arms over the front of his crisp white shirt, he cocked his head at an angle. "Don't be so quick to refuse before you hear what I'm about to offer."

"I'll still pass."

Reaching for her free hand, he folded it in the crook of his arm. "We'll discuss it another time."

She attempted to free her hand, but he tightened his grip. It was not enough to hurt her, but it silently confirmed that he was much stronger than she was.

Her delicate nostrils flared slightly as she struggled to control her temper. "You are that certain there'll be another time?"

He nodded slowly. "Very certain, Jolene."

Whatever she was going to say was preempted by the appearance of Claire McDonald. Her husband stood behind her, grinning from ear to ear. The flash of light from a camera temporarily blinded her as everyone shouted, "Surprise!" The invited guests milled around Claire, laughing at her shocked expression.

Claire's large gray eyes filled with tears. Walter McDonald handed his wife his handkerchief, watching as she touched a corner to her eyes. Paige leaned against Kevin, smiling at her mother, while Damon curved an arm around his fiancée's shoulders.

Claire placed a manicured hand over her ample bosom, which was covered in a flattering shade of royal blue silk. "I'm truly surprised. I can't believe no one let the cat out of the bag." She turned to her husband. "I suppose you knew about this?"

"Of course."

Walter McDonald's resonant voice carried easily. At seventy, he still turned heads whenever he entered a room. Tall, with a full head of white wavy hair, he'd retired as federal judge six months before. He and Claire had met as college freshmen when he'd attended Morehouse and she Spelman. Lowering his head, Walter kissed her gently on the lips.

Claire blushed furiously, turning to quickly embrace her daughter and son-in-law. "Thank you for honoring me with your presence tonight," she said to the assembled. "And before the evening ends, I'm going to come around and thank everyone individually." Paige leaned forward and whispered to her mother. "I've just been informed that the caterers are ready to begin serving. *Bon appétit.*"

Jolene jumped when Michael released her hand and wound his arm around her waist. The motion brought her closer to his body, their shoulders brushing, and she pulled away as if a raging fire had scorched her.

"Come sit down and I'll serve you." He led her to a table in a secluded corner of the patio. Michael pulled out a cushioned wrought-iron chair, seating her; it was then that she realized her heart was pounding an erratic rhythm; she felt the thumping in her chest at the same time it echoed in her ears.

She wanted to jump up and escape into the night, because she'd spent five years telling herself that she didn't want a man, didn't need a man, that there was no room for romance in her busy schedule. She'd devised so many clever diversions that she'd become an expert in keeping any and every man she'd encountered at bay.

The women who came to the Sanctuary for counseling had become the sister she'd lost—a woman who'd died too young. The women needed her, but she also needed them; she needed them to help her exorcise her own personal ghosts.

But within the span of less than thirty minutes the presence of one man had forced her to acknowledge her femininity. All he had to do was stare at her and a terrifying awareness attacked her; for the first time since her divorce she was forced to recognize her own physical needs.

Jolene stared at Michael as he strolled across the patio. Even his walk was sexy. His spine was straight as a soldier's, while his broad shoulders swayed with a slight swagger. She studied him freely, finding him physically perfect—as perfect as a man could get. Why, she wondered, wasn't he seeing a woman? Men who looked like Michael Kirkland did not roam around unattached for long.

What was he hiding? Was there something aberrant under his arrogant manner, tailored clothes, and sensual voice? Was he like the boyfriends or husbands of the women who came to the Sanctuary—abused women favoring sunglasses to conceal blackened eyes, those with rehearsed excuses about how they'd sustained broken arms and jaws and concussions? Women whose boyfriends and husbands took their rage and frustration out on those they claimed to love with their fists, and at times other objects?

Stop it, Jolene! the inner voice of reason screamed inside her head. She had to stop analyzing and compartmentalizing men. The world was filled with good, decent men who loved their girlfriends, wives, and children. She'd grown up with friends who had brothers who adored and protected them. She'd fallen in love and married a man who'd never raised his hand or his voice to her, not even in anger.

She knew her short-lived marriage had not survived a year because she'd been unwilling to compromise. She and Cheney had argued incessantly about Jeanine. Even after so many years she remembered his words: *You can't help your sister, Jolene, if she refuses to help herself. Surely you should know that. After all, you're the therapist. If she doesn't care if her husband uses her face as a punching bag, then why are you getting involved? You're commuting between D.C. and Chicago an average of once a week. You're not my wife anymore; you've become my roommate.*

She closed her eyes, willing the painful memories away. She took a deep breath, held it, and then let it out slowly.

Her eyes opened when she heard approaching footsteps. Standing next to her table was the last man she wanted to talk to. She'd caught a glimpse of him when she'd come in, but had deliberately ignored his presence.

The flickering flame from a candle highlighted his pleasant features. Arthur Lyondell liked to boast that he was the first in his family to graduate college. The grandson of an Alabama sharecropper, Arthur had attended Howard University on full scholarship, earning a coveted degree in economics. He'd subsequently added a graduate degree in tax accounting, married the daughter of a prominent African-American D.C. attorney, and fathered three children in rapid succession. Mrs. Arthur Lyondell was due to deliver her fourth child in a month.

Arthur had worked in the auditing division with the Internal Revenue Service for several years before transferring to the General Accounting Office as an associate director. He thought of himself as a rising star. He was good-looking, highly intelligent, and a hopeless philanderer.

Not waiting for an invitation to join her, Arthur sat down. "I almost didn't recognize you, Jolene. You look very different with short hair."

She stared at Arthur through lowered lids, wishing him gone. The last time they were together in the same room he'd asked her out. He'd waited for his wife to go to the ladies' room before coming on to her. She'd stared at him in stunned silence before walking away without saying a word.

"Where's your wife, Arthur?" she drawled sarcastically. He flinched as if she'd struck him.

"She's eating," he said solemnly.

"I suggest you join her."

"In a few minutes," he snapped, visibly angry. Resting his elbows on the table, he leaned forward, his fingers touching the handle of one of the forks in a place setting. "Why didn't you return my phone calls, Jolene?"

He was beginning to annoy her. "Isn't it obvious?"

"No, Jolene. It's not. Enlighten me, please. I called your office so many times that your receptionist recognized my voice even before I could give her my name."

The tenuous rein on her temper snapped. "Good-bye, Arthur." He reached for her hand, but she pulled it out of his reach. "Get away from me." The warning hissed between her clenched teeth.

"I suggest you listen to the lady."

Jolene's and Arthur's heads snapped up in unison at the sound of the soft but powerful voice. Michael stood motionless, holding a dish in each hand. He had appeared without making a sound.

Arthur glanced over his shoulder, meeting the lethal gaze of the tall man looming over him. The lights ringing the patio revealed a pair of eyes glowing with a savage inner fire.

Bowing gracefully, the motion as fluid as a dancer's, Michael positioned his mouth close to Arthur's ear. "If you're not gone by the time I put down these plates, then I promise you your babies will grow up without a daddy. Now, get the hell out of here!" he whispered.

Jolene couldn't hear what Michael said to Arthur, but she saw fear, wild and naked, cross Arthur's face. He glared at Michael for several seconds before Michael moved back to permit him to stand. He rose to his feet and walked away without a backward look.

Michael smiled, the expression softening his features as he placed the plates on the table. "What's up with the bean counter?"

She averted her gaze. "I don't know."

"You don't know?" His voice was heavy with sarcasm.

Tilting her chin, she glared up at him. "I said I don't know." She'd stressed each word.

Moving closer, Michael hunkered down, studying her closed expression. It was a mask of stone, while the stubborn set of her delicate jaw spoke volumes. It was apparent she wasn't going to explain her relationship with Arthur Lyondell. He hadn't overheard the exchange between Jolene and Lyondell—only her warning that he leave her alone. And he was more than aware of the man's proclivity for sleeping with women other than his wife. His brow furrowed. Was it possible that Jolene also shared Lyondell's bed? Rising to his full height, he set a plate in front of her. She stared at it.

"You can have the *saumon à la crème au muscadet,* or the *gigot d'agneau à la boulangère.*"

Her jaw dropped when she heard the French roll off Michael's tongue as if it were his native language. He could've been cursing at her, but whatever he'd said sounded incredibly beautiful. Paige had mentioned that he'd lived in Japan. Had he also lived in France?

She gave him a dazzling smile. A smile he found so intriguing. "Will you translate what you just said, please?"

Sitting down, he returned her smile, the flickering candlelight illuminating his eyes. "I said you have a choice between the salmon in cream with a muscadet sauce or the leg of lamb with potatoes and onions. If you don't like either, then I'll go back for something else."

"The salmon in the sauce sounds wonderful. You get a gold star."

He halted placing a cloth napkin on his lap, his brilliant gaze burning her face with its intensity. "Thank you very much. I can't remember the last time I got a gold star."

She glanced away, her gaze fixed on one of several lanterns hanging from the branch of a nearby tree. "I want to thank you."

Leaning forward, Michael studied her closed expression, his sweeping raven eyebrows shifting. "For what?"

"For getting rid of Arthur. The situation could've become nasty, and I didn't want to embarrass his wife."

"You're concerned about his wife and not yourself?"

Her head came around, waves of humiliation heating her cheeks. "You think I'm having an affair with *him*?"

"I didn't say that, Jolene."

"You didn't have to, *Michael*. Your expression said it all."

Nodding, he offered an apologetic smile. "Guilty as charged."

"I don't date married men."

Compressing her lips tightly, she inhaled and a swell of sable breasts spilled over her dress's décolletage, drawing his gaze, and Michael wondered what she would look like completely nude. His eyes widened, jade pupils dilating from a rising passion he was unable to control, a passion that aroused an involuntary stirring between his thighs.

What was wrong with him? He was lusting after a woman he knew nothing about. He couldn't remember the last time a woman had actually turned him on, and there weren't so many women in his past that he couldn't remember their names. He'd always been very selective and discriminating. His military training dictated absolute control professionally and in his personal affairs. However, it was not control that stirred his flesh until it hardened and throbbed against the fabric of his briefs. Closing his eyes, he swallowed a groan.

Jolene watched the play of emotions cross her dining partner's handsome face. He looked as if he were in pain. And she noticed the length and thickness of his lashes resting on a pair of high cheekbones for the first time. A woman would be willing to sacrifice a broken fingernail for lashes like his.

"Are you all right, Michael?"

He opened his eyes. "I'm fine," he lied smoothly.

He wasn't all right. He wanted Jolene Walker—in his bed and with his flesh fused with hers. He didn't know her, yet he wanted her.

"I don't want to be disrespectful, but there are a lot of women who make it a practice to date married men and vice versa."

"Well, I'm not one of those who do."

Lowering his chin slightly, he gave her a smile that unknowingly sent her pulse racing. She didn't date married men and he refused to date a married woman. And there had been an occasion when the wife of one of his superior officers had become obsessed with him. He'd done nothing to elicit the woman's attention, but that hadn't stopped her from pursuing him. He was grateful it had ended without incident. Her husband, who was the United States Army attaché with the American embassy in Tokyo, had been officially recalled to stateside.

"Good for you."

She felt a shiver of awareness as if he'd touched her. She had to admit that she liked Michael Kirkland; he was drop-dead gorgeous, wearing what she recognized as a light-weight, charcoal gray Ralph Lauren suit and Hermès silk tie with the aplomb of a male model swaggering down a runway. Coupled with the fact that he spoke fluent French, she had to ask herself, what was there not to like?

Placing her napkin over her knees, she picked up a fork, breaking off a flaky portion of salmon. "Where did you learn to speak French?"

"I studied it in school."

"So did I," she admitted. "But I can't speak it fluently."

"I have an ear for languages."

"Don't be so modest."

"I'm not being modest." There was a hint of laughter in his voice.

"Do you also speak Japanese?"

His fork stopped in midair. "Who told you I speak Japanese?"

"Do you?"

"Yes," he replied, his gaze narrowing in suspicion.

"Paige said Damon told her that he'd met you in Japan when he attended grad school."

"That's true," he confirmed. "We met at a club frequented predominantly by American businessmen and students."

"Were you also a student?"

His lids came down, concealing his innermost thoughts. He couldn't tell her that he'd been on assignment; that he'd been a member of a team of specialized intelligence agents who were trained in counterterrorism.

"No. I worked for an electronics firm." It was a half-truth. "How about yourself?" he asked, deftly shifting the focus.

"I'm a social worker."

Placing a finger alongside his nose, he smiled. "You don't look like a social worker."

Jolene laughed, the sound soft, sensual. "And what should a social worker look like?"

"Definitely not like a fashion model."

Her attention was directed to her plate. When she did look up at Michael, it was through a veil of lashes. "Are you flirting with me, Michael Kirkland?"

He gave her a slow, lazy smile. "I'm surprised you have to ask, Miss Walker."

"You *are* flirting." The question came out like a statement.

"Absolutely. Does that disturb you?"

Jolene forced herself to hold his gaze. The flickering candle was flattering to the rich gold undertones in his brown face. *Yes,* she wanted to scream, he did disturb her. He

disturbed her not because he was male, but because he was
who he was. He was a man who was just a little too sure
of himself, a man who appeared to take charge of any situation, a man who was able to intimidate another man with
his mere presence.

"I've never been bothered by a man flirting with me."

Michael tilted his head at an angle. "You're used to men
coming on to you?"

"A man hasn't come on to me in a long time."

This disclosure surprised him. Women who looked like
Jolene Walker were certain to elicit any man's attention,
anytime and anyplace. "Why not?"

Her gaze widened, fusing with his questioning one.
"Because I don't have time for dating, flirting, or romance.
The work I do has become a priority."

The mention of work garnered his complete attention.
Jolene unknowingly was his female counterpart. Her career
dictated her life in a way the military dictated his.

"What kind of work are you involved with?"

"I'm responsible for the day-to-day operation of a treatment program for victimized women."

He whistled softly. "I suppose you've seen a lot of
abuse."

"Too much," she confirmed. There was no mistaking the
heavy emotion in the two words.

All conversation ended when a waiter approached their
table, pushing a small cart. He placed a platter of vegetable
couscous on the table, along with crystal wineglasses and
goblets. He filled the goblets with sparkling water and the
wineglasses with red wine for Michael and white for Jolene.

Michael nodded. "Thank you."

The waiter, who looked barely out of his teens, smiled.
"Is there anything else I can get you, sir?"

"Two salads, please."

"I'll be right back."

Jolene waited until the waiter walked away before she said in a quiet voice, "This is not a sit-down affair."

Michael shrugged a broad shoulder under the fabric of his exquisitely tailored suit jacket. "I'm aware of that."

She gave him a direct stare. "If you're so aware of it, then why are you requesting personal waiter service?"

Michael stared boldly at the woman sharing the table with him, drinking in her extraordinary natural beauty. There was an undeniable sexual magnetism that drew him to her—one that he could not and did not want to understand.

Picking up his wineglass, he touched it to hers. "Because I can."

The three words hit Jolene in the face with the force of a jab from a boxer's glove. His statement spoke volumes. He was spoiled. He was used to getting what he wanted.

Who was he?

Why did he feel *that* entitled?

Four

The fingers of Jolene's right hand toyed with the stem of her wineglass. She was curious, intrigued by the man sitting opposite her. The therapist part of her wanted to probe, delve deeply into his past. If he'd come to her as a client she would've begun the intake process with a detailed psychosocial, medical, and financial history. But he wasn't a client; he was her dining partner for the evening.

"Have I embarrassed you?" Michael asked. "Do you think I made a social faux pas?"

She shrugged a bare satiny shoulder. "No."

And he actually hadn't, but that no longer mattered, because after tonight she doubted she would ever see Michael Kirkland again. Picking up the glass, she took a sip of the dry white wine, staring at him over the rim. The cool liquid bathed her throat as her defenses began to subside.

They watched each other eat, shutting out everything and everyone around them. For a span of time it was as if they were the only two people sitting on the patio.

The magical spell was broken when she touched the corners of her mouth with a napkin. Gathering her small evening purse, Jolene pushed back her chair. She wanted to wish Claire a happy birthday before departing. She'd fulfilled her social obligation to Paige and Claire by attending, while providing Damon's friend with the requisite dining partner.

Michael pushed back his own chair, coming around the table to help her stand. "Is there something I can get for you?"

She shook her head. "No, thank you. I just want to talk to Claire."

He watched her make her way across the patio and stop at Claire and Walter McDonald's table. A sixth sense told him Jolene was leaving, and he didn't want her to leave—not yet. He wanted to talk to her, schedule a day and time when he could see her again.

His suspicions were verified when he saw her hug Claire and Walter, then move over to Damon's table. Smiling, she spoke to Damon, shook hands with Melissa, and then disappeared. Moving quickly, silently, he left the patio, coming around the Sutton property along a path that wound around the garden. He was waiting for Jolene as she walked out the front door. A slight gasp escaped her parted lips when she saw him looming in front of her.

"Leaving so soon?"

Placing a hand over her chest, she closed her eyes for a brief moment. "You frightened me. I didn't expect to see you."

Michael flashed a half smile. "I'm sorry about that, but I didn't expect you to leave without saying good night."

She recovered quickly. "Good night, Michael." He stepped aside, permitting her to move past him. And much to her surprise, he fell in step with her. "Where are you going?"

"I'm walking you to your car."

She stopped suddenly, and he bumped into her. His hands moved quickly, gripping her shoulders to steady her, her flesh burning under his touch.

"I didn't drive tonight."

Michael's fingers tightened slightly before he released her. His sweeping black eyebrows nearly met over the bridge of his straight nose. "You walked?"

"I live within walking distance." She'd lowered her voice, being purposefully mysterious.

He stared, complete surprise on his face. He also lived within walking distance of the Suttons. He'd returned to the States after a four-year stint in Japan, established a residence within the capitol district, and yet had been totally unaware that he and Damon's sister lived in the same neighborhood.

"Where do you live?" he asked.

"Over on P Street." A low chuckle rumbled in his chest, eliciting a frown from Jolene. "What's so funny?"

He stopped laughing long enough to say, "I live on Q."

She stared wordlessly up at him, her heart pounding. *No!* the inner voice had screamed at her again. The man was practically her neighbor. Had she passed him on the street before? How many times had she walked or driven past his house? What were the odds that she would meet a man she was attracted to who lived only blocks from her?

"Would you mind if I walked you home? To make certain you arrive safely," he added smoothly.

What did he expect her to say? *No, you can't walk me home because you remind me that I'm not as unaffected by you as I would like to be? That just looking at you reminds me that I am a woman—a woman who has been so involved in her work she's forgotten what it feels like to acknowledge desire?*

An uneasiness she hadn't felt in a long time snaked through her. It was the same emotion she'd experienced when she'd met Cheney for the first time. She'd ignored the warning bell telling her that Cheney wasn't all he'd presented to her. At twenty-five, she hadn't come to her marriage a virgin, but she also hadn't had a lot of experience with the opposite sex. Focusing on her education and establishing a career had taken precedence.

However, many things had changed in five years: she'd married, divorced, lost a sister, waged a campaign to make certain the person responsible for Jeanine's death was incarcerated, become responsible for the administrative day-to-day operation of a facility for victimized women, and for the first time in five years she was emotionally balanced.

Then there was Michael Kirkland with the gorgeous face, killer smile, bedroom eyes and voice. She would let him walk her home, and if there was the remotest possibility that he wanted to see her again beyond tonight, then she would accept an offer for dinner or a movie; she would agree to a date—and only one date, because she had no intention of permitting herself to fall under his sensual spell.

A slow smile trembled over her generous lips. "Yes, you may walk me home."

Reaching for her left hand, he curved it into the crook of his elbow. Her fingers were cool, soft. They walked slowly, neither attempting to initiate conversation. They savored the sultry warmth of the summer night, the aromatic fragrance of blooming night flowers over the distinctive scent of chicory.

Jolene loved the smell of the South. It was so different from Chicago or New York, where she associated smells with different neighborhoods. Here it was the damp earth after a thunderstorm or the cloying scent of magnolia and dogwood trees. She missed Chicago, but not its long, harsh winters. D.C. had its share of snow, but the accumulations would never come close to challenging the Windy City's.

There were other couples strolling the Georgetown sidewalks, holding hands, talking and laughing softly. They passed an elderly man walking his dog, who waited patiently as the little Jack Russell terrier examined every blade of grass around each tree he passed.

"How long have you lived in D.C.?" Jolene asked, breaking the comfortable silence.

Michael stared at her delightful profile under the glow of a streetlamp, smiling. "What if I tell you that D.C. is my hometown?"

"I don't think so," she countered. "You still have a trace of Texas in your speech pattern."

"You're close. I'm from New Mexico," he confirmed. "You've got a good ear."

"I'm trained to be a good listener. It's an integral component of the profession. You still didn't answer my question, Michael."

"And that is?"

Stopping, she smiled up at him. There weren't too many men she could look up at while wearing high heels. "How long have you lived here?"

"Four years." He gently urged her forward and they resumed walking.

"Do you plan to return to New Mexico one day?"

Again he shrugged a shoulder, the motion barely perceptible. "I don't know."

He'd told her the truth. He didn't know what he would do after his leave was up. There was one option he'd considered: teaching at a military school. He'd updated his résumé with the intent of mailing copies to military schools in Maryland and Virginia. His original plan was to spend twenty years in the Army, retire, and then apply for a teaching post at his alma mater, West Point.

Michael had confided in his father about his superior officer's salacious conduct. Joshua Kirkland, who had also attended and graduated West Point, and gone on to become a full colonel and associate coordinating chief of the Defense Intelligence Agency, had suggested he follow his instincts—

perhaps he wasn't mentally prepared to make the military his career. He'd wanted to refute his father's allegation but had held his tongue, thinking perhaps he might be right.

"I live here." Jolene's soft voice brought him back to the present. They stood in front of a brownstone building with gleaming oak doors and stained glass insets. "I reside in the penthouse apartment."

Looking up, Michael noted the golden glow from a table lamp radiating from the floor-to-ceiling windows. "I'll see you to your door."

Easing her hand from his grip, she shook her head. "That's all right. The building's very secure. Thank you for walking me home." She extended her right hand.

He ignored it, leaning over to press his lips to her cheek. "Thank you for your company tonight. Can we can share dinner again—this time without Damon and Paige's intervention?"

Her face flamed from the fleeting brush of his mouth on her cheek. His intoxicating cologne lingered in her sensitive nostrils, drugging her with its clean and manly scent. What was there about Michael that made her just a little weak in the knees whenever he touched her? Made her a little too curious? Reckless? And made her aware that she'd felt an immediate and total attraction to him even before seeing his face?

"Call me at the Sanctuary the middle of next week and I'll let you know. We're listed in the telephone directory as the Sanctuary Counseling Center."

Stepping back, he winked at her. "I'll talk to you then."

She smiled. "Good night, Michael."

He returned her smile. "Good night, Jolene."

Turning, she made her way up the steps and opened the door to the building's vestibule. She closed the door and stared at Michael through the colored glass. He hadn't moved. He stood on the sidewalk in front of her building, hands thrust into the pockets of his suit trousers. She wondered what he was waiting for, what he was thinking.

She climbed the three flights, unlocked her door, closed it behind her, and then began the ritual of slipping off her shoes and placing the tiny purse on the chair. Heading for the bathroom, she undressed, cleansed her face of makeup, and brushed her teeth before slipping into a pair of lounging pajamas.

It was ten minutes before two o'clock the next morning when she finally turned off the lamp in her study, making her way down the narrow hallway to her bedroom. Twin emotions of fatigue and elation warred with each other as she pulled back a lightweight quilt. A slight groan escaped her as she collapsed on the bed. She was beyond exhaustion. Her brain felt like mush. She'd completed the first draft of the grant proposal. It would take her only a few days to edit what she'd written. The agency's accountant had promised to give her the proposed budget by Thursday. Reaching over, she turned off the bedside lamp, plunging the room into darkness, smiling a tired smile. Once the grant was submitted, then she would take Michael up on his offer to have dinner together.

And, as it had been since she'd become director of the Sanctuary, her work was paramount.

Five

Michael sat on the loggia to his sister's home, staring out at the different colors painting the Southwest desert. The setting sun fired the peaks of the Organ Mountains, turning them a vibrant bloodred.

He'd arrived in Las Cruces late Sunday night, surprising Emily Kirkland-Delgado and his brother-in-law, New Mexico Governor Christopher Delgado, with his unannounced arrival.

He'd slept for twelve hours, and then woken up to find his three-year-old nephew sitting on his chest, whispering for him to get up and play. Alejandro Delgado II waited patiently while he showered, shaved, and put on his Las Cruces attire: boots, jeans, and a wide-brimmed Western-style hat. The transformation was complete. He had become Uncle Michael.

Alejandro kept him busy riding horses and tossing a base-ball. Even though Esperanza, his year-old niece, had learned to walk unaided a month ago, she was more than content to have him carry her around until Emily warned him about spoiling her.

The door opened and he caught the scent of Emily's perfume as she joined him on the loggia. "You have a telephone call."

He'd always thought her dulcet voice was very pleasant. He didn't move from his lounging position on a *butaca*, one of a quartet of leather sling chairs she'd transported from her in-laws' ancestral Mexican hacienda.

"Who is it?"

"She said her name is Jolene."

Michael forced himself not to jump up and race into the house to answer the call. He hadn't waited until the middle of the week to call the Sanctuary, but called early Sunday morning, leaving a message for Jolene on the answering machine. He'd told her he was leaving for Las Cruces and she could reach him there.

Emily stared at her brother's impassive expression, successfully concealing a smile. "Who is she?" It was the first time a woman had called her home asking for Michael.

"A friend," he replied, deliberately being evasive.

"She sounds nice." Emily stared at his broad shoulders as he rose to his feet and headed for the door.

"She is," Michael confirmed, not turning around. Walking through the entry, he made his way into the kitchen and picked up the cordless phone resting on a countertop.

"Good evening, Jolene."

"Good evening, Michael."

Resting a hip against the counter, he smiled. Minute lines fanned out around his eyes. "How are you?" Her soft laughter sent a shiver up his spine. He missed her. It was amazing. He didn't even know her, yet he missed her.

"I should be the one asking how *you* are? I take it you've been relaxing?"

His smile widened. "I've done absolutely nothing since

I arrived except spoil the hell out of my niece and nephew. My sister's ready to evict me.''

Jolene laughed again. ''I'm glad you're relaxing, because I feel like the mouse I once had to train in an experimental psychology course. If the little bugger wanted to eat, then he had to learn to navigate the maze, and then press a lever for a pellet of food. One time he ran around so much that he collapsed after overeating.''

It was Michael's turn to laugh. ''Are you telling me that you're ready for a little R and R?''

''Big-time.''

''Are you free Saturday?''

''I have nothing on my calendar.''

''Good,'' he said quickly. ''If that's the case, then I'll pick you up Saturday at six.''

''Where are we going?''

''Do you ever get seasick?''

''No. Why?''

''I'd like to take you on a dinner cruise, unless you'd like to suggest something else.''

''That sounds wonderful.''

''I'll see you then.''

''Good night, Michael.''

''Good night, Jolene.'' He stared at the newly installed terra-cotta floor in the expansive kitchen, waiting for her to hang up. It was a full ten seconds before he heard the click, breaking the connection. Depressing a button on the cordless instrument, he placed it on a wall cradle.

What had he been waiting for? What more had he expected her to say? She'd asked him to call her, and he had. He'd left a message for her to call him, and she had. He'd felt more comfortable meeting her for the first time than he did now.

Emily walked into the kitchen, meeting his amused gaze. He had to admit that marriage and motherhood agreed with his older sister. She had married a childhood friend, given birth to two beautiful, intelligent children, and was the wife of the state's incumbent governor. She'd willingly given up a brilliant career as a television journalist to become a stay-at-home mother.

Her bare face, professionally coiffed short, curling black hair, T-shirt, and the fitted jeans hugging her slim hips made her look much younger than thirty-five. She gave him a smile that did not quite reach her large green eyes. There was a sad quality about his sister that he hadn't noticed during their last reunion.

Pushing off the counter, he closed the distance between them, cradling her to his chest. "You miss him, don't you?" he asked perceptively. She saw her husband and the father of her children an average of three nights a week. As governor, Chris commuted between Las Cruces and Santa Fe. He left his wife and children early Monday mornings, and returned late Friday afternoons.

Curving her arms around her brother's slim waist, Emily laid her head on his shoulder. "Not as much as I used to. Chris and I only have another four months before we can live together like a normal married couple."

"Has my brother-in-law talked about running for public office again in another four years?"

Pulling back, Emily's eyes narrowed. "He'd better not. I gave up my career, and now it's time for him to make a few concessions."

Michael's expression sobered. "Do you want me to talk to him?"

"No. There's no need for you to get involved. Chris knows how I feel." Rising on tiptoe, she kissed his cheek. "Thanks for offering to look out for me, little brother."

"I'll always look out for you because I love you."

"I know you do, Michael. And I love you. But this isn't about me, is it?"

His lids slipped down over his penetrating gaze. "What are you trying to say?"

"You show up here out of the blue, with the lame excuse that you miss your family. You have family—a mother and father, aunts, uncles, and at least fifty cousins who live closer to you than Las Cruces, New Mexico. Do I have to remind you that Florida is in the same time zone as Washington, D.C.? What's going on with you, brother?" Her voice had softened considerably, taking on a pleading tone.

He wanted to tell Emily about his undeclared war with General Cooper. That he was considering leaving the United States Army.

"Does it have anything to do with Jolene?" she asked when he avoided her gaze.

His expression brightened at the mention of Jolene's name. Right now she was the only positive thing in his life even though they hadn't had their first official date. Leaning down from his superior height, he dropped a kiss on the tip of Emily's nose.

"No meddling," he warned seconds before he released her and strolled across the kitchen floor. "I think I'll go for a walk."

"Be careful, Michael. There have been coyote sightings. A few have wandered a little too close to the house this summer."

"Okay," he said over his shoulder.

As school-aged children, alternating summers had found him and Emily traveling from Santa Fe to Las Cruces to stay with the Sterlings. Matthew and Eve Sterling had become their surrogate parents, and Christopher Delgado and his sister, Sara Sterling, had validated their best-friends status. Chris and Sara's father had taught them to ride horses, handle firearms, and survive overnight in the desert. Sara and Chris's sojourns to Santa Fe included playing tennis, swimming in the Kirklands' Olympic-sized swimming pool, and skiing during the winter season at nearby resorts. Michael perfected his use of firearms when he attended a prestigious New Mexico military academy, and after entering West Point, he broke and set new records with his outstanding marksmanship.

Michael was always careful, but now his caution was heightened because he wanted to see Jolene Walker again. Making his way into a room where Chris kept a collection of rifles and handguns in a locked armoire, he retrieved a key atop the massive piece of furniture, opened it, and withdrew a small automatic pistol. Slipping in a fully loaded clip, he tucked the gun into the waistband of his jeans. Three minutes later he walked away from the house, and was quickly swallowed up by the blackness of the desert night.

Six

The soft chiming of the downstairs doorbell echoed throughout Jolene's apartment. It was on rare occasions that she entertained in her apartment. The only exception was the annual Christmas gathering for her staff. There had been a time when she saw fewer than a half dozen private clients. However, it had been more than a year since she'd terminated her relationship with the last one. After becoming the executive director of the Sanctuary, she hadn't had the time, so she'd referred her clients to another therapist. Glancing at her watch, she noted the time. It was exactly six o'clock.

Her pulse accelerated as she made her way to the front door. After a hectic week, she looked forward to seeing Michael Kirkland again. When he'd asked her if she was ready for a little rest and relaxation, she was more than ready to admit that she was. She'd completed the voluminous grant proposal and negotiated the purchase of a new car, nearly losing her composure when she saw the salesman drive her old car away. Her last link with Jeanine was gone. All she had left of her sister were photographs and memories.

Pressing a button on the intercom, she spoke into the mouthpiece. "Yes?"

"Michael." The single word was strong and confident.

She pushed another button, releasing the lock on the inner door, and then awaited his arrival. Without warning, he appeared at the bottom of the stairs on the third flight, and her gaze lingered on the top of his head. How had he come up so quickly? She doubted he'd run or sprinted because his chest was rising and falling in a deep even breathing rhythm.

He glanced up, stopping, their gazes fusing. Jolene felt as if someone had reached into her chest and gently squeezed her heart, making breathing difficult. Seeing Michael for the first time in a week was more startling than meeting him for the first time on Paige's patio.

The desert sun had darkened his face to a shimmering chestnut brown; his eyes gave off sparks like flawless jewels, and the contrast was breathtaking; they were much lighter than she'd originally thought. He continued his ascent, coming closer, a slight smile curving his mouth and crinkling his eyes.

She missed the navy blue linen suit, crisp pale blue shirt with French cuffs, red silk tie, and black oxfords, because her gaze was fused with his. There was no mistaking the intangible sexual magnetism that made him so attractive, so self-confident.

Michael mounted the last stair, coming face-to-face with Jolene. He'd spent the week trying to recall the shape of her eyes, mouth, the velvet smoothness of her skin, the curves of her lush body, her sensual smile—and had failed miserably. She was more beautiful and sexy than he'd remembered.

His smile widened in approval as he silently admired the

shimmer of rose pink silk against her exposed sable flesh. Tonight she'd elected to wear a short-sleeved conservative coatdress with tiny covered buttons lining the front. The slim garment ended midcalf. In deference to the sweltering humidity, she'd opted to leave her legs bare. Her groomed toes were visible in black patent leather high-heeled sandals. Reversing, his gaze lingered on a single strand of large pearls spilling over her delicate clavicle. The baubles had a soft pink hue, as if warmed by the heat of her velvety throat.

Leaning over, he pressed a kiss to her cheek, his warm moist breath sweeping over the large gold hoop in her pierced lobe. "Hello again."

Jolene's hands came up involuntarily, resting against the solid wall of his broad chest. Closing her eyes, she breathed in the warmth and intoxicating scent that was exclusively Michael Kirkland's.

"Welcome back." Her voice was low, soft, and unintentionally seductive. "How was your return flight? Did your sister finally evict you?" The questions were running together, but she didn't care. She'd seen him only once, spent about two hours with him, yet she missed him more than she wanted to admit—at least to herself.

Pulling back, Michael chuckled. "Which question do you want me to answer first?" She opened the door wider and he walked into the spacious entry, dwarfing everything with his impressive height.

"It doesn't matter."

"I'll tell you everything on the drive to Alexandria," he promised.

Jolene picked up her small shoulder purse from the chair and her keys from the table. "I'm ready."

And she *was* ready, because she'd decided to lower her defenses and enjoy whatever it was that had attracted her to him. She closed and locked the door, and then slipped her keys into her purse. Michael took her hand, squeezing her fingers gently as they descended the staircase. Her shoulder brushed against his, but she did not pull away as she'd done before. She welcomed him and his touch.

Michael opened the front door and a thick blanket of heat and humidity descended like a scorching blast from a roaring furnace. Even though it would be twilight in another hour, the stifling heat still persisted. A sail along the Potomac River was the perfect place to spend the evening.

He pressed a button on a remote device, and a soft beeping sound unlocked the doors to a low-slung titanium gray convertible parked at the curb. Opening the passenger-side door, he waited until Jolene was seated on the charcoal gray leather seat. Seconds later, he slipped out of his jacket, hanging it up on a hook in the rear; he eased his long legs into the Jaguar and inserted a key in the ignition. With a flick of his wrist, the powerful engine purred to life like a large contented cat; pressing a button, he raised the black top and adjusted the settings for the air conditioner. Within seconds the inside of the automobile had cooled to a comfortable temperature. A navigational system shone brightly in a burl walnut dashboard. All of the roads leading to Alexandria were clearly highlighted on the visual map.

"Let me know if it gets too cold for you."

Luxuriating in the cool air flowing over her moist face, Jolene shook her head. "It's perfect."

She glanced at Michael's perfect profile as he pulled smoothly away from the curb. "Is it safe to say that you never get lost in this car?"

He nodded, giving her a quick glance. "Never. The navigational system is standard with this model."

Her curiosity about her date intensified. Who was he? What did he do for a living? How was he able to afford an automobile which had a sticker price that approached the one-hundred-thousand-dollar mark?

"Where do you work?" she asked.

Michael arched his eyebrows, not taking his gaze off the road. "I thought you wanted to hear about my trip to New Mexico."

"I do. But I also would like to know *if* you work for a living."

This time he did look at her. "You think I'm involved in criminal activities?"

Heat flared in her cheeks as she turned her head to stare out the side window. "I didn't say that." Her head swung around and she gave him a challenging stare when he stopped for a red light. "I just like to know who I'm involved with, that's all."

A slow smile softened the harsh lines in his lean face. His lips parted, displaying a set of perfect white teeth. "How involved are we?"

"You know what I'm talking about."

"No, I don't know what you're talking about. Are you asking me to become involved with you?"

Jolene's eyes narrowed. "Don't put words in my mouth, Michael Kirkland."

The light changed, and he concentrated on his driving. "I'm not trying to put words in your mouth," he said after a prolonged silence. "I just want to know if you want to get involved."

"No. I don't want to get involved."

"Why not?"

"I don't know you. I know nothing about you. In fact, this is only our first date. Besides, I don't need involvement as much as I need friendship."

He wanted to tell her that women who looked like her usually wouldn't be counted as friends; she was more likely to become a lover, wife, or the mother of a man's children.

"Let's see if I can allay some of your curiosity. My full name is Michael Blanchard Kirkland. I'm the second child and only son of Joshua and Vanessa Kirkland. My parents are retired and live in Palm Beach, Florida. I'm thirty-two, never married, and I'm not some baby's daddy.

"I have a law degree from Georgetown, and I'm currently on leave from my job at the Pentagon. I have an older sister, Emily, who lives in Las Cruces. She's married and the mother of a three-year-old son and year-old daughter." He gave Jolene a quick glance. She stared at him, her eyes wide, unblinking. "Is there anything else you'd like to know?" The softly spoken query held a thread of facetiousness.

Jolene forced herself not to glance away. "How was your trip to New Mexico?"

Laughter rumbled in Michael's chest as he shook his head. The woman seated beside him was indeed his counterpart. Under her sophisticated exterior was a spark of defiance that challenged him. And he was one who was never able to resist a challenge.

"It was very nice. My niece is walking and getting into everything she can reach."

"What's her name?"

"Esperanza."

"Is it Spanish?"

He nodded. "When Emily found out she was pregnant for a second time she prayed every day, hoping for a girl. When tests revealed she was going to have a daughter, she decided to give her the Spanish derivation of Hope."

"What's her son's name?"

"Alejandro."

Jolene peered closer at Michael, taking in his deeply tanned olive coloring and raven black hair. "Do you claim Spanish ancestry?"

"I do on my father's side. His mother's parents were born in Cuba."

"And your mother's people?"

"Straight up African-American." She laughed, and seconds later his laughter joined hers. "What about you, Jolene? What dark secrets are you hiding?"

She sobered quickly. "I have no secrets."

"Are you certain you're not a black widow?"

Jolene landed a soft punch on his hard shoulder. "Of course not."

"How old are you?"

"Thirty. I was born and raised in a Chicago suburb. My parents have a few more years before they retire. My dad taught world history before becoming a football coach and dean of boys at a Chicago high school. My mom teaches psychiatric nursing at a local nursing school. I had a sister, but she died in an accident five years ago."

Michael heard the pain in her voice. He wanted to slow down, pull over to the side of the road, and take her in his arms. "I'm so sorry." The three words sounded so empty, so trite. "How about brothers?"

Blinking back the moisture filling her eyes, Jolene shook her head. "No brothers. There was just the two of us."

He remembered two incidents when his sister's life was at risk. Emily had been stalked and shot at by a homicidal maniac who believed she'd spurned him, because she hadn't replied to his on-line marriage proposal; the police had shot and apprehended the man before he'd gained access to the television station where she worked as a political journalist. The second incident occurred when his sister attempted single-handedly to solve the murder of a young woman who'd had an affair with the governor of New Mexico. Her impulsiveness would have cost Emily her life and that of her unborn son if his brother-in-law hadn't intervened.

"I don't know what I'd do if I lost Emily."

"You would survive, Michael. You learn to go on with your life."

He made a right turn, heading in a southern direction. "Is that what you've done?"

"That's what I attempt to do. I wake up every morning, sit up, and then get out of bed. That's the hardest part of beginning a day. After that everything's easy."

The mood inside the luxurious vehicle turned somber, and Jolene regretted prying into Michael's life, which made her a subject for the same. She'd made herself a promise the last time she'd visited Jeanine's grave never to discuss her with anyone ever again. That was last Christmas. She'd been successful—until now.

Michael placed his right hand over Jolene's left knee. His touch was comforting, nonsexual and nonthreatening. She looked at him and smiled. His eyes crinkled attractively as he winked at her. He didn't remove his hand, and she didn't ask him to. It wasn't until he maneuvered into a large public parking lot adjacent to the pier between Prince and Duke Streets on the Strand in historic Old Town Alexandria, that he removed his hand.

He retrieved his jacket, and then came around the car to open the door for Jolene. She placed her hand in his outstretched one. Tightening his grip, he pulled her to her feet. He stared at her upturned face for several seconds, drinking in the essence of her feminine beauty. She returned his intense stare, and both ignored the gazes of others who silently admired the tall, attractive couple.

Curving his free arm around her waist, he pulled her closer. "Thank you for going out with me."

Lowering her gaze, she stared up at him through her lashes. "Thank you for asking."

A barely perceptible sensuous light passed between them as they shut out everything and everyone around them as couples made their way toward the gleaming ship docked at the pier.

"What time are we sailing?" she asked softly, breaking the magical spell.

"Not until 7:30. But boarding is between 6:30 and 6:55."

Michael glanced at the gold watch showing beneath the monogrammed cuff on his shirt. "It's time we board."

He escorted Jolene up the gangplank of the sleek, newly built *Dandy* and into the exquisitely appointed ship. The melodious sound of a piano greeted them as their names were checked on a list of reservations, and then they were shown to a table in the main salon.

Soft lighting, cloth-covered tables, and burning candles set the mood for several hours of gourmet dining and dancing on a four-hundred-square-foot marble dance floor.

Michael picked up a menu, studying the selections. "I hope you brought your appetite, because dinner is a five-course affair."

She glanced at her menu. The dinner offering was more than she would eat for two meals. "If I eat a five-course meal, then you'll have to roll me out of here."

"After we eat we'll go upstairs and dance off the calories."

She smiled at her dining partner over the top of her menu. "You've got yourself a deal."

Michael and Jolene spent the next ninety minutes talking about the upcoming election and sports while eating and sharing a bottle of champagne; the soft sound of live piano playing punctuated the night.

After her second glass of champagne, she couldn't remember the last time she'd felt so relaxed. She temporarily forgot about the loss of Jeanine and the lives of the victimized women at the Sanctuary. She didn't want to forget them, but there was something so powerful and compelling about the sexy man sharing the same space with her that vestiges of guilt crept under the barrier she had set up to protect her vulnerability.

Touching the corners of her mouth with a napkin, she placed it beside her plate. "I can't eat another morsel."

Michael stared at her, unblinking. The flickering candle

highlighted the jade centers of his large penetrating eyes. "What about dessert?"

Shaking her head, she said, "I'm going to have to pass on dessert."

He inclined his head in acknowledgment before touching his mouth with his napkin. "Are you ready to dance off a few calories?"

A sensual smile softened her lush lips. "Yes."

He came around the table and pulled out her chair. Hand in hand they headed for the upper deck. Recorded music ranging from the '40s to the present replaced the piano player. The sun had sunk into the Potomac, taking with it the day's brutal heat.

Curving his right arm around Jolene's waist, Michael led her out onto the dance floor, joining half a dozen other couples. Closing his eyes, he reveled in the crush of her full breasts against his chest as he pulled her closer.

Jolene felt the unyielding strength of Michael's arms around her as her body melted into his. His nearness made her senses spin in a confusing longing. *He's only a man*, the inner voice whispered to her.

He was a man like all of the others she'd encountered in her life, but there was something more about him. His presence made her think about herself and her role in the world. She'd become a social worker with a mission: to make the public aware that adult domestic violence was one of the most serious public health and criminal justice issues facing women today. She'd become a dedicated advocate for victimized women, resulting in her working eighteen-hour days. Her crusade had become her life, and she could not remember the last time she'd thoroughly enjoyed an evening with a man. And the last time she'd danced with a man was on her honeymoon. She and Cheney had taken time off and flown down to Aruba for their honeymoon.

Her left hand moved up around Michael's collar, her

fingers grazing the short straight hair at the nape of his neck. Closing her eyes, she smiled to herself. He looked wonderful, and smelled even better.

"What are you smiling about?"

Her eyes flew open as she missed a step. She would've fallen if Michael hadn't tightened his hold on her waist. "How did you know I was smiling?"

He chuckled softly against her ear. "I felt your cheekbone move." Her velvety cheek was pressed against his clean-shaven jaw.

"I was smiling because even though we're wearing the same fragrance, it smells different on you."

"How?" he whispered.

"It's wonderful, sensual."

"I felt the same way the night I came up behind you at Paige's house. I thought at that moment that you smelled good enough to eat."

It was Jolene's turn to laugh—an uneasy laugh. "I hope not quite that good."

"Yes. *That* good."

Flames of embarrassment warmed her face, spreading lower to her neck and even lower to her breasts. Now she was treading on dangerous ground because their interchange was layered with sexual overtones.

The tempo of the music changed, becoming upbeat and allowing her a respite. Michael swung her out, releasing her hand. Everyone lined up for the macarena, and they joined the others gyrating to the familiar dance number. The electric slide followed the macarena and then the popular "Hot Hot Hot."

Hearing the island rhythms reminded Michael of Jamaica. He wanted to take Jolene to Ocho Rios for a weekend; they would sleep late, swim in the clear blue-green Caribbean, lie on the beach under the sun, and then dance the night away at a few of the more popular clubs. He would ask her at another time—when they were more familiar and comfortable with each other, once they passed the "friends" stage.

The *Dandy* sailed up the Potomac to Georgetown before reversing its course to return to Alexandria, Virginia. Succumbing to dining and dancing under the star-littered sky, Jolene leaned against Michael on the upper deck as the pier came into view. She did not want the night or the magic to end. Resting her head on his shoulder, she looked up at him.

"Can we do this again?"

He stared, complete surprise on his face. "When?"

She shrugged a shoulder. "Next month."

"Are you asking me out?"

She wrinkled her nose. "Yes, I am."

He hesitated, his luminous eyes widening in astonishment. He'd spent the night hoping Jolene would go out with him again, never anticipating she would be the one asking.

"I'd be more than honored to do it again, but I'd like for you to do something for me."

She felt a creeping uneasiness that hadn't been present all evening. Had she made a mistake? Had she become so comfortable and bold that she'd been prompted to solicit a future assignation? What if he hadn't wanted to see her again after tonight? Something cautioned her not to ask, but she knew she had to.

"What, Michael?"

"Come to my house for brunch tomorrow morning."

She swallowed a nervous laugh. "You're kidding, aren't you?"

He sobered quickly, his expression becoming a mask of stone. "No, I'm not kidding."

Rising on tiptoe, she kissed his chin. "You sounded so serious that I didn't know what to expect."

Gathering her closer, he buried his face against her short fragrant hair. What Jolene didn't know was that he was

serious—very, very serious. What he felt and was beginning
to feel for her would frighten her if he made his intentions
known.

"Do you like omelettes?"

"Yes."

"What else do you like for breakfast?"

"Muffins," she whispered.

"What kind?"

"Carrot raisin."

"Coffee or tea?"

She smiled. There was no doubt he wanted to please her.
"I'll drink either one."

Curving a hand under her chin, he raised her face to his.
Lowering his head, he touched his mouth to hers, increasing
the pressure until she responded. The kiss lasted seconds,
but the heat lingered.

Jolene studied his impassive expression, wondering what
he was feeling at that moment, because she was certain he
felt the runaway beating of her heart.

"What time is brunch?"

"Is eleven too late for you to eat?"

"No."

And it wasn't. It would give her enough time to go to the
gym, work out, then return home to shower and change for
church. After church she usually returned home to prepare
breakfast; the following two to three hours were spent reading the Sunday newspaper. Sometimes she prepared dinner
for herself, or she ate out. She always called her parents at
eight, and then prepared herself for the coming workweek.
Her weekends were routine and very parochial. She was
willing to share Friday nights, Saturdays, and Sundays with
Michael, but not the days or hours when the Sanctuary was
operational. The line of demarcation between her private
life and career was unconditional. When it came to her work
she refused to compromise.

* * *

The return ride to Georgetown was accomplished without conversation. Jolene was content to relax and listen to the music selections flowing from the Jaguar's sophisticated sound system. Closing her eyes, she let her other senses take over. The masculine smell of leather mingled with the sensual scent of Michael's cologne. She felt him move when his right foot shifted from the gas to the brake pedal. She imagined him staring at her whenever he stopped for a traffic light.

She opened her eyes, and caught him looking at her. The glow of the lights on the dash wouldn't permit her to see his expression. Was he feeling what she was beginning to feel? Was he aware of an invisible thread that bound them together even if neither wanted it? The answer to why, even though they were practically neighbors, they had never met each other before the night of Claire McDonald's surprise birthday party?

Jolene was the first one to glance away. She stared out the window until he miraculously found a parking space in front of her building. Waiting until he came around the car and opened the door for her, she placed her hand in his. She gave him her keys; they mounted the stairs to the brownstone. He opened the door, leading into the vestibule, and then escorted her up the stairs, their footsteps silenced by the thick pile of the carpeting lining the staircase.

Michael unlocked the door to her apartment and was met with the soft golden glow of a table lamp. He looked around the entryway before handing her the keys. She placed the keys on the table, dropped her purse on the chair, and kicked off her shoes. Without her shoes, her head was even with his shoulder.

''I'll see you tomorrow at eleven, but you'll have to give me your address.''

Reaching into the breast pocket of his jacket, he withdrew a blank business-sized card and a pen. He wrote down his name, address, and telephone number, handing her the card.

"I'll see you tomorrow."

She smiled, nodding. "Good night."

Inclining his head, he returned her smile. "Good night." Turning, he opened the door, walked out, and then closed it quietly behind him.

Jolene stood motionless, staring at the door. He'd left without kissing her. Tracing the outline of her mouth with a forefinger, she closed her eyes. A shocking realization swept over her. She'd told Michael that she did not want to become involved with him, that she only sought friendship. But she'd lied to him and to her herself. She hadn't slept with a man in more than five years because there hadn't been one who could elicit a modicum of desire in her, no one except the tall, raven-haired, green-eyed stranger. A stranger who'd penetrated the wall she'd erected to keep all men out of her life and out of her bed.

She opened her eyes, an expression of satisfaction shimmering in their velvety soft depths. Michael had referred to her as a black widow. Was she that obvious? Did he know that she'd been mourning, mourning the loss of her sister, her failed marriage, her lack of a social life and companionship? Unknowingly she had become a widow—one who continued to grieve for what was, what could never be again.

A warming glow eddied through her. It was time she opened herself to accept whatever life offered.

Seven

Michael sat motionless, staring at the numbers and lighted dials on the dashboard of his car. It had taken only three minutes to drive from Jolene's house to his. He'd pulled into the driveway, shifted into park, but hadn't turned off the engine. He didn't want to go into the house, not yet. His gaze lingered on the clock. It was 11:35.

An inexplicable restlessness assailed him. He had six months to himself, and he had nothing to do. He could go to one of the clubs he normally frequented with some of the young officers who were assigned to the Pentagon, but dashed that notion as soon as it entered his mind. He had requested the leave to divorce himself temporarily from anything resembling the military.

Picking up the cell phone resting on the console, he dialed his own number, listening intently for the programmed voice telling him how many messages had been left at the number. There were three.

"Michael, darling, you could call your mother every once

in a while to let her know that you're well. She loves you very much. Bye.''

His face split into a wide grin. Whenever Vanessa Blanchard-Kirkland left a message on his answering machine, she always referred to herself in the third person. The call probably was the result of Emily telling her that he'd come to Las Cruces. And it had been several months since he'd visited with his parents. Perhaps he would drive down to Palm Beach and spend a week with them.

He listened to the second message. It was from a woman he'd dated briefly a year ago. She wanted to know if he wanted to get together. If he did, then he could call her— anytime or any day.

"No," he whispered into the mouthpiece.

There was a third call, but the caller hadn't left a message. Pressing a button, he erased the messages and turned off the phone. Putting the car in reverse, he backed out of the driveway.

Making certain he stayed under the speed limit, Michael drove through the quiet, tree-lined Georgetown streets, turning right on Connecticut Avenue and heading in a southern direction. Restaurants and cafés along the wide avenue were overflowing with patrons taking advantage of the warm summer night. He lowered the convertible top, drove past Crystal City, and then took Interstate 395. Road signs became a blur and he sped past cars doing seventy as if they were standing still. He hadn't turned on the radio or the CD player. There was just the sound of the rushing wind competing with the slip-slap of tires on the smooth roadway.

He found himself on I-95, losing track of time, of the speedometer, and everything that had happened to him since being recalled from Japan. It was only when the signs indicated the number of miles to North Carolina that he was aware of how far he'd driven. Slowing, he pulled into a service station at a rest area to refuel. The bright lights ringing the station and several fast-food restaurants could be seen several miles from the exit on the interstate.

Waiting for the attendant to pump the gas, Michael closed his eyes. The image of Jolene Walker crept into his consciousness. It was so vivid that he thought he'd conjured her up. She'd come to him, creeping on whispering feet, her approach as silent as the dawn breaking a nighttime sky.

He didn't know what it was about her, other than her incredible natural beauty, that had him so off balance. He'd followed her when she'd left Paige's house because he couldn't bear not seeing her again. That was something he'd never felt with other women. She hadn't rejected him outright, but she also hadn't made it too easy the night he'd walked her home from the McDonald party. He knew where she lived, where she worked, but she still hadn't offered to give him the number to her residence. That wouldn't have presented a problem if he were still at the Pentagon. All he would have to do was type her name and address into a classified database, and pull up statistics gathered on her since birth.

But Jolene wasn't a target; she was a woman who'd managed to stoke a gently growing flame within him without her being aware of it. Physically she was his ideal; however, there was something more. It was the more he had to identify.

The return drive to D.C. was slower, less frantic, his anxiety receding as he recalled his mantra: *Life is easy when you're not controlled by what you can't control.*

He couldn't control his superior officer's feelings toward him no more than he could control his emotions whenever he was around Jolene. With her, his emotions were spinning out of control, and he couldn't remember when he was ever *not* in control, especially when it came to women.

He was not a neophyte when it came to the opposite sex. However, there was one woman whom he'd believed he loved enough to offer marriage. She'd informed him on their first date she would not sleep with him unless they were married. She'd stunned him with her candor, but he'd continued to see her for more than a year. It had ended when she married someone else with whom she *had* been sleeping. Her duplicity had changed him and he'd become a master in his ability to hide his emotions. He'd never wanted to become that vulnerable again.

This was not to say that he ever mistreated or abused a woman. His father had lectured him sternly about respect and being responsible. And whenever he slept with a woman, he always assumed the responsibility for contraception despite her protests that she was using protection. His liaisons always ended quietly, and once he determined it was over, it was truly over.

The Jaguar ate up the surface of the interstate, and by the time he crossed the Potomac, a tiny glow pierced the veil of navy blue, growing and spreading until streaks of mauve, lavender, and pink overwhelmed the dark sky to herald the advent of a new day.

The heat of the rising sun warmed the earth, penetrating the windshield of the sports car, touching his soul. The drive was what he'd needed to clear his head; however, memories of the time he'd shared with Jolene lingered. He was drawn to her—more than any other woman he'd known. Something swept over him, something quiet, not noisy, that couldn't be seen. He felt the strange and disturbing sensation in his mind, blood, and heart. It was foreign, unfamiliar, and he needed to identify exactly what it was. He was confident it would manifest itself once he saw Jolene again.

Jolene woke up feeling more tired than she had before she'd gone to bed. She'd spent most of the night tossing restlessly until she'd given up all pretense of trying to sleep. The bedside lamp had burned for hours while she'd finished the latest Alex Cross mystery, and it was nearly four when she'd extinguished the lamp a second time.

Peering at the clock, she groaned audibly. It was 6:30. She'd planned to be at the gym at six. Now she was forced to rush to complete her Sunday-morning errands.

She quickly brushed her teeth and splashed water on her face before pulling a tank top and sweatpants over an athletic bra and her panties. Socks, running shoes, and a baseball cap rounded out her workout attire. She had planned to swim laps this morning, but doubted she could make it across the Olympic-sized pool for one lap. The treadmill and rowing machine would become her exercise apparatus of choice this day.

Her step was jaunty as she skipped down three flights of stairs, and walked out into bright sunlight and lower humidity. Making her way to her car, she groaned aloud. Birds had used her brand new navy blue Audi as a canvas for their droppings. The car wash was added to the list of her morning stops.

She completed an intense workout in an hour, spending thirty minutes on the treadmill and another thirty on the rowing machine. The exercise revived her, boosting her energy level. Leaving the gym, she drove to a twenty-four-hour car wash in a less-than-desirable section of D.C., waiting patiently while one of the attendants took an inordinate amount of time buffing the Audi until it sparkled like a polished sapphire. He thanked her profusely when she offered him a lot more than her usual tip. His scarred face split into a wide smile; she noticed something that hadn't been apparent before—he'd had extensive dental work to replace his missing teeth.

Jolene had counseled him as a high-school student, warning him about the dangers of joining a local gang. He'd ignored her, displaying a false bravado fancied by boys who seemed convinced they had to prove to the world they were men, indestructible warriors. His gang involvement had led to selling crack to school-aged children. Then he'd committed the ultimate sin—he'd begun using. This had resulted in a savage beating from a couple of thugs associated with his supplier, which had left him close to death. After an extended stay in the municipal hospital, he'd dropped out of school and moved out of his home, taking on odd jobs to support himself. She'd given him a list of referral sources to assist him in finding housing, medical assistance, and treatment for his substance abuse. At eighteen, he'd made the attempt to turn his life around.

On the return drive to Georgetown, she stopped at a local florist to pick up a bouquet of flowers for her brunch date with Michael. She was drawn to a beautifully handcrafted summer wreath. The sea grass, pink coxcomb and roses, tiny seashells, and sand dollars on a base of salal had captured the soft shades of dawn. She stared at the wreath, contemplating whether it was an appropriate choice. Unlike the wreath, fresh flowers usually lasted no more than a few days.

Walking around the elegant shop, she stopped near a shelf displaying bonsai plants. The miniature plants reminded her that Michael had lived in Japan. Picking up the tag attached to a tiny branch, she winced. It was three times what she would spend for a large bouquet of flowers. She picked up the black shiny pot before she was tempted to change her mind, withdrew a credit card from her tiny purse, and paid for her purchase.

The morning sped by quickly for Jolene. She'd returned home to shower, shampoo her hair, and dress for church. A sunny yellow loose-fitting dress and natural straw hat with turned-up brim were flattering to her figure and coloring as she slipped into a pew at the back of the small, homey church. At the end of the service she did what she'd done every Sunday since losing Jeanine—she lit a votive candle, praying her sister found the peace in death that had eluded her in life.

She had less than half an hour until she had to meet Michael when she returned home a second time that morning. A pair of black capri pants, a white silk tank top, and comfortable black leather mules replaced her dress and sandals.

Consciously her thoughts hadn't strayed to Michael, but as she walked from her house to his she felt blissfully happy, fully alive. Brunch was become their second date, one she looked forward to sharing with him. One she hoped would lead to many more in the future. Her response to him was similar to the one she'd had with Cheney—instant attraction. Her response to him was the same, but she wasn't the same woman who'd fallen so blindly in love with a man she'd known less than a month that she refused to acknowledge his shortcomings. Five years, family tragedy, and a new career focus had changed her completely.

She turned down the street where Michael lived, peering at the numbers on the houses in a charming cul-de-sac. There were only six structures on the dead-end street, most large, imposing, claiming spacious front lawns and flowering shrubs.

Nearing the house bearing the address he'd written on the small card, she stared mutely at a structure with a design completely different from the other Colonial and Georgian-style residences. Its simplicity reminded her of a Frank Lloyd Wright Japanese-inspired design. A broad sheltering roof with generous overhanging eaves and glass windows set with colorful geometric shapes radiated warmth, beckoning her closer. A waist-high slate wall covered with a profusion of climbing vines and flowers protected the property, but a gate made of iron pipe painted a Cherokee red stood open, welcoming her.

She walked up the path, then up six steps to the front

door. Her hand was poised to ring the doorbell when the door opened and Michael Kirkland's tall figure suddenly loomed in front of her.

His exposed muscular arms were brown as berries, and his shoulders were broader than she'd remembered; a stark white T-shirt did little to conceal the developed muscles of his wide, deep chest, while pale, well-washed jeans were molded to his slim hips and solid thighs. His tanned arched feet were bare. In a suit he cut an elegant figure, out of it he was awesome. She must have been gawking because when he leaned down to kiss her, his tongue slipped through her parted lips.

Her shock began as he curved an arm around her waist, pulling her flush against his rock-hard middle. Jolene closed her eyes, moaning softly. This was what she'd wanted last night, had missed so much that it had kept her from a restful night's sleep.

Michael deepened the kiss, losing himself in the taste of Jolene's sweet mouth, the clean scent clinging to her soft flesh. Today she wore a different perfume. It reminded him of a fresh spring rain shower. The soft sounds coming from her throat were his undoing. He hadn't kissed her the night before because he hadn't been in control, and if he had then he doubted whether Jolene would have agreed to see him again. He wouldn't have stopped with a kiss; he would've demanded more.

Pushing against his chest, Jolene jerked her head away. Breathing heavily, she pressed her face to his shoulder, inhaling his potent masculine scent.

"Michael, stop!" she gasped. Her pulse was racing uncontrollably. "Your neighbors."

Throwing back his head, he laughed, the sound coming deep from within his wide chest. He'd thought Jolene was angry because he'd kissed her, not realizing her uneasiness came from the possibility that his closest neighbor might be watching the passionate exchange.

"Let's give them something to talk about," he said teasingly, swinging her up in his arms. The decorative bag with the bonsai brushed his shoulder as she curved her arms around his neck to keep her balance. Taking several steps backward, he kicked the front door closed with a solid slam.

Jolene smiled up at him, unaware of the stirring desire warming his blood. This time when he lowered his head, the action was deliberate, calculated.

His mouth covered hers hungrily, communicating the need to possess her, all of her, while Jolene kissed him with a hunger that belied her outward calm. The kiss changed, becoming a slow drugging intimacy that bound them together, making them one with each other.

She was shocked, amazed at the pleasure of his mouth on hers. Shivers of arousal coursed through her breasts, moving lower to the pulsing area between her thighs. The unexpected rush of moisture jerked her from the erotic abyss, and she pulled back. Her mouth was on fire, throbbing with a lingering desire screaming to be assuaged.

There was no way she could continue to let Michael kiss her. Not if she didn't want to beg him to make love to her. In that instant she felt a profound loss—loss of the intimacy she'd shared with Cheney. The best thing she'd learned from being married was that she had come to know her body. The feelings coursing through her at that moment indicated she was fast approaching the point of no return. She did not want to sleep with Michael—not now. They were strangers. What they had shared was too new.

He stared at her, his eyes a deep green. A knowing smile crinkled her large slanting eyes. It was apparent that the color of his eyes changed with his mercurial moods.

"Good morning," she whispered.

"Good morning to you, too," he countered, kissing the

tip of her nose. Bending slightly, he lowered her feet to the floor.

She extended the shopping bag. "A little house gift."

Michael stared at the bag, his expression still and serious. "You didn't have to bring anything."

"I know I didn't. But I wanted to. Please be gracious and take it."

He took the bag from her fingers, peering inside. The vertical lines creasing his high smooth forehead disappeared, then a grin overtook his symmetrical features. Jolene noticed several attractive lines fanning out around his eyes for the first time.

Reaching into the bag, he withdrew a gardenia bonsai protected by clear cellophane. His smile was dazzling. "It's beautiful."

She arched an eyebrow. "I hope you like it."

"I love it. Thank you."

Their gazes met and fused for several seconds. "You're quite welcome."

He put the plant back in the bag, extending his hand. "Have you eaten anything this morning?"

She grasped his proffered hand, feeling its strength and warmth. "No. Not even a cup of coffee."

"You must be starving. We'll eat first, then we'll decide what we want to do with the rest of the day."

"You said nothing about spending the day together."

Michael affected an expression of innocence. "I didn't?"

"No, you didn't. You invited me for brunch."

"Well, in the Kirkland household brunch is normally a twelve-hour affair. Eleven to eleven, or noon to midnight."

Her jaw dropped. "You're kidding, aren't you?" she asked disbelievingly.

"Nope. It's a tradition my parents initiated, and I see no reason to change it."

"What did you do for twelve hours?"

Pulling her gently into the living room, he set the shopping bag with the plant on a table, then turned and cradled her face between his hands. "We used to get up and go to church, then come home and prepare a monstrous breakfast. My sister and mother baked muffins, biscuits, and sweet breads. My dad and I were given the task of cutting up fruit and preparing the ingredients for the omelettes, while Mom and Emily set the table with silver, china, crystal, and flowers.

"Brunch would go on for hours as we all caught up on what had been going on in our lives during the week. We alternated Sundays cleaning up before everyone retreated to the sunporch to read the Sunday newspapers. We'd compromise when listening to music. There was no conversation as we listened to the prerecorded taped selections. There was only the sound of turning pages or someone asking for a section of the paper.

"If the weather was favorable, I usually went for a walk with my father. It was our time for our man-to-man talks."

A slight frown appeared between Jolene's eyes. "Why did you have to wait for Sundays to talk to your father? Didn't you see each other during the week?"

Michael glanced at a spot over her head. He didn't know how much he should tell Jolene about himself. He'd told her that he worked at the Pentagon, but hadn't told that he'd been assigned to the Defense Intelligence Agency.

"I was enrolled in a private military school about thirty miles outside of Santa Fe. Most of the kids stayed on campus during the school year, coming home only during school holidays, but I elected to come home every weekend."

Her eyes widened with his disclosure. "Where did you attend college?"

A sweep of black lashes came down, concealing his gaze from her. "West Point."

"I take it you're a lifer." Her question was a statement.

He hesitated, a muscle throbbing noticeably in his lean jaw. "I'd like to be."

Jolene hadn't expected the cryptic response. Did he or didn't he plan to make the military his lifelong career?

"Were you working for the military when you lived in Japan?"

His gaze widened. Jolene had a mind like a steel trap. He'd told her he'd worked for an electronics firm during his stint in Japan.

Nodding, he said, "I was involved in a military exchange program, assigned to share information about electronic devices."

His answer seemed to satisfy her when she asked, "What did you do after your talks with your father?"

"Everyone usually took an afternoon nap."

"After the nap?" She hadn't realized her heart was beating a little too quickly. Did he actually expect her to sleep under his roof?

"We'd go out for a movie, or select a favorite from our video library. Of course we had to have hot buttered popcorn."

She smiled. "I prefer gummi bears."

"If you decide to spend the day with me, then I'll see if I can get some for you."

"No, please. I really don't need the extra calories."

His penetrating gaze swept over her body, admiring its firmness. She wasn't thin, because her hips and breasts were too full, rounded. Her body was what he thought of as lush. At thirty years of age, Jolene Walker was not a girl, but all woman.

"What happened after the movie?"

"We cooked dinner. Sometimes we barbecued outdoors, and other times prepared a formal dinner. It was usually a rack of lamb, crown roast, fresh ham, or turkey with all the trimmings. I waited all week for Sunday, referring to it as Family Day.''

Jolene wanted to remind Michael that she wasn't a member of his family; they'd only met a week ago. An unexpected panic seized her. Things were moving too quickly. Even more quickly than they had when she'd first met Cheney. What she did not want was a repeat of what she'd shared with him.

She'd lowered her defenses, and in doing so Michael had assaulted her senses with his powerfully compelling presence. *Be careful,* the inner voice warned her. *Be very, very careful.*

And she would be careful.

"What would you like for dinner?" The confidence in his voice was almost tangible. He'd accepted the fact that she would spend the day with him.

"Broiled lobster." It was the first thing that came to her mind. She heard his quick intake of breath as complete surprise swept over his features. "Is something wrong?"

Michael's gaze narrowed. "How did you know?"

"Know what?"

"That I'd bought lobster for tonight's dinner?"

"I didn't know. I suppose it was a lucky guess."

Closing his eyes, briefly, he forced a smile. He wanted to believe it was a lucky guess. What else could it be? Were they that compatible? What invisible force had brought them together?

Ignoring the oddly primitive warning that told him his future and Jolene's were inextricably connected, he asked, "Are you ready to eat?"

"Yes," she replied. And she was. But more important, she was ready for Michael Kirkland—all of him.

Eight

Jolene sat on a tall stool at a cooking island, sipping from a goblet of chilled orange juice and watching as Michael quickly and expertly diced onions and peppers into tiny pieces on a built-in cutting board.

"Are you right-handed or left?" she asked as he wielded the knife with his left hand.

"Both," he said, not looking up from his task. "I eat and write with my right hand, but do everything else with my left."

"Isn't that confusing?"

Wiping his hands on a cloth towel, he picked up his goblet filled with juice. "Not for me. I just do it automatically." He was equally proficient firing a gun or rifle with either hand.

Her gaze swept around the open spaces making up the kitchen. The entire first floor of the house seemed to be constructed without walls, giving it a sense of unending openness. Oak floors, cabinets, and moldings were the perfect contrast to beige walls reminiscent of rice paper.

Michael noticed her glancing around the highly functional kitchen. "I'll give you a tour after we eat."

"Can I help with anything? I don't like sitting around doing nothing."

"Relax, Jolene. You're a guest."

"I thought today was Family Day."

"Today you're *my* guest." His voice was soft, quiet as he emphasized the last two words.

She went completely still, her gaze fusing with his. "When will I stop being a guest?"

Glancing down at the sharp paring knife, Michael's right hand caressed the surface of the cutting board as lovingly as he would her bare flesh. He wanted to touch her—all over.

"That will have to be your decision."

She squinted at him. "Meaning what?"

He picked up the knife again, concentrating on dicing the strips of red, yellow, and green pepper lining the cutting board. "When you decide what we have can be taken to another level."

Jolene detested veiled innuendos. Michael wasn't a client of hers with whom she had to wait until he felt comfortable enough for her to be candid.

"Do you consider sleeping together another level?"

Putting aside the knife, he scrubbed his hands before rinsing them under cold water from the small built-in sink on the cooking island. He dried them on the towel before coming around the island to face her. Reaching out, he pulled her gently off the stool.

She felt the strength in his fingers as they tightened on her bare shoulders. There was something dark and angry in his cold expression that unnerved her. She counseled women who existed in a world of fear when it came to their husbands or significant others. She'd witnessed firsthand the terror in Jeanine's eyes whenever Lamar walked into a room. The abject fear whenever he whispered something in Jeanine's ear.

Michael pulled her up close, her breasts flattening against the unyielding wall of his chest. The rigid tension in her limbs fled as he lowered his head, breathing a kiss under her left ear. Her arms curved around his waist as if she'd done it countless times, holding him possessively.

"I'm not going to lie and say I don't want to sleep with you," he whispered against the column her long, scented neck. "I wanted you the moment I laid eyes on you."

"Why?" she whispered back. Her voice was muffled in the cotton fabric covering his shoulder.

"I don't know, Jolene."

"I can't sleep with you, Michael. Not now."

A soft laugh rumbled in chest. "Did I ask you to?"

"No." The single word came out like a child's reply.

"Then we won't rush it. If it happens, it happens. And if it doesn't, then we can always remain friends."

Closing her eyes, she tried to still the runaway beating of her heart. She was certain he could feel her heart pumping wildly against his chest. What she wanted to tell him was that she did want him. She did want to sleep with him because she wanted to recapture the intimacy she'd missed since ending her marriage.

Resting her cheek over his heart, she counted the strong steady beats. "I want you to promise me something."

"What?"

"Promise me, Michael."

Easing back, he stared at her bare face. She hadn't worn any makeup, yet she still was ravishingly beautiful. There was a pleading in her eyes he could not resist. He didn't know what she wanted from him, but whatever it was, he was willing to concede.

"I promise, Jolene."

"When it's over, I don't want you to come back into my life. I don't believe in repeating mistakes."

Michael wanted to shake her until her teeth rattled. What was she talking about? They hadn't even begun, and already she was talking about it being over. He'd kissed her twice, and it had taken everything in his iron-willed control not to ravish her body. He dared not think of how he would react if she actually invited him to her bed.

"Our meeting each other is not a mistake. My running into Damon after four years was not a coincidence. Your date having to handle a family crisis the other night wasn't a catastrophe. It was divine intervention we met *that* Friday night. And it's providence that we know the same people, fate that we live within walking distance of each other."

"I'm not saying that you're a mistake, Michael."

"What is it then?" The vibrant color in his eyes faded to a pale, harsh green, all traces of warmth missing.

Jolene refused to relent. He could not intimidate her. "I don't know what it is," she said honestly, "but I'm a realist. I believe in living one day at a time. I like you and enjoy being with you. However, when the day comes that I don't want to be with you, or continue whatever relationship we'll share at that time, then you'll be the first to know."

His impassive expression changed, becoming almost tender. "Thank you."

She was amazed at how quickly his moods and expressions changed. The man was a chameleon. Forcing a smile, she said, "You're quite welcome."

I like you and enjoy being with you. Jolene's statement lingered with Michael as he reached for a metal canister, measuring a mixture of rose petals, linden flowers, and chamomile leaves into a small dish. They'd scaled the first hurdle: They liked each other.

He poured boiling water into a pale green ceramic teapot covered with painted black Asian calligraphy. Waiting five minutes, he discarded the water and gently crushed the leaves and flowers to release their flavor, then transferred the mixture to a tea ball, returning it to the pot.

"How long will it have to steep?" Jolene asked. She'd watched the entire tea-making process, fascinated. He executed the task with a minimum of wasted motion. Never had she seen a man with more beautiful hands. They were long, slender, seemingly too delicate for his height and weight.

"Only five minutes," he said.

She glanced over at more than half a dozen matching canisters lining a nook along a countertop. "How many varieties of teas do you have?"

He smiled at her. "Too many. I have a supply packed away in a room off the kitchen. The one we're going to drink is a soothing tea. It's legendary for calming the nerves and promoting restful sleep."

Her gaze widened. "I could've used it last night. I sat up reading until four."

Tilting his head at an angle, he regarded her for several seconds. She, too, hadn't been able to go to sleep after their date. "It was almost four when I found myself thirty miles from the Carolina border."

"Why?"

"After I dropped you off I decided to go for a drive."

"To North Carolina?"

He shrugged a shoulder in the elegant gesture she'd come to look for. "I drove until I was low on gas. I would've called you to keep me company if I'd had your number.''

Her jaw dropped slightly. What was he talking about? ''You have my telephone number.''

Closing the distance between them, he cradled her chin in one hand, pressing his mouth to her parted lips. ''I have your number at the Sanctuary, not the one at your home.''

Jolene met his unwavering gaze, hers drinking in the sensuality of the man looming above her. There was something so potent radiating from him that she found it difficult to draw a normal breath. He exuded a powerful vitality she could not resist. Who was he? Why were they thrown together? Why now and not a year ago?

He'd spoken of providence, coincidence, fate, and destiny. Did he really believe in divine intervention, that a higher power had brought them together for a more noble purpose?

''I'll give it to you before I leave.'' She didn't recognize her own voice. It was breathless, as if she'd run a grueling race.

His lips brushed against hers again in a gentle joining that sent the pit of her stomach into a wild spin. Her right hand touched his clean-shaven jaw as she leaned into him. A swath of erotic heat swept through her celibate body, leaving embers of smoldering passion crying out for assuagement. She had to stop Michael, stop him before she begged him to take her to his bed.

Pushing hard against his shoulder, she tore her mouth away, her eyes wild and dark with passion. Her breasts rose and fell heavily, bringing his gaze to the spot. He knew! He knew he'd aroused her.

Turning, Michael walked over to the refrigerator. He jerked open the door and picked up the pitcher of orange juice. His hand tightened around the glass handle in a savage grip. He had to walk away from Jolene, even if it was for only a minute. Touching her, kissing her had him so aroused, he feared embarrassing himself. It was the second time since meeting her that his body refused to follow the dictates of his brain. It was only when the hardness in his jeans eased somewhat that he returned to the cooking island.

"Come, I'll show you where we're going to eat."

She followed him to a room off the kitchen. She did not know what to expect, but certainly not the scene unfolding before her stunned gaze. The large space reminded her of a Japanese teahouse. Octagonal in shape, the walls were made entirely of screened-in windows. Four of the eight sides were open to take advantage of the warm air. A low lacquer table, surrounded by large black and pale green floor cushions, was set up in the middle of the room. The table was set with clean minimalist white porcelain enhanced by a simple hand-painted black line design. Curving a hand under her elbow, Michael supported her until she sat down on a cushion.

A woven rug made of straw covered the gleaming oak floor, while low tables were overflowing with bonsai plants. Towering stalks of bamboo in glazed containers grew in wild abandonment. Gurgling water from a large indoor corner pool created a soothing mood; water trickled over rocks and pebbles concealed by a profusion of bamboo shoots and water lilies. Her gaze shifted to the landscape beyond the room. What first appeared to be a haphazard overgrowth of trees, brushes, and flowering plants was actually a meticulously planned garden.

A brass clock atop an Oriental chest decorated with antiqued-brass butterfly hardware chimed the hour. It was exactly noon. She counted eighteen drawers in the chest; all were covered with carved Chinese characters and brass ring pulls. What she'd seen of Michael's house was nothing short of magnificent. It was the perfect blend of Eastern and Western cultures.

Brunch lasted two hours. Over several cups of tea, omelettes filled with peppers, onion, smoked ham, chorizo, mushrooms, and pepper jack cheese and covered with a tangy salsa, and mini raisin-carrot muffins, Jolene was drawn into a sensual vortex from which she did not want to escape.

She sat quietly, listening as Michael revealed a little of who he was. He'd purchased the property with a house and attached carriage house a year after his transfer back to the States. A contractor had demolished the house, moved the carriage house forward, added a second story, and expanded it twenty-five hundred square feet. His aunt had designed the interiors and his cousin the gardens. Moving the carriage house provided for more acreage and privacy from his nearest neighbor at the rear of the property.

He gave her a tour of the entire house, confirming her first impression that the classic design was the influence of Frank Lloyd Wright.

Cradling her hand, Michael led Jolene down the winding staircase. "I took a drive to Pennsylvania during my first year at West Point. I went to a waterfall near Mill Run, Pennsylvania, and saw Fallingwater for the first time. I stood there, awed. The house, the trees, the outcropping of rocks, and the waterfall are one—indivisible."

She thought of all the work and money Michael had invested in his Wright-influenced home, wondering if he would ever sell it. "What if you're reassigned again? What would you do with this place?"

Stopping before they pushed off the last stair, he cradled her face between his palms. "I'm on official leave, so your question is moot."

"For how long?"

"Six months."

She flashed her beguiling smile. "At least you'll know that you will spend Christmas here. It must be wonderful to sit in the teahouse and watch the falling snow."

"It is," he said.

Six months was enough time for him to decide whether he would remain with the army or resign his commission. Six months was also enough time to determine whether Jolene Walker would become an integral part of his future.

Nine

Images of her Sunday sojourn with Michael lingered with Jolene as she parked her car in her assigned spot behind the Sanctuary. She hadn't spent twelve hours with him, leaving before eight. She'd wanted to call her parents for their scheduled weekly telephone chat. Michael had walked her back to her apartment, where they'd exchanged a chaste kiss and a promise to see each other again. This time she'd offered to host the next Sunday brunch.

Unlocking the back door, she keyed in the password to deactivate the alarm system, pressed several buttons to turn on the lights, then made her way to her office. She'd been the last to leave on Friday and the first to arrive on Monday, finding it hard to believe all she had encountered and experienced with Michael in just two days. They'd shared a dinner cruise, danced, kissed, and then enjoyed brunch and dinner the following day with a promise to see each other again.

After hanging her suit jacket on a coat tree, she returned to her desk and stared at a stack of reports. The operating

license from one of her federal grants was scheduled to
expire at the end of October. She had to prepare for a quality
assurance review.

She heard a distinctive female voice calling her name,
recognizing it as the clinical director's. Deborah Madison
was her only serious challenger when it came to who logged
the most hours at the counseling center.

Deborah stuck her head through the partially opened door.
"I was certain I was going to beat you in this morning. I
stopped by Sam's deli. I know you like his coffee, so I
bought an extra container."

Jolene waved to her. "Thanks. Come in, sit down, and
relax before the others get here."

Deborah walked into the office and dropped her handbag
and leather case on a love seat. She handed Jolene a large
container of steaming coffee from a bag, then sat down.

Deborah had recently celebrated her thirty-ninth birthday,
but appeared at least five years older. A network of small
lines crisscrossed her face, the result of spending too many
hours in the hot sun. Her straight, uneven mousy brown hair
was mixed with an unbecoming steel gray that she refused
to color. She claimed a small turned-up nose and a narrow,
pinched mouth. Her eyes were her best feature: large, vibrant,
and a sparkling cornflower blue. She was engaged to another
student as an undergraduate, but never married, and had
given up all hope of becoming a wife and a mother. The
Sanctuary had become her husband, and the clients her children. The staff had gotten together and given her a gift
certificate to a fashionable beauty spa for a complete
makeover for her birthday, but she hadn't yet availed herself
of its services.

Jolene had recommended her as clinical director to the
board of directors after an exhaustive search and interview
with more than a dozen candidates. Deborah's credentials,
supervisory experience, and familiarity with victims of

domestic violence were the deciding factors. She'd just completed her first year in the position.

Deborah took a sip from her Styrofoam cup, moaning softly. "I have to agree with you, Jolene. Sam does make the best coffee in D.C. Even if I have to drive two miles out of the way."

"I didn't want to say I told you so. It must be the water, because it can't be the coffee beans."

"The man can give Starbucks a run their money," Deborah mumbled between sips. "How was the surprise party?" She'd received an invitation, but had declined, knowing she wouldn't be able to secure a date.

"Claire was very surprised."

"That's good. How did *Stu* like rubbing shoulders with one of D.C.'s finest families?" There was no mistaking the facetiousness in her tone.

Jolene composed her thoughts before replying. Stuart and Deborah had met once, and they had mixed like oil and water. They'd taken an instant dislike to each other.

"I didn't go with Stuart."

"Who did you go with?"

"I didn't *go* with anyone. I met him there."

Deborah's blue eyes widened until they resembled half dollars. "Who is he?"

"He's a friend of Damon McDonald."

"And?" She leaned forward on the love seat, her eyes shining with excitement.

"And that's it. He was my dinner date for the evening."

"What does he look like?" Deborah asked, continuing with her interrogation.

Closing her eyes, Jolene affected a dreamy expression. "He's tall, dark, and very handsome."

Deborah grunted. "Just my type." Her colleagues and close friends were aware of her preference for African-American men. "Really, Jolene, what does he look like?"

She opened her eyes, staring directly at the clinical director. "He's exactly how I described him."

"Are you going to see him again?"

"Don't forget I'm seeing Stuart."

The older woman rolled her eyes while shaking her head. Jolene did not tell Deborah that she was already seeing Michael, and that there was a distinct possibility that Stuart and his wife might reconcile. She'd made it a point to keep her personal life separate from her professional life, but there were times when the two merged.

"I hate to change the subject," she continued, patting the stack of papers on a corner of her desk, "but we're going to begin reviewing client case records before the Feds get here."

Deborah sobered quickly. "I suppose you want the usual: intake assessments, treatment plans, quarterlies, psychosocials, health and financial histories, and discharges."

Jolene nodded. "Everything. And make certain you check all of the session notes and utilization reviews. We were cited on them the last time. I'm working on the treatment improvement protocol, and there's still the policy and procedure manual to go over. We updated the personnel manual last year, so that's one less thing we have to review."

"When do you expect them?"

"They can show up anytime between now and the end of October. Which means we have less than eight weeks."

Gathering her purse and case, Deborah pushed to her feet. "I guess I'd better get to work. I'll talk to you later." She walked out of the office, closing the door behind her.

Leaning back in her chair, Jolene studied the open day planner on her desk. Her week was filled with supervision and business lunches with two groups of local merchants who'd expressed a willingness to support the Sanctuary's latest fund-raising venture. These donations were earmarked to build a safe house for abused women and their children in a remote section of northern Virginia.

She dialed her administrative assistant's extension, leaving a message on her voice mail to call to confirm her 12:30 meeting. She'd hired and fired three secretaries before Sally Leonard had settled comfortably into the position. A former victim of domestic violence, Sally had left her abusive boyfriend, relocated to Silver Spring, Maryland, and undergone treatment for cocaine abuse at an outpatient program. She'd completed a government-funded vocational training program, then been referred to the Sanctuary for possible employment. Her office skills and maturity levels were exceptional at twenty-four, and after a three-month probationary period, she'd become a permanent member of the support staff.

Glancing around the office, Jolene admired the decor. It was spacious, comfortable, and the furnishings reflected her feminine brand of style and strength. She preferred to hold staff meetings in her office rather than the conference room because it was less formal. One corner of the large space was set up as a sitting area with a sofa, two love seats, and three guest chairs upholstered in taupe suede, while another corner claimed a private dining area. A custom-made oval opaque lacquered-top table had six comfortable chairs in the same taupe suede. The walls were covered with a wheat-covered woven fabric, the windows with matching vertical blinds, and the overall effect was relaxed and friendly, but businesslike. Hanging plants and a potted banana tree added a homey touch.

Shifting to a workstation behind her desk, she turned on a computer, waiting for it to boot up. Completing the treatment improvement protocol was top priority. She slipped in a disk labeled TIP, bringing up the draft, and reading her last entry:

Effects of Domestic Violence on Substance Abuse Treatment: Domestic violence is the use of intentional emotional, psychological, sexual, or physical force by one family member or intimate partner to control another. Violent acts include verbal, emotional, and physical intimidation; destruction of the victim's possessions; maiming or killing pets; threats; forced sex; slapping, punching, kicking, choking, burning, stabbing, shooting, and killing victims. Spouses, parents, stepparents, children, siblings, elderly relatives, and intimate partners may all be targets of domestic violence.

Her fingers skimmed the keyboard as she defined *batterer* and *survivors*, expanded on the connection between substance abuse and domestic violence, and the impact of violence on substance-abuse treatment. The morning sped by quickly. The only interruptions were two calls from Sally, updating her on the location for her luncheon meeting.

Retreating to a private bathroom, she dusted the shine off her nose and cheeks with a bronzer, applied a coat of russet lipstick, and brushed her short curling hair off her forehead and over her ears. After washing her hands, she dried them and returned to her office, stopping when she saw Sally standing in the doorway cradling an enormous bouquet of snow-white flowers to her chest. If it hadn't been for a glimpse of braided hair, Jolene wouldn't have been able to identify the person carrying the flowers.

"These came for you, Miss Walker," Sally announced behind the bouquet.

Galvanized into motion, she walked over and helped her assistant carry the heavy vase. "Did it come with a card?"

"A card and this." Reaching into the pocket of her dress, Sally pulled out a small, square foil-wrapped package, handing it to Jolene, who placed it on the coffee table in the sitting area next to the vase of flowers.

"I'll open it when I get back. I have to leave now, or I'm going to be late for my meeting." She pulled an envelope off the yellow cellophane, slipping it into the pocket of her ice blue linen suit jacket. The flowers were probably from a former client.

Jolene maneuvered into a parking lot alongside a restaurant in the Northwest. Longtime residents who lived within three square miles of Rudy B's believed the eating establishment should've been listed with the National Trust for Historic Preservation. The original Rudy B's, a one-room log cabin, had been constructed behind the small house belonging to Rueben Brown in 1908. It had been expanded after World War I, then again in the sixties, and had undergone extensive renovations in 1998 for its ninetieth anniversary. The family-owned restaurant had earned the reputation of serving the best soul food in the capitol district.

She opened the front door, waiting for her eyes to adjust from coming from the bright sunlight into the subdued shadows. The sounds of rattling flatware, dishes, a jukebox blaring out the latest hip-hop tune, and raucous laughter blended with the voices of sassy waitresses flirting with their regular customers.

"Hey, sugah, you the one who called for a takeout of fried catfish, potato salad, and slaw?" A tall, full-figured middle-aged woman sporting a platinum wig greeted her with a wide grin.

Jolene counted at least six teeth completely covered with gold crowns. Returning the friendly smile, she shook her head. "No, I'm not. I'm here to see Mr. Brown."

"Which Mr. Brown, sugah? Robbie, Reuben, Ronnie, or Reggie?" She'd named all of the Brown brothers.

"Rueben."

"He's in the back," she said, pointing a red acrylic-tipped finger toward a door at the rear of the restaurant marked PRIVATE.

"Thank you."

A swollen silence gripped the interior of the restaurant as Jolene walked to Rueben Brown's private office with long, purposeful strides. The slim skirt to her blue linen suit, molded to firm thighs, offered the admiring male patrons a generous glimpse of her shapely legs in a pair of sheer pale hose. Two inches of black patent leather pumps put her at the six-foot mark.

"Hot damn! Milk sure does a body *good*!" a man crooned as she moved past his table.

Turning her head to hide a smile, she knocked on the door, pushing it open when an authoritative male voice said, "Come in!"

She walked into the room and came face-to-face with Reuben Brown. Extending a hand, she flashed an open, friendly smile. "Good afternoon, Mr. Brown."

Rueben, one of four grandsons of the original owner, shook her hand, smiling, the gesture not quite reaching his sparkling golden eyes. He was a handsome man with smooth dark brown skin, a shaved head, and a solid body for a fifty-four-year-old man who'd spent more than half his life as a chef.

"I really don't know how good it is," he said cryptically.

Jolene sobered, vertical lines appearing between her eyes. "What's the matter?"

Cradling her elbow, Rueben led Jolene to a leather sofa. "Please sit down."

Waiting until he sat beside her, she stared at his strained expression. "Where are the other men?" She'd expected to meet with him and three other local businessmen.

Rueben blew out his cheeks. "They're not coming."

"Why not?" Her voice rose in surprise.

He glanced away, his gaze fixed on the lamp on a desk littered with bills and orders. "They claim they don't want to contribute to a foundation that won't benefit black women."

Jolene sat there, shocked, shaken. "What are you talking about?"

Rueben gave her a direct stare. "This safe house you're thinking about building." She nodded. "How many black women and their children do you expect will be housed there?"

"I . . . I don't know. That's something we can't predict or project."

"Exactly. You want us, black businessmen, to contribute to a project that will probably exclude black families."

"That's not true."

"Don't delude yourself, Miss Walker. We all know that it's mostly white men who beat their wives."

Her temper flared, shock yielding to anger. "You think white men have a monopoly on domestic violence?"

"How many sisters do you know that will let brothers kick their butts on a regular basis?"

"More than you'll ever know, Mr. Brown. Domestic violence doesn't favor any race, religion, ethnicity, or socioeconomic group." Struggling to keep her temper from exploding, she stood up, glaring down at his shaved pate. "I hope and pray no woman in your family will ever have to take advantage of the Sanctuary's services." Slipping the strap of her purse over her shoulder, she forced a polite smile, one she did not feel.

Reuben rose to stand beside her. "Please, Miss Walker. Stay for lunch and we'll talk about it."

"There's nothing more to talk about, Mr. Brown. I'm sorry about taking up your time."

Spinning on her heels, she walked out of the cluttered office, closing the door softly behind her. Staring straight ahead, she walked out of Rudy B's and to the parking lot, seething. Rueben Brown and the three missing officers of the Northwest Black Businessmen's Association had pledged to support the safe house when Claire McDonald had approached them for their civic and financial backing. However, they'd reneged, and now it was her responsibility to inform the board chair of their decision.

She sat in her car, staring through the windshield with sightless eyes. A heaviness settled in her chest. Previous fund-raising events had yielded enough money to purchase the land, but the outstanding balance for the construction of a house with sixteen-bedroom suites had exceeded the originally projected amount by $1.2 million. The board had hoped to raise enough money before the end of the year to break ground and lay the foundation the following spring. Late summer was the expected date for completing the project. Now, that appeared to be an even more remote possibility.

Turning the key in the ignition, she started up the car and drove back to the Sanctuary. Maybe, she thought as she maneuvered into her parking space, she'd been too hasty to leave Rudy B's. Perhaps she should've stayed and talked to Reuben. But he'd told her that the others weren't willing to donate their money to the building of the safe house, and there was one thing she hadn't done in the past and did not intend to begin now—and that was beg.

Entering through the back door, she made it to her office without encountering anyone. This was one of those times when she didn't want to see or talk to anyone. She slipped out of her jacket, hung it up, walked over, and sat down on one of the love seats. Staring at the vase of flowers, she remembered the card. Pushing to her feet, she retreated to the coat tree, retrieving the envelope from her jacket pocket.

Slipping a finger under the flap, she withdrew a small card and read the neat, handwritten missive: *Thank you for a*

*wonderful weekend. I'm giving you my heart for safekeeping.
Affectionately, Michael.*

Her mood lightened as she moved over to the coffee table
and picked up the small foil-wrapped box next to the vase
filled with snowy white roses, mokara orchids, white asters,
Queen Anne's lace, and mini carnations.

He'd sent her flowers and what else?

She unwrapped the box, opened it, and went completely
still. Cradled in cotton was an exquisite tiny Limoges heart.
Her fingertips grazed the fragile porcelain surface, tracing
the hand-painted flowers on a white background, bordered
in blue, and with an antique copper clasp. Opening the clasp,
her surprise was complete. A pair of heart-shaped diamond
studs winked back at her.

Placing a hand over her mouth, she sat down, staring at
the bouquet of flowers as Michael's written message whispered to her. *I'm giving you my heart for safekeeping.*

She'd informed Michael she wanted friendship, but it was
apparent he wanted more—much more. And she wasn't able
to offer him more.

Not now.

Not at this time in her life.

Ten

Jolene moved over to the desk, slipping the Limoges heart with the diamond studs into her purse concealed in a drawer. Picking up the telephone, she dialed Michael's number, an expression of determination radiating from her dark brown eyes.

"Hello."

The sound of his deep voice startled her. How had she forgotten the sensual timbre? "Michael, this is Jolene."

"How are you?"

"Good," she said. But she wasn't good. She was still berating herself because she'd failed to secure the Northwest Black Businessmen's pledge for a donation for the safe house.

"I'd like to thank you for the flowers, but I cannot accept the earrings."

"Why not?"

Swiveling in her chair, Jolene stared out the window behind her desk. "We're just friends."

"You've never accepted a gift from a friend?"

"Yes . . . but—"

"But what?" he asked, interrupting her.

"Not diamond earrings."

"Lighten up, Jolene."

A lingering frustration surfaced from her aborted meeting with Rueben. "Don't ever tell me what to do, Michael."

There was a noticeable pause before his voice came through the earpiece again. "What's going on, Jolene? What happened to you today?" His tone was soft, coaxing.

How did he know? Was he that perceptive that he could sense her moods over the telephone? Suddenly she felt like a chastised child. He didn't deserve to be the object of her frustration and disappointment. The Northwest businessmen had pledged a generous donation of fifty thousand dollars. It was not often the Sanctuary realized that lump sum amount. Most times donations ranged from ten dollars to several thousand from individuals and more from groups or corporate sponsors.

"I'm sorry. I didn't mean to snap at you."

"Have you had lunch?"

"No." And she hadn't. She'd declined Rueben's offer to eat at Rudy B's.

"Have lunch with me. If you want you can cry on my shoulder. I won't even charge you."

She laughed softly, wanting to refuse, to tell him that she didn't need to see him more than once or twice a week. She wanted her interaction with Michael to be on a social level, not a repeat of what she'd shared with Cheney. With him she'd brought her work and her cause home. It had destroyed their marriage.

But she and Michael weren't married. They didn't live together. They were friends. And that's what friends were for—to confide to one another, to vent, and to lend a shoulder to cry on.

A sensual smile curved her mouth. "Okay."

"I'll be there in half an hour."

"I'll be ready."

Hanging up, she closed her eyes while shaking her head. What was the matter with her? Why was she fooling herself, trying to rationalize that he was only a friend? Why was it she couldn't resist him? What was there about Michael Kirkland that had her running to him whenever he called? And was she really ready for him?

Opening her eyes, she let out her breath in an audible sigh. She knew the answers to her questions even before they were formed in her mind. She was lonely, she missed the tender intimacy between a man and a woman, and she'd matured enough to realize that she couldn't completely eradicate domestic violence or substance abuse. Her efforts could effect change in an individual's life, but in the end she would only be remembered not as a miracle worker, but as a social worker.

Michael opened the door, walking into the Sanctuary's expansive reception area. He'd been impressed by the exterior of the building housing the program. It was centrally located two blocks from Connecticut Avenue and four blocks from the Metro's Dupont Circle station. An overwhelmingly homey feeling was enhanced by a sloping manicured front lawn, blooming rose bushes, vinyl siding in a soft, sand beige, and navy blue shuttered windows. A colorful summer wreath on the door bore a sign reading, WELCOME.

A woman with graying red curly hair and bright blue eyes stared at him from behind a glass partition. Her eyes narrowed in suspicion, and he suspected not many men came to or were welcomed at the Sanctuary. There was a network of lines around her eyes, but he knew they hadn't come so much from smiling as from squinting.

"Good afternoon. May I help you?" Her voice was strong, demanding. She hadn't bothered to slide back the partition.

Leaning down, Michael forced a polite smile. The nameplate on her desk read, Angela Reilly, Receptionist.

"I'm here to see Miss Walker."

"Do you have an appointment?" Her brusque tone hadn't softened with his smile.

He shifted an eyebrow. "I spoke to her less than thirty minutes ago."

"Your name?"

She should've been a sergeant, he mused. "Michael Kirkland."

"Have a seat, Mr. Kirkland. I'll let Miss Walker's assistant know you're here."

Sitting down on a beige cushioned chair, he stared at a trio of framed Impressionist prints on a wall covered in a pale textured fabric. The reception area was as inviting as the building's exterior. Live hanging plants, a wood-burning fireplace, an area with two small tables with chairs, bookcases filled with children's books, cubbies with toys and games, and several low tables covered with magazines geared toward women beckoned one to stay awhile.

A door opened, and a young woman with flawless brown skin stepped into the reception area. She stared at the tall man sitting on a chair idly flipping the pages of a magazine. Her gold-flecked gaze swept over him as she successfully concealed a smile. It was on rare occasion that a man, other than the one or two husbands or partners of clients who electively joined them in treatment, came through the doors of the Sanctuary.

"Mr. Kirkland?"

Michael's head came up. He replaced the magazine on a table and rose to his feet. His gaze met Sally Leonard's. She was a petite woman with a profusion of braided extensions that reached her tiny waist.

Smiling, Sally extended her hand. "I'm Sally Leonard, Miss Walker's assistant."

Returning her smile, Michael shook her hand. She was a refreshing contrast to the dour receptionist. "It's a pleasure, Ms. Leonard."

"Miss Walker is expecting you." She nodded at Angela, who pressed a buzzer under her desk, releasing the lock on the door. "Please follow me."

He followed Sally down a wide, beige and dark blue tweed carpeted hallway, past a staircase to the second level, visually cataloging the offices. The doors to some were closed, others stood open, offering a glimpse of spaces filled with modern functional office furniture. However, each was identified by individual touches: walls covered with diplomas, licenses, awards, and prints by favorite artists. Credenzas held personal photographs, plants, and vases with fresh flowers. Every door had a brass plate with a therapist's name, title, and credentials. Jolene's office was at the end of the hallway, tucked in a corner, at the rear of the two-story dwelling.

She sat behind her desk, talking softly on the telephone. Her solemn expression brightened as he walked through the door. She waved him in as Sally walked out, closing the door softly behind her.

Michael moved over to the sitting area, folding his tall frame into a suede chair. His features did not change when he saw the large bouquet of flowers on the coffee table. It had taken him more than twenty minutes to personally select the flowers he wanted in the bouquet.

I'd like to thank you for the flowers, but I cannot accept the earrings. His expression grew hard, brooding, as he recalled her statement. Jolene Walker was making it very difficult for him to court her. He'd gotten up early, driven to a twenty-four-hour sports club in downtown D.C. to work out, then returned home to shower. It had been 8:30 when he'd found himself on the road, driving to Chevy Chase, Maryland. He'd waited until the elegant shops along Wisconsin Avenue had opened for business, and an hour later he'd returned to his car with a pair of diamond earrings and the porcelain heart-shaped Limoges collectible. The earrings were a smaller version of an exquisite pair with a total weight of two carats. They would've looked spectacular in Jolene's pierced lobes with her perfect face and short hair. Today, her jewelry was the single strand of pearls she'd worn during their dinner cruise, and matching pearl studs.

His gaze lingered on her impassive expression. She looked different, very professional. He admired her slim toned arms and the length of her long graceful neck under a white linen vest that doubled as a blouse. She drew in a deep breath, closing her eyes, while nodding. Executing a half turn on her chair, she stared through the vertical blinds lining the window behind her desk.

He didn't miss the expression of frustration cross her face as she pulled her lower lip between her teeth. There was no doubt whomever she was talking to had upset her. Seeing Jolene's beautiful face distorted by uneasiness disturbed him. He liked her, more than he wanted to, and he cared for her, much more than he realized. And in an instant all of his protective instincts were in full throttle.

Even though Jolene looked nothing like the woman he'd pledged a year of his life to with a fervent hope that they would spend the rest of their lives together, his feelings for her were similar. What he refused to acknowledge was that he'd lowered his defenses, opening himself up for rejection again. He had to be careful—very, very careful—not to repeat the mistake. With Jolene there would be no compromise.

She ended her call and he stood up, closing the distance between them. Waiting until Jolene rounded the desk, he reached for her, folding her gently against his chest.

"How are you?"

Tilting her head, she smiled up at him. "Much better. Now that you're here."

His black curving eyebrows shot up in surprise. "Should I take that as a compliment?"

Her eyes crinkled in a smile as she drank in the essence of his masculine beauty. He was casually dressed in a pair of tan slacks, black loafers, and a black silk T-shirt.

"A compliment of the highest order." Leaning forward, she pressed her lips to his clean-shaven jaw. "I'm glad you called me, because I need to put some distance between myself and this place for a few hours." She'd just gotten off the phone with Claire McDonald. Rueben Brown had called Claire with the disappointing news that his business organization had reneged on their promise to become a contributor for the safe house project.

Lowering his arms, Michael released her. "Your wish is my command. I'm ready whenever you are."

Waiting for her to retrieve the jacket to her ice blue linen skirt and a black patent leather shoulder handbag, he silently admired the woman who unknowingly had captured his heart. He'd seen her in evening dress, casual and business attire, concluding he liked her equally in all three. She was elegant, feminine, and shockingly sexy.

Jolene walked into an adjoining office, informing Sally that she would be out of the office for a few hours, and that she should refer all emergencies to Deborah.

"Do you have your cell phone with you, Miss Walker?"

"Yes, I do. Why?"

"Please leave it on."

Sally had confided to Jolene that she did not like Deborah Madison. She couldn't identify what it was, but she surreptitiously kept her distance from the Sanctuary's clinical director.

"Refer all my calls to Miss Madison." There was an

edge of authority in the directive that Sally recognized immediately.

"Yes, Miss Walker."

Jolene curved her arm through Michael's. "Where are you parked?"

"I found a space on N Street."

"Would you prefer we take my car?"

He stared at her heels. "We'll have to take my car. If you don't want to walk, then I can go get it while you wait here."

She shook her head. "I don't mind walking."

What he didn't tell Jolene was that their lunch was in the trunk of his car. He'd stopped at a gourmet shop and ordered a picnic basket filled with salad, fresh fruit, and a sparkling beverage.

Slipping her hand in his larger one, Jolene said, "We'll go out the back door."

They walked hand in hand, enjoying the summer heat and each other's closeness. They turned down the block where he'd parked his sports car. He'd purchased the Jaguar based upon his uncle's fervent claim that it was one of the finest driving machines in existence. Martin Cole had bought his first automobile at nineteen. It had been a vintage Jaguar sports car. Sixty years later, he still owned and drove the same model car.

Martin had accompanied Michael when he'd purchased the XKR convertible last spring. He'd flown to West Palm Beach, purchased the car, then driven back to Washington, D.C., taking pleasure in its easy handling. He liked driving his sports-utility vehicle, but enjoyed the sports car more.

Pressing a button on a remote device, he unlocked the doors. Leaning down, he opened the passenger-side door and helped Jolene into the low-slung seat. Seconds later, he slipped behind the wheel, and pulled away from the curb in one continuous motion.

Jolene stared at his distinctive profile. "Where are we going?"

Reaching for a pair of silver oval, wire-rimmed sunglasses on the dashboard, he placed them on the bridge of his straight nose. "Virginia."

"Oh." The single word was filled with awe and surprise.

Smiling, she settled back against the leather seat and closed her eyes. The cooling air from several vents feathered over her face, and she felt a calmness invading her mind and body for the first time since she stalked out of Rudy B's.

Michael Kirkland was good for her—very, very good. He'd become an equalizer, someone who helped her to achieve the perfect balance between her career and a social life. He was a friend, but each time she saw him he became more. What she did not want to think of was the *more*.

Brick, concrete, and recognizable monuments gave way to spacious grassland as Michael drove over the Key Bridge to Virginia. Turning off onto a local, less populated, narrow, winding road, he increased his speed. Jolene felt the powerful thrust of the engine as it literally ate up the asphalt. She stole a glance at Michael's profile. His gaze was fixed on the road in front of him, long fingers curved loosely around the steering wheel. There was no doubt that he was skilled in driving at high speeds.

She had to remind herself that he was a soldier—an officer, who planned to make the military his lifelong career. There was no doubt that he claimed above average intelligence to have been accepted at West Point, but she wondered what it was in his psychological profile that made him select a regimented lifestyle. What he'd shown her was Michael Kirkland the man, not Michael Kirkland the soldier.

Michael slowed, maneuvering into a campsite with a

nearby amusement park. Hundreds of cars were parked in an area several hundred feet from various rides ranging from Ferris wheels to carousels and bumper cars. The distinctive aroma of popcorn, grilling franks, french fries, corn on the cob, cotton candy, and many other unidentifiable mouthwatering foods wafted in the humid afternoon air. Childish screeching rose above the whirring sounds of the mechanical gears driving the rides.

"We'll park here and find a shady spot to eat," he said in a quiet tone.

Jolene waited for him to turn off the engine and then come around the car to help her out. The blazing sun beat down on her exposed head. She felt overdressed in her suit, stockings, and heels.

Michael retrieved a large wicker basket from the trunk of the Jaguar. Shifting it to one hand, he reached for her hand with his free one as he led her out of the parking lot to the campgrounds. Wooden tables, benches, and grills were set up under a copse of towering trees that provided maximum shade from the intense summer sun. Baskets, ice chests, and other personal items littered the tables and benches. People had claimed every table.

"I don't mind sitting on the grass," she said, as she and Michael stood at the last table.

He let go of her hand. "Wait here while I go back to the car. I have a blanket in the trunk." He placed the basket on the corner of the table.

Jolene watched him retrace his steps to the parking area, again silently admiring his sexy walk. She recalled the television commercial sponsored by the U.S. Army. Michael Kirkland was indeed an army of one. He was definitely one of a kind. His face and body were exceptional, his home uniquely reflecting his preference for Asian architecture and furnishings.

He thought of their meeting as divine providence, because

they'd been invited to the same dinner party and knew the same people, while she thought of it as a twist of fate. And she hadn't lied to him—she was a realist. She liked Michael, more than she was willing to openly admit, but if and when whatever she shared with him ended, she was certain not to look back with regret.

Michael returned with a patchwork quilt, spreading it out under the sweeping branches of an oak tree. He knelt, emptying the basket and setting out pale blue plates on straw place mats. Flatware and serving pieces followed.

Jolene slipped out of her shoes and jacket, watching in amazement as he opened a container filled with a spinach salad with pears, gorgonzola cheese, and walnuts. Another revealed asparagus with sun-dried tomato vinaigrette, and the main dish was a Chinese shredded chicken salad. Chilled watermelon balls and a canister filled with carbonated lemonade added the finishing touch.

Removing his sunglasses, Michael smiled at her. "Does it meet with your approval?"

"You're wonderful."

He inclined his head. "Thank you." He wanted to tell her that she was not only wonderful, but also perfect. As perfect as any woman he'd ever met.

Sitting back on her heels, she shifted, trying for a more comforting sitting position. "Michael, I have a problem."

He met her direct gaze. "What is it?"

"I need to go back to the car and take off my pantyhose."

"Why don't you take them off here?"

Her eyes widened. "I can't do that," she whispered, even though there was no one around to hear her.

"Why not?" He moved closer, placing a hand on her shoulder and pushing her gently down onto the quilt.

His laser green gaze fused with hers as his hands slipped up her thighs under the slim skirt. His fingers caught in the elastic waist, and before she could exhale he'd eased her pantyhose down her hips, legs, and feet. He dangled them from one finger.

"Mission accomplished." He was grinning so broadly that she could see his molars.

Sitting up quickly, she reached for her stockings. "Give me those."

He pulled them out of her reach, winding the wisps of nylon around his fist. She reached for them again, and he shoved them into a pocket of his slacks.

"Let me know when you're ready to put them back on, and I'll accommodate you."

A blast of heat raced over her face, and it had nothing to do with the summer temperature. Folding her hands on her hips, she glared at him. "Give them back."

"Only if you say pretty please and give me a kiss."

"No!"

He shrugged a broad shoulder under his black silk T-shirt. "Oh, well. I suppose you'll have some explaining to do if you return to your office without your stockings."

Her humiliation yielded quickly to frustration. "Forget it, Michael."

Leaning closer, he brushed his mouth over hers. "I didn't think you'd be so stubborn," he whispered against her parted lips.

Jolene's hands came up, pushing against his chest to create a modicum of space. "Get away from me." Her voice was a breathless whisper.

Curving an arm around her waist, he pulled her even closer. "Do you really want me to go away?" he asked, peering down at her through his lashes.

Their gazes met, fusing, each cataloging the gamut of emotions crossing the other's face, as they shared an intense awareness of each other. There was no denying the sensual magnetism pulling them together.

Jolene felt herself succumbing to his clean, masculine

scent, the raw, unleashed power in the arm around her waist, and the shimmering gold undertones in his deeply tanned olive skin. The blood roared in her veins like molten lava, eliciting a giddying sense of physical arousal.

Michael stared down at the woman pressed to his chest, glorying in the crush of her breasts. He saw the rapidly beating pulse in her delicate throat, its pulsing matching the throbbing in his groin. He wanted her, wanted to make love to her on the grass, under the tree, with nature's glory as their silent audience.

Lowering his head, he took her mouth, gently, his tongue parting her lips. He swallowed her groan of delight as her arms came up and circled his neck. Curving one hand under her chin, he held her, making her his willing captive.

You're falling in love with her, a silent voice crooned to him. He didn't know how or why, but he wanted Jolene Walker in his life. He deepened the kiss, trying to absorb her into himself.

Michael's kiss sent spirals of ecstasy through Jolene as she kissed him with a hunger that she hadn't thought possible. She wanted him—all of him. Not just a caress or a kiss, but she wanted to share his bed while offering up her long-celibate body.

The sound of children's voices shattered their passionate exchange. Both were breathing heavily as they eased back. His lips left hers to nibble at her earlobe, and then brushed a tender kiss along the silken, scented column of her long neck. His right hand slipped down her skirt, gathering fabric until his fingertips grazed the flesh on her inner thigh. They moved higher, sweeping over the satin hiding her femininity.

"What are you doing to me?" he gasped in her ear.

Closing her eyes, she smiled. "The same thing you're doing to me."

Pulling back, he stared at her wide-eyed expression. A slow smile made his eyes crinkle when her lashes swept down across her cheekbones. "Are you willing to let me court you properly, Miss Jolene Walker?"

Opening her eyes, she was stunned by the intensity in the green orbs. Michael Blanchard Kirkland had revealed to her what few saw—his vulnerability.

Leaning forward, she rested her head on his shoulder. "Yes, Michael. I will permit you to court me properly."

They shared a quick, hard kiss, then settled down to the blanket to enjoy their picnic lunch.

Eleven

Jolene lost track of time as she lay on the quilt next to Michael, holding his hand. Their picnic lunch had become a leisurely affair as afternoon shadows shifted with the movement of the sun.

Turning to her right, she laid her left arm over his hard, flat middle. "I should be getting back," she slurred in a drowsy voice.

Ruffling her short hair, Michael pressed a kiss to her forehead. "Why do you have to rush back?"

She raised her arm and peered at her watch. It was almost four. "I've been gone more than two hours."

"How often do you take two-hour lunches?"

"Hardly ever. I'm lucky if I take lunch."

He chuckled, pulling her closer. "Please stay with me a little while longer."

"We're going to have to leave soon. I want to get back by five."

"Okay," he conceded.

Half an hour wasn't much, but he considered himself fortunate to have spent most of the afternoon with her. "Why did you decide to focus on domestic violence?"

Closing her eyes, Jolene counted slowly to five. She had to compose her thoughts. "It was because of my sister. I was a twin. An identical twin."

Michael went completely still. When Jolene had told him she'd lost a sister, he'd never suspected it would be her twin. "What happened, sweetheart?"

She took a deep breath. "Her husband was responsible for her death."

"He killed her?"

Jolene shook her head. "No, but he was responsible for her falling off the balcony of her high-rise building to escape him. Jeanine met her future husband when she was just fifteen. He was six years her senior. My sister was vivacious and incredibly beautiful. Everyone kept telling her that she should become a model, so she asked my father for money so that she could put a portfolio together. He refused to give her the money, and she went to our grandparents, who also refused. My family's rather old-fashioned about career choices."

"Did she ever get the money?"

"No." The single word was a sob. "She paid for the photographs by offering the photographer her virginity." The muscles in Michael's body tensed. "The man she slept with eventually became her husband once she turned eighteen. And it wasn't until after she'd married Lamar that she told me that she'd been sleeping with him for three years.

"I also found out that during that time Lamar had turned her onto drugs. She began with smoking pot before she moved up to freebasing and snorting cocaine. When she began to accept more important modeling assignments, Lamar became more than verbally abusive. She spent a month in Paris, modeling an up-and-coming designer's creations, and from the moment she hit the runway all eyes were on her and not on what she was wearing. Everyone wanted to know who the new African-American model with the long legs and curly hair flowing to her hips was.

"She returned to the States in shock. She'd made it. Her joy didn't last long because when the agency called to book her for a show in Milan, she had to turn it down. Jeanine told them she had slipped in the shower, but in reality Lamar had beaten the hell out of her. And he always hit her in the face."

Rising up on an elbow, Michael supported his head on a fist. "What did your parents say?"

Jolene met his penetrating stare. "They didn't say anything, because they didn't know. No one knew. I'd call her house and Lamar always had an excuse. His career was going downhill because most times he was so high that he didn't know whether it was night or day. Jeanine always waited for the bruises to heal before she visited the family. I knew something was wrong, but I couldn't quite identify what it was. I'd moved to New York to attend social work school, and after graduating I moved to D.C.

"Jeanine called me one night and finally disclosed the truth about the years of abuse. I'd been married six weeks when she flew down to see me." Jolene saw Michael's gaze widen when she mentioned she'd been married. "Cheney and I picked her up at the airport. We watched heads turn as she strutted down the terminal like she was on the catwalk. We may have looked alike, but Jeanine was so beautiful— she had a special glow that radiated from within. She sat in our guest bedroom, took off her oversized sunglasses, and I started screaming hysterically. Both eyes were so swollen and blackened that I don't know how she could see out of them.

"Cheney walked out of the room, leaving me to take care of my sister. She confessed everything: how Lamar would systematically punch her in the face to keep her from accepting modeling assignments because he was jealous of other men. I pleaded with her to leave him, but she said she couldn't because she loved him. She begged me not to tell my parents. And if I did, then I would never hear from her again."

"You believed her?"

Jolene nodded slowly. "Yes."

"Didn't you think she was bluffing?"

"She never bluffed. Jeanine always followed through on her threats. She stayed with me for week before she started dropping hints about going back to Chicago. I begged her to stay in D.C., promising her that Cheney and I would help her until she got on her feet. I woke up one morning and she was gone.

"I heard from her a week later. Lamar had beaten her again. I was on the first flight leaving for Chicago. I began commuting between D.C. and Chicago so often that flight attendants recognized me on sight. Meanwhile, my marriage was falling apart, but I couldn't desert my sister. Jeanine decided to listen to me and got a court order of protection once she found out that she was pregnant. Carrying a child had jolted her into reality. I rented an apartment for her, bought furniture to furnish it, while Lamar was served with a summons and arrested for assault. The judge issued the order for Lamar to stay away from her at the same time I was back at their house directing movers to remove her personal possessions. They didn't know that I wasn't Jeanine Moore, but Jolene Clarke.

"Jeanine settled into her apartment, living off money she'd secreted away during her modeling career. She knew if she'd given Lamar all her earnings he just would've snorted it up his nose.''

''Was she abusing drugs at this time?''

''No. Lamar began his physical abuse after she stopped using. I believe she was only able to stand up to him when she was clean. She said he'd turned her onto drugs to control her. I returned to D.C. and was greeted with divorce papers. My ex-husband said he couldn't compete with my sister, so he wanted out of the marriage. I agreed to a quick and amicable divorce.

''A month later Jeanine was dead. Somehow Lamar found out where she was living and went to see her. The police report says there was no forcible entry, which meant she had to have let him in. A neighbor said she heard a scream, and came out onto her balcony to investigate. She saw Jeanine with her back to the railing, screaming at Lamar not to touch her. He reached for her, but Jeanine scrambled over the railing to escape him. She fell sixteen stories to her death. She died instantly, along with the tiny life in her womb.''

Michael's eyes paled to a frosty green. ''The punk son of a *bitch*!''

''I called him that and every other dirty name I could think of. The shock almost killed my father. He suffered a mild heart attack once he found out that Lamar had been beating his daughter. Being hospitalized for two weeks prevented Daddy from becoming a murderer. I contacted an assistant district attorney, and we began a campaign to make Lamar pay for Jeanine's death. Because he'd violated the order of protection, he was sentenced to five years in an Illinois state prison. He's scheduled to be paroled at the end of September.''

''How's your father taking the news of his release?''

''Very calmly.''

''And you?''

She stared up at pinpoints of light filtering through the leaves of the tree. She redirected her gaze to Michael's impassive face. "All I can say is that I'm ready for him."

"He knows you live in D.C." The question was a statement.

Nodding, she said, "He knows."

Michael sat up, pulling her across his lap. Her hips burned his groin, but this time the press of her body did not arouse him. What she'd disclosed was too chilling a tale to be dismissed lightly.

Burying his nose in her hair, he breathed a kiss on her scalp. Jolene didn't have a husband or brother to protect her if Lamar Moore decided to exact revenge for his imprisonment. Even her father was miles away. But she did have him; he would protect her.

Tightening his hold around her waist, he breathed close to her ear, "I won't let anything happen to you."

She shivered despite the heat. Michael had just appointed himself her protector, and in that instant she believed he would protect her. They held each other for several minutes, and then rose to clean up the remains of their picnic lunch before driving back to D.C.

Jolene walked back into the Sanctuary at 4:50. Sally met her, handing her a stack of telephone messages. She'd prioritized them.

"Mrs. McDonald wants you to call her about an emergency board meeting."

"Has she set a day and time?"

"Tomorrow, 7:30, at her home. Enid Thompson's in the hospital again. This time her husband broke her nose. Once again, she refused to press charges. The others are from people who said they'll call you tomorrow."

She gave her assistant a warm smile. "Thanks, Sally."

"Do you want me to stay late tonight?"

"No. And thanks for asking. Have a good evening."

"You, too, Miss Walker."

Cradling her jacket in the crook of her arm, Jolene walked into her office, closing the door. Instead of sitting at her desk, she went to the sitting area and sat down on a love seat. She'd spent most of the afternoon with Michael without experiencing one iota of guilt. Stretching out her long legs, she kicked off her shoes and dug her bare toes in the deep pile of the carpeting. Her eyes widened. She'd neglected to retrieve her pantyhose from Michael.

The sensual image of his fingers searching under her skirt to remove her hose sent erotic shocks through her body. She recalled how her skin had tingled when he touched her, his fingers feathering up her inner thigh.

She pressed her knees together, waiting for the throbbing at the apex of her thighs to subside. But instead of weakening, the pulsing came faster, harder until her traitorous body betrayed her. Biting down on her lower lip, she moaned softly. She wanted Michael Kirkland, wanted him with a passion that bordered on hysteria.

Her legs were trembling when she finally pushed off the love seat, locked the door to her office, and made her way to her private bathroom. Stripping off her clothes, she stood under the spray of a shower, luxuriating in the water splashing over her fevered flesh, and when she stepped out of the shower stall and wrapped a towel around her naked limbs, she was back in control.

A shelf on a narrow built-in closet held a collection of trial and travel-sized grooming aids. She creamed her body before selecting a pair of bikini panties and a matching bra from another shelf. A T-shirt and a pair of loose-fitting drawstring cotton pants replaced her blouse and skirt. Slipping her bare feet into a pair of leather thongs, she returned to her office and turned on the computer.

She had to complete the first part of the treatment improvement protocol. It would take hours, but she was prepared to stay and complete it—even if it meant spending the night at the Sanctuary.

Twelve

Jolene ran a hand over her hair and down the nape of her neck. She rolled her head on her shoulders, trying to alleviate the stiffness. Her neck was the most vulnerable part of her body. All of her tension settled in that region.

Staring out the window through the partially opened blinds, she had to decide whether to close the Sanctuary early this evening. More than half the counseling staff and many clients had succumbed to a very contagious summer virus. One counselor had been hospitalized for three days with pneumonia. She'd given Sally the task of canceling individual sessions and rearranging groups to accommodate the absences.

A soft knocking on the door brought her out of her reverie. Turning, she saw Sally in the doorway. "Yes?" The single word was filled with resignation.

"One of Mrs. Bell's clients needs a letter for a court appearance tomorrow morning. She was promised the letter would be ready today. I told her that Mrs. Bell and Miss

Madison were out sick, and that she may not be able to get it until next week. She says if she shows up without the letter, then she's going to be sent back to jail."

A slight frown marred Jolene's forehead. "Who's the client?"

"Thelma Jeter."

Nodding, Jolene recalled the name. She was a mandated parolee. "Give me her case record, and I'll dictate the letter."

Three minutes later, Sally returned with the folder. A Post-it was attached to the file with a judge's name. Jolene spent a quarter of an hour reviewing the session notes, lab reports, and quarterly treatment plans for Thelma Jeter. The twenty-two-year-old high-school dropout had been arrested for shoplifting jewelry to support her three-hundred-dollar-a-day cocaine addiction. She'd been sent to jail for a year, but paroled after serving half the sentence because of overcrowding.

Picking up a small handheld tape recorder, she dictated the letter: "Sally, please address this to the Honorable Judge Hubert Miller. This letter is in regard to Thelma Jeter, who has been a client in our full-time, outpatient day treatment facility since April 18th. Our program requires full-time participation five days a week in a structured, therapeutic community setting.

"In addition to comprehensive rehabilitation services and a clinical emphasis on group therapy, clients are also involved in a behavior modification module. Positive attitudes and improved levels of functioning must be demonstrated in order for clients to advance through the progressive phases of treatment.

"After successfully maintaining abstinence in full-time treatment, clients must become eligible for the reentry phase. The total length of treatment will vary according to the individual's needs, but will require a minimum of six months.

"At this time, Ms. Jeter has an excellent attendance record and her urine analyses have been negative. She has maintained good grades through our on-site tutoring module. Please see attached teacher evaluation. Although Ms. Jeter had a slow start to the therapeutic process, she has been participating more and more and has learned to express her feelings and has begun trusting both staff and other clients. It is our clinical opinion that Ms. Jeter would benefit from completing this program.

"If we can be of any further assistance, please do not hesitate to call us at . . . Sally, please close with the usual and I'll sign the letter."

She removed the tiny cassette, slipped it into a small envelope, clipped it to the file, and left it in a wire basket for Sally. Taking a quick glance at the clock on her desk, she noted the time. It was only after eleven. Why, she asked herself, did she feel as if she'd been working for eight hours instead of three? She hadn't felt this fatigued in a long time, and she hoped she wouldn't be the next one to come down with the virus.

The pain in the back of her neck intensified. Maybe it wasn't just stress. Reaching into a drawer in the desk, she found a bottle of an over-the-counter pain reliever. Shaking out two tablets, she popped them into her mouth, and then picked up a bottle of spring water and swallowed them. She'd give herself an hour for the pain to subside, and if it didn't, then she would go home and lie down. The last time she'd ignored the pain she'd found herself incapacitated for a week. And with the upcoming review, she could not afford to spend a week away from the program.

*   *   *

Jolene lay in the cool dimness of her bedroom, finally drifting off to sleep, when the phone on the bedside table chimed softly. Rolling over, she opened her eyes and picked up the receiver.

"Hello." Her voice was low, sultry.

"Jolene?"

The corners of her mouth curved upward, the expression more like a grimace than an actual smile. "Hi, Michael."

"What's wrong?" He didn't disguise the concern in his voice.

"I have a pain in my neck."

"From what?"

"Tension."

"Are you certain it's only tension?"

She nodded, and then realized he couldn't see her. "Yes. I've had it before."

"I'll be over in five minutes."

"There's no need for that," she slurred. "I'll be all right."

"Buzz me in when I ring your bell."

"Michael, I . . ." What she was going to say was lost on him because he'd hung up. Seconds later she hung up as well.

She knew why he'd called her. He wanted to confirm the time they would meet Damon McDonald and Melissa Kyoto for dinner later that evening at Hisago, an upscale Japanese restaurant located on the Georgetown waterfront with spectacular views of the Potomac River.

It appeared as if she'd just closed her eyes again when she heard the intercom. Swinging her legs over the side of the bed, she slid gently to the cool wood floor. It rang again as she made her way on bare feet out of the bedroom, down the hallway, and to the front door.

"Stop ringing the bell," she whispered as the annoying buzzing resounded in her head. She pressed a button on the wall, disengaging the lock on the downstairs door. Unlocking the door to her apartment, she opened it and waited for him.

This time she did not have to wonder whether he'd run up the stairs, because he had. And judging from the moisture pasting a stark white T-shirt to his chest, she knew he'd jogged from his place to hers.

Michael took in Jolene's appearance in one, sweeping glance. A floor-length silken nightgown failed to conceal the curvy lushness of her body. Narrow straps held up the bodice to a lacy rose pink garment whose décolletage revealed a soft swell of full, firm breasts. His gaze shifted to her face, seeing what she vainly tried to conceal: pain.

He took a step into the entryway, sweeping her up in his arms. He closed the door with a shoulder, his gaze fused with hers. "Where's your bedroom?"

Jolene closed her eyes, shutting out his deeply probing gaze. "Down the hall and to your right."

He carried her, supporting her weight as if she were a small child and realizing, as he took furtive glimpses of a living and dining room, that it was the first time he'd been past Jolene's entryway. Seeing the furnishings told him a lot about the woman he'd unofficially given his heart to. She was very traditional and a romantic.

His assessment was verified once he walked into her bedroom. It was as if he'd stepped into an English country manor house. Yards of lace sheers covered the floor-to-ceiling windows, while the fabric was repeated on the canopy of a massive four-poster mahogany bed, pillowcases, bed skirt, edge-trimmed sheets, and bedspread. Even the lampshades on matching bedside tables were decked with lace. A decorative screen in a corner provided a place for a retreat with a mahogany table that doubled as a desk. Several books, a small Waterford lamp, a vase filled with pale pink roses, and a quartet of black-and-white photographs covered the table's surface. A matching chair with a plump tapestry seat cushion was pushed under the table.

Lowering her gently to the sheet, he inhaled the scent clinging to the linen. The smell of Jolene was everywhere in the room. Sitting down on the side of the bed, he placed a hand alongside her cheek.

"Where does it hurt?"

She placed a hand on her nape. "Right here."

Curving his arms under her shoulders, he gently turned her over to lie on her stomach. His gaze lingered on the outline of her hips under the clinging fabric. He swallowed, briefly closing his eyes.

"I'm going to touch you, and you have to let me know where you're experiencing the most pain."

He bent down, untied the laces to his jogging shoes, and kicked them off. Then he straddled her body, his hands braced on either side of her head. His touch was as light as the gossamer brush of a butterfly's wings. His fingers grazed the base of her skull in a soft massaging motion.

Jolene groaned once, closing her eyes. She forgot about Michael poised over her body, forgot that she was lying in bed wearing a skimpy nightgown, and forgot that it was the first time in more than five years that a man had shared her bed—even if it was only to comfort her.

Michael concentrated on the tight muscles in Jolene's neck and shoulders as his fingers worked their healing magic. Her arms lay limply at her sides as he slipped the delicate straps off her shoulders and eased the gown down around her waist. He froze, staring at the flawless velvety skin on her back. The color and texture reminded him of whipped mousse.

When she'd told him about her twin sister, he'd found it difficult to fathom that Jolene had referred to Jeanine's beauty while she hadn't attributed the same physical characteristic to herself. After all, they were identical twins.

A thoughtful smile curved his mouth. Jolene had been a twin, and there were twins in his family. His uncle David claimed a set of fraternal twins—Ana and Jason. And Emily's in-laws, Salem and Sara Lassiter, had welcomed identical twin daughters two years ago. After an ultrasound had shown evidence of two babies in her womb, Sara had confessed that twins were prevalent in her father's family.

If he married Jolene, would they, too, expect to have twins? He went completely still, the heels of his hands resting gently on the small of her back. Where had that thought come from? Why was he thinking about marriage when he hadn't even come to terms about his feelings toward her? He was still trying to identify whether his attraction for Jolene was lust or infatuation.

He continued massaging the knots in her neck, back, along her spinal column, and still lower to her hips. She moaned softly as he kneaded a muscle at her narrow waist. Her waist was small enough for him to span with two hands.

Returning to her neck, he leaned in closer. "How does it feel now?"

Shifting her head from one side to the other, she smiled. The pain and tightness were gone. "You're incredible."

Michael lowered his body until he lay flush on her back while supporting his greater weight on his elbows. "You won't think so once you get my bill."

"I thought you said that you wouldn't bill me," she teased, reminding him of what he'd said the day they shared the picnic lunch.

"That's true if I make an office visit," he crooned against her ear. "House calls are different."

Savoring the comforting weight pressing her down to the mattress, she exhaled audibly. "How much are you going to hit me up for?"

Sliding his arms under her middle, Michael tightened his hold on her waist and reversed their positions, her bare breasts cradled to his chest. Only the cotton fabric of his T-shirt separated their nakedness. Jolene wiggled, and the silk gown rode up around her thighs. She found a comfortable position in which her legs were cradled between his denim-covered ones.

"Come away with me over the Labor Day weekend."

She went completely still and at the same time held her breath. "Where?"

"Ocho Rios, Jamaica."

Her head came up slowly and she rested her chin on his breastbone as he stared down at her through lowered lids. Labor Day was less than two weeks away, and she still wasn't ready to sleep with him.

"What's there?"

"My parents' vacation home."

"Will they be there?"

"No."

"Are you certain?"

He chuckled softly. "Very certain." He planned to spend a week in Palm Beach with his parents before flying down to Ocho Rios for a few days.

Jolene worried her lower lip between her teeth. She wanted to take him up on the offer, but something prevented her from sharing his bed.

"No strings attached," he said perceptively, reading her mind.

"I don't know."

"Have you made plans for the holiday weekend?"

"No," she answered truthfully. She'd planned to stay home and relax.

Michael studied her face, seeing indecision in her wide-eyed gaze. Was she afraid of men? Was she distrustful of them because of the abuse her sister had experienced at the hands of her husband? Had she heard so many horror stories from the battered women at the Sanctuary that she was turned off by the opposite sex?

"I want to go, but . . ."

"What's stopping you?" he asked when her words trailed off.

"I don't want a repeat of what I had with Cheney."

"What does your ex-husband have to do with *us*?" A thread of hardness had crept into his tone.

"I haven't known you a month and already you're planning for us to go away together."

A shadow of annoyance crossed Michael's face. "Don't confuse me with your ex, Jolene, because if you'd been my wife I never would've placed you in a situation where you had to choose between your sister and me. It would've never come to that, because the first time Lamar Moore hit Jeanine would've been the last time he would've raised a hand to her. I would've considered your sister *my* sister, and therefore I would've protected her."

"It's not about Cheney and Jeanine."

Moving with the speed of a pouncing cat, he reversed their positions again. "What is it?" he whispered against her ear.

Her arms came up and curved around his neck, as she breathed in his intoxicating scent. "It's me. It's about not wanting to like you as much as I do. It's about not wanting to relive the pain when it ends. I fell in love with Cheney the first time I saw him. We met in March, and married in April. And despite the declarations of undying love, it didn't last a year. I don't want to take that roller-coaster ride again. What I need is a relationship that is measured and leisurely."

Closing his eyes, Michael tightened his hold on her slender body. He felt her anguish, her despair as surely as if it were his own. Since meeting Jolene he'd become a prisoner of his own tormented emotions. Whenever they were apart, he felt detached and frustrated until he saw her again. He wanted to tell her that she wasn't the only who'd loved and lost, the only one carrying emotional scars.

The fingers of his left hand played with the soft curls covering her scalp. "Are you capable of loving me, Jolene?"

She heard the deep voice in her ear, his query in her heart. He was asking a question she had refused to acknowledge for more than a week now. At first she'd thought her attraction to Michael was merely physical, but dashed that notion the night they'd sailed up and down the Potomac on the *Dandy*. Everything about the night had been magical, so magical that she hadn't wanted it to end.

Shifting her head, she buried her face against his shoulder. "Yes, Michael. I believe I can love you."

Pulling back, he smiled down at her. "That's good, because I *know* I can love you."

"You're that certain?"

He nodded. "Very certain."

She stared wordlessly at him. The tenderness in his gaze brought tears to her eyes. She blinked them back before they fell. "What's going to happen with us?"

He dropped a light kiss on the end of her nose before reaching down to pull her gown up over her naked breasts. "We're going to enjoy it. Every second, minute, day, month, and year," he whispered, placing light kisses over her eyelids.

She giggled like a child. "That sounds like a long time."

"All we have is time, *mi amor*," he whispered before his mouth covered hers.

The heat from his rapacious mouth burned her lips and throat before moving lower to her breasts. Pushing aside the lacy fabric, his tongue swept over a distended nipple, causing her to arch off the mattress.

Tremors shook Jolene from head to toe as Michael worshipped her breasts with his mouth, giving each equal attention before sliding down her trembling limbs. A passion she'd forgotten spread over her, leaving her shaking uncontrollably as his tongue caressed her thighs, stopping inches from the moist, throbbing entrance to her femininity.

Michael moved slowly up her silken body, reclaiming her thoroughly kissed mouth. He'd stopped himself just in time. He didn't have any protection with him. If and when he got Jolene pregnant, he wanted her to be Mrs. Michael Kirkland.

Sinking down to the mattress, he pulled her to his side, waiting for his respiration to resume a normal rate. Now that he'd tasted her flesh he wanted more—much more. And the next time he would be prepared to claim all of her, her body and her heart.

Thirteen

Jolene moved closer to Michael, feeding on his strength. She hadn't wanted to reveal her vulnerability, but it had surfaced without warning. She was always prepared for setbacks, disillusionment, and frustration with her work at the Sanctuary, but not for herself.

Jeanine's death, followed by the dissolution of her marriage, had shaken her to the core. It was as if she'd had to mourn twice. She'd loved Cheney unconditionally, but in the end he'd deserted her. He'd walked away when she'd truly needed his love and support, compounding their breakup when he'd refused to attend his sister-in-law's funeral.

Resting her left arm over Michael's flat middle, she closed her eyes and pressed her nose to his hard shoulder. She was drawn to the man sharing her bed—his strength, sexiness, and powerfully compelling personality. He was candid and forthright about how he felt about her. He'd admitted that he wanted to sleep with her, while she'd balked and made excuses to him and herself for why she wanted to wait. The truth was she didn't want to wait. She wanted all of him, his body pressing down on hers; she wanted to feel his hard flesh inside her, filling her until they ceased to exist as separate entities. And she wanted his lovemaking to exorcise the ghost that had lingered for five years; the ghost that came to her in the middle of the night, whispering that she should've ignored her sister's threat to run away if Jolene told of the abuse; the ghost that reminded her of her cowardice because she should've confronted, challenged, and threatened Lamar Moore about hitting Jeanine.

Angling for a more comfortable position, she smothered a soft sigh; she was exhausted. Not physically exhausted, but mentally fatigued. She worked twelve-hour days, brought work home, attended board meetings, and scheduled lunch or dinner meetings with local business people and civic organizations to solicit donations. She also had to maintain her professional certificates by taking continuing education credits. And her social life, if she could call it a social life, was usually linked to Sanctuary-related activities. However, meeting Michael Kirkland had changed that and changed her.

Now, she lay in bed with him in the middle of the afternoon without obsessing about what was going on back at the program. She'd called the senior therapist into her office, telling her to cancel all evening sessions and close at six before she'd gathered her purse to leave. It was the first time since becoming executive director that she'd walked out with just her personal belongings. Her ever-present leather case filled with computer disks, reports, and relative informational data lay on a table beside her computer workstation. The increasing pain and stiffness in her neck had been a blatant reminder that she had to slow down.

"Michael?" The soft whisper of his name filtered through the swollen silence.

"Yes?" he replied without opening his eyes. The warmth of the delicate body molded along his length was intoxicatingly sensual. He'd catalogued her smell, the texture of her bare flesh, and the curves and firmness of her limbs. Everything about Jolene Walker had seeped into his consciousness, making them one with each other; he wanted to spend every second, minute, and hour in her arms until hunger or thirst forced him out of her scented embrace.

"I'd like to decline Damon's offer to eat at Hisago's tonight."

He opened his eyes with her disclosure. Was she still in pain? His gaze lingered on the swell of flesh rising above the lace neckline of her nightgown. "Are you all right?" There was no way he could disguise the concern in his voice.

"I'm fine. It's just that I'd prefer staying home tonight."

A satisfied smile lifted the corners of his mouth. She'd read his mind. Pulling away from her, he sat up. "May I use your phone? I want to call Damon."

She pushed up on an elbow, staring at Michael. "Sure."

He picked up the telephone on the bedside table, punching in the numbers to the largest Japanese-American financial institution in the United States. He spoke to Damon's private secretary, identifying himself before he was transferred to her boss. The call ended two minutes later. He and Damon promised to connect again after Labor Day. Replacing the telephone in its cradle, he smiled over his shoulder at Jolene.

Wrapping her arms around his slim waist, she pressed a cheek to his broad back. "Thank you."

"You're welcome. What do you plan to do with the rest of the afternoon?"

She smiled a dreamy smile. "Hopefully spend it with you."

His hands covered hers. Tightening his grip, he pulled her effortlessly off the mattress and across his knees. The motion was executed so quickly that he hadn't given her time to protest or catch her breath.

Cradling her head to his shoulder, he kissed the top of her head. "That's the best offer I've had in years."

She smiled at him. "If you give me a moment of privacy, I'd like to change into something more appropriate."

His hands dropped, while his gaze bored into hers. "I happen to like what you're wearing."

A warming heat burned her cheeks and she dropped her head to stare at the finely woven lace barely concealing her nipples. "Go. Please."

Gathering her tightly, her breasts pressed against the hardness of his chest, Michael kissed her passionately. His demanding lips caressed hers, signaling desire and possessiveness. He ended the kiss, easing her off his lap; rising gracefully off the bed, he walked out of her bedroom.

Jolene retreated to the private bath adjoining her bedroom and took a quick shower. She washed away the lingering scent of Michael's cologne and aftershave. She'd stopped wearing Angel after meeting him. The fragrance was a constant reminder of his blatant sensuality that made it difficult for her to concentrate on her work.

Twenty minutes later she walked into the living room and found Michael staring at a series of photographs lining the fireplace mantel. Her admiring gaze lingered on the pale blue jeans molded to his slim waist, hips, and long legs. The pristine whiteness of his T-shirt was a brilliant contrast against his dark brown arms. Her gaze moved up to his head. His short, straight coarse hair was a shocking coal black. She wondered, if he let it grow out, whether it would claim a wave or curl.

Shifting his position, he turned and stared at her with his penetrating laser green eyes. How did he know she was standing there? She'd entered the carpeted room on sock-covered feet without making a sound.

The fine lines at the corners of Michael's eyes crinkled in a smile when he saw Jolene dressed in a pair of fitted, well-worn jeans she'd paired with a red V-neck T-shirt. He liked seeing her in that color.

"I can't believe how much you and your sister looked alike. I couldn't tell you apart in these photographs."

Walking over to the fireplace, she pointed at a picture of her and Jeanine taken the day they'd celebrated their tenth birthday. "I'm the one on the right."

Curving an arm around her waist, Michael pulled her closer to his side, studying their smiling faces. Their curly hair was braided in two thick plaits that hung over their narrow flat chests. The beauty that had manifested itself in adulthood was evident in the prepubescent girls. "Was it easy for your parents to tell you two apart?"

"Not at a glance. It was only when we opened our mouths to speak that they were aware of the difference. Jeanine's voice was a slightly higher register than mine. We couldn't fool Mama, but it took poor Daddy years before he called us by the right names."

Jolene had a wonderful voice, Michael mused. It was a therapist's voice: soft, even, and comforting. He even liked her Midwestern accent with the distinctive flat *A* sound.

There was a roll of thunder, followed by a loud crack of lightning. The oppressive summer heat and humidity had spawned an afternoon thunderstorm. Mysterious shadows gathered in the expansive living room, and Jolene pulled away from Michael to turn on several table lamps, filling the space with soft golden light.

He rested a hand on the marble mantel. "The furnishings in your place are magnificent." The chintz-covered sofa, tables, and chairs reminded him of some of the antique pieces in the house on Ocho Rios.

She smiled at Michael, saying, "I'd like to take the credit for choosing them, but I won't. With the exception of a few pieces, everything here belonged to my grandparents. As a child I thought of them as ugly and old-fashioned, but what did I know.'' Both sets of grandparents favored the style known as English country. She glanced at the mantel clock. It was after one. "Have you had lunch?"

Crossing muscular arms over his broad chest, Michael shook his head. "No, I haven't."

Jolene placed her hands on her hips. "I'll offer you a choice. I can call for a delivery, or I can prepare something." The sound of rain assaulting the windows preempted her suggestion that they eat out.

Closing the distance between them, Michael cradled her face between his palms. "We can prepare something together."

"I don't mind cooking. After all, you're a guest."

"Guest or not, I'd like to help."

"Okay," she conceded, reaching up and capturing his left hand. She tightened her grip on his long fingers, directing him out of the living room toward the kitchen.

He followed Jolene into a large functional kitchen furnished with off-white cabinets boasting gold-tone handles and a double sink with gold faucets. All of the backsplashes, as well as the counters, were covered with marble; a serviceable cooking island was strategically placed for easy access to a built-in dishwasher and the sink. A large vase filled with a profusion of sunflowers added warmth to the dark clouds concealing the afternoon sun. Added decoration was evident from blue-and-white transferware with an Oriental motif, a favorite of collectors since it first appeared in the eighteenth century. Several terra cotta pots bordering the sink were filled with dwarf trees with an overflow of vines. Everything was so clean, meticulous, that he doubted whether Jolene ever cooked or ate in the kitchen.

"Do you ever cook?" he asked, voicing his thoughts aloud.

"Of course." She managed to look insulted. "I cook all the time."

"Why does this place look so untouched?"

"Because I clean it," she drawled sarcastically.

"I have a cleaning service, and yet my kitchen doesn't look like this," he mumbled under his breath. Now that he thought of it, her apartment did not appear lived in, except her bedroom. But then, if she hadn't been in bed, it, too, probably would've looked as if it belonged in a museum exhibit. Was she more obsessive-compulsive than he was, though his personality trait had been reinforced by a lifetime of military training?

Opening the door to the freezer portion of a side-by-side refrigerator-freezer, Jolene peered at shelves stacked with labeled and dated packages of meat, fish, and poultry. "What do you want?"

Moving behind her, Michael's moist breath swept over the back of her neck. He spied a package of labeled shrimp. "How about a Caesar salad and pasta with shrimp?"

"I have some romaine lettuce, but not the dressing."

"If you have olive oil, vinegar, eggs, anchovy fillets, garlic, and Parmesan cheese, then I'll make the dressing," Michael volunteered.

She pointed to a double-door cabinet at the opposite end of the kitchen. "Check in there. I'm certain I have several tins of anchovies."

Flicking on overhead track lights, Jolene and Michael worked side by side defrosting and deveining shrimp before marinating them in a spicy mixture. He quickly and expertly mixed the ingredients for the dressing in a food processor while she cut up small cubes from a loaf of fresh French bread for garlic-flavored croutons. Soon the kitchen was filled with the mouthwatering smell of grilled garlic-encrusted shrimp and crisp deep-fried croutons.

He concocted a tomato sauce with basil, oregano, and

parsley, adding chopped onion and a half cup of dry red wine, while Jolene set the dining-room table with china, silver, crystal stemware, and tapers in sterling holders. She hadn't bothered to turn on the overhead chandelier. The flickering candles threw long and short shadows on the decorative floral wallpaper. A steady rain tapping against the windows created a cloistered mood from which she did not want to escape.

Walking back into the kitchen, she returned Michael's sensual smile as he stood at the cooking island, stirring linguine. "Do you like yours al dente?"

"Yes, please. Do you prefer wine or sparkling water?"

He arched a raven eyebrow. "I think wine would do quite nicely."

It was several minutes before three o'clock when they finally settled down to eat. They bowed their heads to say a silent grace, and then raised glasses with a chilled white wine in a toast. The soft strains of classical music flowed from speakers hidden within a massive breakfront filled with several patterns of china and crystal stemware.

Jolene bit into a tender shrimp, savoring the piquant spices on her tongue. "You're an incredible cook."

Michael swallowed a mouthful of an excellent vintage of dry white wine. "Thank you. I love cooking."

"Who taught you?"

"My father."

"Is your mother a good cook?"

He smiled. "She's good, but my father's better. All of the men in my family are great cooks. The only exception is my brother-in-law, but he's coming along. He's learned to grill hamburgers without overcooking them until they resemble hockey pucks. How's your neck?" he asked, smoothly changing the subject.

She rolled her head from side to side. "The pain's gone."

"Are you always so tense?"

"Not usually," she replied, sprinkling freshly grated Parmesan cheese over her pasta.

Jolene told Michael about the Sanctuary's board of directors' fund-raising efforts to erect a safe house in Virginia. She left nothing out when she told him of the Northwest Black Businessmen's Association's refusal to donate monies to a project they felt would not benefit African-American women and children. She revealed that they'd raised enough monies to purchase the land, but needed an additional $1.2 million to house sixteen families in the proposed two-bedroom apartment units.

"So, at any given time, you'll be able to take in sixteen women and their children?"

She nodded. "Each woman can bring up to three children with her. But none of the children can be more than five years old."

"Why five?"

"Five and under are considered preschool. By the age of six, children are enrolled in first grade, and hopefully they'll be in a stable environment by that age."

Michael stared at the food on the plate in front of him. Jolene was stressed because her program needed a little over a million dollars to complete a project, while he'd lost count of the number of millions in various accounts bearing his name.

As the grandson of the late, self-made billionaire Samuel Claridge Cole, he'd come into a five-million-dollar trust fund at the age of twenty-five, and another twenty-five million after his grandfather's death. His retired accountant mother handled his portfolio, sending him quarterly statements updating his various investments. Most times he merely glanced at the bottom-line figures before filing the papers. His uncles and cousins were businessmen, something he never wanted to become. Even his father had traded in twenty years as a lifer to become a businessman. With Michael it was the military, and only the military.

"When is the deadline for raising the one-point-two million?"

"The end of the year. That way the construction company can dig the foundation as soon as the ground thaws, and hopefully complete construction by late summer. We're sponsoring a fund-raising dinner dance at the Four Seasons in mid-October. We hope to raise a minimum of two hundred thousand from that event alone."

He picked up his fork, winding a portion of pasta around the tines. He wanted to write her a check for her beloved cause, but balked at doing so because he didn't want her to misconstrue his intentions. He didn't want her to think he was buying her. What he wanted was for her to come to him without any strings attached.

Staring at her through lowered lids, he fixed his gaze on her generous lower lip—a lip he wanted to pull between his teeth and suck gently until she begged him to stop. Once again his body betrayed him, and he was grateful that he was sitting. For if he had been standing, then Jolene wouldn't be able to miss the solid bulge in the front of his jeans.

There came another roll of thunder, followed by lightning, and then complete silence. The music had stopped. The storm had caused a power failure.

"How many candles do you have?" Michael asked, smiling at Jolene across the lace-covered mahogany table. The flickering candlelight was flattering to her dark skin.

"Enough to last for a couple of days."

"If they don't restore power before the sun sets, then you'll have a houseguest."

She returned his mysterious smile. "I've survived blackouts by myself."

He bit back a grin. "What if I tell you that I'm afraid of the dark?"

"You're kidding, aren't you?"

He shrugged his shoulders. "Could be."

She noticed the slight crinkling of his eyes. He was just joking. There was something about Michael Kirkland that silently announced that he wasn't afraid of anything or anyone.

His promise whispered in her head: *I won't let anything happen to you.* And she believed he wouldn't.

How different, she mused, would her life have been if she'd married Michael instead of Cheney? She wondered as she took a sip of her wine, would Jeanine still be alive if Jolene had been Mrs. Michael Kirkland instead of Mrs. Cheney Clarke.

Yes, the silent voice whispered. Jeanine would be alive, and Jolene would be an aunt of a niece or nephew.

Aunt Jolene.

An expression of sadness and loss swept over her features. That was a privilege she would never claim.

Fourteen

Jolene was not given the opportunity to uncover whether Michael was actually afraid of the dark, because the electrical power was restored an hour after it went out, saving the capitol district from a rush-hour traffic nightmare.

He spent the rest of the day with her, sprawled on the futon in her study, viewing two movies. She'd wanted to see *The End of the Affair*, and he *Gladiator*. In the end they compromised and saw both.

The rest of the week passed slowly as she looked forward to the weekend for their scheduled Sunday brunch. He came to her house at eleven, bearing a bouquet of flowers and another Limoges collectible. This one was a Lilliputian picnic basket. She opened the petite hamper to find handmade, hand-painted porcelain replicas of bread, wine, cheese, and two plates. Michael was taken aback when she threw her arms around his neck and gave him an open-mouthed kiss that left them both breathing heavily. They spent the morning lingering over oven-fried fish, grits, homemade cheese biscuits, and several cups of herbal tea.

Their magical time together ended when he announced that he was leaving for Palm Beach later that afternoon. She successfully concealed her disappointment, wishing him a safe trip. It wasn't until she closed the door behind his departing figure that she broke down and cried. She'd wanted him to ask her to come to Jamaica again; he'd given her a chaste kiss, and then walked down the staircase without a backward glance.

Friday afternoon she took her frustration out on the heavy bag. Each time she hit it, she felt pain radiating up her arms to her shoulders, but this time she welcomed it. Her jabs became pounding blows before she spun around on the balls of her feet, the right one connecting with the bag with a resounding thud. Balancing herself on her left leg, she hit the bag with her right foot three times in rapid succession. The bag had become Lamar Moore's face. Each time her foot made contact with the bag, she gritted her teeth. The solid blows were redemption, payback for all the times his fist had connected with her sister's face.

After a session with the bag, she returned to the locker room, took off her gloves and hand wraps, and changed into a swimsuit. She ignored the admiring glances of several men standing around the Olympic-sized pool as she walked to the deep end, diving in without a splash. Losing count of the number of times she crisscrossed the pool, she felt her tension easing.

She'd finally completed the preliminary draft of the treatment improvement protocol. What had surprised her was that she hadn't worked on it in the office, but had brought the disk home, where she didn't have the constant interruptions from telephone calls and staff members requesting her

attention. Working at home also made it easier for her not
to think about Michael. It was now Friday, and she hadn't
heard from him once since he'd walked out of her apartment
Sunday afternoon.

Wading over to the shallow end of the pool, she pulled
herself up out of the warm water and returned to the locker
room. She dressed quickly in a pair of sweats, not bothering
to shower. That she would do once she returned home.

She turned the key in the lock at the same time she heard
the soft chiming of the telephone on the table in the entryway.
Pushing open the door, she reached for the receiver after
the second ring.

"Hello."

"Hello, yourself."

A brilliant smile spread across her face. "Michael." She
didn't care whether he could hear her breathless sigh.
"Where are you?"

"I'm at the house in Ocho Rios waiting for you."

She closed her door and sank down to the floor. "You
want me to come?"

"Why do you think I'm calling you?" There was a hint
of laughter in his voice. "Well, miss, are you or aren't you
coming?"

Closing her eyes, she bit down on her lower lip. She
missed him, missed him so very much because she'd fallen
in love with him. That much she could admit to herself.

"How do you expect me to come if I don't know how
to get there?"

There was a pause before he spoke again. "I've made a
reservation for you. Just—"

"You ... you made a reservation without consulting
me?" she sputtered, interrupting him.

"Yell at me when you get here. Please write down what
I'm going to tell you."

Rising to her feet, she picked up the pen that lay beside

the pad on the table, writing down everything Michael told her. He'd arranged for her to leave Reagan Washington National Airport for a flight to West Palm Beach, Florida, at 8:10. From there she would board a private jet for her arrival in Kingston, Jamaica, where he would meet her at the airport. He ended the call, reminding her to pack light and bring her passport.

She hung up, staring at her watch. It was almost six. That meant she had less than two hours to pack and make it to the airport. Her pulse fluttered, bringing with it a warm glow of excitement. She would yell at Michael, but only after she told him that she loved him.

Jolene walked over to a young woman with curly, shoulder-length red hair, holding a sign bearing her name. She was dressed in a white blouse with a navy blue skirt and matching jacket.

"I'm Jolene Walker."

"Welcome to West Palm Beach. I'm Bryn Landis." Her Southern drawl was even more pronounced than what Jolene usually heard in D.C. She reached for Jolene's carry-on. "Please, come with me, Miss Walker."

Adjusting a garment bag over her shoulder, Jolene followed the woman as she wove her way through the throng waiting for luggage arrival and others waiting for arriving passengers. At the end of the terminal, Bryn punched several buttons on a security lock on a door. She opened it, leading the way down a flight of stairs to a Tarmac, where a sleek jet stood waiting, its engines revving.

"Mr. Kirkland had you precleared through customs here in the States, but you'll have to check in when we reach Jamaica."

A shock spread through her. How had he cleared her when

everyone leaving the States for certain foreign countries had to go through customs? And who owned the private jet?

A pilot met them at the top of the stairs, welcoming her aboard. He introduced himself as the copilot. Her luggage was taken and she was shown to a sofa at the front of the luxurious aircraft.

"As soon as we're airborne, Ms. Landis will serve you dinner."

Jolene managed a smile she did not quite feel. Who was this man she'd fallen in love with? How had he arranged for a private jet to fly her to Jamaica?

"Thank you."

"Please fasten your belt. We've been cleared for takeoff."

In a trance, she snapped the belt around her waist as the copilot made his way to the cockpit. Bryn Landis took a seat at the back of the aircraft, buckling herself in.

Jolene stared out the large oval window, focusing on the sparkling lights lining the runway. What she felt toward Michael was similar to what she'd felt when she met Cheney, only stronger. They'd met for the first time exactly four weeks ago on the patio at Paige Sutton's house. He'd come up behind her like a specter, weaving his magical spell so she was unable to resist him. He'd followed her home, coming into her home and into her life, while reminding her that she was a woman—a woman with a strong passion begging to be assuaged.

The jet taxied down the runway before picking up speed. She closed her eyes as it lifted off, climbing rapidly into the nighttime sky. After they leveled off, the seat-belt sign was turned off and she opened her eyes. Glancing around the cabin, she saw seating for at least a dozen passengers along with two large flat-screen televisions.

Forty minutes into the flight, Bryn served her an exquisite dinner of salad niçoise, mushrooms grilled with garlic and parsley, and herb-roasted chicken. She ignored the glass of chilled champagne, preferring instead to drink bottled water. She wanted her head clear once she and Michael were reunited.

Her eyelids were drooping by the time the jet touched down at the Kingston airport. The squeal of rubber hitting the Tarmac jolted her awake and she couldn't deny the pulsing knot forming in her stomach. She'd been in the air for hours, flown hundreds of miles to see the man who'd managed to make her fall in love with him despite her determination to resist his dynamic personality. She thought she was immune to all men since her divorce, but one had proven her wrong.

Michael saw her first. He couldn't move as he sat staring at the woman who'd captured his heart. His penetrating gaze lingered on the length of her shapely legs each time she took a step. A slim peach-colored cotton skirt with a generous front split displayed an expanse of bare flesh from ankle to knee. He noticed men turning to glance at her as she made her way into the area for arriving flights, and was reminded of her story about her sister. A cold chill swept up his spine. Was Jolene destined to share the same fate as her twin? Would her brother-in-law, seeking revenge, come after her? He mumbled a silent prayer for protection as he stood up.

Jolene's smile was radiant when she spied Michael. He was dressed entirely in black: slacks, shirt, and shoes. He moved toward her with a minimum of effort, reminding her of a stalking cat. He stopped less than a foot away, holding out his arms. She dropped her bags and moved into his embrace.

Ignoring the curious stares of hundreds of people crowding the terminal, Michael lifted Jolene off her feet and devoured her mouth with a hungry kiss. Her hands cradled his lean jaw, feeling the stubble of an emerging beard under her fingertips. She moaned softly as he kissed every inch of her face.

"I have something to tell you," she whispered between his nibbling kisses.

"Tell me later," he moaned against her parted lips.

"No, Michael. It has to be now or I'll lose my nerve."

Lowering her feet to the floor, he cupped her face between his palms, making passionate love to her with his eyes. The brilliant heart-shaped diamond earrings winked at him from her pierced lobes. She'd come to him wearing his gift.

"What is it, sweetheart?"

Jolene stared up at him, noting that his face was darker than it had been before he'd left Washington. He looked glorious, magnificent. She'd fought her own battle of personal restraint and lost. Her secret vow not to become involved with a man was shattered completely, because she'd known from the very beginning there was something special about Michael Kirkland. She'd known it even before seeing his face.

"I love you." The three words were a hushed whisper.

His eyelids came down, hiding his gaze from hers. A fringe of long black lashes touched a pair of highly sculpted cheekbones. She stared, frozen in place. The blood pounding in her temples turned into an unwelcome roar as she struggled to save what was left of her pride. She'd just blurted out that she loved him, and he'd reacted as if she'd driven a knife into his chest.

He opened his eyes after what seemed an interminable amount of time, when actually it was only seconds. A hint of a smile tilted the corners of his firm mouth. He'd spent the time waiting for her arrival, praying—praying that she would come to love him as much as he loved her.

"Let's get back to the house where I will show you exactly just how much I love *you,* Miss Jolene Walker."

Releasing her, he leaned over and picked up her garment and carry-on bags. Reaching for her hand, he led her out of the terminal and into the warmth of the Jamaican night to the airport parking lot, stopping beside a late-model, dark-colored Mercedes-Benz. Opening the passenger-side door, he seated her before putting her luggage in the trunk.

Jolene pulled the seat belt over her chest at the same time Michael slipped behind the wheel. He leaned over and kissed her again. "Thank you for coming."

"You're quite welcome," she said against his firm mouth. The stubble of hair on his chin was shockingly masculine.

Turning the key in the ignition, Michael maneuvered out of the parking lot. His right hand rested on Jolene's knee while he steered with his left hand. He had to hold on to her, wanting to make certain she was actually in Jamaica with him, and he hadn't imagined it.

He'd spent five days in Florida, interacting with his parents, aunts, uncles, and countless cousins, laughing, talking, eating, and drinking. He'd mouthed the appropriate responses, fooling everyone except Vanessa Blanchard-Kirkland. His mother had found him distracted and on edge, and after his third night in Palm Beach, she'd confronted him.

He'd been open and forthcoming when he told her everything about Jolene. Vanessa had smiled, kissed his cheek, and told him to follow his heart and instincts. Taking his mother's advice, he'd made the arrangements to fly Jolene to Jamaica, risking what was left of his masculine pride if she once again rejected his offer to spend the weekend together. Not only had she come, but she had also confessed her love for him.

I love you. Eight letters that made up three simple words—words torn from his heart and into the universe. She knew he loved her, and now there was no turning back.

"How long will it take us to get to Ocho Rios?" Jolene asked, smothering a yawn.

Michael savored the breathless quality of her voice. It

seemed to come from a long way off, even though she sat only a few feet away.

"About ninety minutes."

"That far," she slurred, trying vainly to keep her eyes open.

"That far," he repeated, giving her a quick glance. She was sound asleep, her chest rising and falling gently under her peach-colored blouse.

Removing his hand from her knee, he pressed a button on the dashboard. The soft sounds of reggae came through the speakers, and he found himself humming along with a Jimmy Cliff composition. He and Jolene would have all of Saturday and Sunday together before they flew back to the States late Monday afternoon. It wasn't much time, but he considered himself lucky because he'd been allowed two full days with her. Lucky and very blessed that she had come into his life.

Fifteen

Jolene did not stir as Michael carried her into a bedroom, placing her gently on his bed. He removed her sandals, blouse, and skirt. She moaned once, but did not wake up. Staring at the scraps of pale pink silk and lace covering her nakedness, he felt pride and possessiveness well up in his chest. The beautiful, intelligent woman asleep in his bed was his—his to love and protect, his to honor and cherish. And he would until he breathed out his last breath.

He didn't know why Jolene had come into his life at this time, and he didn't care. All he knew was that he'd fallen in love with her and he did not plan on losing her, not to anyone or anything.

Leaning over, he pulled a lace-edged sheet over her before he turned off a bedside lamp, plunging the room into darkness. A sliver of light from a three-quarter moon shone through the jalousie shutters. Removing all of his clothes, he slipped under the sheet next to her. She moaned again, moving closer to his heat, her buttocks pressing intimately against his groin. Gritting his teeth against the exquisite erotic torture, he held his breath. He was forced to release it, and when he did he registered Jolene's soft breathing in the stillness of the room. After a while, he joined her in sleep.

Jolene woke up, thoroughly disoriented. Her eyelids fluttered wildly as she stared up at yards of sheer mosquito netting shrouding a four-poster bed. Turning her head, she stared into a pair of clear green eyes framed by long black lashes staring back at her.

She was in Ocho Rios!

She was in Michael Kirkland's bed!

Her gaze swept from his face to a smooth, dark brown muscled chest. Heat crept into her face as she smiled shyly, clutching the edge of the sheet to conceal her lacy demibra. Now she remembered. She'd fallen asleep soon after they'd driven away the airport.

Michael smiled the slow sexy smile she'd come to love. "Good morning. Welcome to Ocho Rios."

Glancing at a spot over his shoulder, she mumbled, "Good morning." He turned to face her, resting his head on a folded arm, and she sucked in her breath, holding it until her burning lungs screamed for relief. The black stubble on his lean jaw and chin made him so overwhelmingly virile that she wanted to flee the bed and Ocho Rios.

Jolene had thought she was ready for Michael, but she wasn't. She found him to be even-tempered and generous. He was fastidiously fashionable in his choice of attire, vehicle, and home furnishings, spoke several languages, and claimed above average intelligence. He had it all, but there was something about him that was menacing—the quiet lethal menacing of a stalking panther.

Something he'd said the night they'd met for the first

time sent a shiver up her spine despite the Caribbean heat: *I can assure you that when I play, I play very, very hard.* Was it warning, or a threat?

She closed her eyes, shutting out his intense stare. Who or what had she fallen in love with?

The fingers of Michael's free hand feathered over her cheek. "How about a swim before breakfast? You did bring a suit, didn't you?" he asked when she opened her eyes.

"Yes."

He didn't tell her that it wouldn't have mattered if she hadn't, because when his father had purchased the house, he'd also bought the beachfront. Their closest neighbor was five miles away. Most of his relatives who visited the house the locals called Sunderland had confessed to swimming naked in the clear blue-green waters of the Caribbean.

"Are you ready to get out of bed, *mi amor*?" His voice had lowered to a seductive drawl.

Lifting an eyebrow, she said, "Am I really your love, Michael?"

He lowered his lashes, smiling. "You're my love and much more."

"Can you explain the more?" Reaching out, he pulled her over his chest. She gasped not from the sudden motion as much as the heated contact of her belly with his flaccid sex. The only thing separating her femininity from his maleness was a triangle of silk and lace. The heat from his body added a layer of moisture to her already fevered flesh.

Tightening his grip around her waist, he lowered his head and kissed her tousled curls. "The more is having you in my life—forever. The more is my wanting to take care of you, wanting to protect you from all seen and unseen. The more is you having my children and my growing old in your arms. That, Jolene, is the *more*."

She'd asked and he'd answered. Raising her head, she

rested her palms on his breastbone. Her gaze was direct, unwavering when it met his.

"I don't know why I've fallen in love with you, because that wasn't my intention when you introduced yourself to me at Paige's house. I don't know why I've let you become a part of my life, because that also wasn't my intention. I've rationalized, telling myself that you're good for me. You've offered me the perfect balance of romance and career, and for that, I'm eternally grateful. But . . ." Her words trailed off.

"But what, Jolene?"

Closing her eyes, she laid her head on his pectorals, feeling and listening to the steady pumping of his heart under her cheek. "All I can offer you is right now—today. I can't even plan for tomorrow or the next day."

He tightened his hold around her waist. "Don't you want to marry again? Have children?"

"I don't consciously think about it."

Michael felt as if she'd pierced his heart, leaving him to bleed slowly to death. He loved her! He wanted to marry her! What was wrong with him? Why was he destined to fall in love with women who claimed to love him but refused to marry him? What wasn't he offering them other than himself?

His mood changed, his face becoming a glowering mask of rage. He'd stripped himself bare, opening himself up for rejection, a rejection that left him naked and vulnerable. In that instant he made a silent vow: Jolene would become the last woman in his life who would claim his passion and his love.

He'd give up his life before he let her go.

Turning her head slightly, Jolene kissed Michael's chest, her tongue sweeping over a flat dark nipple, eliciting a sharp gasp from him. "Please be patient with me, Michael," she pleaded between soft, moist kisses. "I love you, but I need time to learn to trust again."

His hands moved lower, cradling the curve of her firm hips. Her silken flesh burned his palms through the tiny scrap of fabric. He'd wanted to wait to make love to her, but that decision had been taken out of his hands when his flesh stirred to life.

"You can have all the time you need," he said between clenched teeth. He'd waited thirty-two years for her, and would willing wait another thirty-two if it meant having her in his life.

"Thank you," Jolene whispered as her mouth swept over one nipple, then the other. "Thank you, thank you, thank you," she repeated; it had become a litany as her breathing deepened.

The rising heat and natural scent of his body mingling with his cologne pulled her in where she did not want to escape. Tasting, touching, and smelling him had become a sensual, flavorful, tactile, and olfactory feast. Her need made her bold, unashamed as her hands moved over his upper body, committing everything about him to memory.

A jolt of desire swept through Michael with the force of a sirocco wind sweeping across the desert. One second he was soft, and suddenly his limp flesh was rigid and throbbing with desire. He'd wanted it to go slowly, but that decision was now beyond his control.

Reversing their positions, he reached around her back and unhooked her bra, his gaze fused with hers. He tossed it onto the floor. He did not look away as he sat back on his heels and pulled the matching bikini panties down her hips, legs, and off her feet. Only when she was as naked as he did he attempt to survey what lay before him.

"Sweet angels in heaven. You're perfect." There was no mistaking the awe in his voice, the words torn from his constricted throat.

Never would he have imagined the unabashed perfection of her body. Full, firm breasts rose and fell heavily above a narrow rib cage. He laid a hand on her flat belly, moving lower until it rested on the triangle of tightly curling hair concealing her femininity from him. Her skin was flawless, from head to toe.

Jolene stared at the straining length of dark pulsing flesh jutting between Michael's thighs before closing her eyes. He was large, so much larger than he'd appeared fully dressed. She prayed he would be gentle with her. It had been more than five years since she'd lain with a man.

She opened her eyes when he moved over her, while supporting his greater weight on his arms. Her breasts brushed his chest, the nipples hardening with the slight pressure.

Her fingers curled around a strong wrist. "I don't want a baby, Michael. Not now."

He closed his eyes, shutting out the expression of desperation radiating from her pleading gaze. She'd told him what he already knew; he would have to assume the responsibility for contraception.

Burying his face between her scented neck and shoulder, he breathed a kiss over her velvety skin. "I'll take care of everything."

Shifting slightly, he reached in the drawer of a bedside table, withdrawing a small square plastic packet. He opened it, removed the condom, and rolled the latex covering down his rigid sex, certain he registered a sigh of relief escaping Jolene's parted lips.

Placing his hands on her thighs, he parted them as he lowered his body until she felt comfortable with his weight. "I'll try not to hurt you."

Jolene nodded. She didn't trust herself to speak. What could she say when she wanted Michael with a craving she'd never known before? Her arms curved around his strong neck, holding him close. She felt him when he positioned himself at the apex of her thighs, inhaling sharply.

"Relax, baby," he crooned in her ear. "Let me do this." Waiting until let she out her breath, he pushed gently. She stiffened momentarily, and then exhaled again. "I'm going to go slow, and I want you to tell me if I'm hurting you. If I hurt you, then I'll stop."

"Don't stop," Jolene whispered, trembling with a rising desire that made it almost impossible for her to breathe.

What she felt was much more than sexual desire. It was a desperate yearning to love and be loved. She was fully aware of the hardness pushing into her body, slowly and deliberately. There was discomfort, but it did not lessen the passion skimming along her nerve endings as a hungry spurt of ecstasy swept over her.

She moaned aloud with erotic pleasure. "Now, Michael," she pleaded. "Now!"

Pulling back, he impaled himself in her tight body, awakening the dormant sexuality she had guarded protectively since her marriage had ended. A gush of moisture bathed the tight walls gripping his sex, her body vibrating with liquid fire.

She wrapped her long legs around his waist, and he felt the turbulence of her passion sweep him up in a flood tide of the hottest fire, clouding his brain. He was lost—completely lost in the flames that threatened to devour him. And in that moment he knew he'd never love another woman. What he'd felt before was infatuation or lust. With Jolene it wasn't only passion; it was love—a true love, an uncompromising love.

Jolene welcomed the powerful thrusting of Michael's hips, meeting each one with her own upward thrusts. Her well-toned, well-conditioned body took everything he offered, giving as well as receiving. She wanted to yield to the burning sweetness that held her prisoner, but knew it was only a matter of minutes before she was forced to succumb to the raging inferno singeing her mind and body.

His rigid, throbbing hardness touched the walls of her womb, and she screamed out her release, shaking uncontrollably as the screams turned to moans of a sweet satisfaction she had never known before.

Electricity seemed to arc through Jolene's body and into Michael's as he tried holding back his own release. He didn't want it to end—not yet. What he wanted was for it to go on for an eternity. But as her breath came in long, surrendering moans, it was his undoing. He had to let go, or his heart and lungs would explode. Gripping the pillow behind her head in a death grip, he lowered his head and groaned as the explosions erupted in his lower body, leaving him gasping, mewling, and weak as a newborn. He collapsed heavily on Jolene, waiting for the lingering shivers of delight to wane.

Opening his eyes, he stared at her moist face. Her eyes were closed, her breasts rising and falling heavily, and never had he seen her look more beautiful. She'd been created for love.

He slid off her body, collapsing to the mattress. Placing a muscular arm over his forehead, he stared up at the mosquito netting draping over the antique canopy bed, while at the same time he reached for Jolene's hand with his free one. Threading their fingers together, he savored their oneness.

"I love you," he stated simply.

"I know," she replied in a quiet tone.

Those were the last words they exchanged before succumbing to a sated sleep reserved for lovers.

The sun was high in the heavens when Jolene woke up for the second time that morning. A weighted lethargy made it difficult for her to keep her eyes open. Turning over, she reached for Michael, but he wasn't there. She sat up, parting the sheer netting, and swung her legs over the side of the bed. A soft gasp escaped her parted lips as an unexpected soreness between her thighs reminded her of what she'd shared with her lover.

Lover! The word wrung a smile from her. Her relationship with Michael Kirkland had reached another level. They were friends and lovers. Her smile widened as she recalled their passionate coupling. Making love with him was everything she'd expected, and then some. After her prolonged period of celibacy, it had been well worth the wait.

She spied her bags by a rocker and eased her feet to the wood floor. Her first priority was to take a bath and unpack. Taking ginger steps she made it over to her carry-on bag, opened it, and withdrew a small canvas case filled with her grooming supplies. She opened one door, discovering a closet with shelves of bundled linens wrapped lovingly in tissue paper.

A second one revealed a private bath. The charming space claimed a claw-foot blue-veined marble bathtub hidden behind an Oriental ornamental screen. An oval basin sat on a decorative pedestal. White wicker stools, covered with cushions in aquamarine added a tropical accent to the room. Hidden away in a far corner was a shower stall.

Jolene turned on the tub's faucet, letting the water run clear before she added her lavender crystals. She brushed her teeth, rinsed her mouth with a wintergreen mouthwash, and splashed cool water on her face. The tub was half-filled when she stepped in and sank down to the soothing warm water. Waiting until the water cooled, she reached for a bottle of scented gel, squeezed a small glob on a bath sponge, and scrubbed her body, but avoided the tender area between her legs. She rinsed away the lingering scent of Michael's cologne, along with their lovemaking, then stood up and stepped out of the tub.

As she reached for a towel on a nearby stool, she saw

movement out of the corner of her eye. She held the towel in front of her, concealing her nakedness.

Turning, she saw Michael's broad shoulders under a tropical print shirt filling the doorway. Her gaze swept quickly from his gleaming smooth-shaven jaw to his sandaled feet. He was dressed for the tropical climate: loose-fitting shirt, walking shorts, and sandals. She forced herself not to stare at his powerfully built legs.

They stood motionless, staring at each other as if they were strangers instead of lovers. Jolene managed a small, tentative smile, ending the tense moment.

Closing the distance with three long strides, Michael eased the towel from her loose grip. He wrapped it around her body, tucking it in over her breasts, and swung her up in his arms. She held onto his neck as he reentered the bedroom and placed her on the neatly made bed. It was apparent he'd changed the linen while she was in the bathtub.

His expression was impassive as he blotted the moisture clinging to her warm flesh. Jolene stared up at him through her lashes, luxuriating in the feel of his hands moving over her body.

"Don't move," he whispered close to her ear.

He moved off the bed, returning less than a minute later with a bottle of her perfumed body cream. The side of the bed dipped under his weight as he sat down, pouring the thick, rich liquid into the palm of one hand. She drew in her breath when he lathered her body with the cream, massaging it into her thirsty flesh while kneading the muscles in her neck, back, legs, and feet.

Jolene lost track of time as she savored the full body massage. She was so relaxed she doubted she would be able to move. Resting her head on folded arms, she moaned when he used short chopping motions on the back of her thighs.

"Where did you learn to do this?"

"I studied with an elderly gentleman who'd lived in Hong

Kong. Massage is one of the oldest forms of remedial therapy. Hippocrates wrote around the fifth century B.C. that the way to health is a scented bath and an oiled massage every day."

She smiled. "I'll take one once a week."

"Are you asking for a weekly massage, sweetheart?"

Affecting a salute, she said, "Sir, yes, sir!" Resting his forehead on her back, he dissolved into a spasm of laughter. "I need to get dressed, Michael," she whispered.

"I like you naked," he crooned, placing light kisses along her straight spine.

"I'm hungry, darling."

"So am I."

"No-o-o!" she screamed as he turned her over, slid down her body, and buried his face between her scented thighs.

Sixteen

Jolene sat opposite Michael at a massive, scarred mahogany table in a large kitchen, spooning bite-sized portions of fresh fruit into her mouth. She stared at him as he sipped steaming coffee from a fragile china cup.

"Aren't you going to eat something?"

His gaze met hers, his smile slow in coming. "I ate already. I had *you*."

"Michael!"

Waves of embarrassment and humiliation made the blood roar in her ears. He'd introduced her to another form of lovemaking she'd been unfamiliar with—something she'd never shared with the two men in her past. Michael had shocked her when he'd positioned his face between her thighs, but her shock had been short-lived once his tongue had bathed her tender flesh as she writhed on the bed, pleading with him to stop. But he hadn't stopped until she was hurtled beyond herself to a place where she'd never been. She'd floated on a cloud of uncontrollable joy while Michael had retreated to the bathroom, returning with a warm cloth to bathe her delicate, pulsing flesh.

She'd lain in bed, staring up at the diaphanous fabric falling around her like a shroud until pangs of hunger had forced her to get up.

Michael peered at Jolene, noting her downcast gaze. "Did I embarrass you? I did, didn't I?" he asked when she turned away from him. His left eyebrow froze a fraction. He'd misjudged her, believing she was more experienced than she actually was. After all, she had been married.

"If you didn't like it, then I won't do it again," he continued in an apology.

Jolene's head swung around, meeting his direct stare. "Did I say I didn't like it?"

Both black sweeping eyebrows rose inquiringly. "No, but—"

"But nothing," she interrupted, pulling her lower lip between her teeth and drawing his gaze to linger on the spot. "It was the first time a man has ever made love to me in that manner, but I did enjoy it."

He tried not to smile. There were times with Jolene was so proper that he either wanted to laugh or shake her until her teeth rattled. At the Sanctuary, she was the very proper Ms. Walker, CSW, but under the business suit and professional demeanor was a sexy woman who turned him on until he found it difficult to stay in control of his mind or his body. Without her clothes and in his bed she sent him into overdrive.

"Are you telling me that you're going to be an eager student?"

Clamping her jaw tight, she glared at him. "Don't flatter yourself, Michael Kirkland."

This time he did laugh, a deep laugh that erupted from his belly, and much to his surprise, Jolene's laughter joined his.

She took a sip from a cup filled with what Michael had called *café con leche*. He'd brewed a pot of Jamaica Blue Mountain coffee, then added a generous portion of evaporated milk, reheated it and added sugar to taste. The result was a rich, full-bodied, flavorful coffee beverage.

Her gaze swept around the kitchen, noting the furnishings from a bygone era. "I love this kitchen, this house."

"Some of the pieces remind me of the ones in your apartment."

"English country."

"More like English manor house," he countered softly.

"Who maintains it when your family's not here?"

"My father pays someone to come in once a week to air out the rooms, making certain the electricity and plumbing are working. We usually give three days' notice when someone is coming down. That way the refrigerator is stocked with the necessary staples of meat, fish, bread, and dairy."

"When was it built?"

"Eighteen thirty-six. It was a honeymoon retreat for a family named Abington. They were descendants of wealthy British shipbuilders, who made their fortune in the New World by growing sugar cane."

Resting her elbow on the table, Jolene supported her chin on a fist. "Your father bought this place for his honeymoon?"

"No. He purchased it several years before he met and married my mother."

He wanted to tell Jolene that he stood to inherit the house, all of its priceless furnishings, and five miles of private beach. Joshua and Vanessa Kirkland had willed him all of their Ocho Rios holdings. His sister and brother-in-law had inherited a four-hundred-year-old Mexican hacienda, set on two hundred acres, from Christopher's father, Alejandro Delgado-Quintero.

Jolene lingered over her second cup of *café con leche*,

listening intently as Michael told her about the mysterious curse that had befallen generations of Abingtons. She was transfixed by the deep timbre of his mellifluous voice as he spoke of slaves, voodoo, and mixed-race children of slave owners and African women. They sat for hours, talking comfortably about everything—everything but themselves.

It was late afternoon when they walked hand in hand down to the beach, shed their clothes, and frolicked like children in the crystal-clear waters of the Caribbean until angry storm clouds filled the sky. She followed him back to the house, her gaze fixed on a decorative red-and-black Chinese dragon tattooed on the small of his back. They made it inside just as the heavens opened, soaking and enriching the earth with life-giving moisture.

Jolene forgot about everything back in the States as she lay in bed beside Michael, listening to a CD on a portable stereo system. The steady tapping of rain against the closed shutters complemented the relaxing piano selections. The only illumination came from an oil-filled hurricane lantern. She lay in his protective embrace, eyes closed, savoring the peace she'd found with him.

"You owe me a tongue-lashing." His resonant voice was a shivery whisper against her ear.

She smiled, nodding. "I know I do, but I've decided to give you a reprieve this time."

"Thank you, madam warden."

"What I would like to know is whose jet I flew down on?"

"It belongs to a cousin. It's his company's jet."

Timothy Cole-Thomas, his aunt Nancy's eldest son, had assumed the presidency of a company their grandfather had begun more than half a century ago. The GIV Gulfstream belonged to ColeDiz International, Ltd., and the family mandate was that all who claimed Cole or Kirkland bloodlines were forbidden to fly on commercial airlines. The edict was still in effect after forty years, following the abduction of nine-year-old Regina Cole. Martin Diaz Cole, the family's reigning patriarch, had stubbornly refused to lift the ban even though Regina would soon celebrate her fiftieth birthday this upcoming July. Only Michael was exempt because of his military status.

"It's an exquisite aircraft."

He pulled her closer. "We'll fly back together."

Jolene shifted into a more comfortable position until her silky smooth leg was nestled between his hair-covered ones. "Don't talk about going back. I just want to enjoy the little time we have left." They would have all of Sunday together before preparing to leave on Monday.

"You don't want to go out dancing?"

"We can dance here," she argued softly.

"I want to take you to Dunn's River Falls. It's a spectacular six-hundred-foot climb to the top over slippery rocks and ledges. All day, long chains of tourists wend their way up the falls, getting thoroughly drenched in the process. A bathing suit is required attire."

"The next time, Michael."

He smiled in the dimness of the bedroom. "Will there be a next time, Jolene?" It was the same question she'd posed to him when he'd teased her about all work and no play.

"Yes. I'm certain of that."

And she was. She had fallen in love with Michael, wanted to marry him, and bear his children. But she wanted to wait, wait until she knew him longer than a month. What she did not want was a repeat of her marriage to Cheney. And if her marriage to Michael failed, she knew she would never marry again.

* * *

Jolene stood in the entryway of her apartment, cradled against Michael's chest. Their magical Caribbean sojourn had ended forty-five minutes ago, the moment the Gulfstream jet had touched down on a private runway at Washington Dulles International Airport. They were reflective during the return flight, each lost in private thoughts. She'd feigned sleep while Michael had stared with unseeing eyes at a movie on the flat-screen television. They'd passed through customs without having anything to declare except their love for each other. Even the cab ride back to Georgetown was accomplished in complete silence.

Cradling her face between his hands, Michael forced a smile he did not feel. It had taken only three nights for him to get used to having her sleep beside him. Jolene Walker was a drug—a slow, addictive, potent drug that had hooked him.

"How about dinner tomorrow night?"

"Tomorrow is my late night."

"Wednesday?"

She nodded, smiling. "Wednesday it is."

"Seven?"

"Seven is good."

"I'll pick you up here at seven." Tightening his hold on her delicate jaw, he lowered his head and tasted her mouth—tentatively at first, and then he devoured her mouth like a starving man taking his first bite of food after being denied for days.

Jolene's fingers curved around his strong wrists, her nails biting into the tender flesh. Jerking her head back, she gasped for breath, her chest rising and falling as if she'd run a grueling race.

"Go, Michael. Please go."

He saw the shimmer of tears fill her large eyes, and at

that moment he didn't want to go. He wanted to stay with her throughout the night. His hands fell away.

"Good night, Jolene."

Lowering her head, she said quietly, "Good night."

She didn't raise her head until she heard the soft sound of the self-locking device. Reaching out, she slid the security chain in place. Not moving, she stared at her luggage on the floor next to the chair, her handbag on the chair, and her keys on the table. Pushing off the door, she bent over and removed her sandals.

She didn't know how or why, but she could still see Michael, smell him. His intoxicating presence lingered with her until she made her way to her bedroom. The flashing light on her answering machine on a bedside table had recorded five calls. Pressing a button, she listened to the first message. It was from Claire McDonald, asking her to return her call as soon as she came in.

Shaking her head, she smiled. For three days she'd lost herself in a magical kingdom with a handsome prince. And during that time she'd managed to keep everything to do with substance-abusing, victimized women out of her mind. But the call from the Sanctuary's board president was a blatant reminder that not only was she back home, but back to a real world—a world with its share of evil and ugliness.

Part Two

The Chase

Seventeen

A light rap on the door garnered Jolene's attention. Her head came up as a smile softened her lush mouth. "Come in, Deborah."

Deborah Madison walked in, cradling several folders and her appointment book. "Can you see me now? I know I'm early, but I'm still not feeling well. I'd like to get home and go to bed."

Glancing at the clock on her desk, Jolene noted the time. It was 6:20, forty minutes earlier than she usually met with Deborah for their Tuesday-night supervision.

"Sure."

Gathering a folder, she followed the clinical director over to the sitting area. Once seated next to Deborah on a love seat, she handed her a sheet of paper.

"I'll try to make it quick. Look this over and give me your feedback—positive or negative."

Deborah's intelligent blue eyes perused the page as she

chewed her lower lip. "I like the concept, but how easy will it be to implement?"

Jolene had restructured the services for their day treatment modality. "I think we can accomplish the change quite easily. Morning meetings and seminars will meet five times a week for sixty minutes each. The work component will meet five times a week for a total of three hours. The encounter group will meet once a week for two hours. Individual counseling sessions will continue to be once a week for fifty minutes, group three times a week for two hours, and other support groups like AA and NA twice weekly for two hours. It's intensive, but I believe it will work."

Deborah stared at her boss. "What about the evening program?"

"It will continue with group counseling twice a week for two hours."

"Why are you restructuring the day program and not the evening?"

"Because you know our clients for the evening program don't have the same needs as the ones in the day component. Most of the women who come to us during the day don't work, are abusing prescription drugs as well as illegal substances; they are the wives and girlfriends of politicians, high-priced lawyers, and corporate executives. And they are the ones who become punching bags when their partners or husbands seek to rid themselves of their failures and frustrations. Once they walk in here seeking help, we have to get them into counseling as quickly as we can. They're not going to make it coming twice a week for a group counseling session."

She handed Deborah another sheet of paper. "This is for the evening program. When you check the client records I would like all treatment plan short-term goals to contain the following language: eliminate all substance and alcohol use; develop outside support systems, improve self-esteem, and for those who don't have one, work toward getting a GED. Long-term goals will include: remain drug and alcohol free, continue to develop outside support groups, obtain GED, secure meaningful employment, and continue to improve self-esteem.''

"I have to recheck the ones I've reviewed to make certain they all read the same." Her voice was still raspy from a lingering cough.

"Why don't you go home? You look as if you're going to fall over."

Gathering her folders, Deborah grimaced. "I feel like a piece of crap."

"If you don't feel better tomorrow, please stay home."

"I can't. I have an encounter group with four new intakes."

"I'll lead the group."

Deborah gave her a stunned look. "When was the last time you led a group?"

Jolene smiled. "Not so long ago that I don't remember how to be a facilitator. You forget that I represented D.C. on a panel at the national conference for the prevention of domestic violence last year in San Francisco."

Gathering her papers, Deborah stood up. "Right now I can't even remember my own name."

"Do you want me to drive you home?"

She shook her head. "No, thanks. I think I can make it. I'll call you to let you know that I'm still alive," she said, walking slowly toward the door.

"Feel better."

"Thanks."

Jolene stared at her clinical director's departing figure. Despite the extra day off because of the holiday weekend, half the Sanctuary staff was still out sick. She'd been one of the luckier ones not to succumb to the debilitating virus that had decimated not only the staff but also many of the clients.

The intercom on her phone buzzed softly, and she left the love seat to answer it.

"Yes?"

"I have someone out in the reception area who wants to see you."

"Who is it?" she asked the part-time evening receptionist.

"She won't give me her name. I tried to refer her to our intake counselor, but she insists on seeing you."

"Tell her to wait."

Jolene slipped her arms into her suit jacket as she walked out of her office with long, determined strides. Opening the door to the reception area, she stepped out into the inviting space, spying the lone figure of a young woman with long dark brown hair wearing a shapeless sweatshirt and baggy jeans sitting stiffly on the edge of a chair near the door. Dark glasses shielded her eyes, and she looked as if she was ready to bolt at any sudden motion.

Maintaining a comfortable distance of four feet, Jolene flashed a warm smile. "Good evening. I'm Jolene Walker."

The woman jumped to her feet, reminding Jolene of a puppet on a string. There was no doubt she was wound tight—very, very tight.

"I would like to speak to you, Miss Walker." The words spilled over themselves as they tumbled out of her mouth.

Jolene extended a hand. "Please come with me." Turning, she nodded to the receptionist to buzz her in. She stood aside as the petite woman preceded her. "My office is down the hall."

April Stansfield followed Jolene Walker, her heart pounding uncontrollably in her chest. What she felt was similar to the sensations that lifted her beyond herself after she'd snorted several lines of cocaine. The only difference was the white powder elicited a feeling of euphoria; it had the power to make her temporarily forget the horror and the shame she'd endured over the past ten years. What she felt now wasn't euphoria but fear. A cold breath of air swept over the back of her neck, and in that instant she was tempted to turn around and run back through the doors and out into the warm late summer night.

She couldn't run—not now. Not when it had taken her more than two months to work up the nerve to walk into the Sanctuary. It was in moments of lucidity that she pulled out the articles she'd collected on Jolene Walker's program, a program that catered to victimized women with a history of substance abuse. And that was what she was. At twenty-two she'd abused so many substances that she surprised herself that she was still alive when the sun rose to herald a new day.

She was an abuser and a victim of domestic violence.

Jolene entered her office. "Please have a seat. You can sit anywhere you want."

April stared at her through the lenses of her sunglasses. "Aren't you going to close the door?"

"I only close the door when I'm in session." April moved toward the door, but Jolene blocked her escape. "Okay, I'll close the door." She closed it, watching the woman move cautiously around the room before choosing a chair beside her desk.

Jolene sat down behind the desk, lacing her fingers together. "You told my receptionist that you wanted to speak to me."

April nodded as she studied the face of the executive director staring directly at her. Her gaze lingered on the soft black curling hair before moving lower. She stared at her eyes. They were eyes she could trust. Large, dark, tilting upwards at the corners, and set in a flawless brown face that had the appearance of whipped mocha. Her nose was small, much too delicate for her large eyes and wide mouth, yet it hadn't detracted from her startling beauty.

"I'd like to come here for counseling."

"When would you like to start?" Jolene asked, wishing she would take off her glasses.

"Tonight." It had to be tonight or she would lose her nerve and never return.

"I need to call my intake counselor—"

"No!" April sprang to her feet. "Either you see me or I'm walking out of here."

Jolene stood up. "We have a certain protocol for intakes."

Curving her arms around her body in a protective gesture, April shook her head, the stiff hair falling around her shoulders barely moving with the motion. "I know all about intakes. You ask hundreds of questions, I fill out a dozen forms before I sign a contract saying I must remain drug and alcohol free as long as I'm in treatment."

"You've been in treatment before?"

"More times than I can remember. I want this to be my last time." Unfolding her arms, she pulled up the sleeves to the oversized sweatshirt and extended her hands, palms upward. Faint white lines crisscrossed the blue veins showing through her pale flesh. "I call these my cries for help, Miss Walker. I never cut deep enough to end my life, because I don't want to kill myself. All I want is to wake up and make it through the day without popping a pill to help me get out of bed, or taking another to help me sleep."

Jolene pulled her stunned gaze away from the scars on wrists so small they could've belonged to a child. "Sit down. Please, Miss—"

"April."

"April what?"

"April is all you need to know for now."

Struggling to remain in control with the manipulative

woman, Jolene forced a smile. "Okay, April. I'd like for you to sit down." The two women eyed each other suspiciously, and then sat down simultaneously.

"Tell me what you want, April."

Lowering her head, she studied her hands folded on her lap. She curled her fingers into tight fists to stop their trembling. "I want your help. I want you to help me."

"Help you how?"

"I want to stop using."

"How do you want me to help you stop using?"

Her head came up and she glared at Jolene. "I want you to take me on as a client."

"I can't take you on as a client without you going through an intake process."

"No!"

"Yes, April! This is a licensed facility, and because it is I have to follow regulations. I will not risk losing the Sanctuary's license, or jeopardize my own because you want to play the game your way."

April's jaw quivered as she struggled to hold back the tears welling up behind her eyelids. She'd risked her life by sneaking out and coming to the Sanctuary.

"I can't go back. I won't go back unless you help me." Hot tears overflowed, spilling down her pale cheeks.

Something in the younger woman's voice touched Jolene. She didn't know why, but she sounded so much like Jeanine after she'd discovered she was pregnant.

Could she send April home without accepting her as a client? And what was waiting for her at home? Mixed feelings surged through her as she struggled for an answer to what had become an impasse. April slashing her wrists was a cry for help, which meant she was definitely suicidal. How many times had she attempted and failed? And would she try again? Reaching into a drawer of her desk, Jolene pulled out several tissues and handed them to the sobbing woman.

"What if I take you on as a private client?"

April removed her glasses for the first time, blotting the moisture staining her face. She stared at Jolene with a pair of blue-gray eyes that seemed too old for her, eyes filled with years of pain.

"A . . . private client?"

"Yes. I can't see you here."

"Where will we meet?"

"In my home."

"Where do you live?"

"Georgetown. Will getting there pose a problem for you?"

"I . . . I don't know. I'll have to make arrangements."

"Do you drive?"

She nodded. "Yes. I have a license." What she didn't have was a car.

Jolene picked up a business card and wrote her private number on the back. "Call me and let me know when you're available and we'll set up a schedule."

"I can pay you, Miss Walker."

Her head came up slowly and she gave April a cold stare. "I'm not taking you on because of money. I'm doing it because I want to save your life." She handed her the card.

A wave of color suffused her face for the first time. "Thank you." She pushed the card into the pocket of her jeans. A hint of a smile lifted the corners of her mouth. "I'll call you."

"I'm the only one other than my administrative assistant who will answer if you call that number. Her name is Sally Leonard."

April's smile widened as she stood up. "Thank you again, Miss Walker."

"Are you going to be all right when you get home?"

"Oh, yes," she said confidently.

"Good. Then I'll be waiting to hear from you."

"You will."

Pushing back her chair, Jolene rose to her feet. "I'll walk you out."

She escorted April out to the reception area, watching as she opened the front door and closed it gently behind her. Closing her eyes, she mumbled a silent prayer for the young woman with the misshapen clothes and sad eyes.

The clock on a wall in the reception area read 7:50. The Sanctuary was scheduled to close in another hour. Then she would go home, close her door, and shut out all of the Aprils until the next day.

Eighteen

April Stansfield always dreamed in color: vivid reds, vibrant yellows, shocking pinks and blues. It was always that way after she swallowed two of the tiny capsules. After she washed them down with a glass of red wine, she'd told herself it would be the last time—the very last time, because she was going to get help. Miss Jolene Walker had promised to help her get clean.

She floated in and out of consciousness, and still she heard him. Even if she swallowed half a dozen capsules, she would always hear him. Holding her breath, she waited for him to approach her bed. She waited for the heat of his body, the scent of the expensive cologne she found so repugnant, and then his touch. The room was pitch-black, the way she preferred it. That way she wouldn't have to see his face, or the other revolting part of his body. He placed a hand over a bare breast. He forbade her to wear a nightgown or pajamas.

"How was your day, precious?"

She wanted to scream at him that her name was April,

not precious. "Good." The single word was flat, emotionless. She hated his voice. It was soft, comforting, unlike the cruel man who claimed it.

The side of the mattress dipped from his weight. "I was told that you went out tonight."

April found it hard to breathe with him so close. "Your spies are right," she spat out.

The hand on her breast tightened. She clenched her teeth instead of screaming in pain. "I was told that you went out tonight," he repeated.

"Yes," she hissed through the excruciating torture.

His grip lessened. "That's a good girl. Where did you go?"

"I went to meet a friend."

"Where?"

"We met at a Starbucks not far from Dupont Circle."

She'd told him a half-truth. Before she worked up enough nerve to go to the Sanctuary, she spent more than an hour at Starbucks, drinking cup after cup of latte. It had become her favorite hangout for the past two months.

"Who is this friend?"

"It's no one special."

"Who's the friend, precious?"

"His name is Joe."

"Joe what?"

"I don't know his last name."

"Why?"

"Because I never asked him. He must be a student, because every time I see him he's reading or studying. We shared a table the other day, and we struck up a conversation."

"You like this Joe?"

"Not really. He's just a nice boy. Someone to talk to."

A swollen silence ensued. April wanted him to leave so she could return to her psychedelic dream world. She'd just drifted back into her drug-induced slumber when she felt his mouth cover hers, praying she would not gag.

"I leave you alone too often. There's no reason why you should have to seek out strangers to talk to."

Her hands curled into tight fists to keep from pushing him away. Whenever she attempted to push him away, she woke up bruised and bloody. And when he hit her, he never stopped at one or two slaps. The blows would rain down until she passed out.

"Please, not tonight," she pleaded softly against his marauding mouth.

"Why not?" There was no trace of the former softness in his voice.

"I'm bleeding."

"You had your period last week."

"I still have it," she sobbed. "You know I always have it for seven days." She'd prayed for a tumor, that way she would bleed every day and he would never touch her.

He moved off the bed as if she had come down with a contagious disease. "Let me know when it's gone. And another thing, please lose the wig. I'm told it's hideous."

His footsteps were muffled in the deep pile of the carpeting as he made his way to the door. A sliver of light pierced the darkness before it was quickly extinguished as the door closed behind his departing figure.

It was then that April Stansfield put her hands over her mouth to cut off the screams exploding in the back of her throat. She cried without making a sound, her tears flowing into the long, pale blond hair fanning out on the pillow under her heaving shoulders.

Jolene hadn't realized how much she'd missed Michael until he walked into her apartment. She put her arms around

An important message from the ARABESQUE Editor

Dear Arabesque Reader,

Because you've chosen to read one of our Arabesque romance novels, we'd like to say "thank you"! And, as a special way to thank you, we've selected four more of the books you love so well to send you for FREE!

Please enjoy them with our compliments, and thank you for continuing to enjoy Arabesque...the soul of romance.

Karen Thomas
Senior Editor,
Arabesque Romance Novels

Check out our website at
www.arabesquebooks.com

3 QUICK STEPS
TO RECEIVE YOUR "THANK YOU" GIFT
FROM THE EDITOR

Send this card back and you'll receive 4 FREE Arabesque
novels! The introductory shipment of 4 Arabesque novels – a
$23.96 value – is yours absolutely FREE!

There's no catch. You're under no obligation to buy anything.
You'll receive your introductory shipment of 4 Arabesque
novels absolutely FREE (plus $1.50 to offset the costs of
shipping & handling). And you don't have to make any
minimum number of purchases—not even one!

We hope that after receiving your books you'll want to
remain an Arabesque subscriber. But the choice is yours to
continue or cancel, anytime at all! So why not take us up on
our invitation to receive 4 Arabesque Romance Novels, with
no risk of any kind. You'll be glad you did!

Call us
TOLL-FREE
at 1-800-770-1963

THE EDITOR'S "THANK YOU" GIFT INCLUDES:

- 4 books absolutely FREE (plus $1.50 for shipping and handling)
- A FREE newsletter, *Arabesque Romance News*, filled with author interviews, book previews, special offers, and more!
- No risks or obligations. You're free to cancel whenever you wish... with no questions asked.

BOOK CERTIFICATE

Yes! Please send me 4 FREE Arabesque novels (plus $1.50 for shipping & handling). I understand I am under no obligation to purchase any books, as explained on the back of this card.

Name _____

Address_____ Apt. _____

City _____ State_____ Zip _____

Telephone ( ) _____

Signature _____
Offer limited to one per household and not valid to current subscribers. All orders subject to approval. Terms, offer, & price subject to change. Offer valid only in the U.S.

Thank you!

AN022A

Accepting the four introductory books for FREE (plus $1.50 to offset the cost of shipping & handling) places you under no obligation to buy anything. You may keep the books and return the shipping statement marked "cancelled". If you do not cancel, about a month later we will send 4 additional Arabesque novels, and you will be billed the preferred subscriber's price of just $4.00 per title. That's $16.00 for all 4 books for a savings of 33% off the cover price (Plus $1.50 for shipping and handling). You may cancel at any time, but if you choose to continue, every month we'll send you 4 more books, which you may either purchase at the preferred discount price. . . or return to us and cancel your subscription.

his neck, pulling his head down, giving herself freely to the passion of his kiss.

Her day had gone well. She'd filled in for Deborah, interacting with four anxious, uncertain middle-aged women who'd undergone years of domestic abuse. During the two-hour session she'd covered three major topics, telling the women, You are not alone, you are not to blame, and you do not deserve to be abused. They'd gone through two boxes of tissues but emerged from the session feeling better about themselves than they had when they'd tentatively entered the group room.

She'd returned to her office to find a message on her desk that Michael had called. She'd returned the call, confirming their dinner plans and agreeing to spend the night with him.

Michael's tongue outlined the shape of her mouth, her lips parting and allowing him access to the honeyed sweetness he'd spent days trying to recall. Everything about Jolene Walker seeped into him, making them one.

Pulling back, he stared at her wide-eyed expression, unable to fathom how she could look so innocent and provocatively wanton at the same time. He'd impulsively asked her to spend the night with him, and she hadn't hesitated when she'd agreed. He'd then tried to think of ways to make the night memorable, but had given up once he realized that he didn't have to try to impress Jolene. He'd come to her as Michael Kirkland, a civilian, not United States Army Captain Michael Kirkland. And it was the first time since he'd entered West Point that a woman had become more important than his military career.

She flashed her winning smile, pointing to a garment bag thrown across the chair and a small overnighter on the floor. "I'm ready."

He picked up both bags, waiting while she closed and locked her apartment door behind them. "You have a choice to either eat out or in." It was a little past seven, and a weekday, so it probably wouldn't be too difficult to find a table at a restaurant now that most tourists had returned to their home cities.

Jolene stared at the back of Michael's head as she followed him down the staircase. "What's on the menu at your place?"

"I can throw a couple of steaks on the outdoor grill."

"I like that idea." She did not want to go to a restaurant and wait to be served, because she hadn't eaten anything all day except for several cups of coffee and a package of crackers she'd found in the employee lounge. The women who attended their day program were always served lunch, and they'd ordered in pizza, which wasn't on her favorite foods list.

"Where are you going?" she asked Michael as he walked past her car parked several doors from her building.

Stopping, he turned, staring at her. "We're going to my place."

"But I need my car."

"What for?"

"How am I going to get to work in the morning?"

"I'll drop you off."

"I might need my car during the day."

Shrugging a shoulder, he walked back to where she stood beside the blue Audi. She opened the doors with the remote device and handed him the keys. He waited until she was seated, then placed her bags on the backseat. He sat down, adjusting the driver's seat to accommodate his longer legs.

After turning the key in the ignition, he pulled away from the curb in a burst of speed, maneuvering into the driveway at his house within two minutes. He smiled at Jolene when she stared at him, her mouth gaping.

"You like speeding, don't you?"

Unbuckling his seat belt, he winked at her. "Not as much as I like you."

He helped her out of the car, carrying her bags with one hand while his free arm curved around her waist. He pressed several buttons on a hidden panel concealed under decorative wood facing, and the front door opened silently.

"It beats using a key," he explained, seeing her shocked expression. He left her bags on a chair near the door, and then closed the door.

Jolene walked into the living room, completely awed by its beauty. She didn't think she would ever get used to the architecture and meticulously chosen furnishings. Illumination from recessed lights built into a ledge above the many narrow rectangular windows cast a warm glow over wood surfaces. A layered light fixture of squares and rectangles was suspended above a dining room table with seating for eight. A smaller matching table and chairs with seating for four was positioned near a wall of windows with the Wright-inspired Tree of Life design. The high-back chairs had oak vertical slats with red seat cushions dotted with gold geometric motifs.

A gleaming black concert piano sat near a massive column, dividing the living room from the dining room. Michael admitted that he'd learned to play as a child, yet hadn't been motivated to play much since purchasing it a year ago.

The two-story, three-bedroom house would provide enough space for a family of four to move about comfortably without stepping over one another. She stood there, shocked and shaken by her thoughts. Why was she thinking about children? Did she really want a child? Did she want to become the mother of his children?

Michael moved silently, stopping in front of her, and as their eyes met, she felt a shudder run through her. Did he know? Could he read her thoughts?

"What's wrong?"

"What makes you think something's wrong?"

"Something about your expression. You looked as if you'd zoned out for a minute."

"It's probably hunger. I haven't eaten all day."

Reaching for her hand, he pulled her gently toward the kitchen. "If that's the case, then I'd better feed you. I can't have you fainting on me."

Jolene leaned back on a cushioned teakwood chair and closed her eyes. The aroma of grilled meat lingered in the humid night air. It was the first week in September, yet the summer heat and humidity hadn't abated.

Lighted candles in several Kobi lanterns bathed the garden in an eerie glow. She and Michael had decided to eat under a pergola with an overhang of grape leaves. He'd grilled steaks to succulent perfection while she'd prepared a salad of field greens with a vinaigrette dressing. She'd opted for a rice pilaf instead of baked potatoes. He'd shown her how to use a pair of black lacquer chopsticks, but she'd wound up leaving more food on the plate than in her mouth. The sound of a cat's howling, the incessant chirping of crickets, and the intermittent hooting of an owl were magnified in the stillness of the night.

"It sounds as if that cat's in heat," she said softly.

The cat's not the only one in heat, Michael thought.

He'd spent the past hour and a half feasting on Jolene's beauty. They'd lingered over dinner, neither wanting the evening to end. He was so relaxed that he could've spent the night in the garden, sleeping on one of the loungers. She offered him a chance to love and capture the peace that had always seemed to evade him.

He smiled when he saw her conceal a yawn behind her fingers. Raising his arm, he stole a glance at his watch. It was nearly ten. "Why don't you go in and get ready for bed?"

Her eyes opened, meeting his gaze, his eyes glowing in the darkness like a cat's. "I'll go after I help you clean up."

Pushing back, he came around the table and placed a hand under her armpit, easing her gently to her feet. "I'll clean up. You're the one who has to go to work tomorrow."

Leaning forward, she rested her forehead on his shoulder. "I keep forgetting you're a goldbrick."

He curved a hand around the back of her head, dropping a kiss on her hair. "Don't you forget that this goldbrick loves you."

Rising on tiptoe, she pressed a kiss to his smiling mouth. "I don't think you'll ever let me forget it."

His smile widened. "How right you are."

He released her, watching as she walked back into the house and disappeared from his line of vision before he began the task of clearing the table and taking everything into the kitchen. It didn't take him long to rinse dishes and pots, stacking them in the dishwasher. Then he put out the garbage and set the alarm. His footsteps were silent as he mounted the staircase for the last time that night.

The soft sound of classical music coming from the stereo unit in the sitting area of his bedroom greeted him as he walked in, his gaze fixed on the king-sized bed. Jolene had changed the radio station from his favorite one featuring contemporary jazz. She lay on her side, one arm thrown over her head. All of the light in the room had been extinguished except for a mounted sconce on a wall next to the adjoining bath.

Walking into the bathroom, he stripped off his clothes, brushed his teeth, and then stepped into an oversized shower stall. Ten minutes later he returned to the bedroom, flicked off the light, and slipped under the sheet.

Jolene turned toward the source of heat like a sunflower facing the sun, climbing atop Michael's naked form. "What took you so long?" she whispered against his lips.

Reversing their positions, he had her on her back before she could exhale. One hand feathered over her inner thigh. "Next time leave the nightgown off."

"I'll try to remember." She gasped when his fingers slid between the delicate folds of flesh to find her wet and ready for him.

Groping for the drawer to the bedside table, Michael managed to retrieve a square packet, open it, and slip the latex protection over his swollen flesh without turning on the light. It had been days since he'd sampled her silken body, and it had only served to heighten his need for her.

He kissed her mouth as he slipped the delicate straps to her nightgown off her shoulders, down her arms, and lower until it pooled at her ankles. He pressed a light kiss over her throat, measuring the rapidly beating pulse under the delicate flesh. Her soft moans intensified his craving when he caught a distended nipple between his teeth.

Jolene's fingernails sank into the rock-hard muscles in Michael's biceps, holding him fast. She was the cat in heat, mewling and howling for her mate. Her need bordered on insanity as she kicked off the offending silk fabric around her legs. Once freed, she wrapped her legs around his waist, making him her willing prisoner.

Michael managed to free himself from her long limbs, pulling back and entering her with one, smooth, sure thrust of his hips. Then his world stood still before tilting wildly. He rode her deep, he rode her hard, wanting to fuse her flesh with his. They reversed positions once, twice, and then a third time. Jolene sat astride him, eyes closed, neck arched, while setting a high-speed rhythm that gave no sign of slowing.

She felt alive, every pulse in her body humming with the mounting pleasure seeking and searching for a means of escape. Michael's arms flailed wildly as pillows, shams, and the duvet landed on the floor. The soft groans in his throat escalated until he was gasping painfully for each precious gulp of air.

They raced faster and faster, moisture pouring off their labored bodies and soaking the Egyptian cotton sheets. Their passions rose higher and higher like the funnel cloud of a powerful twister, sweeping up everything in its path. Then, without warning, the storm broke, their cries echoing in unison as they exploded and melted all over each other.

Jolene tasted droplets of salt on her tongue. At first she thought it was perspiration, but as she collapsed on Michael's heaving chest, she realized it was her tears. She'd exorcised herself. She'd given Michael all of herself, holding nothing back.

He held her to his heart, one hand moving up and down her damp spine in a comforting gesture. "Shhhh, baby," he crooned softly. "It's all right. I'm here for you." He kissed her forehead. "I love you," he repeated over and over until her sobbing eased.

Waiting until he heard the soft sound of her even breathing, he gently eased her off his body. Reaching over, he picked up two pillows, placing one under her head.

As he pulled her to his side, he stared up at the ceiling, unable to believe what had just occurred between him and the woman asleep in his embrace. Their lovemaking had become a raw act of possession. He tried dismissing the word that nagged at his brain, but it persisted.

They'd *mated* with each other.

Jolene was not his girlfriend or his lover. She had become his mate.

Nineteen

Jolene sat in her study at her apartment, staring at April Stansfield, shocked at the transformation. A curtain of shiny blond hair, parted in the middle, framed her tiny heart-shaped face. She looked fragile enough to shatter into hundreds of tiny pieces if someone pushed her.

Jolene's day had begun when she'd awaken in a cocoon of sensual bliss that had lasted for hours until the younger woman's arrival.

She'd opened her eyes to find Michael reclining on a chair in his sitting room, drinking coffee and reading the *Washington Post*.

Realizing she was awake, he'd come over and kissed her, and then gone downstairs, returning with breakfast on a tray. He'd joined her in bed, reading her the top news stories while she ate. She'd loathed having to get up, but reluctantly had left the bed to shower and prepare to go to the Sanctuary. She'd kissed Michael, promising to call him later, then gotten into her car and driven away. She'd watched him in her rearview mirror as he waved until she was out of sight.

It had been a few minutes after nine when a call had come in on her private line. It had been April Stansfield, asking if she could see her. They'd agreed to meet at Jolene's apartment at three o'clock.

An oversized shapeless long-sleeved cotton pullover nearly concealed April's tiny trembling hands as she sat on the edge of her chair. She had yet to make eye contact.

"How old are you, April?"

Her head came up, her eyes narrowing in suspicion. "Are you secretly recording this session?"

Jolene's expression did not change. "Do you want me to?"

She shook her head. "No. No tapes, no notes."

"I'll agree to your wishes if you answer my question. How old are you?"

"Twenty-two."

"Tell me about your family."

April looked away, staring at a framed reproduction of a mural by John T. Biggers. She seemed transfixed by the detail of a mother and child, the central figures in the painting titled "The Web of Life."

"There's nothing to tell."

"How about your father?"

"He's dead."

"When did he die?"

Her head spun around, her gaze brimming with rancor. "How should I know?"

Jolene decided not to press her. "Is your mother alive?"

April gritted her teeth, her lips thinning in a hard line. Her gaze returned to the painting. Ten minutes passed without a verbal exchange, Jolene waiting patiently for her patient to open up again.

"My mother is a tramp."

It wasn't the response Jolene sought, but she mentally filed it away in her mind. "A tramp in which way?"

"She's a whore!"

She needed information, answers, not name-calling. "What substances are you taking?" she asked, smoothly changing the focus.

"Everything—except heroin. I don't like needles."

"When was the last time you used?"

April stared at Jolene as if she'd taken leave of her senses. "Last night. I needed something to help me sleep." She jumped to her feet, reaching into the pocket of her jeans. She threw five new twenty-dollar bills on the coffee table. "I have to go. I'll call when I can meet with you again."

Turning quickly, she ran out of the room, Jolene in pursuit. She caught up with her at the door. "Try to go to sleep without the pills tonight."

Placing a hand on the doorknob, April nodded without turning around. Reaching over her thin shoulder, Jolene turned the lock. One minute April stood staring at the door, then she opened it and was gone.

Jolene was rooted to the spot, unable to move. She saw the pain in April's eyes. Heard the venom in her voice. *My mother's is a tramp! She's a whore.* What had her mother done to her? Was it possible her mother had turned her onto drugs?

Gathering her handbag off the chair, Jolene checked her cell phone for messages. She hadn't told Sally where she was going, just that she was taking a late lunch. There were no messages. She dropped the tiny phone in her bag, gathered her keys, and left her apartment to return to the Sanctuary.

April called her the following morning, again setting up an appointment for three. The second session was a repeat of the first. April was practically monosyllabic, her rage evident whenever she had to speak about her family. Jolene felt her frustration, deciding not pressure her to disclose before she was ready. And as with the first session, April threw five new twenty-dollar bills on the table before their fifty-minute session ended.

Picking up four of the bills, Jolene held them out to April. "I only charge sixty an hour."

A slow smile curved April's mouth as she shook her head. "Keep it. Consider the extra forty a donation to the Sanctuary. And before you say it, I'll tell you. I'm still taking the pills. I can't get to sleep without them."

Jolene stared at her for several seconds. "You came to me because you want me to help you get clean. That's not going to happen if you don't talk to me. We need to identify what it is that makes you medicate yourself."

April closed her eyes, clenching and unclenching her jaw. "I'm not ready to talk. Not now." When she opened her eyes, determination radiated from the blue-gray depths. "Please give me time, Miss Walker. Meanwhile, I'll try not to OD."

"That's not funny," Jolene snapped angrily.

"I didn't mean for it to be." Turning on her heels, she walked out of the study and out of the apartment.

Crumbling the bills in a tight fist, Jolene flung them in the air. The girl was playing with her. April had come to her for help; meanwhile, she'd become the master puppeteer pulling strings and making her therapist bend to her will. She'd established the days and time when they met, determined the fee for service, and walked out whenever she tired of her questions.

Next time it would be different—very, very different.

Monday morning Jolene deactivated the alarm at the Sanctuary, walked into her office, and nearly collapsed from the

shock of seeing her computer lying on its side on the carpet.
Drawers to her desk were turned upside down. Even seat
cushions on the chairs and love seats were slashed.

Her hand shook so much that when she knelt down to
pick up the telephone, it slipped from her grasp. She finally
grabbed the receiver and put it to her ear, but there was no
dial tone. The line was dead.

Someone had vandalized the Sanctuary!

"Get it together, Jolene," she whispered, trying not to
panic. *Get out!* the voice in her head screamed at her. What
if whoever had broken in was hiding somewhere on the
premises?

Looking over her shoulder, she backed out of the office,
retreating to the parking lot. Leaning against the side of her
car, she found her cell phone and dialed 911. She gave the
information to the clerk, who warned her not to attempt to
reenter the premises until the police arrived.

She left the parking lot, walking across the street to where
she could observe the front of the building. How, she thought,
had someone broken in without setting off the silent alarm?
Had one of the staff returned and forgotten to set it?

All of the questions floated around in her head as she
tried remembering who was the last one to leave Friday.
She'd left at 2:15 to return home in time to meet April. The
Sanctuary's hours of operation were nine to nine Monday
through Thursday, and nine to two on Fridays.

Her fingers gripped the cell phone until it left a distinct
impression on her palm. She stared at it, then dialed
Michael's number. She'd only left him twenty minutes
before. He'd spent Friday and Saturday nights at her apartment, and she'd reciprocated by staying over on Sunday
night.

"Hello."

She swallowed when she heard his voice. "Michael, this
is Jolene."

There was a noticeable pause before he said, "What's going on?"

"Why would you ask that?"

"Something's wrong. I hear it in your voice."

Closing her eyes, she bit down on her lower lip to stop its trembling. "Someone broke into the Sanctuary. They destroyed—"

"Where are you?" he shouted, interrupting her.

"I'm outside, across the street. I'm waiting for the police."

"Get away from the place. Go stand on the corner if you have to. I'll be there as soon as I can."

She held the phone to her ear until she realized he'd hung up. Moving farther down the block, she saw Deborah drive up seconds before the police arrived. Waving to Deborah, she shouted at her not to pull into the parking lot. The clinical director found a spot on the street, then jumped out of her car, racing toward her.

"What's the matter?"

"We were burglarized."

The color drained from Deborah's normally tanned face. She mumbled a raw expletive under her breath, then caught Jolene's arm in a death grip.

Two cruisers stopped in front of the Sanctuary, and four uniformed police officers emerged, hands resting on their firearms. A tall, light-skinned black officer glanced at the two women holding onto each other. He walked over to them while the others moved cautiously around the two-story structure.

"I'm Sergeant Tompkins. Who placed the call?"

Jolene pried Deborah's hand off her arm. "I did. I'm Jolene Walker, executive director of the Sanctuary."

"What happened?"

"I deactivated the alarm and walked in to find my office trashed. I left before checking the others."

The officer pulled a leather-covered notebook from his back pocket. "We're going to check to see if anyone's still inside before we can allow you to go back in."

His gaze lingered on Jolene's face longer than necessary, silently admiring the light cover of makeup highlighting her best features: her eyes and mouth. He liked her short, fashionable hairdo, and the lush curves of her tall, slender body, which a tailored silk blouse and linen slacks failed to disguise. His attention was diverted when a racy Jaguar screeched to an abrupt halt behind the cruisers.

Jolene turned, spying Michael as he jumped out of his car and sprinted over to her. She knew he had exceeded the speed limit to arrive that quickly.

He wore what he'd put on that morning after they'd shared a shower: jeans, T-shirt, and running shoes. His brilliant green eyes were hidden behind a pair of oval sunglasses.

Ignoring the police officer and the other woman standing next to Jolene, he reached out and pulled her to his chest. "Are you all right?"

Burying her face against his warm brown throat, she nodded. "I'm all right now."

Michael didn't believe her. He felt the little tremors shaking her body despite her outwardly calm appearance.

"You work here?" Sergeant Tompkins asked Michael.

Michael stared at him over Jolene's shoulder. "No. I'm responsible for *this* woman."

"If you don't mind, I need to talk to Miss Walker."

Michael released Jolene, watching as she and the police officer moved several feet away. He couldn't overhear their conversation as Sergeant Tompkins busied himself taking notes. She shook her head, then gestured, pointing in the direction of the building that housed the treatment program.

Deborah Madison stared numbly at Michael, her admiring gaze moving languidly over his tall physique. *So,* she mused, *he's the reason why Jolene stopped logging so many hours at the office.* A knowing smile parted her spare lips. Maybe he had a friend somewhere who wouldn't mind becoming *responsible* for her.

Extending her right hand, she smiled. "I'm Deborah Madison, the Sanctuary's clinical director."

Michael offered her a polite smile, shaking her hand. "Michael Kirkland."

Nice name, voice, teeth, hair, face, and very nice body, Deborah thought as he stared at her through the lenses of his small oval sunglasses. She wished he'd take them off so she could see his eyes.

Michael's gaze lingered briefly on Deborah before it returned to Jolene. He'd known something wasn't right the instant she'd said, *Michael, this is Jolene.* There had been an obvious panic in her voice when she'd called his name, because whenever she called him, her first greeting was usually a sultry hello.

He wondered who could've broken into the place—an angry husband or boyfriend seeking revenge, or a petty criminal looking for something to fence easily? He was aware that no one could enter any of the therapists' offices without being buzzed in. And he knew that the Sanctuary was wired with a silent alarm system. How had the burglar—or burglars, if there were more than one—been able to bypass the alarm system? Or had someone left without activating it?

These were questions the police would ask. His concern was, would Jolene have the answers?

Twenty

The Sanctuary's staff spent more than two hours milling around the parking lot while two members from D.C.'s Crime Scene Unit dusted every surface in the structure for fingerprints and clues to who may have vandalized the center. The arriving clients were met by their respective therapists, and sent home with a promise they would call them as soon as a structural problem was resolved. Jolene and Deborah decided it best not to advertise the break-in.

The break-in had been labeled an act of vandalism instead of a burglary because nothing appeared to have been stolen. Seat cushions were slashed, locks ripped from desks and file cabinets, client case records strewn about the water-soaked carpet, phone jacks smashed, and computer files deleted. State-of-the-art computers and printers housed in a resource room were damaged beyond repair. Several inches of water stood in the kitchen and rest rooms, soaking the carpeting in the front of the house when open faucets had overflowed sinks and basins.

The question of the security alarm was answered when Sally Leonard verified that she was the last to leave Friday afternoon. And yes, she *had* set the alarm. The police confirmed that there had been no forcible entry, which meant someone either knew the code to disable the alarm, or someone familiar with the system had been able to bypass and breach the security code.

Michael waited in his car in front of the Sanctuary while Jolene conducted business on her cell phone in the parking lot. She'd sent the staff home at eleven, and then sat in her car talking to Claire McDonald. She persuaded Claire not to come to survey the damage, suggesting she call the telephone company to restore phone service, and the insurance company to arrange for an adjuster to estimate the damage. She told Claire that the alarm company had sent a technician to check the system, declaring it operable.

It was exactly noon when she walked over to Michael's car, slipped into the passenger seat, and fell into his arms. She didn't cry, because she couldn't. Her anger was burning too hot for tears.

"I wish I could've walked up on whoever did this," she said through clenched teeth.

Pulling back, Michael stared at the rage radiating from her gaze. "You don't know what you're saying."

She met his cold glare, refusing to back down. "I know exactly what I'm saying."

"Oh, yeah? So, instead of a break-in, then it could've been a homicide." He tightened his hold on her shoulders. "I didn't fall in love with you to place flowers on your grave, Jolene."

"Let me go, Michael." Her voice was low, void of emotion.

He complied, falling back against the leather seat, running his left hand over his face in a weary gesture. "What are you going to do now?"

''There's not much I can do.'' She stared out the windshield. ''I have to wait for a call from the insurance company. They have to let me know when they're going to send an adjuster to assess the damage. Until then, we're closed for business.''

Turning his head, he stared at her profile. She could've been carved out of granite. ''Come back to the house with me.''

''I'm sorry, Michael. But I need to be alone right now.''

''That's what you don't need.''

Jolene wanted to scream at him, telling him he had no right to tell her what she needed or didn't need. But she'd called him right after she'd called the police because she needed him. And he'd come. He'd told Sergeant Tompkins he was responsible for her. It was not the first time he'd appointed himself her protector.

He cradled her chin in his right hand, leaning over and kissing her cheek. ''Come stay with me until all of this is over.''

She stared at him, not blinking. ''You think this break-in has something to do with me?''

''I'm not saying that. I just don't want you to go through this alone.''

Her lids fluttered wildly. ''What I can't understand is how someone broke in without tripping the alarm.''

Vertical lines appeared between his eyes. ''Did the alarm company verify that?''

She shook her head. ''The technician said everything was okay. He checked with his office, and they said their records show that no one deactivated the alarm over the weekend.''

''How the hell did they get in?''

Sighing heavily, she shook her head again. ''I don't know.''

''How long have you had this security system?''

"Just a little more than year."

"How about the alarm company?"

"At least four years. We contracted with them right after I was hired as executive director."

"Can you switch companies?"

"I can't do it without board approval. Why?" She saw his gaze fixed on her mouth. "What are you thinking?"

"I'd like to install a more sophisticated system to monitor all activity at the facility."

"What kind of system?"

"Cameras and beams similar to those used in museums."

"We can't afford that. Right now we're operating on a shoestring budget because of the safe house project. This will be the first year staff won't receive a salary increase."

"I'll take care of it."

"What do you mean you'll take care of it?"

"I'll pay for the cameras *and* install them."

"No. I can't ask you to do that."

"You didn't ask. I'm volunteering. Consider it a donation."

Her lids fluttered again. "Why, Michael?"

He hesitated, measuring her for a moment. "I'm surprised you have to ask why."

"But I am asking."

His left eyebrow arched as he stared through her. "I'm a very selfish man, Jolene, and I always take care of what belongs to me."

She registered his words, but it wasn't what he said that unnerved her—it was his tone. It was quiet and menacing, menacing and lethal as the man who'd spoken.

"I'll think about it," she said noncommittally.

A muscle throbbed spasmodically in his lean jaw. "What the hell is there to think about, Jolene?" he shouted, his voice bouncing off the ceiling of the low-slung car.

Her temper rose to meet his. "Don't you dare take that tone with me, Michael."

Dipping his head slightly, he leaned closer to her. "I have a bad feeling about this ... this break-in." His voice was low, calmer. "Things are just not adding up."

Her eyes widened. "What's wrong?"

"It's not a robbery, so the police have identified it as vandalism. What vandals do you know who have the ability to breach a sophisticated security system?"

What he didn't say was that whoever had broken into the Sanctuary was an expert. He or she knew exactly what they were doing. And it was apparent they were looking for something.

"I have to talk to Claire about it."

"Claire doesn't have to know. There's no need for anyone to know other than you and myself. I can do it after hours. Just call the security company and tell them that you're going to be working after closing time. I probably can wire the whole building in about four hours."

She wanted whoever had vandalized the Sanctuary caught and prosecuted. What she didn't want to believe was that someone on her staff had given out the code. As soon as the place was up and running again, she would change it.

"Okay, Michael. I'll let you install the cameras, but I will be the only one who'll be able to view the film, because our clients' identities are protected by federal confidentiality."

Bowing his head, he brushed a kiss over her lips. "Thanks."

Grazing his smooth cheek with her fingertips, she smiled. "Thank *you*. I'm going over to see Claire and find out if there's any feedback on how soon we can expect to be operational." Burying her face against his throat, she pressed a kiss there. "I'll come by later."

Pulling away, Michael stared at her. Even though his mouth was smiling, his eyes were pale and forbidding. "I'll be waiting."

Pushing open the door, she stepped out and walked across the street to retrieve her car. Michael waited until he saw her drive out of the parking lot before he turned the key in the ignition. He waved as she drove past him, his expression tight and strained.

He sat motionless, staring out the windshield and wanting to ignore the inner voice telling him that the police's conclusion that someone had broken into the Sanctuary to vandalize the place wasn't ringing true. He thought about what Jolene had said about client confidentiality. Did someone break in because they were looking for privileged data on a client?

Stanley Willoughby peered through the tinted glass of his limousine, his gaze narrowing when he spied the man standing outside Union Station.

"Stop here," he directed his driver.

The Lincoln Town Car eased up along the curb, and the man lounging against one of D.C.'s most magnificent architectural jewels straightened. The driver put the car in park, stepped out, and came around the vehicle to open the rear door. The well-dressed man slipped onto the velour backseat, and sixty seconds later the limo cruised smoothly in the steady flow of late-afternoon traffic.

Leaning forward, Stanley Willoughby closed the partition separating him from his chauffeur. "What do you have for me?"

Preston James hated—no, he loathed Stanley Willoughby. The man was rude, brash, and above all condescending. But he was also very wealthy *and* very powerful. He had influential friends in high places, and high places meant the

White House. Stanley and the president had attended college and law school together. Their close association had been cemented when the president had selected Stanley as his son's godfather.

"I found nothing."

Stanley's gray eyes grew cold, the only indication of his rising anger. "What do you mean, you found nothing?"

Preston stared at his hands resting on his knees. "There was nothing there. I checked every folder and scanned every computer program. I even found time to read about some of your friends' wives. You'd be surprised who's beating the crap out of their trophies." His head came up and he looked at Stanley for the first time since getting into the luxurious vehicle. "I could earn a nice penny from that kind of information."

The attorney moved back several inches, as if he feared contamination. He hated scum like Preston James, but he needed the man. He'd been paying Preston for years to do his dirty work. Perhaps it was time to fire the man—permanently.

"If you try blackmailing any of my associates, then you'd better kiss this life good-bye. Unless you want to end up like Jimmy Hoffa, I suggest you forget what you read."

Preston had no intention of blackmailing anyone. His little gig with Willoughby had proven to be too lucrative to try his luck elsewhere. "As I said, I found no record of the girl coming there."

Reaching into the breast pocket of his suit jacket, Stanley withdrew an envelope and tapped it against his palm before handing it to Preston. "I still want you to keep an eye on her."

Preston took the envelope, pocketing it in a motion too quick for the eye to follow. "I'll be in touch." He glanced out the side window. "You can let me out here."

Stanley picked up a telephone and buzzed his driver. "Pull over here."

Several blocks from the White House, Preston got out and disappeared in the crowd strolling along Pennsylvania Avenue.

Twenty-one

Dusk was descending on the city by the time Jolene returned to her apartment. She retrieved her mail, then made her way up the three flights of stairs. Her afternoon with Claire had yielded success. Judge Walter McDonald had intervened, using his clout with the insurance and telephone companies. Telephone repairs were scheduled for nine the following morning, while the insurance adjuster had confirmed a ten o'clock inspection.

Unlocking the door to her apartment, she spied an envelope that had been slipped under the door. She picked it up and dropped her keys on the table, her handbag on the chair, and kicked off her shoes. Walking slowly down the hallway to her bedroom, she scanned the stack of mail. She stared at the small plain envelope with her name printed on the front.

Slipping a fingernail under the flap, she withdrew a single sheet of paper, her gaze racing across the scrawled message:

Miss Walker. I tried calling you today, but the phone just rang. I needed to see you, because now I'm ready

to talk. Contact me tomorrow morning anytime after
eight. The number is for my beeper. After I leave here
I'm going home to take a pill to help me sleep.

The letters in Jolene's hand floated to the floor as she
reread the handwritten missive. She wanted to beep April
and plead with her not to take the pills; tell her to wait until
after they talked, but she did not want to put her at risk.
She didn't know enough about the young woman—who she
lived with, or if her significant other was violent.

Returning to the entryway, she retrieved the cell phone
from her handbag and turned it on. The signal indicating
low battery flashed intermittently. She'd used up most of
the battery talking to Claire while waiting for the Crime
Scene Unit to complete their investigation. She walked into
the kitchen and snapped the tiny phone into a charger on a
countertop.

"Dammit!" The word exploded from between her
clenched teeth. April was ready to disclose and she hadn't
been there for her. The break-in at the Sanctuary had turned
her day upside down.

Unbuttoning her blouse, she eased it off, draping it over
the back of a chair. An audible rumbling in her stomach
reminded her that she hadn't eaten anything since breakfast.
She'd been too upset to share lunch with Claire and Walter,
opting instead to drink a glass of orange juice. Dropping
down onto a tall stool, she reached for a wall phone and
dialed Michael's number.

He answered after the third ring.

"Hello." Her voice was soft, breathless.

"Hello back to you," came his reply.

She tried imagining his sensual smile. "Is your invitation
to spend the night still in effect?"

He chuckled softly. "The invitation isn't just for one
night."

It was her turn to laugh. "I'll see you in a little while."

"I'll be here."

Jolene hung up, retreating to the bathroom to shower while her phone charged itself.

Michael took Jolene's bags, setting them on the floor beside the door before sweeping her up in a strong embrace. He spun her around and around until she pleaded with him to stop.

He went completely still, smiling down at her. She smelled wonderful. The soft scent of lavender wafted to his delicate nostrils. Moisture clung to her shortened curls, glistening like diamonds on a luxurious black pelt.

His smile faded. "Is that your stomach growling?" Closing her eyes, she rested her head on his hard shoulder, nodding. Vertical lines appeared between his eyes. "When did you eat last?"

"This morning."

"Are you telling me you haven't eaten anything since breakfast?"

"I had a glass of orange juice at Claire's." He mumbled a curse under his breath. "I heard that," she teased.

"You're lucky that's all I said. How do you expect to keep your strength up if you don't eat?"

Michael continued to grumble as he carried Jolene into the kitchen, depositing her on a stool at the cooking island. Quickly, expertly, he concocted a mushroom omelette smothered with a spicy salsa, a small plate of sliced melon, strawberries, and seedless white grapes, and a cup of soothing chamomile tea.

She ate everything, kissed him tenderly, then climbed the winding staircase, leaving him to clean up the kitchen. Pulling back the taupe duvet with black Asian characters, she fell asleep within minutes of her head touching the pillow.

Michael slipped into bed next to Jolene, pulling her close to his side. He'd gotten so used to sleeping with her that he couldn't remember when she hadn't been in his bed or his life. He loved everything about her: her beauty, passion, intelligence, smile, and her dedication to her profession. She was strong-willed and independent—traits he admired most in a woman.

Burying his nose against her fragrant curls, he breathed a kiss onto her scalp. She knew he wanted to spend the rest of his life with her even though he hadn't asked her to become his wife. She'd asked him for time, and he'd willingly conceded. But what he didn't know was how much time he'd have to wait for her to become his bride, wife, and the mother of his children.

Jolene heard the voice, felt the heat as she struggled to surface from a deep, dreamless slumber. Opening her eyes, she stared up at Michael looming over her.

"What time is it?" Her voice was heavy with sleep.

"It's only four."

Rising on an elbow, she looked over her shoulder, peering at the lighted numbers on the clock on his side of the bed. "Why are you up so early?"

He sat down beside her. "I'm going to Lexington."

Falling back to the pillow, she closed her eyes against the stream of light coming from the bathroom. "What's there?"

"Your security equipment."

"You have to drive all the way to Lexington for it?"

Leaning over, he kissed her forehead. "Yes. I left a set of keys for you on the kitchen countertop to lock up when you leave."

She opened her eyes, unable to see his shadowed expression. "What about your alarm?"

"I've reprogrammed it to activate automatically sixty seconds after you lock the front door." He kissed her again. "I have to go because I want to be here when you come back later."

"I'm not certain whether I'm going to come back tonight."

"And why not?"

The three words were thrown at her like stones hurled from a slingshot. "Because I have *things* I have to do." Her waspish tone had matched his. She wanted to be available in case April wanted to see her.

Rising off the bed, Michael glared down at her. "Then I'll see you when I see you." Turning on his heels, he stalked out of the bedroom.

She became instantly wide awake, biting back the acerbic words poised on the tip of her tongue. How dare he try to monitor her whereabouts! The last man she'd had to answer to had been her father. And Michael Kirkland looked nothing like her daddy.

Swinging her legs over the side of the bed, she stood up. There was no way she could go back to sleep now. Making her way to the bathroom, she decided she would shower, dress, and then return to her own apartment. She'd neglected doing laundry for days, and now was as good a time as any to put in several loads. She had time to spare because she didn't have to be at the Sanctuary until nine.

Streaks of dawn painted the early morning sky with glorious color as Jolene backed her car out of the three-car garage constructed at the rear of the house. Michael had driven his sports-utility vehicle to Lexington instead of the Jaguar.

Droplets of water fell from the leaves of an overhead tree. It had rained overnight, resulting in a drop in temperature of at least fifteen degrees. The air was crisp, reminding her that autumn was only two weeks away.

Georgetown was just stirring. A smile curved her lips when she saw two dog walkers talking quietly, while their canines greeted each other with licks and sniffs. The distinctive sound of a woodpecker tapping on a tree trunk echoed loudly in the hushed silence.

She drove up and down her block twice, unable to find parking. She finally located a space several blocks away, and managed to squeeze into it with more maneuvering than she'd anticipated. It wasn't until she arrived at her building that she realized she'd walked the three blocks glancing over her shoulder. The break-in at the Sanctuary had left her skittish.

She grimaced when she thought of the scene that would greet her once she opened the door to the two-story structure housing the program. There was no doubt the carpeting on the first floor would have to be ripped up and discarded. Then, there were the client files floating in several inches of water. She wasn't certain whether any of them could be salvaged. A violent shudder shook her as she made her way up the brownstone steps. The case records had to be retyped before the quality assurance reviewers arrived. And as she opened the door to the vestibule, she prayed the vandals hadn't found and destroyed the program's backup disks.

Michael maintained his deathlike grip on the steering wheel until he felt his hands tingling from impeded circulation. He unclenched his jaw and his fingers, reaching for a pair of sunglasses in the compartment near his right hand. Watery rays of the rising sun fought valiantly to pierce the cover of blue-gray clouds, and won.

His dark mood lifted with the warmth and light penetrating the windshield of his truck. He'd walked away from Jolene before he lost his temper and said something to her he would regret for the rest of his life. He'd called on his iron-willed control, summoning up his father's warning when dealing women: *"Just walk away, Son. Never argue because you'll lose. There are other ways to win the battle, if not the war. Remember, a brilliant general always knows when to retreat."*

And he had retreated rather than tell Jolene that he did not want to control her life. All he wanted to do was protect her, protect her from something to which she appeared oblivious. The break-in still bothered him, bothered him so much that he was willing to drive to Lexington to purchase the most sophisticated state-of-the-art surveillance equipment. The army had recently declassified it, making it available for nonmilitary installation.

Entering local Route 211, he set the cruise control for seventy, removed his foot from the gas pedal, and settled back to enjoy the lush scenery as he drove westward. He enjoyed driving through the picturesque Shenandoah National Park. The region's natural beauty was humbling, as he tried imagining the land inhabited by First Nations Americans decades before the arrival of Europeans. Before all of the game had disappeared; before the rivers and streams had been polluted with the advent of modern technology; before wholesale destruction of portions of forested areas because of greed.

The cynical thoughts stayed with him until he left the park for the interstate. Cool, clean autumn-like air flowed from open vents as he sped southward with the Blue Ridge Mountains in the distance. He read the sign indicating the number of miles to the Virginia Military Institute. An envelope addressed to the historic military college containing his résumé lay on the table with a stack of others in his sitting room. He had yet to mail them, because he was waiting, waiting for a commitment from Jolene as to their future.

Before meeting her, his career had been uncertain; since meeting her, his future had become uncertain.

Entering Lexington's city limits, he followed the directions Bobby Ridgewell had given him when he'd called his former army buddy to tell him that he needed to place an order for surveillance equipment. Bobby's soft suggestion of "come on down and take a look at what I got" was all he'd needed to set up the appointment. Major Robert Ridgewell had given the U.S. Army thirty-five years of his fifty-five years of living, then retired to sell military surplus. He took umbrage at being referred to as an arms dealer, so Michael respected his wishes and never called him that.

He found Bobby's house easily. It was built on the top of a hill with the Shenandoah Mountains as the backdrop on the west. Bobby sat on his porch, rocking slowly. He did not rise from his seated position, not even when Michael stepped out of his truck, walked up the four steps, and stood in front of him. Michael snapped a perfect salute, then Bobby eased his solid bulk from the rocker, returning the salute.

"At ease, captain." Reaching out, he wrapped his massive arms around Michael, smothering him in a bear hug. Michael stood six-four and weighed one-ninety, but retired Major Robert Ridgewell lifted him off his feet as if he were a small child.

Releasing the younger man, he peered up at him. "You look good. What did you do, fall in love?"

Michael placed a finely boned hand on a thick shoulder covered by a plaid cotton shirt. "Where are your manners, Bobby? You expect me to spill my guts after a long ride and no tea?"

Bowing from the waist, Bobby extended an arm. "I'm sorry, but I seem to have forgotten my manners," he said with a very proper British accent. "Please come into my humble domicile and have a spot of tea before I fleece you for every shilling in your pocket."

The two men laughed loudly while slapping each other's backs. Bobby opened the screen door, permitting Michael to precede him into the log cabin he'd built with his own hands.

Michael sat across the solid wood table, hewn from a tree trunk, enjoying his second cup of tea. Bobby's tea was strong enough to grow hair on his smooth chest.

Staring at the former Green Beret, he had to admit that retirement favored the former career officer. His sable brown face was still smooth, although there was a liberal sprinkling of gray in his close-cut coarse black hair. He'd come from a family of military men. His father had been a pilot with the Tuskegee Airmen during World War II, and subsequent to graduating the ROTC, Bobby had been inducted into a special forces training program and shipped out to Vietnam. He'd earned several medals for bravery during the fierce and bloody Tet Offensive when he'd rescued six civilians attached to the U.S. embassy in Saigon after its brief occupation by Vietcong and North Vietnamese forces.

Twice-divorced, Bobby became Michael's mentor a week after he'd been reassigned to the Pentagon. Bobby had helped to ease his transition from being a highly trained intelligence expert to that of a glorified military clerk.

Bobby stared at Michael over the rim of his mug. "I heard you're out for six months."

Michael's expression didn't change. "Good news travels quickly, even out in the boonies."

"I still have my contacts back in Arlington. The word was Coop nearly burst a blood vessel when your leave was approved."

Coop's lucky I didn't kill him, Michael mused, forcing a smile he didn't feel.

"Don't let the bastard make you retreat before you're ready," Bobby continued.

"It's not a question of retreating. What Coop fails to realize is that I'm not obligated to spend the rest of my life in the army."

No one knew, other than family members, that he had enough money to last him the rest of his natural life, even if he never collected another paycheck.

Bobby put down his mug. "Tell me what you need."

"Cameras. They shouldn't be any larger than a quarter."

This time Bobby's expression remained impassive. "How many?"

Michael didn't know because he hadn't examined the architectural blueprints for the Sanctuary. "How about two dozen?"

Bobby's full lips parted in a wicked grin. "Do you have any idea how much those little puppies cost on the retail market?" Michael shook his head. "They're selling between fifteen and eighteen hundred a piece. But, because I know you, I'll charge you twelve."

Reaching into the back pocket of his jeans, Michael withdrew an envelope. He placed it in front of Bobby, waiting for him to open it. He was hard-pressed not to smile when seeing the man's eyes practically pop out of their sockets.

"Will that cover it?" He'd given him five checks, payable to CASH, in the amount of $9,900 each. "Please throw in all of the extra equipment I'll need to install them. And don't forget the laptop and disks."

Bobby slipped the checks back in the envelope, covering it with a pepper mill. "You're a strange man, Captain Kirkland. You keep the IRS from breathing down my neck by writing checks under ten thousand dollars, yet you ask me to sell you a piece of equipment that hasn't been declassified."

Michael folded his arms over his chest. "Don't try to jerk

me around, Bobby. I know you have at least one laptop hidden away somewhere.''

Scratching his head, the older man pursed his lips as his forehead furrowed. "You know, I think you're right. I was checking my inventory the other day and I believe I did see one.''

Pushing back his chair and rising to his feet, Michael nodded in acknowledgment. "Even though I always enjoy talking with you, I'd like to pick up my purchases and return to D.C. before the next millennium.''

Bobby stood up. "Come with me and I'll hook you up.''

Twenty-two

Jolene could not begin to imagine the damage wrought by the vandal or vandals. The wanton destruction to the property was astounding. The insurance adjuster checked off *damaged beyond repair* over and over as he made his way through offices, meeting rooms, rest rooms, staff and client kitchens and dining rooms. Computer monitors, terminals and printers, and lamps were shattered, seat cushions were ripped open, and tables and desktops had been gouged with a sharp object. Only the walls and window blinds remained untouched.

"I'll file my report as soon as I return to my office. You can expect a hand-delivered check for the replacement cost within thirty-six hours. Meanwhile, I suggest you call your respective vendors to begin replacing any equipment that will help you get up and running again."

She accepted a copy of his report, offering him a grateful smile. "Thank you for coming out so quickly."

The bespectacled adjuster shook his head as he stepped

over a tray to a laser printer. "Whoever did this is an animal," he mumbled as he walked out the front door.

Leaning over, Jolene righted a lamp in the reception area, placing it on a scarred side table. She'd spent most of the morning with the adjuster while a telephone technician worked feverishly rewiring each office. As she turned to retreat to her own office, the front door opened, and Deborah walked in. She was casually dressed in a pair of jeans, running shoes, and a faded Redskins sweatshirt.

"I thought I'd stop by and help clean up."

"You're just in time, because the adjuster left a few minutes ago."

"What did he say?"

"Almost everything has to be replaced."

Shaking her head, Deborah swore softly. "I think we better call a salvage company for a Dumpster."

"The upstairs telephones are working. You call while I begin with the case records."

"Are they salvageable?"

"I don't know. Most of them are soaked. Thankfully they weren't torched or shredded."

"Bite your tongue," Deborah said sarcastically. "When do you think we'll be back in business?"

Jolene ran her fingers through her shortened curls. "It's going to be at least a week."

"It could've been worse." Wincing, Deborah realized what she'd said. "I better get started calling for that Dumpster." She opened the door leading from the reception area to the therapists' offices, climbing the stairs to the second story.

Walking into the receptionist's cubicle, Jolene picked up a soggy case record. Despite the damp pages, the client numbers were still legible. A sense of strength flowed through her as her despair lessened. The vandals hadn't discovered the Zip disks containing all of the program's confidential backup data. Every Friday afternoon, Sally copied every therapist's floppy onto a Zip. It was a policy she'd instituted more than a year before. Every Zip was labeled, dated, and then concealed in a hidden panel behind the vanity in Jolene's private rest room.

It probably would take the administrative assistant a week to pull up the data and print it out, but at least the case records would be available whenever the reviewers arrived.

Jolene knew she was in denial, but she did not want to accept the possibility that a partner of one of the women in treatment was responsible for the carnage.

She'd stacked the files, putting them in numerical order, when the front door opened again. Her head came up, her pulse racing as she recognized the tall figure. Michael stood motionless, staring at her, and she returned his penetrating look with one of her own.

He was so breathtakingly virile that she found it hard to breathe. Resting long fingers on his waist, he angled his head, smiling at her. The slight lifting of his firm mouth, the crinkling of the lines around his brilliant eyes, and the arching of a curving black eyebrow galvanized her into action. Rising slowly to her feet, she moved from the cubicle to stand in front of him.

"Good afternoon, Michael."

He looked at her as if seeing her for the first time. Her hair was growing out, and her body was slimmer than it had been when he'd met her on Paige's patio. Even her exquisite cheekbones were more pronounced.

His lazy gaze roamed over the pale yellow cotton pullover she'd tucked into a pair of well-washed jeans. The denim fabric outlined the soft curves of her feminine body, and her narrow feet were encased in a pair of low-heeled black leather boots.

"Hello, Jolene."

"How was your trip to Lexington?"

His expression was one of faint amusement. "Successful."

She kept her features deceptively composed. "What are you smiling at?"

"The question should be who am I smiling at?"

"Then who, Michael?"

"You," he whispered, his sonorous voice dropping an octave.

"Why me?"

"Just looking at you takes my breath away."

A tiny flame flared in her face, spreading lower until she doubted whether her legs would support her trembling body. Her eyelids fluttered as she swayed unsteadily.

"Oh." She sighed, falling against his chest.

"Darling," he crooned in her ear. *"Mi amor, mi corazon."*

And she was his love and his heart. He didn't know what he would do if some harm befell her.

Holding her to his heart, he dipped his head and breathed a kiss along the column of her neck. "When do you think I'll be able to wire this place?" He would feel more comfortable once he installed the cameras.

"I'd like for you to wait until we get rid of the debris."

Pulling back, he stared at her upturned face, his gaze making sensual love to her. "Do you think that will be completed by the weekend?"

"I'll make certain it is."

The cellular phone she'd left on the receptionist's desk rang. Excusing herself, she rushed over to answer the call. She'd left the number on April's pager earlier that morning.

Picking up the tiny instrument, she pressed the Talk button. "Yes?"

"Miss ... Miss ..." A soft sobbing came through the earpiece.

Jolene felt a shiver race down her spine. "What is it?"

she whispered, trying to keep the rising panic out of her voice.

"He . . . he beat me again," came April's halting voice.

"Where are you?" A surge of anger replaced her uneasiness.

"I . . . I don't know."

"Are you home alone?"

"Yes." The single word was a long sigh.

It was apparent April was under the influence. "Listen to me," Jolene said in a quiet voice as she noticed Michael staring at her. "Can you get to my house? I need to see you."

"I don't know," April slurred.

"As soon as you hang up I want you to call a taxi."

"I don't know, Miss Walker."

"Call the taxi," she ordered with quiet, but desperate, firmness. She wanted April out of that house before her attacker returned.

"Okay. I'll do it."

"I'm leaving now to return home. If I'm not there when you arrive, then wait for me."

"Okay," April repeated.

Jolene ended the call, pushing the phone into the front pocket of her jeans. She ignored Michael as she opened the door and raced up the staircase, finding Deborah in the large group room. She was talking on the phone while making notations on a yellow pad.

"I have a crisis situation. I'm not sure when I'll be back," Jolene told Deborah when she put her hand over the mouthpiece.

Her blue eyes widened. "Who is it?"

"Someone not connected to the Sanctuary."

Deborah removed her hand, telling whomever she was speaking to to hang on. "I plan to be here until at least six or seven. I'm going to call some of the other counselors and tell them to come in and help with the clean up.''

"Good. But don't forget to lock up before you leave.''

She retraced her steps, going to her office for her handbag. She knew she was wasting precious time, but she had to tell Michael that she had to leave.

He was where she'd left him, arms crossed over his broad chest. His gaze shifted to the leather bag slung over her shoulder. "I have to go see a client. I'll call you later.'' Rising on tiptoe, she kissed his cheek, and without a backward glance, she walked down the hallway to the rear exit and the parking lot.

Preston James was a man with very few admirable traits— if any. But he was one thing, and that was patient. He'd parked the rental car across the street from Stanley Willoughby's sprawling Colonial-style home, watching and waiting for April Stansfield to leave. Several times he had to duck down in the car when an elderly man strolled past not once or twice, but three times. It wasn't the norm for a black man to sit in a car in their affluent community, spying on their neighbors.

The front door opened, and then he saw her. He had to admit that she was pretty, but too tiny for his tastes. Her pale, blond hair, caught up in a flowing ponytail, reminded him of a palomino he had once ridden as a young boy in Texas. He sat up straighter, watching as she walked down the street to the end of the block, where she slipped into the back seat of a waiting car. He had to smile. She'd called a car service.

Preston started up his car and executed a U-turn, following at a comfortable distance. Willoughby paid him well because he was the best at what he'd been hired to do. And he'd been trained by the best—the CIA. He'd been one of their top independent operatives until an incident had led to his voluntary resignation. In a brief moment of weakness, he'd become involved with a woman, and it had cost him his career, while teaching him a harsh lesson: Never trust a woman.

Preston let two cars maneuver between his and the taxi, but never lost sight of the fast-moving vehicle. He drove past the taxi when it pulled up in front of a brownstone building in Georgetown, noting the address. It took him a minute to circle the block and cruise past the brownstone again. He saw April waiting in the vestibule. It would take him less than an hour to ascertain who owned and/or occupied the building and apartments. Then he would pass the information on to Stanley. His contract with Stanley was due to expire at the end of the year, and what the high-powered attorney didn't know was that he hadn't planned to renew it. He'd deposited enough money in several banks in the Cayman Islands to live like a king for the rest of his life.

Yes, he wanted out. All he had was another three months. Then he would voluntary resign for a second time. A feral grin curled his lip under a neatly barbered mustache. Mrs. Asa Brown's boy had done well for himself. At forty he would look forward to spending the rest of his life reclining on a beach sipping tropical concoctions. Perhaps, just perhaps, he would marry an island girl and father a couple of children.

Twenty-three

Jolene paced the floor, staring at various objects she'd seen hundreds of times that now appeared foreign, strange. She used to refer to the space as her office, because it was where she'd counseled her private clients. But now, it was her study. A futon, with a reversible black kente cloth cushion-mattress covering a highly varnished oak frame, had replaced the maroon leather couch; her video library held an extensive collection of commercial movies, while the damaged educational ones on domestic violence and alcohol and substance abuse had once lined shelves at the Sanctuary.

She loved this room. It was where she retreated to shut out the outside world. It was where she lay on the futon viewing her favorite movies; it was where she extinguished all light, lit several candles in oil cylinders, and filled the room with the soothing scents of lavender or sandalwood; it was where she lay on the carpeted floor listening to music. It had become *her* sanctuary.

But, her cloistered peace was shattered by April Doe. She'd begun referring to her as that. The mysterious, manipulative twenty-two-year-old had come into the Sanctuary, into her home, and had inexorably entwined her life with Jolene's.

Glancing at a small digital clock on the étagère cradling a large-screen television, VCR, DVD, and components for a high-tech stereo system, Jolene noted the time. She'd been home for more than ninety minutes, and April still had not rung her bell.

April stared at the bells on the shiny brass panel in the vestibule. She'd raised her trembling hand twice to ring the bell to apartment 3, but couldn't bring herself to complete the action.

Her body throbbed with pain. He'd beaten her again, but this time where it wasn't visible. After the last assault, he'd promised never to touch her face again. But she would've preferred the black eyes or swollen jaw to the blows to her midsection that made it difficult for her to draw a breath without wincing. Sucking in her breath, she moaned audibly, suspecting that she might have a broken rib.

Turning, she opened the door and made her way slowly back down the stairs to the black sedan waiting at the curb where she'd instructed the driver to wait for her. Holding her right side, she managed to open the rear door and collapse on the seat. The driver moved from behind the wheel and closed the door before retaking his seat.

He stared up at the pale face of the woman lying across the back seat in his rearview mirror. "Where to, miss?"

Her eyes filled with hot tears. "Take me back."

* * *

Jolene lay on the futon, eyes closed. It was after six, and she'd given up on April. The phone rang, startling her. She sprang up, reaching for the instrument.

"Hello." There was a thread of anticipation in her voice.

"Hi, Jolene. This is Paige."

Sighing, she cradled the cordless instrument between her chin and shoulder, sinking down to the futon. "How are you?"

"Round and very pregnant. I should be asking how you are. Mother told me about the break-in and how someone trashed the place."

"Trashed is putting it mildly. It was more like total destruction. All of the office equipment was damaged beyond repair."

"Do you think it had anything to do with one of your clients?"

Jolene sat forward. Had Paige heard something? "What are you saying?"

"Kevin and I were talking last night, and he believes it may have been some guy whose wife or girlfriend is a Sanctuary client."

"That's what I don't want to believe."

"Why not, Jolene?"

"Because that would make us more vulnerable. Now, if it is vandalism, then there's the possibility that it was a random act."

There was a pause before Paige spoke again. "Who are you trying to convince?"

Closing her eyes, Jolene bit down on her lower lip. "Myself," she said. A random act committed by someone skilled enough to breach their security system?

"Exactly," Paige countered. "Promise me you'll be careful, girlfriend."

She emitted a nervous laugh. "I'm always careful."

"Please promise me, Jolene."

"I promise, Dr. Sutton."

"Don't be facetious or cynical, Miss Walker. Those are not good traits for a therapist. To change the subject—I called because I'm putting together a little dinner party at my place on Sunday at three."

"How little?"

"Just three couples: Damon and Melissa, you and Michael Kirkland, and of course Kevin and I."

"Who told you I was seeing Michael?"

"You just did."

"Come on, Paige. Who told you?"

"Damon."

"I didn't know he was a gossipmonger," she said laughingly. Sobering quickly, she wondered what Michael had told Damon about them. Had he revealed that he was not only seeing her, but sleeping with her, too?

"Well, can I expect you and Michael Sunday?"

"I'll have to ask him."

She chattered with Paige about her pregnancy and her plan to take an extended leave from her practice. Paige said she'd contacted an oral surgeon who was looking to form a partnership. Jolene ended the call, promising to get back to her about the proposed Sunday dinner party.

Pushing off the futon, she headed for her bedroom to change her clothes. She had to get out of her apartment, even if it was only for a few hours. It was too late to visit her favorite beauty salon to get her hair trimmed, or get a manicure and pedicure. Tomorrow, she told herself as she opened drawers to pull out a set of underwear. The perfect remedy for her uneasiness was an intensive workout at the gym.

She arrived at the two-story building housing the sports club to find the parking lot filled to capacity, but she managed to find a space almost half a block away from the entrance. It wasn't often she came to the gym at night, because she usually had to wait to use certain machines.

Walking down a flight of stairs to the locker rooms, she changed into her swimsuit, pulled on a pair of sweatpants, then draped a towel around her neck and made her way to one of the three pools. Scantily clad men and women stood around the deck, laughing, flirting, and making deals. Ignoring them, she took off her pants and lowered herself into the tepid water, then began swimming laps in long, measured strokes, losing count of the number of times she touched one end before pushing off again.

She followed her vigorous swim by lifting weights in the weight room until the straining muscles in her biceps burned from the exertion. Her workout left her feeling energized. But she refused to stop, pushing herself to complete sixty sit-ups. Reaching for her towel, she wiped away the perspiration dripping into her eyes, meeting the admiring gaze of a tall, attractive, well-built black man cradling a ten-pound weight in each hand.

"You're good." His soft voice was filled with awe.

Draping the towel around her neck, she affected a smile. She'd made it a practice not to talk to any of the men at the gym. Not even idle chitchat. Most who joined the sports club were serious about staying in shape, but there were always some who used it for a more social purpose: to meet the opposite sex.

"How much can you bench-press?" he asked.

"I don't know," Jolene threw over her shoulder as she headed for the door. She'd lied. She did know. It had taken time, but she was now able to bench-press twice her weight. There wasn't an ounce of fat on her five-eight, one-hundred-thirty-pound frame, only tightly coiled muscle that did not detract from her femininity.

Preston James watched Jolene Walker's gently swaying

hips under the sweatpants until she was out of his range of vision. A computer search from a classified database had revealed a lot about the beautiful social worker. He knew where she lived, worked, and where she worked out. And he knew she was the one April Stansfield had come to visit at the Georgetown brownstone.

Now, all he had to do was wait—wait and uncover what April had revealed to Miss Walker. He hadn't asked Stanley Willoughby why he wanted his ward followed, and he really did not want to know. Willoughby told him what he wanted him to do and he did it. He didn't think he would ever be caught, but if he was, then the less he knew, the better it was for him.

He'd paid the woman at the security company that monitored the silent alarm system at the Sanctuary more money than she earned in three months to delete the entry from their computerized log that he'd gained access to the Sanctuary by simply punching in the code she'd given him. There hadn't been a need to cut wires, remove a window, or jimmy a lock. A sinister smile curled his lip under the mustache. Everyone could be bought—for a price. Only his price was higher than most, because he was the best.

Twenty-four

Jolene drove around for hours, not wanting to go home. She found herself in Baltimore in bumper-to-bumper traffic as thousands of baseball fans filed out of Oriole Park at Camden Yards; and judging by their high spirits, the Baltimore Orioles had won the game.

She parked near the harbor and got out for a walk, enjoying the feel of the damp air on her face. A full moon hung in the air like a wheel of pale yellow cheese. Smiling, she remembered Jeanine sitting up at night staring out the window at a full moon. Jolene would lie in bed, silent, while her twin sister spun imaginary tales about trips to the moon and other planets in the solar system. Each planet had its own topography, alien creatures, and sets of laws governing the unique world. Jeanine was a wonderful storyteller, and Jolene had told her on more than one occasion that she should write children's books. She'd shrug a shoulder, saying her stories were private—only for her and her twin.

A smile touched her mouth as she remembered the elegant

gesture that had become Jeanine's trademark: a slight lifting of a shoulder, while she smiled over it with a long, arched neck.

Jolene's smile vanished as quickly as it had come. Michael on occasion executed a similar shrug with his broad shoulder. A gesture she liked, one for which she had come to look.

She sucked in her breath, and then let it out slowly. She'd left him at the Sanctuary when she'd raced out to return home to await April's arrival. Why, she asked herself, had her life become an instant replay of her past? She had fallen in love with Cheney, but had chosen to sacrifice their marriage for her sister.

Now, more than five years later, April had replaced Jeanine as another helpless victim with a need to be rescued from her dark world of violence and substance abuse. She'd been offered a second chance at love when Michael Kirkland had come out of the night and into her life. Did she want to risk losing again?

"No," she whispered softly.

If she lost April to violence or substance abuse, then it was beyond her. But it wasn't beyond her to hold on to the man who professed to love her as much as she'd come to love him.

Her stride was determined as she made her way back to where she'd parked her car. She got in and turned on the ignition, noting the time. It was almost eleven. If she was lucky she'd make it back to Georgetown by midnight.

Jolene pulled into the driveway to Michael's house, stopping in front of the three-car garage. Sensors brightened as she passed them, flooding the area with intense light. She left her car, walked around to the front door, and rang the doorbell. Melodious chimes echoed within the expansive structure, and seconds later the door opened. A sensual smile

parted her lips as she looked up at Michael staring at her
as if she were a stranger. He wore a pair of black sweatpants
with a drawstring waist, but had left his feet and chest bare.
His upper body was as toned as those men she saw at the
sports gym.

"If you don't let me in before the clock strikes midnight,
then I'm going to disappear."

His eyes crinkled in a smile as he bent slightly, sweeping
her effortlessly into his arms. "Now, I can't let that happen
can I, Cinderella?"

Curving her arms around his strong neck, she pressed a
kiss to the emerging stubble darkening his lean jaw. "No,
prince."

Chuckling softly, Michael closed the door, adjusted
Jolene's weight so he could lock it, then turned and headed
for the staircase. He'd stayed up waiting for her. He didn't
know how, but he'd known she would come.

The next two days passed in a blur. The Sanctuary's staff
arrived early and stayed late, working nonstop to return their
workplace to its former state of efficiency. After filling one
Dumpster, another arrived and it, too, was soon carted away.
The first-floor carpeting was ripped up and replaced. Cartons
containing computers, monitors, and printers were delivered
and set up over a twenty-four-hour period. Sally began the
onerous task of printing out all of the backup disks before
setting up new client folders.

Jolene kept her cell phone charged and turned on, but
April hadn't called her again. Even though her mind was
filled with more pressing matters like making certain the
Sanctuary was partially operable by Monday, the sound of
the young woman's sobbing that she'd been beaten was
never far from her thoughts. It was only when she lay beside

Michael at night that she replayed the scene over and over until she wanted to scream.

She and Michael hadn't made love since the time she'd come to his house just before midnight. The onset of her menses, along with severe cramps and lower back pain, made her feel out of sorts. Minutes after she walked through his door, he helped her undress, then gave her a cup of tea while she soaked amid the pulsating jets in an oversized Jacuzzi. He pampered her, massaging her body with a perfumed oil, and it always ended with her falling asleep under his sensual ministration.

She loved him, his gentleness, generosity, and his selflessness. They'd met six weeks ago, and she couldn't remember when she didn't know or love him.

"Paige is having a small, intimate dinner party on Sunday."

Michael turned to his left, resting his right arm over Jolene's hip. Her scent wafted to his sensitive nostrils. He wanted her. He wanted her so much he'd pulled on a pair of silk pajama pants to remind himself that he would have to wait a few more days to claim her fragrant body.

"How small is small?" Moving closer to his body, Jolene pressed her buttocks to his groin. He gasped as if she'd burned him. "Don't do that!"

She smiled in the dimness of the bedroom. "Do what?"

Smothering a groan, Michael felt his flesh stirring. "Don't play the innocent, Jolene. You keep wiggling like that and I'm going to have you on your back before you can bring yourself to remind me so very delicately that it's 'my time of the month,' " he said in a falsetto.

She felt a wave of heat suffuse her face as she inched away from him. "Have you no shame?"

He laughed, the deep rich sound floating up and enveloping her in a cocoon of sensual warmth. "Nope."

"Be serious, Michael."

"I am."

"Back to Paige. Are you coming with me?"

Pressing his nose to her softly curling hair, he kissed the nape of her velvety neck; he made certain the lower portion of his body did not touch hers. "Was I invited?"

"Of course you were invited."

"Then, I suppose that means I'm coming with you."

There was a comfortable silence broken only by the sound of their soft breathing. "What did you tell Damon about us?"

"If you're asking me whether I told him that I'm sleeping with you, then the answer is no. He asked about you, and I told him that we were seeing each other."

"I suppose this means we're a couple?"

There was a pregnant pause before Michael answered her. "We're more than a couple, Jolene. You should know that by now."

Her heart pounded rapidly under her breasts. How much more could they be without marrying? Several days each week she slept under his roof, shared his bed and his body, but she still had not committed to sharing the rest of her life with him.

She knew Michael was waiting for her to tell him that she would marry him and become the mother of his children. And it wasn't as if she did not want it, too. The only thing holding her back was time—the short time they'd known each other. Time had changed her, making her less impulsive and more patient.

Closing her eyes, she whispered a silent promise. She would wait, and with the coming of a new year, she would consent to becoming Mrs. Michael Kirkland.

Jolene sat, staring up at Michael as he inched his way along the heating-cooling vent in her office, installing fibers so thin they reminded her of silk threads. They'd come to the Sanctuary at seven that morning, and it had taken him more than ten hours to complete setting up cameras no larger than a coin, then put the fibers in place in overhead ceiling panels. He'd refused to eat anything, stopping only to drink water, while she busied herself with the task of printing out data for the new client folders Sally had set up to replace the soaked ones.

She was awed, astounded by his skill, until a shiver of uneasiness shattered her stunned silence. She remembered him saying he'd worked with a team of electronic technicians in Japan, but his wiring the Sanctuary with highly sophisticated state-of-the-art surveillance equipment revealed more about him than he'd disclosed. Michael was forthcoming with details about his personal life, family members, but was somewhat reticent about his career. She knew he was on a six-month leave from the Pentagon, but nothing beyond that.

What did he do at the Pentagon? What was his specialty? Was he in surveillance? Military intelligence?

Slumping against the suede-covered love seat, she closed her eyes. The cushion on which she sat was one of two that had been repaired and returned. She still awaited another four.

Who are you, Michael Kirkland? She barely had the time to pose the question to herself when she felt his heat. He'd replaced the ceiling tiles, descended the ladder without making a sound, and stood over her, smiling.

She opened her eyes, staring up at him. Smudges of dirt streaked his forehead and minute particles of light-colored cork dotted his inky-black hair. He'd worked tirelessly for hours, yet his eyes shimmered with banked excitement, and she knew this was what he loved doing. This was his passion.

"How long has it been since you've done something like

this?'' Her question seemed to catch him off guard when his eyes widened, but he recovered quickly.

"It's been a few years." His tone was neutral.

"How long is a few years, Michael?"

"It's just that," he replied, sinking down to the carpeted floor beside the love seat.

Jolene stared at the clearly defined lines of his profile. The bloodlines of his African and Cuban ancestors had compromised, resulting in an incredibly handsome man who, whenever he looked at her, never failed to take her breath away.

"Are you an intelligence officer?"

Michael steeled himself not to react to Jolene's query. What he'd been trained to do was classified, and although he'd been reassigned, a folder at the Pentagon bearing his name and rank was stamped CLASSIFIED in bold red letters.

"No," he said in a quiet voice. "I'm a glorified clerk for a general. My job description says I'm a researcher."

"Did you go to West Point to become a military researcher?"

"No. I applied to West Point believing I was going to give the United States Army twenty or thirty years, then retire and hopefully teach at my alma mater."

"Where did you get the cameras?" Jolene asked, continuing with her questioning.

"From a friend."

Leaning forward, she placed a hand on his shoulder. "Is this friend also in the military?"

Turning his head, Michael glanced up at her, his gaze pale, cold, and forbidding. He stared without blinking, and for the second time since meeting him, Jolene felt a shiver of real fear—a fear that reached deep inside her, holding her prisoner.

"What is it you *need* to know, Jolene?" His deep baritone

voice was soft and challenging. "Do you still suspect I'm involved in something illegal?"

Her cheeks burned from his veiled reprimand. It was the second time he'd reminded her that he wasn't a criminal. "No, Michael. I don't believe you're a criminal."

Shifting, he rested his head against her thigh and closed his eyes. "There're some things I can disclose about my work and some I can't—"

"Can't?" she said, interrupting him.

He opened his eyes. *"Cannot,"* he repeated, stressing the two syllables. "The equipment I just installed is military issue. Which means it's the best. It was declassified last year. I'm going to show you how to access the surveillance film, which in reality isn't film at all. The cameras are digital devices."

"Won't I need a computer or something similar to one?"

This time he smiled, his eyes darkening to a lush green. "You're way ahead of me, darling. I'm going to give you a laptop that's about the size of a paperback novel. It weighs less than thirty ounces. The disks are programmed for your laptop only. The password will be your right thumbprint."

Her eyes widened. "I will be the only one who'll be able to access the pictures?"

Michael nodded. "The one and only." He didn't tell her he'd programmed it that way. "I installed additional cameras in the front and rear offices on the second floor. You'll be able to view who comes in and who leaves. The system will activate once you set your regular system at night and deactivate the mornings you come in. This way your clients' identities are not compromised, which eliminates the possibility of lawsuits if someone breaches their confidentiality."

"Do I have to change our system's code?"

"No. In fact, I suggest you not change it. Whoever broke in has the code." The police had not been able to identify any of the fingerprints found at the scene with those in their files. "And if they didn't find what they were looking for the first time, maybe they'll try again."

Jolene shook her head. "Please don't mention another break-in. I don't think the insurance company would cover our losses a second time." She worried her lower lip. "Will the digital system interfere with the other one?"

"Not at all. It's virtually undetectable."

Lowering her head, she rested her chin on the top of his head. "Show me how to use the computer. I've had enough of the Sanctuary today."

Twenty-five

Jolene walked into her apartment, kicking off her shoes. Michael had dropped her off, promising to return at seven to take her out to dinner. She made her way to her bedroom and checked the answering machine. There were two messages.

She pressed the play button. "Jo, I'm calling to let you know that Lamar was released yesterday. The parole board mentioned something about overcrowded conditions at the prison. Please be careful, baby."

"Oh, no," she whispered as her mother's voice faded, followed by the programmed voice verifying the time of the call. She barely had time to recover from the news that Lamar Moore had been released two weeks early when she recognized April's voice: "I'm sorry about the other day. I couldn't see you. I'll see you Monday at one, if that's okay with you. Thank you, Miss Walker."

Something in the young woman's tone was different. She

sounded remorseful, apologetic. What had happened since their last meeting?

Picking up the telephone, she dialed her parents' number. It rang three times before the answering machine switched on. She left a message, reassuring them she was okay and would be on alert just in case Lamar decided to leave Illinois. She knew he had to check in with his parole officer if he wanted to leave the state. But then, she was aware of his total disregard for the law when he'd violated the order of protection to stay away from Jeanine. Had five years in prison rehabilitated him or hardened him? She was certain it was the latter, because usually men who abused women were dealt with by the unwritten code of jailhouse justice.

Stripping off her blouse and khakis, she headed for the adjoining bath. She and Michael planned to share dinner at a Chinese restaurant in downtown D.C. before going to the Ritz Nightclub on NW E Street. The upscale, predominantly black crowd, always dressed to the nines, was offered a choice of reggae, soca, progressive R&B, live jazz, and Top 40 while gyrating on one of five dance floors in the four-story building. Michael said he wanted to sample all of them before the four A.M. closing time.

Jolene opened the door, waiting for April. The warm glow from her weekend lingered. She and Michael had left the Ritz Nightclub at three, returning home blissfully exhausted. They'd slept for a few hours, gone to the gym to work out, and then returned home to prepare for early Sunday morning mass. After church, they'd ordered a light brunch at Patisserie Café Didier, an elegant Georgetown French restaurant on Grace Street between Wisconsin Avenue and Cecil Place. After brunch, they'd departed to their respective homes to catch up on some much-needed sleep before Paige and Kevin's three o'clock gathering. She and Michael had walked to the Suttons, arriving in time to see Damon assisting Melissa from his car.

Jolene had watched Michael bow to Melissa as he greeted her in fluent Japanese. After they'd been seated in the Suttons' formal dining room, he'd translated a few of the expressions. *Konnichi wa* meant *good afternoon, hajimete ome ni kakarimasu* meant *I am very happy to meet you,* and *hai, genki desu* meant *I'm fine, thank you.* During the course of the evening, conversations had been conducted in two languages: English and Japanese. Melissa, Damon, and Michael had argued good-naturedly about the influence of Japanese baseball players in the major leagues, while Jolene, Kevin, and Paige had discussed the merits of the leading candidates for the next presidential election.

Dinner had ended at six with cordials, cappuccino, and divine French pastries. Michael had promised the two couples that he and Jolene would host the next gathering, eliciting shocked expressions from everyone. She'd recovered quickly from his unexpected announcement, slipped her hand in his, and smiled sweetly up at him. Within a span of sixty seconds, they'd validated their status as a "twosome."

"Good afternoon, April." Stepping back, she opened the door wider.

April flashed a shy smile. "Good afternoon, Miss Walker."

Jolene closed the door, waiting while April walked in and made her way to the office for their session. She wanted to give her time to relax. The young woman looked different. She'd curled her ash-blond hair, pulling it off her delicate face with an elastic band. Her clothes were still too large for her petite frame. She wore a white tailored man's shirt over a pair of baggy khakis.

Jolene walked into the room and took her usual seat. She effected a warm smile. "How are you today?"

Running her tongue over her lower lip, April said, "Much better."

"Better how?"

Her pale eyebrows knit in a frown. "The pain is gone."

Leaning forward, Jolene gave her a direct stare. "Who beat you?"

The glow faded in April's luminous blue-gray eyes. "I can't tell you his name. Not now, anyway."

"Why not?" The two words were spoken very softly.

April stared at the Biggers mural. "Because he would kill me."

"Would you believe me if I said I could protect you?"

"No." The single word was emphatic.

Jolene decided to try another approach. "Why did he beat you?"

April's face paled, becoming ghostly white, as she closed her eyes. "Because I told him that I didn't want him to touch me again."

She took in a quick sharp breath. "He beat you because you wouldn't sleep with him?"

Shaking her head, April opened her eyes. "I never want to sleep with him."

"Are you telling me that this man—this person rapes you?"

An expression of hardness settled into April's features— a hardness filled with a loathing for Stanley Willoughby. "He always rapes me. The first time was a week after my twelfth birthday. I used to keep count, but stopped after twenty-five."

Jolene felt hot angry tears prick the back of her eyelids. The man had to be an animal to sleep with a child. "Does your mother know?"

"I told you before that my mother is a whore!"

"You may think of her as a whore, but she's still your mother."

April moved closer to the edge of her chair. "I told her and she slapped me for lying. After that time I never mentioned it again."

"Do you live with your mother?" She shook her head, the golden ponytail sweeping over her back. "Do you see her?" Again, April shook her head. "You live with this man?"

Her mouth tightened. "Yes."

"How do you get your drugs?"

"He gets them for me."

"What are you taking?"

This query made her smile. "Everything."

"Do you care to elaborate?"

"My current drug of choice is black beauties, washed down with red wine. But I've smoked weed, snorted and freebased cocaine, smoked angel dust, and dropped acid a few times. I don't like Special K, roofies, or Ecstasy."

Jolene's impassive expression masked her shock and horror. It was amazing April was still alive. "Did you ever OD?"

"Once. I experimented dipping a joint into some PCP and wound up in the hospital."

"How many times have you been in treatment?"

She sighed, smiling. "Five or six times."

"How many times have you relapsed?"

"Five or six times."

"When was the last time you used?"

"Three days ago."

Jolene smiled. "Good."

"What's good is that he's away."

"How long will he be gone?"

"A week."

"I can get you away from him. A place where he can't find you." She knew of a safe house in western Pennsylvania.

"You just don't understand, Miss Walker. There's no place I can go where he can't find me."

"That's what he wants you to believe, April. That's one of his ways of controlling you."

She stood up, her hands tightening into fists. "You know nothing! You know nothing about me or him."

Jolene forced herself to remain calm. "Perhaps you can tell me about him."

April blew out her cheeks. "He's a powerful man."

"There are a lot of powerful men in Washington," she countered.

"This one is more powerful than the others."

"Why is that, April?"

"Because he has ties to the Oval Office."

It was Jolene's turn to sit on the edge of her chair. "Is he a member of the president's cabinet?"

April knew she had revealed too much. She'd told Miss Walker more than she needed to know at this session. She'd planned to tell her how she hadn't taken any of the pills or drank wine for more than seventy-two hours. The first night had been the hardest to get through without reaching for the pills in her bedside table drawer. But she'd made it because she'd known he wasn't there. She just wanted to wake up without the pain and shame; shame from when her body betrayed her, shame that even though he raped her she enjoyed his lovemaking, shame that the pills blurred fantasy and reality, wherein she couldn't leave him even if she wanted to.

Reaching into a pocket of her khakis, she pulled out five

new twenty-dollar bills, dropping them on the table. "He's not a member of the president's cabinet, Miss Walker."

Jolene waited for her to give her the answer, but was disappointed when April turned and walked out of the room. Rising to her feet, she followed her to the door.

"Can I see you tomorrow at the same time?"

"Yes, April. I'll be available for you." She would *always* be available for her. And it was the first time she'd asked, the first time she hadn't exhibited her usual manipulative manner.

Jolene stood motionless, staring at the door long after April left. *He has ties to the Oval Office. He's not a member of the president's cabinet.*

"Who is he, April?" she whispered to the door. Who was this perverted cretin who would take a twelve-year-old girl to bed and systematically rape and drug her for a decade?

Jolene mentally replayed everything April had told her in this session and the prior ones. Her story wasn't a new one. The women in treatment at the Sanctuary related episodes of being raped and physically abused as children, the suffering continuing for years and overlapping adulthood. And the abuse did not discriminate by race or socioeconomics. That was apparent with April. She doubted whether the young woman worked, yet she tossed twenties around like confetti.

Her expression changed. It wasn't what April had disclosed in the session that bothered her as much as her method of payment. She always gave her crisp new twenty-dollar bills.

Retracing her steps, she picked up the bills from the table, examining the serial numbers. They were sequential. She walked over to the black lacquer box on a side table in a corner. Opening the box, she removed the other bills April had given her. Her pulse quickened when she saw the numbers. They also were sequential.

Where had the money come from?

It was something she would ask April tomorrow.

She couldn't ask April on Tuesday, because April did not call or show for their session. Jolene waited until four before returning to the Sanctuary. She was tempted to call the girl's pager, but decided against it. April had asked her to page the one time only, while on the other hand, two-thirds of the women treated at the counseling center put down phone numbers for family members, pagers, and cellular phones on their client data files rather than the ones to their private residences.

The remainder of the afternoon and early evening went by quickly. They were close to being fully operable. The second-floor copier still hadn't arrived and two desks were promised for delivery before the end of the week. All of the desks and table surfaces had to be sanded and refinished.

The tiny control circuitry for the digital equipment concealed within her office's baseboard heating was a constant reminder of their vulnerability. She carried the tiny laptop in her tote rather than leave it in the office.

It was after three o'clock Friday afternoon and Jolene still hadn't heard from April, knowing she would not hear from her over the weekend. A tapping on her door garnered her attention. Her head came up. It was Sally.

"I thought you'd left."

"I'm leaving now. I wanted to finish all the client folders."

Nodding slowly, Jolene flashed a wide grin. "You did it."

Sally wagged her braided head. "No, Miss Walker. We

did it. If you hadn't come in last weekend and did what you did I'd still be putting folders together."

She wanted to tell Sally that printing out the data on the backup Zip disks was the alternative to watching Michael Kirkland wire the Sanctuary for optimum safety measures.

Reaching into a desk drawer, she withdrew an envelope, extending it to Sally. "Just a little something to express my gratitude for you going the extra mile."

Sally stepped into the office, her eyes widening in surprise. "What is it?"

Jolene wrinkled her nose. "Open it and find out."

Sally took the envelope, slipped a nail under the flap, and withdrew a gift certificate to her favorite salon for a full day of beauty. She could get her hair rebraided, a pedicure, her nails filled in, a facial, and a full-body massage. The hand holding the single sheet of paper trembled as she closed her eyes.

"Thank you so much, Miss Walker."

Pushing back her chair, Jolene stood and hugged her assistant. "I should be the one thanking you."

Sally returned the hug, tears glistening in her eyes. "You're the best, Miss Walker."

"How come I wasn't invited to this love fest?"

The two women sprang apart. Deborah stood in the doorway, hands on her hips, smiling. The clinical director had finally taken advantage of her birthday gift from the staff. She'd had her hair cut into a becoming style, the dark strands highlighted until they blended with the gray, creating an overall frosted look. A light cover of makeup took five years off her face while bringing out the brilliance of her blue eyes.

"I was just leaving," Sally mumbled under her breath. "Have a good weekend." She walked out of the office, barely glancing at Deborah.

"Are you working late?" Deborah asked, taking a seat next to Jolene's desk.

She glanced at the small brass clock. "Not too late."

"How late is not too late?"

"Six. Why?"

"I met someone, and I want you to tell me what you think of him."

So, that's why she effected the new look, Jolene mused, smiling at Deborah. "Where did you meet him?"

"I met him in a restaurant near Woodley Road. Some of my friends got together last Friday for happy hour. He was at the next table, and we started talking, and before I left he asked me if I'd come back this Friday."

Jolene shifted her eyebrows. "So? Are you going?"

Deborah twisted her mouth. "Yeah, I guess so. But, there's something about this guy that makes me uncomfortable."

"What is it?"

"I don't know. You'd think as a clinician I'd be able to pick up on certain indicators, but with him I draw a complete blank. That's why I want you to come with me. Just as an observer."

"What time do you plan to meet him?"

"I told him 4:30."

"I'll go with you, but—"

"Thank you, Jolene," Deborah said, cutting her off.

"I'll go with you," she repeated, "but I'll leave my car here. If you don't feel comfortable with him, then tell him you have to drive me back to my car."

"But what if he turns out to be Mr. Wonderful?"

"Then I'll call for a taxi."

Deborah grabbed her hand, squeezing her fingers. "You're the best."

"I'm a hopeless romantic and you know it."

* * *

Preston James watched the two women as they drove away. Again, his patience had paid off. The fact that Jolene Walker left her car in the Sanctuary's parking lot meant she would be coming back. And when she did, he would be waiting for her.

He'd spent two weeks, gathering information on Ms. Walker and Deborah Madison. A slight smile curved his handsome mouth. He was amused to discover that Ms. Madison had a penchant for black men. He'd followed her to the Woodley Road restaurant and engaged her in conversation. Despite her homely appearance, he liked her. She was friendly and extremely intelligent, traits he admired in a woman. Unfortunately for Ms. Madison, she was missing something—she was not the right color.

He much preferred women who looked like Ms. Walker. And it was also unfortunate that Ms. Jolene Walker would not live to make the elder Walkers grandparents. Something perverse nagged at him to call Oliver and Frances Walker in Chicago and tell them that they should prepare to bury their last surviving child.

Glancing at his watch, he estimated that Ms. Walker would return before six. That was more time than he needed to disable her car.

Deborah finished her second strawberry martini while Jolene still sipped her wine spritzer. They'd arrived minutes after 4:30, and it was now close to six and there was no sign of Deborah's admirer.

"I'm going to have to leave now," Jolene shouted to Deborah. The noise level in the restaurant was deafening. The throng at the bar was three-deep.

"I'm sorry, Jolene. I brought you here for nothing."

She saw the pain her colleague tried so desperately to conceal and silently cursed the man who had deliberately stood up the vulnerable woman.

"I have a call for a Deborah Madison," a waiter shouted loudly. "Miss Deborah Madison."

Deborah's expression brightened. "I'm Miss Madison."

"There's a call for you at the bar."

"It's probably him," Jolene said with a wide grin.

"Cross your fingers," Deborah replied.

Instead of crossing her fingers, Jolene fished in the bottom of her handbag for her phone. Punching a button, she scrolled through the directory until Michael's name appeared. She pushed another key, waiting for the connection.

"Yes, darling?"

"Don't you know how to say hello?" she shouted into the tiny mouthpiece.

"Why should I when I recognize your number on my caller ID."

"Are you still cooking tonight?"

"Why? Do you want to go out?"

"No. I'd like a quiet evening at home after screaming at the top of my lungs to be overheard in this place."

"Where are you?"

"I'm at a restaurant on Woodley Road. Their happy hour has just gone off the jubilant scale. I have to go back to the Sanctuary to pick up my car, then I'll be over."

"I'll be here waiting."

"Bye."

She ended the call as Deborah returned, a smile of enchantment softening her mouth. "What's up?"

"He ran late and couldn't call me until now. He's on his way over. Do you mind taking a taxi back across town? I'd like to be here when he comes in."

"Of course I don't mind." Pressing her cheek to Deborah's, she whispered, "Enjoy."

"Thanks."

Jolene managed to secure a taxi within minutes of leaving the restaurant. Twenty minutes later she stood in the parking lot at the Sanctuary, staring at a flat right rear tire.

"Damn!" she moan.

Unlocking the car, she sat behind the wheel and retrieved her wallet for the card for her road assistance member number. She placed the call and then sat, waiting for someone from a nearby garage to come and fix the flat.

"Do you need help with your car?" Turning to her left, she stared at a man leaning down close to the open window. His warm eyes sparkled in an attractive nut-brown face. "I just parked my car when I noticed your tire."

"Thanks for the offer, but I'm waiting for road service."

His full lips curved seductively under a neatly barbered mustache. "I insist." His gaze lowered, coming to rest on her mouth. "Get out." The two words, though spoken quietly, shouted at her when she noticed the small caliber handgun in his right hand. "Easy, Miss Walker."

She felt her heart drumming in her chest, certain he could see it beating through her suit jacket. He knew her name! And it was apparent it was he who'd flattened her tire. Who was he? What did he want? The questions assaulted her senses as she pushed open the door, placing one foot on the concrete surface, then the other. She stood inches from him, her head almost level with his.

If he thought she was going to stand there and let him shoot her, then he was a bigger fool than she thought to accost her on a street where anyone could drive by and witness the scene.

"Who are you?" she asked, as anger singed the thin thread of her self-control. There was something about him that was familiar. She'd seen him before, but couldn't remember where.

"No questions, Miss Walker." He reached for her upper arm, pulling her close to his body. "Just come with me."

Rage made her reckless. "If you think I'm going with you because you say so, then you're a sick puppy."

Preston shoved the barrel of the gun against her ribs. "I'll kill you here if you don't do as I say."

"Then do it!" she shouted.

Preston's composure slipped with the force of Jolene's rage, allowing her an advantage. Whirling, she drove an elbow into his side, causing him to drop the automatic. Her knee came up, crashing into the soft organs between his thighs. He went to his knees, holding his genitals and moaning in pain. Then she kicked him, the point of her heel connecting with his chin, snapping his head back.

Preston had underestimated her as he rose on trembling legs to regain his balance. The burning pain between his thighs paled in comparison to his rage. Dancing lightly on the balls of his feet, he hit her with a well-aimed deliberate jab to the left side of her face. He thought he heard bones crack, but it wasn't her jaw. He'd hit her once before she kicked him twice in rapid succession, breaking his nose and his jaw.

He registered someone shouting, then the screams of sirens. Looking around wildly for his gun, he spied it several feet away. He lunged for it, slipping it into the pocket of his slacks.

"Until the next time!" he spat at Jolene as he ran from the parking lot to where he'd parked his rental car. Starting up the car, he drove away casually, holding a handkerchief to his bloodied nose while passing a police cruiser with flashing lights coming in the opposite direction. He'd escaped and so had Jolene Walker.

He didn't know which hurt worse, his jaw or his groin. If the amazon had ruined his chances of fathering a child, then he would torture her until she begged to die.

Twenty-six

The sixth sense that allowed Michael Blanchard Kirkland to be so good at what he'd been trained to do nagged at him. When Jolene failed to walk through the door to his house at seven o'clock, he knew something had happened to her. She'd called him from Woodley Road before six and told him she was going back to the Sanctuary to pick up her car. She could've made the trip twice during that time. He'd called her apartment and the Sanctuary, hanging up when he heard the answering machines click on.

Then he went to retrieve something he hadn't carried in years—a handgun. Opening a wall safe concealed behind a Japanese print in his bedroom, he removed a compact automatic pistol. The ERMA EXCAM RX-22, a very compact "sleeper," was a favorite of his. Not as well known as it should've been for its many virtues, it held eight rounds of .22 Long Rifle, and with hypervelocity ammunition, it was a formidable weapon. He slipped in a clip, pushed it into a Renegade Ghost holster, and fitted it under his shirt at the small of his back. The indentation of his spine successfully concealed the weapon from prying eyes. He then deactivated the alarm just in case Jolene arrived before he returned.

Michael forced himself not to speed as he drove through the quiet Georgetown neighborhood. He maneuvered into the Sanctuary's parking lot and saw Jolene's car and the flat tire. Getting out of his automobile, he walked over and examined the tire. Running his fingers along the rubber treads, he located a wide slit. Someone had deliberately slashed her new tire.

Sensing a presence, his head came up at the same time he reached around his back for the handgun. His hand froze when he looked up at an elderly man with a scraggly-looking dog tied to a leash.

"You looking for Miss Walker?"

Rising to his full height, Michael forced a smile he didn't feel. "Yes, I am."

"She was here, but the police took her to the hospital."

He went completely still. "Hospital? Which hospital?"

The old man scratched his freckled bald pate. "I don't know which hospital, but they took off going west with their sirens wailing like the dickens."

"What happened here?"

"My neighbor told my wife that some Afro-American man attacked her, but she put up a good fight. Someone said they saw him running away with blood all over his face. Serves him right. Women can't walk the streets in the daytime without some animal attacking them. That's why I don't let my wife walk Scruffy after six. It just ain't safe."

"Thank you for the information. By the way, we're African-American, not Afro-American."

The man bobbed his head. "Thanks. I'll remember that the next time."

Michael walked back to his car, reaching for the phone. He dialed Paige's number, hoping to reach her husband.

Detective Kevin Sutton would be able to find out where the police had taken Jolene without Michael having to call or drive to every medical facility in the capital district.

He was in luck when he heard Kevin's voice. He quickly identified himself. "I need a favor from you."

"What is it?"

"Someone attacked Jolene in the Sanctuary's parking lot sometime around six. The police took her to the hospital, but I need to know which one. Can you help me out?"

Kevin smothered a savage expletive before saying, "Hold on while I call headquarters."

Michael sat half-in and half-out of the Jaguar, his feet firmly planted on the ground as he stared at what appeared to be drops of blood in the waning daylight. He looked up, his grim expression softening slightly. He'd installed the cameras just in time. Whoever had attacked Jolene would be recorded on the digital camera positioned to survey the parking lot.

It was a full five minutes before Kevin's voice came through the earpiece again. "They took her to St. Ignatius. That's a small Catholic hospital on . . ."

"I know where it is," Michael said, cutting him off. "Thanks, Kevin. I'll call you back after I see her." He hung up abruptly, and when he pulled out of the parking lot, it was practically on two wheels, as he reversed his direction. If the police stopped him for speeding, he would simply show his military license and identification verifying his status at the Pentagon. Officially he was still assigned to defense intelligence.

He found a parking space half a block from the tiny hospital that was reminiscent of a plantation from the antebellum period. Forcing himself not to run, he slowed his pace, pushing open the front door. The interior was cool and quiet. There were only the swishing sounds of rubber soles from passing nurses on the highly polished vinyl tiles.

Walking over to the information desk, he smiled at the middle-aged clerk. "I'd like to check on someone who was brought into your emergency room."

"What's the name?"

"Jolene Walker."

The clerk checked her computer. "Miss Walker checked in at 6:42. Go down this hall," she said, pointing to her left, "and follow the blue stripe. You should find her there."

He thanked her, this time not concerned if anyone saw him running. His long legs covered the tiles, and when he stepped out into a large waiting area, he saw her. She had her back to him, as she stood listening to a doctor. It was only when she turned in his direction that he felt as if his legs would not support his body. The left side of her face was grotesquely distorted.

His hands curled into tight fists. *The police better find him before I do, because I'm going to kill him!* The silent vow roared in his head, shutting out all sound.

Jolene saw Michael and went completely still. How had he found her? Moving slowly, she walked toward him, falling into his embrace when he held out his arms. Closing her eyes, she inhaled his distinctive scent, telling herself it was really him. He had come for her. He hadn't waited for her to walk out of the hospital to use her cellular phone to ask him to pick her up.

"Michael," she sobbed against his shoulder. She repeated his name over and over until it became a litany.

"Baby, baby, don't," he crooned. His hand cradled the back of her head, holding her as she wept. Easing back, he held her chin, his gaze sweeping over her face. Her left eye was swollen so badly that he marveled she could see out of it. "Did he break your jaw?"

Closing her one good eye, she shook her head. "No. The doctor said the swelling should go away in a few days."

"Are you in pain?"

"Not really. I've had worse."

"Did they give you anything for pain?"

Reaching into her shoulder purse, she pulled out a small brown envelope containing six pills. "The nurse gave me Tylenol with codeine."

"Come," he urged softly. "I'll take you home." He took her purse, holding it under his arm.

Leaning heavily against his side, Jolene wound an arm around his waist, feeling the bulge at the small of his back. "What's this?"

"A little extra protection."

She stopped, forcing him to stop also. "I don't like guns."

He stared down at her. "Sometimes they're a necessary evil."

"I don't want to see it, Michael."

"And you won't."

They continued down the corridor in silence. It wasn't until they were seated in the moving Jaguar that Jolene spoke again.

"I left my car at the Sanctuary."

"I'm glad you did or I wouldn't have been able to track you. I checked your tire. It was slashed. Some old man on the block told me what happened, and then I called Kevin to check to see where the police had taken you."

A dull throbbing began in her temple, radiating down to her chin on the left side of her face. Then her stomach roiled angrily. If Michael didn't stop, then she was going to throw up in his car.

"Pull over," she groaned against a spasm of pain.

He crossed two lanes of traffic to blowing horns and curses, pulling up to the curb in a no parking-no stopping zone. Moving quickly, he jumped out of the car and raced around to the passenger side. He'd just opened the door and pulled Jolene gently from the seat when she opened her mouth, losing the contents of her stomach. Holding her gently to his chest, he blotted her face and mouth with a handkerchief.

A couple passed them, pointing and whispering that she probably had had too much to drink. But when Michael glared at them, they quickened their pace and moved down the sidewalk.

"I'm sorry, Michael." She was ashamed to be seen regurgitating in public.

"Don't be," he crooned. "Are you all right now?"

"I think so. I'm probably better than the guy who hit me."

He helped her back into the car, adjusting her seat belt. Then he crossed to the other side of the Jaguar and slipped in behind the wheel. Waiting until traffic slowed, he pulled away from the curb. This time he drove slower, avoiding the occasional pothole.

Jolene sat motionless, eyes closed, and he thought she'd fallen asleep until she said, "I wonder what kind of excuse he's going to give an emergency room doctor when he comes in with a busted jaw, nose, and jacked-up family jewels."

Taking his gaze off the road, Michael gave her a quick glance. "You hurt him that bad?"

"I'm certain I broke his jaw."

"What did you hit him with?"

"I kicked him. And if he comes at me again I'm going to do worse. The S.O.B. made me rip my pantyhose."

Michael frowned at her. "The guy knocks the hell out of you and the only thing you're concerned with is your pantyhose?"

She glared at him with her uninjured eye. "You have no idea how hard it is for me to find a pair that'll fit. If I find them for my height, then they sag in the calf and ankle. But on the other hand, if they fit my legs, then the waistband stops just below my crotch. That's on top of my having to drive to Maryland and pay eight dollars a pair for them."

He didn't know why, but he felt like laughing. She could've lost her life, but that wasn't as important as her clothes. "I'll pay for your damn pantyhose, Jolene."

Turning her head, she stared out the side window. "I don't need you to pay for anything for me."

His jaw tightened. "What is it you need from me?"

"Nothing."

Michael struggled to control his temper. She had fallen into his arms sobbing when she'd seen him walk into the waiting area of the emergency room, but now she didn't need him. His expression was one of pained tolerance.

"It's been a long time since I've been able to open up to a woman and let her into my life. Why you, I don't know. Yet you want nothing from me when all I want is for you to need me. I want to be able to wake up and go to sleep with you beside me every night. I want to be your fantasy, reality, and everything in between. I love you, Jolene Walker. I love you more than I've ever loved any woman. And in loving you I'd willingly give up my own life to keep you safe. But there's someone out there who wants to either hurt or kill you. But that's not going to happen. Do you know why?"

His voice was so soft and ominous that she hadn't realized she was holding her breath. "Why?" she asked after she recovered enough to speak.

"Because I'm going to kill him."

"Please don't."

"Don't what?" he said in a nasty tone. "Don't protect you? I'm sorry, Jolene, if you're the therapist who's been trained to talk things out. But I'm the soldier who's been trained to serve, protect, and kill my enemy. And whoever this bastard is who attacked you is my enemy. Get used to the gun, because where I go, it goes. And where you go, I go."

She wanted to scream at him that he had no right to give

her orders, but the pain in her face intensified with each passing second. The Michael Kirkland sitting beside her had become a complete stranger, a man she'd slept with but did not know.

Closing her eyes, she tried to will the pain away. But it did not go away, not until Michael handed her one of the pills and a glass of water. By the time her head touched the pillow beside his, she forgot the frightening scene in the parking lot when the man had pointed the gun at her. It was as if she'd blocked out the attack in her mind. She slept throughout the night unaware that Michael held her protectively in his arms while the small powerful handgun lay on the table on the side of his bed.

Twenty-seven

Stanley Willoughby reclined on a club chair in Preston James's hotel suite, scowling. His hired thug looked as if he'd run into a wall. James had come to his home, bruised and bloodied and unable to open his mouth more than a few inches. He'd ordered James to check into a hotel room and await a doctor, who tended his injuries, wiring his jaw, then walked away as surreptitiously as he'd come.

"What the hell do I need you for if you let a woman kick your butt?" His voice was soft, his manner condescending.

"She caught me off guard," Preston said through his teeth.

"I could've given a crackhead in the Southeast three bags of rock, and he would've taken his mother out for the promise of another three."

Preston glared across the space at Stanley Willoughby. That's why he truly hated the man. He sat there like a pompous prig, looking down his pencil-thin nose at him.

The attorney was a racist and a bigot, and Preston suspected he might have a few other latent tendencies. And why did Willoughby have to make reference to Southeast D.C.? After all, he had a rental unit in that section of the city.

"Did you expect me to blow her brains out in broad daylight?"

"I expected you to kill her. If you can't do it, then I'll find someone else." What he did not say was that not only would *that* someone kill Jolene Walker, but Preston James, too, because he couldn't afford to leave any witnesses.

"Give me some time to heal, then I'll do it."

Willoughby rose to his feet, brushing off a piece of lint from the sleeve of his navy blue suit jacket. "You have a week, and no more."

Preston wanted him gone, gone so he could ice down his swollen scrotum. The doctor had assured him that his jaw and nose would heal, but wouldn't confirm whether his testicles were severely damaged. He told him he would have to wait.

The door closed quietly with Willoughby's departure, and Preston used the arms of the side chair for support as he pushed to his feet. Every step was agony, but he finally made it over to the wet bar for some ice.

It wasn't until hours later when he went to the bathroom that he saw blood in his urine. Tears filled his eyes and streamed down his face. She'd ruined him—for life. He would kill Jolene Walker, not because Stanley Willoughby wanted her dead, but because Preston James wanted her dead.

Jolene existed in two worlds the day following the assault in the parking lot. The real world was when Michael carried her from the bed to the bathroom where she shared a bath with him while he washed her body. She remembered sipping a fruity concoction through a straw, and she also remembered talking to two police officers who interrogated her about the attack. She was able to give them an accurate description of her attacker.

What she did not remember was Paige and Kevin coming to see her, or talking to Claire. It was early Sunday morning when she awoke lucid and clear-headed for the first time in more than twenty-four hours.

Michael stirred as she slipped out of the bed, but he did not wake up. Making her way on bare feet to the bathroom, she stared at her face in a mirror.

The face looking back at her wasn't hers, but Jeanine's. The swollen, discolored eye, the distended jaw. A man had hit her! It hadn't mattered that she'd broken his nose and jaw. What mattered was that all of her training hadn't stopped him from hurting her. Working out at the gym twice a week wasn't enough. Perhaps she needed to go three or four days each week.

Slowly, painstakingly, she washed her face and brushed her teeth before retreating to the bedroom to dress. Opening a massive armoire in a dressing room at the far end of the bedroom, she searched a drawer for her underwear. She slept at Michael's house an average of three nights a week, and had decided to bring over several sets of underwear, sweatpants and shirts into which to change. Cradling her clothes to her chest, she tiptoed out of the room. She hadn't made it halfway down the winding staircase when she heard the powerful voice behind her.

"Where do you think you're going?"

She stopped, not turning around. "To the gym."

"No, you're not."

This time she turned around to find Michael standing at the top of staircase, resplendently naked in all of his masculine glory. "This is the last time you're going to tell me what I can and cannot do."

His footsteps were silent on the carpeted stairs as he descended like a sleek black panther. He stopped one stair above hers, snatched the clothes from her loose grip, and threw them over the railing. Jolene's right hand came up, but he was quicker, stronger. He held her, his eyes paling to an almost colorless green.

"No," he warned softly as her left hand moved.

Before she could blink, he swung her up over his shoulder and mounted the staircase. She tried to free herself to pound his back, but found herself completely helpless and defenseless. Why was it she could disarm a man with a weapon, but found herself impotent against her naked lover?

Without warning, he released her, setting her gently on her feet, giving her the advantage she sought. Pivoting, her right leg shot up, but again he thwarted her when he flipped her, cushioning her fall with his arm as she came down hard on the carpeted hallway.

Holding both wrists between the fingers of one hand, he lowered his body, making her his prisoner. "Don't fight me, Jolene."

Closing her eyes against his wild, intense stare, she drew her lips back over clenched teeth. "Let me go."

"Not until you promise to stop fighting me."

"No!"

Michael felt his passion rising, spinning out of control. He lay atop her naked body, their rage and passions rising and merging to where they were inseparable. Lowering his head, he took her mouth, ravishing it with an explosive kiss.

Jolene felt shivers of pure electricity pulse and explode in her body. She met his punishing mouth with her own brand of detonating passion. Opening her mouth, she let her tongue speak for her. It met and dueled with his, danced and parried, and whenever she inhaled, he exhaled, and vice versa. He released her wrists and her arms curled around his neck, holding fast.

Her fingernails left tracks down his back before he moved lower, his mouth sampling every inch of her body in his quest to stake his claim for all time. She moaned and screamed as he put his face between her thighs, drinking until satiated, and then retraced his sensual journey. His tongue tantalized her breasts as her nipples peaked and trembled with each labored breath she drew.

Reaching between their thighs, she caught his straining hardness, pulling him into her burning flesh. They groaned in unison, their heated bodies melding as one.

Michael pulled her up from the carpet, their bodies still joined, pressing her back to the wall. Cradling her hips, he lifted her easily and she wrapped her long legs around his waist. It was flesh against flesh, man against woman, as his hips drove into hers.

Nothing mattered—nothing except the unbridled passion escaping beyond the boundaries of common sense. Michael braced his hands against the wall over her head, his soaring lust rising higher and higher.

Jolene felt the pleasure swirling between her thighs. She gasped in sweet agony with each thrust of his hips. She felt her breasts swell against the hardness of his chest. She wanted to get closer, absorb him into her body until they ceased to exist as separate entities. Their bodies moved in perfect rhythm, exquisite harmony with one another.

"Michael!" She screamed out his name when she felt him touch her womb seconds before her love eddied through her like heated honey. The explosions continued until she melted all over him.

Michael heard his name in his ear, felt the heat of her breath against his jaw, and gloried in the tightening of her flesh around his rigid sex. The strong pulsing pulled him in, milking him until he, too, groaned deeply in erotic pleasure, moaning her name over and over.

He eased her down to the carpet where they lay, limbs

entwined, waiting for their breathing to resume a normal rate. Supporting his greater weight on his elbows, Michael cradled her face between his palms, placing light kisses over her swollen jaw.

"Did I hurt you, *mi amor*?"

A satisfied smile curved Jolene's thoroughly kissed mouth. "No."

He kissed the end of her nose. "What were we arguing about, love?"

Her smile widened. "I can't remember."

He chuckled deep in his chest. "Neither can I."

He stared down into her dark velvety eyes, smiling. "I love you, Jo."

"I love you, too, Mikey."

Arching his curving black eyebrows, he shook his head in amazement. How was she able to make him so angry and happy within a span of minutes?

She'd just offered him the most exquisite lovemaking he'd ever experienced in his life, a lovemaking that made him forget everything he'd been taught since his first sexual encounter. He hadn't used protection.

He did not want to think of Jolene carrying his child now. Not when someone wanted to kill her. He knew he couldn't watch her all the time, but knew of someone who would when he couldn't. It had been more than a year since he'd last spoken to or seen Merrick Grayslake. It was time he gave his elusive friend a call.

However, viewing the digital pictures of the Sanctuary's parking lot was now a priority. Jolene would have to retrieve the disk and load it in the specialized computer. If they were able to get a clear view of the attacker's face, it would make the police search much easier. He would also print out a copy for Gray. A slight smile tilted the corners of his mouth, because he was willing to bet Gray would find the man before the police did.

* * *

April braced herself for the blow that never came. She knew Stanley was enraged because of the small tic torturing his right eye.

"What did you tell her?"

Lifting her chin in a defiant gesture, she said, "Nothing about you."

Standing over her, he smiled a cold smile. "Why is it I don't believe you?"

"I don't know. You never believe me."

His smile faded. "You're right about that, because you're a liar. Just like your mother."

His words elicited the reaction he sought. All Stanley had to do was mention Holly Stansfield's name and it would spark resentment and rage in April—a rage so close to passion it was almost indivisible. That's when he liked to take her. That was when she fought him most. He did not know why, but he liked to take a woman by force. It was his way of continuing his dominance in and out of bed. But he did not want April's rage and passion—not tonight. He wanted and needed answers.

"Why were you seeing Miss Walker?"

"I want her to help me."

Hunkering down in front of her, Stanley took her tiny hands in his, turning them over and studying her palms. *Beautiful hands,* he mused. *Just like Holly's.*

"Help you how?" His voice was soft and comforting.

"I'm tired, Stanley," April said, closing her eyes against his intense stare. "I don't want to take the drugs anymore. I want to go to bed and wake up clearheaded. I like myself when I'm clean."

Stanley tightened his grip on her delicate fingers. "Would you come to me willingly if you don't take the pills?"

She opened her eyes, staring into eyes that were vacant, hollow, unfeeling. "No. You know I won't."

"But I love you, precious."

A spark of defiance swept over her. "You don't love or want me. It's my mother you want. And it's my mother you can't have. So, I've become her replacement."

He froze, his expression impassive. "Is that what Miss Walker told you?"

"Miss Walker and I don't discuss you or my mother."

"What do you talk about?"

"Me. Only me."

"That's going to end, precious. You're going to stop seeing Miss Walker. Because if you don't, then you'll be the one carrying the guilt for her death."

What he did not tell April was that he'd already placed a hit on her therapist and her contract killer. Preston James had become a useless liability. The man had lost his edge. He was getting sloppy.

April's eyes grew larger, filled with a wild fear she couldn't hide. She knew Stanley was not mouthing an idle threat. She'd lived with him long enough to know this.

"Do you understand what I'm saying?"

Blinking back tears, she nodded. "Yes, Stanley, I understand."

"Meaning?"

"I will not see her again."

He patted her cheek with one hand. "That's my good girl. You don't have to take your pill tonight, because I'm going out."

"Are you coming back?" Her voice was as soft as a small child's.

Leaning forward, he pressed a kiss to her parted pink lips. "No, precious. I'm not coming back tonight."

April stared at Stanley Willoughby's even features. He was not a handsome man, but then again, he wasn't unpleasant to look at either. His fair coloring and light brown close-cropped hair made him somewhat nondescript. His eyes were his most distinguishing feature. They were a startling gray with glints of blue, reminding her of the sky after a storm. And they could be dark and stormy whenever some-one crossed him. He wasn't large in stature, but he compen-sated for that with veiled intimidation. He was a very powerful man in Washington, regardless of who occupied the Oval Office. Insiders often said that Stanley Warwick Willoughby was the power behind the throne, and because of his close friendship with the current president, she was beginning to believe the rumors.

"Good-bye, Stanley."

Releasing her hands, he rose to stand. "Good-bye, pre-cious."

Waiting until he left the room, locking the door behind him, April pushed off the chair and walked over to her bed. She lay across it, staring up at the ceiling with unseeing eyes. He'd locked her in again. She'd become a prisoner for the second time in her life. The first time had been the week after her twelfth birthday, when he'd come to her room and taken her virginity and her youth.

She would not take a pill, because she wanted to be clearheaded so that she could think—think about escaping Stanley Willoughby for good.

Twenty-eight

Deborah Madison sat under the pergola in Michael Kirkland's garden, staring at Jolene's bruised jaw. The swelling around her left eye had gone down enough for her to regain full vision. When Jolene had called her earlier that morning, telling her of the assault, it had made Deborah's bad weekend even worse.

Her Friday-night date had never shown. She'd waited in the restaurant for another two hours, and after downing three martinis, she'd been slightly under the influence once she'd stumbled to her car to drive to her condominium. She'd arrived safely, without incident, fallen across her bed fully clothed, and cried herself to sleep. She'd awoken hours later to a throbbing headache and churning stomach, vowing never to drink the potent concoctions again.

Jolene handed her a photograph of the man's face as he stood in the Sanctuary's parking lot. "Do you remember seeing this man hanging around the center?"

She and Michael had gone to the Sanctuary earlier that

morning, retrieving the disk and loading it into the tiny
personalized laptop. She had to relive the nightmare all over
again when she stared at her attacker's face on the screen.
Pushing another button, the image was instantly transferred
onto a two-by-three photograph from a built-in printer.

Placing a hand over her mouth, Deborah shook her head,
unable to believe that the face staring back at her belonged
to the same man who had come on to her at the Woodley
Road restaurant.

"What is it, Deborah?"

Lowering her hand, she whispered, "It's him. He's the
one I was supposed to meet Friday night."

Jolene's pulse quickened. "You know him? You know
his name?"

Deborah's head bobbed as if it had been attached to a
string. "He said his name was Asa Brown."

"Does he live in D.C.?"

"I don't know."

"Where does he work?"

"I don't know."

Jolene wanted to shake the woman. How could she talk
to a man, set up a date to meet him again, and not find out
anything about him?

"What *did* you talk about?" There was an obvious harsh-
ness in her tone she didn't bother to disguise.

Deborah lifted her shoulders. "Everything: politics,
sports, the latest Hollywood gossip."

"Did you tell him where you worked? What you did for
a living?"

An expression of realization filled Deborah's eyes. "He
did ask me about my job."

Leaning closer, Jolene glared at her. "Did you tell him?"

"I think I did."

"He set you up, Deborah. The man singled you out and

set you up, so he could come after me. He knew exactly who I was when he called me Miss Walker.''

"Why you?"

Settling against the cushioned back on her chair, Jolene stared at a late-blooming rose bush. She had come to love Michael's garden. It was where she sat for hours, reading. It was where she liked to take her meals, and it was where she could escape to shut out the horror stories of the women who came to the Sanctuary. It was here that she did not have to think about April and wonder whether the man she lived with had beaten her so severely she couldn't leave the house, or if she had overdosed on her black beauties.

"I don't know, Deborah," she said slowly.

"Do the police have a photograph of him?"

Jolene nodded. "Yes."

Michael had given the photograph to Kevin Sutton, who had given the search for her attacker high-priority status.

Deborah blinked back tears. "I'm sorry, Jolene. I had no idea he planned to kill you."

Reaching over, she held her colleague's hand. "You didn't know. You couldn't know."

"I feel like such a fool."

"Don't beat up on yourself. Just take this as a lesson not to be so open and trusting the next time."

"There's not going to be a next time, Jolene."

"I'll give you your words back seconds before you exchange vows with the man of your dreams."

Deborah smiled through her tears, her vivid blue eyes sparkling like priceless sapphires. "From your lips to God's ears." Sobering quickly, she smiled. "Does Michael have an older brother?"

Jolene laughed, then grimaced when she felt the slight ache in the left side of her face. "No. But, I'll ask him if he has a friend."

"No! Please don't. I don't want to appear desperate even

though I am. I'll celebrate my fortieth birthday next year, and my biological clock is tolling down to its last gong. I'd like to squeeze out one baby before nature shuts down my reproductive mechanism completely. Am I not entitled to marrying once and bearing a child?"

"Yes, Deborah. You're more than entitled. Please, let's not get maudlin. Now, are you staying for dinner? Michael's making one of my favorites—an herb encrusted leg of lamb."

Deborah whistled softly under her breath. "He cooks, too."

"That he does."

The two women rose in unison and retreated to the house, where Michael was putting his finishing touches on what would become a very elegant dinner.

"Why are you so restless?"

Turning over, Jolene tried making out Michael's features in the darkened bedroom. The only illumination came from a nightlight in the adjoining bathroom. She laid her head on his solid shoulder.

"I don't know," she said, her moist breath sweeping over his throat. "I suppose I slept enough yesterday to last me for a couple of days."

He wrapped an arm around her waist, pulling her to his hard chest. "Do you believe Deborah's story about meeting Asa Brown at the restaurant?"

"She has no need to lie about that. I believe whoever this Asa is—if that's his real name—stalked her. He had to know that she worked at the Sanctuary and that she frequented that restaurant with her friends. She assured me that she did not breach any client confidentiality."

"Why didn't he go after you directly?"

"I don't know. We probably won't know until we catch him. I owe him one for messing with her head."

"I take it she's into black men?"

"She's obsessed with them. She wanted to know if you had an older brother and I told her no. But I promised to ask if you had a friend."

"I'm not into matchmaking."

"Neither am I. Deborah's sole focus right now is to get married and have a baby."

There was a swollen silence until Michael said, "Speaking of babies."

"What about them?"

"Our lovemaking this morning . . ." He didn't finish his statement.

"What about our lovemaking, Michael?"

"I lost control and didn't protect you. There is a possibility that I could've gotten you pregnant."

Another prolonged silence ensued. "I've thought about that, too."

"What if you are? Do you plan to have it?"

She stiffened in his protective embrace. "Of course I'd have it."

"Would you marry me?"

"I wouldn't agree to marry you, Michael Kirkland, just because I was pregnant."

"Will you marry me even if you're not pregnant?"

Her heart thudded wildly in her chest as a quiver of uneasiness seized her limbs. He'd confessed his love, hinted that he wanted her in his life, but he hadn't actually come out and mentioned the *M* word.

"Are you proposing marriage, Michael?"

Lowering his head, he breathed a kiss at the base of her throat. "Yes," he whispered as he moved lower. *"Hai,"* he repeated in Japanese before he took a nipple into his mouth. *"Oui, sí,"* he continued in French and Spanish. She didn't understand the German, Arabic, and Russian.

Pushing against his chest, she managed to get him to stop his sensual assault on her body. "I'll marry you. But not now."

His head came up, his body vibrating with banked passion. "When?"

"Soon."

"How soon?"

"Before the end of the year."

"Next week?"

She landed a soft punch to his chest, laughing softly. "No."

"That's before the end of the year."

"That's not what I mean and you know it."

"Then tell me what you mean, Jolene Walker. Give me a date."

"New Year's Eve."

Michael calculated quickly. They were nearing the end of September. That meant he had to wait three months to make her his wife. He would marry her the next day if that were possible. But he was willing to wait only because she was worth it.

"When do you want to make the announcement official?"

"I'll let you know," she whispered, molding her soft curves to his lean body.

Cradling her hip in the palm of one hand, Michael offered up a silent prayer of gratitude. He'd gotten his wish; his solemn prayer had been answered.

"I want you to live with me until the police catch Asa Brown."

"Okay. But only until they catch him."

He chuckled softly. "You're a hard woman, Jolene Walker."

"Only because you're a hard man, Michael Kirkland."

"No, I'm not. I'm a pussycat."

"Yeah, right. A pussycat with claws and teeth."

"I'd never hurt you."

"What were you doing this morning when you flipped me on my back?"

"Subduing you. If I'd wanted to hurt you I would've broken your neck before you hit the carpet."

She shivered again, but this time it wasn't so much from passion as from fear. She'd known Michael the civilian, but since the attack she'd become familiar with the soldier, a military officer—one trained to serve, to protect, and to kill.

Twenty-nine

Michael sat, waiting for Jolene to walk into the Sanctuary before he drove away for his meeting with Merrick Grayslake. He'd convinced her to stay home until most of the swelling in her face faded, but after the third day her mood veered from boredom to complete restlessness.

It rained for two of the three days, forcing her to remain indoors instead of sitting out in the garden. He wouldn't give her the keys to her car or drive her to the gym, eliciting a fit of temper that stunned him with her virulent outburst. He'd called his mechanic to replace the slashed tire on her car with a new one, then had it towed to his home and garaged.

She'd alternated pacing and checking her cell phone every hour like a guard on duty, leading him to suspect she was waiting for a call from someone. He did not ask who that someone was, because he knew she wouldn't tell him.

Kevin Sutton had reported that the D.C. police had decided

not to publicize the attack, thereby not alerting the attacker that they'd begun an exhaustive search for him.

Deborah Madison had filled in for Jolene during her absence, informing the staff their executive director had had an accident that would keep her out of the office for a few days. Jolene had instructed her not to disclose any details of the parking-lot assault, because she saw no need to alarm the staff or the clients of the imminent danger stalking their executive director.

Michael had given Jolene a pager similar to the one clipped on the waistband of his jeans. All she had to do was press a button, a panic button, and he would be able to pinpoint with absolute accuracy her whereabouts. The pagers were programmed with a digital navigational tracking system first utilized by intelligence agents on assignment more than a decade ago. It was now deemed obsolete by the military, but would serve his purpose well.

The weather had changed with the rain, lowering the temperature and humidity. The cooler air coming through the vents of his car whispered over his face, reminding him of Santa Fe's higher elevations. He'd enjoyed the weekends he'd spent skiing with his childhood friends Chris Delgado and Sara Sterling. A smile softened his stoic expression. Not only were Chris and Sara friends, but they were also his in-laws. Before leaving Las Cruces, he'd promised his sister that he would return for a Thanksgiving celebration.

The second generation of Coles, Kirklands, Lassiters, Spencers, and Delgados had established their own legacy of coming together with their husbands, wives, and children to celebrate Thanksgiving. However, the entire clan usually met in West Palm Beach, Florida, for Christmas. The weeklong festivities always culminated with a raucous New Year's Eve blowout to welcome in the new year, before everyone disbanded to return to their respective homes.

This upcoming New Year's Eve would become even more

momentous with a wedding. His parents had mumbled for more than a year that Emily had cheated them out of a wedding when she'd secretly married Christopher Delgado in Mexico. Joshua and Vanessa Kirkland had taken him aside, lecturing sternly that when it came time for him to marry, they expected to become participants in the celebration.

And they would be. But first he had to convince Jolene that they should officially announce their upcoming nuptials. He had to purchase a ring for her, meet her parents, and add her name to all of his financial documents, thereby making her financially independent for the rest of her life.

He entered the town limits of Bolivar, a small town south of Harper's Ferry, West Virginia, marveling at its quaintness, while wondering why he was drawn to men who'd fled the bright lights of large cities for secluded locales known only to those who'd inhabited the region for generations. Bobby Ridgewell and Merrick Grayslake looked nothing alike, but their personalities were more similar than dissimilar.

Michael found Gray's modest two-story house in the middle of a grassy pasture easily. His friend had given him excellent directions. Merrick was standing in the open doorway when he maneuvered into the driveway behind a pickup, coming to a complete stop.

Even if Gray had sounded the same on the phone, he did not look the same. A light breeze lifted heavy auburn-streaked waves off his broad shoulders. His normally clean-shaven jaw was covered with a short beard two shades darker than his long hair. The hot summer sun had burned his khaki-colored skin to a deep, rich rosewood brown. The intense color made his piercing silver-gray eyes appear lighter than they actually were. The weight he'd lost when convalescing after a gunshot wound ended his career as a CIA agent gave him a lean, almost gaunt appearance, while the beard and long hair made him look mean, dangerous.

Gray flashed a wide white-toothed grin. "You're right on time, Kirk. Even down to the minute."

Michael closed the car door, returning the warm grin with one of his own. "How would you know what time it is? You're not wearing a watch." Gray always complained about living his life by days, hours, minutes, and seconds.

He pointed a long finger upward. "I can tell the time by the position of the sun."

Striding forward, Michael extended his right hand. "Cut the bull, Gray. You're beginning to believe your own hype about being a throwback to the mountain men who came here two hundred years ago to trap bear and beaver for their pelts."

Ignoring Michael's hand, Merrick Grayslake wrapped an arm around his neck, holding him tightly. "What are you trying to do, brother? Destroy my reputation?"

Rubbing his knuckles over the heavy wavy hair, Michael gave him a playful tap. "What reputation? You gave that all up when you walked away from your career with the Company."

Merrick grimaced, shaking his head. "Don't start with that Kirk. Not this morning. You know I was never one to sit behind a desk, unlike someone else I know. Now, tell me what is so important that you had to leave the craziness of D.C. for the sanity of the West Virginia woods?"

"I need your help, Gray." He'd decided to be direct.

"How?"

"It's a woman."

Merrick arched a pair of curving dark eyebrows. "A woman? You and a woman?"

"A woman I plan to marry before the end of the year."

Merrick stared at Michael's impassive expression. For a man who supposedly had fallen in love and planned to marry within the next three months, he didn't appear to be too enthused. "Whoa, Kirk. When did all this come about?"

"A couple of months ago."

"Come on in and tell me what you need."

He followed Merrick through a spacious living room filled with modern functional furniture and into a large modern sun-filled kitchen. "I like this." His green eyes took in everything in the room in one sweeping motion.

Merrick pointed to a chair against a table near an expansive window. "So do I. Sit down and relax. Have you had breakfast?"

"Yes." He'd shared breakfast with Jolene. "But I will have a cup of coffee."

He sat, staring out the window at the peaks of the Allegheny Mountains less than three miles from the house. The view was spectacular, breathtaking, and he tried imagining waking up to miles and miles of pristine, untouched wilderness. Perhaps Gray and Bobby were right when they chose to leave D.C. for the unspoiled beauty of the mountains.

Merrick placed a mug of steaming black coffee on the table in front of Michael. "I hope you don't mind that it's instant and black. I usually don't keep milk in my fridge."

He picked up the mug, nodding. "Not a problem." Michael stared at Gray when he took the chair opposite him. His friend was only thirty-four, two years older than himself, but appeared much older. It had to be the weight loss. At six-four, his own weight fluctuated between one-ninety and one-ninety-five, and he doubted whether Gray, an inch shorter, topped the scales at one-fifty. Had the man moved to West Virginia to die?

"I need you to watch my fiancée," he began without preliminary. He told Gray about the break-in at the Sanctuary and the subsequent attack on Jolene, watching a shimmer of excitement light up the silver-gray eyes. He left nothing out.

"I can't watch her twenty-four-seven, Gray," he continued. "So that's where I'd like for you to come in."

"Has she agreed to let you follow her?"

"No. She's agreed to live with me until they catch this punk, and let me drop her off at work and pick her up. Aside from that, she won't cooperate."

"It looks as if you've picked a winner."

"She's perfect, except that she's bullheaded."

Merrick shook his head slowly. "How exciting would she be if she bowed and scraped every time you gave her an order?"

"Not exciting at all." It wasn't his style to order a woman about. He had fallen in love with Jolene because of her spirit, her independence.

"Exactly, my brother. Do you have a name or a face for your punk?"

Michael pulled the computer-generated photograph from the pocket of his denim shirt. Merrick took it, his eyes widening in recognition. "You know him?"

"I know the face. Give me a few minutes to come up with a name."

Merrick Grayslake had enlisted in the Marine Corps at eighteen to escape his foster parents, distinguishing himself during his basic training course at Parris Island. His antisocial behavior in high school had masked a superior IQ, which was fully utilized during his stint in the corps. He'd earned the nickname "Lock and Load" because if he saw something or someone once, he was able to file the information away in his mind and recall it at will. This gift served him well once he was recruited by the Central Intelligence Agency. His overall physical appearance also proved to be an asset. Even though his birth records listed him as black, he was able to blend in well with many other ethnic groups. On assignment he managed to conceal his unique eye color with tinted contact lenses.

But his short celebrated career ended after he was mugged by a trio who'd lain in wait for him when he'd left a woman's house in a less-than-desirable section in D.C. He'd sustained a gunshot wound to the abdomen that tore through his spleen and left kidney. Michael had driven past, found him bleeding on a street corner, and taken him to the hospital. A team of surgeons had repaired his spleen, but could not save the kidney. After his recovery, he was transferred from the field to a desk position. He'd sat at the desk for three days, then walked into the director's office and handed in his resignation. He invested his meager savings in the stock market, resulting in windfall profits that afforded a simple but comfortable lifestyle.

"James," he mumbled to himself. "That's it. His name is Preston James."

"He told the clinical director that he was Asa Brown. Now, which one is the alias?"

"Brown has to be the alias."

"He worked for the Company?"

Merrick nodded. "He *was* a wet boy. He was booted out because of an incident with a woman. He blew almost two years of undercover surveillance when he tipped her off about her brother, who was planning with some army generals the overthrow of a president of one of the few democratic African countries."

A rush of fear gnawed away at Michael's confidence. Preston James, aka Asa Brown, was a wet boy, an assassin who'd been trained by the CIA. But if he no longer worked for them, then who was it who had hired him to kill Jolene? And why?

"He was one of the best, Kirk. I'm surprised he let your woman get the drop on him."

Attractive lines fanned out around Michael's eyes when he smiled. "I suppose he didn't count on her training as a kickboxer. I knew she worked out, but I had no idea she kickboxed. She finally admitted it's her secret weapon."

"You're a better man than me, because I don't think I'd

ever lie down next to a woman who could jack me up with her hands and feet.''

The two men laughed, and then put their heads together to plan how to thwart Preston James if he decided to come after Jolene again.

Thirty

A week after Merrick Grayslake checked into a comfortable suite at the Washington Hilton and Towers on Connecticut Avenue and Columbia Road, he called Michael Kirkland for a face-to-face meeting.

Michael met him minutes after he'd dropped Jolene off at the Sanctuary. Merrick answered his knock, opening the door. He looked nothing like the man he'd visited in West Virginia. He'd cut his shoulder-length hair, shaved his beard, and replaced his jeans and flannel shirt with a pair of dark tailored slacks and a stark white shirt. A matching suit jacket lay over the back of a sofa. It even appeared as if he had put on a few pounds.

Michael embraced him warmly. "What do you have for me?"

Merrick waved a hand. "Sit down and relax. After all, you're the one paying for this opulence." Waiting until Michael sat down on a matching love seat, he crossed one leg over the other. "Preston James sleeps in the morgue."

Leaning forward, Michael stared numbly at his friend, complete surprise freezing his features. "How?" He wanted to ask Gray how he'd found out about Preston James when Kevin Sutton had yet to call him to give him the news. It was obvious he still had his D.C. contacts.

Merrick pinched the nostrils of his aquiline nose. "The coroner ruled it a suicide."

"Did he leave a note?"

"No note. No sign of a struggle. He was dead at least three days before the police broke into his apartment and found the body after the other tenants began complaining of the odor. He was found hanging from a ceiling fixture in his living room. You don't believe he killed himself?" he asked Michael, noting his skeptical expression.

He shook his head. "No. It just wouldn't fit his psychological profile. A man trained to kill would never hang himself. He'd rather do it the macho way: eat his gun."

"I'm with you, friend. I believe someone took James out because he botched his assignment."

"But who?" Michael asked softly.

"Therein lies your mystery."

"Can you spare a little more time?"

"Why? Preston's gone."

"Something tells me Jolene is not out of danger."

"How much more time?"

"Until whoever is responsible for taking out James is caught."

Running a hand over his face, Merrick gave Michael a direct stare. "I can hang out here as long as you want, but I'd rather not. I miss the quietness of Bolivar. I miss getting up in the morning and walking. I've been away too long to feel comfortable in this milieu. Once you drop Jolene off in the morning, she stays inside until you come for her at night."

Ignoring the inner voice telling him that Gray was wrong,

Michael nodded. "Okay. But can you hang around until the weekend?"

"What's happening?"

"Jolene and I are throwing a little something at the house. I'd like for you to come. You do remember how to use a fork and knife, don't you?"

Merrick scratched the top of his head. "I believe I do."

A social gathering was what he needed to break the monotonous routine of sitting across the street from the Sanctuary watching people coming and going. He'd bribed the superintendent of the three-story building to grant him access to a vacant front apartment, telling the man he was a private detective hired by a foreign diplomat to watch his wife, who had abducted the two children a judge had placed in his custody. The greedy man had barely glanced at his fake identification, his gaze fixed on the wad of bills he held in his fist. For the one-hundred-dollars-a-day fee, the superintendent offered to bring him lunch and dinner gratis. Merrick had turned him down the first two days, but accepted on the third day once he discovered his wife was from the Dominican Republic. He spent a glorious three days wolfing down copious amounts of white rice, red beans, fried sweet bananas, baked chicken, and spaghetti with spareribs.

"Why don't you check out of here and spend the night with us?"

"When's the get-together?"

"Late Saturday afternoon. If the weather holds, then we'll cook outdoors."

"You've got yourself a deal." He rose and walked Michael to the door. "She's beautiful, Kirk. You're a lucky man."

Turning, his gaze caught and held Gray's. He'd just verbalized what Michael had felt the instant he'd seen Jolene on Paige Sutton's patio. "I know," he said without a hint of boastfulness. "And thanks for the compliment."

* * *

Clasping her hands together in a prayerful gesture, Jolene visually examined the contents of the living room. Vases overflowed with flowers from the garden, complementing those delivered by a neighborhood florist. She'd gotten up early, making certain she had enough plates, napkins, and serving pieces for their invited guests.

She caught a whiff of Michael's cologne, and then she felt his body's heat as he came up behind her. He wrapped his arms around her waist, pulling her back against his chest.

"Tell me, Michael, how did three couples, including us, turn into more than eighteen people?"

He pressed his mouth along the side of her long, graceful scented neck. "Don't blame me, darling. I told you I was going to invite a couple of folks, then you added to the list—"

"Oh, now you're blaming me for the extra folks." She laughed, interrupting him.

Turning her around in his loose embrace, he kissed the end of her delicate nose. "I'm not blaming you. More of your friends will be here than mine."

"Our friends," she crooned, kissing his ear. "Don't forget they're going to become our friends once we're married."

Michael stared down at her upturned face, making passionate love to her with his hot gaze. She looked exceptionally beautiful tonight. Her hair was growing out, curling softly over the tops of her ears and forehead. Warm sparks of delight shimmered from her bottomless dark eyes, and the smile curving her lush mouth reminded him of what they'd shared the night before.

They'd come together with an insatiable lust that had left them shaking uncontrollably while struggling for each breath. And it was the second time since he'd taken Jolene to his bed that he'd failed to protect her. It was as if they were tempting fate, playing Russian roulette with contraception. After he'd rolled off her body, he'd lain facedown on the bed while she'd straddled him. She'd revived him all over again as her tongue traced the tattooed dragon at the base of his spine. He'd begged, pleading for her to stop, but she'd been relentless. They'd made love a second time, and before he'd exploded in her body, he'd forgotten his name, who he was, and where he'd come from. She had stripped him bare—her power over him absolute and complete.

Cradling her face between his hands, he smiled. "Will your parents mind if you don't spend the Thanksgiving holiday with them?"

She arched an eyebrow. "What do you have planned?"

"My sister is hosting Thanksgiving this year. I promised her I'd be there."

"You didn't tell her you'd be bringing me, did you?"

He shook his head. "No, not yet. Last year those of us in our generation decided to bond by getting together for Thanksgiving because we're spread out all over the country. We get together with the rest of the family for Christmas. We all gather in Florida on Christmas Eve, exchange gifts, and then spend the week with relatives until New Year's Eve, where we party until well into the next day."

"Thanksgiving shouldn't be a problem, because Mom and Dad usually go away that weekend. But I cannot not see them for Christmas."

"They can spend Christmas in Florida with us. I am certain your mother will appreciate my mother's assistance in planning our wedding."

"You want to marry in Florida?"

Michael heard the censure in her voice. "The choice is yours, *mi amor*. Either it's Florida's sunshine or a Chicago blizzard."

Her gaze narrowed. "You're not giving me much of a choice."

"It was you who selected the date."

"Oh, now I'm to blame for that, too."

"No, Jolene," he said softly. "I'm not blaming you, baby. I agreed to the date because everything I say and do, I do it for you. I love you just that much."

Curving her arms around his neck, she pulled his head down. "I don't know why I keep forgetting that."

The doorbell rang and they pulled apart. Their first guest had arrived. Jolene made her way to the teahouse while Michael answered the door. At first she'd planned for a sit-down dinner, but quickly abandoned that plan when the guest list kept growing.

She'd invited Deborah, then added Sally and the other full- and part-time therapists. Michael had countered with his assistant from the Pentagon, then a few more friends— some from the Pentagon and others from law school. Sit-down became buffet and home-cooked catered.

Black silk-covered mules peaked out from under the hem of her long, black silk dress with capped sleeves and a Mandarin collar. Michael wore a matching tunic blouse over a pair of black slacks and slip-ons. Scented candles and votives flickered on every flat surface, lighting up the open spaces like stars in a desert night sky, while prerecorded music flowed from small powerful speakers distributed throughout the first level.

She stared out through the screen into the garden, whispering a prayer for Asa Brown. She still called him that, although Michael had told her that his actual name was Preston James. Even though he'd tried to kill her, she prayed for his soul. What pain or guilt had tortured him to make him take his own life?

Closing her eyes, she thought about April. It had been weeks since she'd seen or heard from her. And there was never a moment when she was very far from Jolene's thoughts.

She heard a strange man's voice. Turning, she walked back to the living room to meet her future husband's friend.

Jolene liked Michael's friends. Especially retired Major Robert Ridgewell. And it appeared as if Deborah liked him, too. It hadn't mattered that she was twenty years his junior or that he'd been married not once, but twice. Sally seemed equally enthralled with Lieutenant Kyle Franklin. The moment the young officer walked into the garden and spied Sally, he headed for her. She seemed rather shy at first, but quickly warmed to his friendly manner. One of Michael's law school buddies assumed the role of bartender, mixing powerful concoctions that had most refusing a second round.

The food was as varied as their guests: sushi, crab cakes, sweet and sour chicken, shrimp, meatballs, pork brochettes with a peanut sauce, lemon-garlic herbed chicken, grilled marinated flank steak, grilled vegetables, and an assortment of cheeses, grapes, flatbreads, and green salads. Dessert included individual apple crisps, strawberries with crème fraîche, fresh figs, and excellently prepared tart lemon custard.

Paige settled down on a chair in the teahouse and permitted Kevin to feed her as Damon teased his brother-in-law about having his nose so wide open he could drive an eighteen-wheeler up it. Melissa looked perplexed when everyone laughed. Even when Michael translated what Damon had said into the equivalent Japanese, she still did not find it as funny as the hysterically laughing Americans.

Jolene hadn't decided whether she liked or was frightened by Merrick Grayslake. Dressed completely in black, he appeared quiet and sinister. It was as if he hung around on the periphery listening to conversations without contributing to any of them. Michael told her that Merrick would be spending the night, and that simply added to her uneasiness.

After a while she realized it wasn't the man but his eyes that disturbed her. They were a silvery gray that didn't look at you, but through you.

A hand closed over hers at the same time a familiar voice said, "Come with me."

She followed Michael out of the living room, through the teahouse, and into the garden, leaving the lights, lively conversations, music, and their guests behind. They walked deeper into the undergrowth of a trio of massive weeping willow trees. Spanning her waist with his hands, he picked up her and stood her on a stone bench.

Resting his forehead against her flat middle, he wrapped his arms around her hips. "I needed you all to myself for a few minutes."

Placing a hand on his head, she grazed the short straight raven strands with her fingers. How did he know? How did he know she wanted their guests gone so she could have him all to herself?

It was if she wanted him inside her at the most inconvenient times. He'd elicited a longing that had gone beyond craving. It was now an obsession.

One hand trailed down the side of her dress, finding the generous side split, then reversed itself under the fabric, moving slowly up her bare leg and thigh. His long slender fingers inched under the tiny triangle of sheer black nylon, finding her moist and ready for him.

Jolene did not have time to gasp when she felt the cool air sweep over her exposed thighs. She collapsed over Michael's head as he pushed her dress up around her waist. His mouth burned her flesh; he brushed light kisses over her belly, thighs, and ribs.

He readjusted her dress, lifted her from the bench, lowering her feet to the narrow slate path. "I could devour all of you right here," he growled against her moist parted lips.

Before she could recover from his erotic confession, he

released her and walked away, disappearing into the night like a specter. She stood there, shaking uncontrollably, waiting for her traitorous body to return to its normal state.

"No, Michael," she whispered angrily.

If he hadn't walked away, she would've taken off her clothes to lie down with him in the grass, unmindful of their guests. She would not have thought of the shame until after she'd had her fill of him. The only thing that frightened her was that she didn't think she would ever get enough of Michael Kirkland.

Thirty-one

Stanley Willoughby couldn't believe what he was hearing. "You're telling me she's hired a bodyguard?" The short, squat man with a bulletlike head nodded. "Who is this cowboy?"

"I don't know. I ran his license plate through the DMV and got his name. But when I put the name through my computer it came up with ACCESS DENIED."

"Who's he with?"

"The Defense Intelligence Agency."

Stanley swore under his breath. He'd gotten rid of a former CIA assassin, but couldn't get close to a mere social worker because of some hotshot soldier. And it hadn't mattered that April hadn't seen her in two months; what mattered was that Jolene Walker was still alive.

He blew out his breath, forcing a smile. "Take your time. In fact, take all the time you need, because the cowboy's going to slip up. One day he's going to get careless, and when he does, eliminate him and Miss Walker."

Swiveling on his chair, he turned his back. When he turned around again he was alone in the room. He hadn't heard the man move off the chair or walk out of the office. This time he'd hit the jackpot. It was only a matter of time before he would be able to go to bed and sleep without waking up in a cold sweat.

Michael stood up when Jolene walked into the doctor's waiting room, his gaze fixed on her drawn face. His concern was evident by the lines furrowing his high forehead. She gave him a half-smile and extended her hand. He took her hot, dry fingers, folding them into the crook of his arm.

"Feeling any better?" Closing her eyes briefly, she shook her head. "Did he write you a prescription?"

"He couldn't."

Leading her down the one flight of stairs to the street level, Michael curved an arm around her shoulders, offering his body's heat. He'd finally convinced Jolene to see a doctor. She'd come down with a cold a week after the Sanctuary's annual fund-raising dinner-dance because of exhaustion. She'd stayed in bed for two days before returning to work.

Deborah had called her at ten o'clock, rousing her from her much-needed sleep to inform her that the reviewers had come to the program like locusts. Feverish and sniffling, she'd forced herself out of bed and gone in. After a weeklong review of every chart and manual, the Sanctuary's operating license was renewed for an additional three years, which perked up everyone's spirits. A license renewal equated the continuance of local and federal grants, and therefore a continuance of services and jobs.

Waiting until he'd settled Jolene in the car and sat beside her, Michael said, "Why couldn't he?"

"Because I'm pregnant."

The three words hit him in the face with the force of a sledgehammer. He registered a buzzing sound and, believing a bee had gotten into the automobile, he looked around for it. The buzzing escalated, and after awhile he realized the sound was in his own head. Leaning forward, he rested his forehead on the leather-covered steering wheel as he forced air into his lungs.

Jolene was pregnant! She was going to have his child.

Sensing his disquiet, Jolene stared out the side window. What she had suspected for weeks, for almost a month, was confirmed. She'd missed her menses in October, but its absence hadn't alarmed her. There were occasions when it failed to appear whenever she embarked on a strenuous workout regimen. But she hadn't worked out or been to the gym since the parking-lot attack. Most times she was too exhausted to do anything except come home and fall into bed.

She hadn't slept in her own bedroom in months. Michael picked up her mail everyday, and he accompanied her to the brownstone building on weekends when she stopped in to dust and pick up clothes for the week. She continued to pay rent on a space she no longer occupied.

"I suppose it's time we make the announcement official." Her voice was soft, hushed in the cloistered confines of the car.

Raising his head, Michael stared at her averted head. "When are you due?"

"Mid-June."

It was now mid-November. They had seven months to plan for a baby—a new life they'd created through the very intimate act of love.

"Jolene?"

"Yes, Michael."

"Look at me, *mi amor.*" She turned to look at him, her gaze open and trusting. He smiled. "Congratulations."

They sat only inches apart, yet there was a tangible bond between them—the new life growing within her. A delicious shudder heated her limbs with his sensual smile.

"Thank you. And congratulations to you, too."

He nodded, fighting his own emotional battle not to lose his composure and dissolve into tears of joy. "Are you happy? Really happy about the baby?" He didn't know why, but he had to know, had to ask.

Reaching over, she placed her right hand over his cheek. "Yes, Michael. I'm very, very happy."

He covered her hand with his. "Do you feel up to going somewhere to celebrate?"

"Not tonight. All I want to do is go to bed and sleep." She had a temperature of 101.

"Aren't you hungry?"

"I'll eat whatever we have at home." She knew she did not sound or appear excited that she was expecting a baby, but she was too tired to pretend. "Can we celebrate tomorrow?"

"Of course."

He started up the car and headed toward Georgetown. She'd given permission to announce their engagement. What he'd wanted was to announce the engagement before he informed everyone that he was going to become a father. Stopping for a red light, he suddenly realized he was a traditionalist. He believed one fell in love, married, then planned for children.

Glancing over at Jolene, he saw she had fallen asleep. He loved her, more than he'd ever loved any woman. And now that she carried his child beneath her heart, it made the love even more precious.

Jolene did not know what to expect as the taxi stopped in front of a sprawling one-story adobe-style structure. Michael had tried to describe Las Cruces, but she couldn't fathom the combination of the desert and mountains until she saw the arid landscape with her own eyes.

When they left Washington, D.C., the temperature registered in the midforties, but once they'd landed at Las Cruces International Airport, the mercury was in the high seventies. She'd slept more than halfway through the flight on one of the sofas that folded out into a bed, waking as the GIV Gulfstream jet flew over Texas. She and Michael planned to spend a week in New Mexico. It was the first time in a long time she'd taken a vacation of more then three consecutive days.

She'd called her parents the day after her pregnancy was confirmed, informing them she was to be married in Florida on New Year's Eve. Her father had interrogated her relentlessly about this *boy* who wanted to marry his daughter. She'd told Oliver Walker that the man she planned to marry was as perfect as any she'd ever met. This seemed to satisfy her father. Just before hanging up, she told them they were going to be grandparents the following summer. Her mother said she wanted to come to D.C. to see her over the Thanksgiving holiday weekend, but Jolene had reassured Frances Walker they would all get together for Christmas. She had not asked them about Lamar Moore, and neither of them had mentioned him. The last time they'd discussed Lamar, Frances informed Jolene that he was rapidly losing his sight from a degenerative eye disease.

A woman stood on the loggia, awaiting their arrival. She waved at them, and Michael returned the wave. "That's my sister, Emily."

He helped Jolene out of the cab, leaving the driver to retrieve their luggage. The setting sun fired the peaks of the nearby mountains, showering the slopes with a dazzling spectacular flaming red.

Stunned by nature's colorful masterpiece, her delicate jaw dropped. "Oh, goodness. It's incredible."

"Sunrise is just as awesome." Winding an arm around her waist, he directed her toward the house. "Come meet *your* family. They can be somewhat raucous and unorthodox, but they're fiercely loyal and supportive."

Emily Delgado offered Jolene a friendly smile. "Welcome to New Mexico. Let's go inside where we'll have proper introductions before we sit down to eat." Raising her arms, she hugged and kissed Michael. "You're looking good, little brother."

Picking her up off her feet, he swung her around, kissing her soundly on her smiling mouth. "Thanks." Releasing Emily, he took Jolene's hand and led her through an entryway into the living room.

Jolene walked into a living room filled with exquisite furnishings reflecting a mix of African, Native American, and Spanish styles. She moved closer to Michael when she noticed everyone staring at her.

It was obvious Emily and Michael were brother and sister. Their resemblance was startling. Both claimed coal black hair, green eyes, and rich olive coloring.

Emily clasped her hands behind her back. "Well, Michael. Why don't you make the introductions?"

He nodded. "This is Emily Delgado, my sister. Standing next to her is her husband, New Mexico Governor Christopher Delgado. The little boy hiding behind his leg is my nephew Alejandro, and the precious angel in his arms is Esperanza."

Jolene smiled, nodding numbly. Michael hadn't told her that his brother-in-law was a governor. Chris nodded, flashing a warm smile. His dark wavy hair was liberally streaked with gray.

"These are the Lassiters: Sara, Salem, Isaiah, and Mistresses Nona and Eve. These two carbon copies are named after their respective grandmothers. Salem is the family veterinarian and psychic, and Sara is Chris's sister.''

Jolene noted that Chris had married a woman who looked a lot like his sister. Sara Lassiter appeared stunningly chic even though she, like the others, wore jeans with a classic white man-tailored shirt. Salem was so breathtakingly handsome that she forced herself not to stare at him. His long straight hair was secured at the nape of his neck. And like Chris's, it was also streaked with gray. Who she did stare at were the petite twin girls. They'd inherited their father's straight black hair and their mother's gold-green eyes. They reminded her of herself and Jeanine.

Michael led her to an attractive older couple. ''These two are my first cousins—Aaron and Regina Spencer of Bahia, Brazil. Aaron is the family pediatrician, and Regina can take credit for designing the garden you love to relax in. They have a twenty-one-year-old son and nineteen-year-old daughter, who elected not to make the trip this time.''

Regina flashed a dimpled smile at the same time she rested her head on her husband's shoulder. ''Hello.'' Her voice was low, almost breathless in quality, reminding Jolene of warm brandy.

''Standing behind Regina is her brother, Tyler Cole,'' Michael continued with his introductions. ''Tyler is the family OB-GYN. He's responsible for delivering all of the babies you see here, with the exception of Alejandro. Master Delgado decided not to wait to make his scheduled entrance into the world. He's always been a little advanced.''

Tyler flashed a dimpled smile similar to his sister's. If Tyler wasn't married, then Jolene felt sorry for the women who were the recipient of that smile. It was erotic and sensual enough to melt Arctic icecaps.

''Last, but definitely not least, is another cousin, Gabriel Cole.''

Another shock rippled through Jolene as she stared

numbly at Gabriel. She remembered viewing the Grammy and the Academy Awards, watching Gabriel Cole as he stepped up in front of the cameras to accept his many awards for his *Reflections in a Mirror* movie soundtrack.

Gabriel stared at her with a pair of large gold-brown eyes that made her inch closer to Michael's side. It was only when he smiled, revealing the trademark Cole dimples, that she felt his unspoken welcome.

"There are a few more cousins, but they decided to stay in Florida," Michael continued. "Everyone, I'd like you to meet Jolene Walker, my fiancée." A chorus of gasps followed his announcement.

Regina's dark eyes sparkled with excitement. "When are you getting married?"

"New Year's Eve," Jolene said, speaking for the first time.

"Next year?" Emily asked.

She shook her head. "No. This year."

Resting her hands on her hips, Emily glared at Michael. "You're not giving us much time, are you?"

"I'm giving you more time than you and Chris gave us. At least Jolene and I are not eloping."

Emily looked at her husband, then opened her mouth to come back at her brother, but Regina Spencer waved a hand, preempting whatever it was she wanted to say. "I'm going to pull a little rank here tonight." She smiled sweetly at Emily. "I don't mean to disrespect you as mistress of this house, but I suggest we sit down to eat, put the children to bed, then discuss Michael and Jolene's upcoming nuptials."

"I agree," Chris said, shifting his daughter from one arm to the other. "Sara, please show Jolene where she can wash up." He gave his sister a direct stare, hoping to diffuse a confrontation between his wife and brother-in-law.

"Come, Jolene," Sara said, smiling. She held out her hand and wasn't disappointed when Jolene took it. Leading her down a hallway, they turned off to a large bedroom. "Emily decided to put you in here. This was my bedroom when I was growing up."

"You grew up in this house?"

"Yes. My parents owned this place before they sold it to Chris and Emily. Salem and I live less than a mile away. This part of Las Cruces is known as the Mesilla Valley."

Walking into the expansive bedroom, Jolene was delighted with the floor-to-ceiling windows offering a view of the mountains. "I won't take too long."

Sara smiled. "I'll be in the living room with the others."

Dinner was very relaxed as everyone gathered in a formal dining room. Emily, Sara, and Regina held each of the little girls on their laps, while Alejandro climbed onto Michael's. All of the little girls and Isaiah Lassiter had inherited their parents' dark hair, but not Alejandro Delgado. He claimed his mother's green eyes, but instead of her black hair, his was a shimmering silver-blond.

Jolene realized a ravenous hunger the moment she bit into, chewed, and swallowed a tender slice of pot roast. She was halfway through dinner when her fatigue became evident. Michael shook her gently; she had fallen asleep at the table. Handing Alejandro to his father, he picked her up off the chair. There was complete silence, all gazes trained on him as he cradled her in his arms and carried her to her bedroom.

He placed her on the bed, removing her clothes. Sitting on the side of the bed, he stared at her naked body, seeing the most obvious change. Her breasts were fuller. Leaning over her, he kissed her parted lips, the tips of her breasts, and then her flat belly. He still found it hard to believe that there was a tiny baby growing in her womb. Reaching for a lightweight blanket at the foot of the bed, he covered her with it. Despite the intense daytime heat, the desert was always cool at night.

Pushing off the bed, he stood there for another full minute, then turned and walked out of the room. He wanted to wait for the shock that he and Jolene would marry in another month to subside before he informed everyone that they were expecting a child. His parents knew about the baby, but he'd sworn them to secrecy.

Michael returned to the dining room to find Emily and Regina clearing the table. "Where's Sara and Salem?"

Emily smiled at him over her shoulder. "They went home. The girls were getting cranky. Isaiah is staying for a sleepover with Alejandro."

He caught Regina's eye, motioning with his head. "Why don't you hang out with the others, Regina? I'll help my sister." Regina winked at him as she retreated to the sunporch to join her husband, brother, and cousin.

"Why the attitude?" he whispered close to Emily's ear.

She stopped stacking plates, staring up at him. "I don't have an attitude, Michael. I just don't want you hurt again."

"This time it's for real."

"How can you be sure? You dated that other . . . other woman and she twisted you into knots. You gave her a year of your life and she left you high and dry."

"Jolene's different."

"How different?"

"I love her and she loves me."

Closing her eyes, Emily shook her head. "I can see why you'd be attracted to her," she said, opening her eyes. "She's incredibly beautiful. Didn't you see all of the men staring at her with their tongues hanging out? Yes, my husband included. Poor Gabriel was so stunned he couldn't even smile. Please don't be blinded by her beauty."

Michael felt a shiver of annoyance snake up his spine. "Can't you be happy for me, Emily?"

She wound her arms around his waist. "I am happy for you. I just want you happy."

Holding her tightly to his chest, he kissed the top of her head. "I am happy, more happy than I've ever been in my life. I've found my soul mate, and next summer we'll celebrate the birth of our son or daughter."

Emily went still. "She's pregnant?"

"Yes."

"Is that why you are getting married?"

"No. She agreed to marry me before I got her pregnant. We'd already set the date, but decided to make it official after we found out she was going to have a baby.

"I knew she was the one the first time I laid eyes on her," he continued passionately. "I ran after her, chasing her relentlessly until I caught her. She complained that we were moving too quickly, so I had to wait until she came around."

"Does she know who you are? How much you're worth?"

"That's something I'll tell her while we're here."

Pulling back, Emily gave him a long, penetrating look. "She's going to be a lovely bride, and you two will make wonderful babies."

"Thank you, sis. Speaking of babies, do you and Chris plan on having any more?"

She shrugged a shoulder. "Maybe. I know you're not going to stop at one."

He laughed. "I'm new at this. Let me get the hang of the first one before you start talking about two or three."

"I love you, Michael."

"Love you, too."

"Let's get this table cleared, then we can sit down and put our feet up. We have a lot to talk about."

Thirty-two

Jolene woke up early Monday morning, her stomach growling for food, and her body's circadian rhythm still on Eastern Standard Time. She showered and changed into a pair of jeans, a cotton pullover, and a pair of low-heeled leather boots. Walking into the kitchen, she found Emily cracking eggs into a large bowl.

"Good morning. Can I help with anything?"

Emily's clear green eyes sparkled in a warm smile. "Not until you get something into your belly. Michael confided to me that you're going to make me an aunt next summer," she said in a quiet voice.

Feeling the heat in her face, Jolene nodded. "We hadn't planned to start a family so soon, but—"

"There's never really a right time for the first one," Emily said, cutting off her statement. "It's the subsequent ones that are planned. Is there anything you can't eat?"

"No."

"Good."

Walking over to a massive walk-in refrigerator-freezer, Emily retrieved several plastic containers. Quickly, expertly, she prepared a small dish of sliced fruit; then she filled glasses with freshly squeezed orange juice and chilled milk and set a bowl of shredded wheat on the table in a breakfast nook.

"Eat," she urged when Jolene stared at the food in front of her. "I know it looks like a lot, but after a while you'll inhale twice that amount. I literally blew up with Esperanza. Whenever Chris was home, he had to hide food from me."

"You don't look as if you've had two babies." A pair of fitted jeans emphasized Emily's flat belly and trim hips.

"That's because they keep me running around most of the day. Chris always comes home on weekends, but before this summer I used to walk to Sara's and back."

"You don't now?"

Emily shook her head. "It's too dangerous. There've been too many coyote sightings this past summer. The children aren't allowed off the loggia, and when we sit out, we have to keep a firearm close by."

Jolene's eyes widened. "You know how to shoot?"

"Anyone who grows up here learns how to handle a rifle or handgun. Chris's father taught us. But my dad is no slouch either. It's Michael who's the expert. He can hit a target dead-center at three hundred feet."

Closing her eyes, Jolene recalled the gun Michael wore in the small of his back. At first she'd been repulsed by it, but after a while she simply ignored its presence.

Emily busied herself slicing oranges in half before she placed them in a juicer, while Jolene ate. The gnawing hunger in the pit of her stomach subsided as she finishing eating everything placed in front of her. Picking up the dishes, she walked over to the sink, rinsed them, and then placed them in the dishwasher.

Resting a hip against the countertop, she stared at Emily

staring at her, the two women measuring each other. Jolene decided to break the strained silence. "What's on your mind, Emily?"

Emily Kirkland-Delgado held her gaze. "Michael."

"What about Michael?"

Emily's gaze narrowed slightly. "I don't want you to hurt him."

"Why would I hurt him? I love your brother."

"You're not the first woman to tell me that you love him."

Jolene struggled to contain her temper. "Don't confuse me with his other women."

"Michael has never had a harem. It was *one* woman in particular. She kept him on hold for a year, then married another man. Her betrayal sent him into an emotional tailspin I never want to experience again. I'm warning you, Jolene. If you dare . . ."

"If I dare what?" she countered quietly, stopping Emily's words.

Emily glared at the tall elegant woman who looked like a fashion model, her eyes a frosty green. The seconds ticked off to a full minute as they faced off in a silent impasse.

Then, without warning, Emily smiled. Extending her arms, she hugged Jolene. "Welcome to the family."

Jolene smiled in spite of her annoyance. "I suppose I just passed the test."

Emily pulled back, flashing a dazzling smile. "You passed the test when you got Michael to fall in love with you. I never thought he would ever open up again to let a woman into his life."

"So, he did propose to another woman?"

"That relationship was doomed from the start, because they were complete opposites." Emily had deftly side-stepped Jolene's query.

"And you think we're compatible?"

Emily nodded again. "You've changed my brother. He doesn't have the intensity that used to make everyone uncomfortable whenever he entered a room. In other words, he's not as uptight as he used to be."

"He's fun to be with," Jolene admitted.

"You've picked one of the best guys in the family, and I'm not saying that because he's my brother. Like my dad, he's going to make a wonderful husband and father."

"What about Tyler and Gabriel?"

"Tyler is married to medicine, while Gabriel's too temperamental for a serious relationship."

"How old is Tyler?"

"Thirty-nine. Gabriel and Michael are only two weeks apart."

"Does Tyler really deliver all of the babies?"

"Yes. He delivered Esperanza and Sara's twin daughters."

"Did Michael tell you that I'm an identical twin?"

"No, he didn't! I have first cousins who are twins, which means you and Michael could also have twins."

She did not want twins, at least not the first time. "Whatever we have, I just hope it's going to be healthy."

"I know it's going to be beautiful. And it's not vanity that allows me to say that we have beautiful intelligent babies. I wish you and Michael a long and happy life together. You two remind me of my parents. You'll know what I'm talking about once you meet them.

"Not to change the subject, but I want you to know that I have quite a few outings planned for this week," Emily said, not taking a breath. "Chris will be home until Sunday, which means I get a break from the children. I've made arrangements for you, Sara, Regina, and myself to go up to Santa Fe for a full day of beauty at my favorite spa on Wednesday. Then we can have dinner at a wonderful restaurant."

Jolene's eyes glittered with anticipation. "How far is Santa Fe from here?"

"About three hundred fifty miles."

"Do you drive up?"

"Most times I do. But this time we're going to hire a driver."

"What about the children?"

"The men will take care of them. Chris and Salem are quite adept with disposable diapers, while Michael, Tyler, and Gabriel will take care of the cleaning and cooking duties. Aaron will make certain everyone stays in line."

"I like that plan," Jolene said, laughing.

"I thought you would," Emily agreed.

"What plan is this?" asked a soft baritone voice.

Jolene turned to find Michael standing under the arched doorway, a pair of well-washed jeans hugging his slim hips and long legs like a second skin. She forced her gaze to linger on his face, because she didn't want Emily to see her lusting after her brother.

"Nothing," Emily and Jolene said in unison.

"Yeah, right," he countered, walking into the kitchen. He brushed his mouth over Jolene's, and then he kissed Emily's cheek. "I know you two are up to no good. Whatever it is you're planning, I hope you leave time for Jolene and me to go look at rings."

Emily flicked a button on an automatic coffeemaker. "Where are you going to look?"

Folding his arms over a blue plaid shirt, Michael stared at Emily. "Chris gave me the name of the jeweler where he bought your ring."

Jolene had noticed the exquisite three-stone anniversary band on her soon-to-be sister-in-law's left hand.

Emily glanced down at her hand. "But he's in Santa Fe."

"Then we'll have to go up to Santa Fe," Michael said,

smiling. "If you don't mind, I'm going to borrow a car and we'll drive up after breakfast."

Emily shrugged her shoulder in a gesture that mirrored Michael's. "I don't mind at all. Try to be back in time for dinner. We're going over to Sara's tonight."

It took less than twenty-four hours for Jolene to feel as if she truly had become a part of Michael's extended family. They'd returned from Santa Fe to find the house empty, and a note on the table in the entryway indicating everyone had gone to the Lassiters.

It had taken hours before she and Michael were able to decide on an engagement ring and wedding bands. He'd taken her on a walking tour of downtown Santa Fe while the center stone was set. It had been after three when they'd returned to the jeweler. A shiver of nervousness had rippled along her spine when Michael had slipped the ring on her finger for the first time. Prisms of light reflected off the princess-set diamonds in a platinum band. The total weight was a little less than three carats.

They hurriedly shared a shower, changed clothes, and drove the short distance to the Lassiter home.

Michael parked behind one of several cars lining the curving driveway. "Don't move too quickly," he cautioned when he saw Salem's wolf-dog creep from the shadows.

Jolene froze, her fingernails biting into the tender flesh on Michael's wrist. "It's a wolf." There was no mistaking the fear in her voice.

"Shadow is a hybrid," Michael corrected softly. He got out of the car, then came around to help Jolene. "Let him sniff you."

"Noooo."

"He's not going to hurt you, darling."

She felt the tremors in her legs move up her body until

she was frozen to the spot. The large canine moved forward slightly, his head lowered. He pressed his nose to Michael's leg, then he crept slightly behind him. He caught Jolene's scent, and as quickly as he'd appeared he disappeared.

Placing a hand over her chest, she leaned against Michael's side. "Just because Salem's a vet, that shouldn't permit him to keeping a wild animal as a pet. What do the children play with—rattlesnakes?"

The sound of Michael's laughter carried easily in the desert night air. "Sara forbids her children to have a pet. She claims that if they're anything like their father, then her home would become a zoo."

Jolene stared up at the two-story structure. Brightly lit, it shimmered like a jewel in the desert. She followed Michael over a flagstone walk into an atrium with rare cacti and native plantings. He opened a set of massive carved doors and stepped into a grand foyer that showcased primitive-looking pieces of sculpture, each placed on its own freestanding block of wood. An artfully designed dramatic lighting technique cast shadows on the carved figures, which appeared to dance playfully along the smooth white backdrop of the walls. Recessed lights and polished hardwood floors contributed to the entry's streamlined look, while a neutral palette imbued the space with elegant sophistication.

Everyone had gathered in the formal dining room. A large table was set with fine china, sterling, and crystal stemware. A smaller table was positioned nearby for six-year-old Isaiah Lassiter, his two-year-old twin sisters, and four-year-old Alejandro. The very chatty year-old Esperanza was seated in a high chair at the children's table. All of the adults were casually attired in slacks, shirts, and blouses. The men had foregone ties and jackets.

"Here they are," Governor Delgado announced loudly in Spanish. "We were taking bets that you two would be late because you'd be somewhat *busy.* Emily told me

Michael was a little ticked off because she assigned him a bedroom in a wing opposite Jolene's.''

"Daddy, what was Uncle Michael busy doing?" Isaiah asked in a Navajo dialect. His little jaw snapped closed as Salem shook his head, frowning his disapproval.

Jolene looked perplexed while Sara glared at her brother. "Chris! The children understand Spanish!"

"For your information," Michael said in English, "Jolene and I were delayed in Santa Fe. It took us a long time to decide on a ring."

Regina walked over to Jolene, grasping her left hand. The light from a large overhead chandelier highlighted threads of silver in her short curly hair. Her dimples twinkled when she smiled. "It's so incredibly beautiful." She kissed Jolene's cheek. "Congratulations."

The women hugged and kissed Jolene, then Michael, offering their good wishes on their engagement. Jolene was hugged, kissed, and lifted off her feet by Tyler, Gabriel, and Aaron. Staring at the men, she realized all were tall, over six feet, broad-shouldered, handsome, and elegant. Their wives were perfect complements: tall, slender, and attractive. It was obvious Salem, Chris, Aaron, and Michael shared similar tastes in women. And she wondered about Gabriel and Tyler. What "type" were they drawn to?

Salem filled fluted glasses with a premium champagne, handing them to all the adults. He poured sparkling water into a goblet for Jolene after she refused his offer of wine. Smiling, his slanting eyes crinkled attractively.

Curving his free arm around Sara's waist, he smiled down at her. "Sara and I would like to thank everyone for coming under our roof this evening to celebrate another family gathering." He extended his glass, looking directly at Jolene. "Welcome and congratulations. May you and Michael be blessed with many strong and healthy children to continue the legacy which we've been given."

"I second that," Tyler said in a soft drawling voice that verified he was a son of the South.

"Here, here," Gabriel said, tugging at one of the tiny gold hoops in his pierced lobes.

Jolene smiled through the hot tears welling up behind her eyelids. "I want to thank everyone for making me feel so welcomed even before I officially become a family member."

Michael swallowed a sip of champagne, his gaze fixed on his fiancée's profile. "Jolene and I have another announcement to make. We're expecting our first child next June."

Regina laughed. "You don't have to have a wedding to make it official. The fact that you're carrying a Kirkland is enough." She'd waited until after she'd given birth to her son to marry Aaron, who officially had been her stepson. And she had never regretted falling in love and marrying the Brazilian-based doctor.

"When in June?" Tyler asked Jolene. "I have to note it on my calendar."

"Anytime between the 15th and 22nd."

Michael kissed Jolene's ear. "How about you, Aaron? You want to fly in and examine the baby?"

Tall and elegant, Dr. Aaron Spencer would celebrate his sixtieth birthday in May, but he could easily pass for a man ten years younger. He and Regina divided their time between Bahia, Brazil, Mexico, and visiting Florida. Their children had decided to pursue their higher education in the States. And like his father and Uncle Tyler, Clayborne had decided on a career in medicine, while Eden hadn't decided what she wanted to be when she grew up.

"I promise to be in the delivery room with Tyler."

Sara put down her flute. "Now that we've made all of the arrangements for mom and baby, I suggest we all sit down to dinner."

Jolene, seated opposite Michael, was flanked by Aaron on her right and Gabriel on her left. Conversations floated around the table in English and Spanish, making her aware that even though she was considered a family member, she truly wasn't. There was so much about Michael's family she did not know.

Both her parents were professionals, as had been her maternal and paternal grandparents, but they weren't elected officials or celebrated musicians. Michael revealed that Emily had been a television news journalist before she gave up a promising career to stay home and raise her children. Sara Sterling-Lassiter had distinguished herself as a federal prosecutor before she returned to New Mexico to marry Salem Lassiter.

And Jolene wondered about Salem's toast. What had the brilliant Navajo veterinarian meant when he'd mentioned the legacy they'd been given? She would be certain to ask Michael later.

Dinner was relaxed, unhurried. Champagne flowed, conversation was lively. The menu was a cornucopia of various regions: Southwest, Mexican, and Texan. She sampled a Navajo staple: Indian fry bread. Salem told her if served with honey or confectioner's sugar, then it was considered a snack. But topped with chilies, stews, or cheeses and vegetables, it became a meal in itself. She sampled fiesta shrimp with thinly sliced Spanish onion, lime, black olives, and diced red pepper chilled in a marinade of vegetable oil, minced garlic, chili, fresh lemon juice, balsamic vinegar, cayenne pepper, and fresh finely minced cilantro, the fry bread with vegetables, and a flavorful black bean soup.

By the time Sara placed platters of Cornish hens with a mango sauce, white rice with fried plantains, and a mixed salad with an avocado dressing on the table, Jolene was ready to push herself away from the table and lie down.

"Do they always eat like this?" she asked Aaron in a quiet voice.

He nodded, grinning. Angling his head closer to hers, he said, "You're marrying into a very passionate family. And their passions are infinite. And that includes food, music, and procreation."

"But you and Regina only have two children," she countered softly.

"I was thirty-eight the day my son was born, much too old to think about fathering four or five children. Michael's only thirty-two, which means the two of you can have at least three or four children before you're forty."

Did she want four children? She hadn't even planned on the one growing in her belly. After falling in love with Michael, she knew she wanted to marry him and bear his children, but she hadn't expected everything to happen so quickly.

Sara slipped away from the table, followed by Emily as they gathered their children and took them upstairs. Jolene excused herself and followed them, surprising Sara when she reached for one of the twins cradled on each hip.

"Who are you?" she whispered to the little girl staring at her with large slanting gold-green eyes.

"Eve," came her soft reply.

"Has anyone told you that you're a beautiful little girl?" Her head bobbed up and down. "My daddy," she said proudly.

Folding the child to her breasts, she kissed her silky black hair. "Your daddy's right about that."

Emily took Isaiah and Alejandro into one bedroom, while Jolene and Sara took the girls into another. Sara filled the bathtub with water, adding an assortment of rubber toys.

Sara made a big production of brushing their teeth as they giggled uncontrollably when she told them to spit before they were seated in the oversized bathtub. Jolene made quick work of bathing Esperanza, Nona, and Eve. She washed, while Sara dried and dressed the girls for bed.

Esperanza was placed in a crib and her cousins were bedded down in twin beds with detachable side railings. Lamps were extinguished, and soft lights off the baseboards were illuminated.

Sara went to her knees between the twin beds, crossed herself, and said a short prayer. Jolene smiled when she heard the two-year-olds trying to repeat the words. She felt her heart swell and nearly explode with joy. And when Sara said, "Amen," Jolene whispered her own prayer for a daughter.

They returned to the lower level. All of the food had been put away and the dishes in the dishwasher. The sounds of music filled the living room. The acoustics were perfect. Salem sat at a magnificent black concert piano, accompanying Gabriel, whose fingers literally rippled over the keys of a synthesizer.

During their drive from Santa Fe earlier that evening, Michael had updated her on the members of his family. Gabriel had taken a much-needed break from performing with his band to retreat to Las Cruces to write new music. He'd had his recording equipment shipped from Florida, and then settled into one of the cabins built on the land belonging to Christopher and Emily Delgado, spending days cloistered in a world where notes spoke to him in the way he heard humans speak. One day he'd driven to a Las Cruces mall, gone into a music store, and exited with more than five hundred dollars' worth of CDs and sheet music.

He'd emerged a week later, gaunt from missing meals but euphoric. He'd decided not to write new music, but to record a collection of classic compositions from Bruce Hornsby, Jonathan Butler, Marc Cohn, Van Morrison, George Benson, Eric Clapton, the late, great Bob Marley, and a few other musical geniuses. And because of the regional and cultural mix, he decided to name it *Kaleidoscope*.

Jolene stared at Michael as he stared back at her when Gabriel played and sang Cohn's "True Companion." The words reached inside her, echoing the depth of emotion she felt for the man with whom she'd fallen in love. She hadn't realized her face was streaked with tears until the song ended. Michael's face swam before her eyes as he pulled her gently from her chair and held her until she lay against his broad chest, smiling. All gazes were trained on them as they held each other.

"I know what song to play for their wedding," Gabriel said with a wide grin.

If Emily needed proof that Jolene Walker loved her brother, she had just witnessed it. There was a collective sigh when Michael brushed his mouth over his fiancée's.

Thirty-three

Michael came to Jolene's bedroom later that evening. She had just fallen asleep when he shook her gently. "Jolene, wake up. I have something to give you."

Rolling over on her back, she stared up at his shadowed features. The soft light in the base of a bedside lamp provided enough illumination for her to walk about the room without bumping into things.

"What is it?" she asked, taking a piece of paper from his hand.

"Read it."

Holding the paper close to the lamp, she recognized Michael's handwriting. It was a check for a million dollars, payable to the Sanctuary. The October fund-raising dinner had generated two hundred thousand dollars, leaving a balance of a million dollars for the completion of the safe house.

"Is this some kind of joke?"

The mattress dipped when he sat down. "No, it's not a joke."

"Where did you get a million dollars?"

"From my account."

Sitting up, she anchored two pillows behind her back, ignoring Michael's hungry gaze as the tops of her breasts spilled over the lacy bodice of her nightgown.

"Talk to me, Michael Kirkland."

"Have you ever heard of ColeDiz?" She shook her head. "ColeDiz International, Ltd., is a privately held family-owned conglomerate that owns and operates coffee and banana plantations in Belize, Mexico, Jamaica, and Puerto Rico. They also own vacation and private properties throughout the Caribbean."

"What's the connection?"

"Are you familiar with the name Samuel Cole?"

"Yes, I've heard of Samuel Cole. What does he have to do with you?"

"He was my grandfather."

Her eyes widened until they were as large as silver dollars. "Oh, my heaven."

Holding her shoulders firmly, Michael pulled her up against his chest. "I came into a five-million-dollar trust fund the day I turned twenty-five. I inherited five times that amount when my grandfather died four years ago. I wanted to give you the money the day you talked about building the safe house in Virginia, but I didn't want you to think I was trying to buy you. This check is my wedding gift to you for your very special cause."

She blinked back the tears that seemed to come so easily now that she was pregnant. "How can I thank you?"

He placed a light kiss over each eyelid. "By marrying me and becoming the mother of our children."

"That should be easy. Very, very easy," she crooned as she moved onto his lap.

"This donation will have two stipulations attached to it."

Easing back, she stared at his solemn expression. Her gaze was filled with uncertainty. "What are they?"

"I remain an anonymous donor, and that the safe house be named in memory of your sister."

Her smile was as bright as a two-hundred-watt bulb. "I'm certain the Sanctuary's board will adhere to those stipulations."

The check floated from her fingers to the mattress and onto the floor when he joined her in the bed, holding her to his heart until she fell asleep for the second time that night.

She awoke the next morning, finding Michael sprawled across the bed fully dressed. The rays of the rising sun pouring through the windows provided enough light for her to see the stubble of inky black whiskers on his lean cheeks and the sweep of thick lashes touching his high elegant cheekbones. Staring at him made her wonder who their child would resemble. Despite his hair coloring, Alejandro Delgado looked like his mother and uncle, while delicate little Esperanza had inherited her mother's eyes and her father's dimpled chin.

Closing her eyes, she whispered a silent prayer. She wanted to bring to term and deliver a healthy baby—one who would grow up in the shadow of the White House and spend his or her school holidays and summers in Las Cruces, Chicago, or West Palm Beach. Her family was small, but that was about to change when she exchanged vows with Michael. Her family would become his, and his hers.

Without warning, Michael's eyes opened and he stared up at her staring down at him. Smiling, attractive lines fanned out around his incredible eyes.

"Buenos días, mi amor."

She returned his smile. "And good morning to you, my love."

"You don't have much time to learn to speak Spanish."

Running her forefinger down the middle of his chest over a navy blue T-shirt, she shook her head. "You truly have gone and lost your mind. I struggled with four years of French and you expect me to learn Spanish in seven months."

She'd felt left out when everyone sitting at the table in the Lassiter dining room had joined in a conversation punctuated with phrases in English and Spanish. She'd sat mute, listening to the musical language floating around her. Even the children understood Spanish. The Lassiter children—Isaiah, Nona, and Eve—were also familiar with a Navajo dialect they had picked up from Salem, their African-American-Navajo father.

"It's easy."

"It's easy because you know it."

"My mother can barely string ten words together, yet Emily and I speak it fluently."

"Who taught you?"

"My father. Of course, our grandmother spoke only Spanish to us whenever we visited her in Florida. Speaking of my grandmother, she's going to turn one hundred on December 27th. My aunts and uncles are planning a blowout of a birthday celebration for her."

"Your father's last name is Kirkland, yet he speaks Spanish."

Michael wondered how much he should tell Jolene about his family. He knew she was overwhelmed meeting so many of them at one time; it probably was as good a time as any to make her privy to the Cole family secret.

"My father is Samuel Cole's illegitimate son. My grandfather had an affair with a young secretary who worked for his company, which resulted in her becoming pregnant with his child. She didn't want to bear a child without a husband, because she feared her very devout Catholic Cuban family would disown her. So, Samuel paid one of his corporate vice presidents to marry her. Teresa Maldonado hated Everett Kirkland as much as she loved Samuel Cole.''

Jolene knew her mouth was gaping, but she couldn't help it. "Did Teresa and Everett ever have children together?''

"No. They finally divorced when my dad was a teenager. Everett had served his purpose. He gave Teresa respectability and saved his boss's reputation. The men were winners while poor Teresa wound up a victim in a loveless marriage. My father carried a lot of bitterness for years, but after marrying my mother, he and his biological father called a truce.''

"Is the grandmother you speak of your biological grandmother?''

He shook his head. "No. She's Samuel Cole's widow. Emily and I think of her as our *abuela*. She treats us no differently than she does Regina, Tyler, or Gabriel.'' Leaning over, he kissed the tip of her nose. "What's on your agenda for today?''

"Salem promised to show me his horses this morning. Then Sara, Regina, Emily, and I are going to begin baking pies and cakes and marinating meats for Thursday.''

"Why don't you do that on Wednesday?''

"We can't, because the ladies are going up to Santa Fe for a day of beauty.''

Michael smiled. "How can you improve on perfection, Miss Walker?''

She touched the attractive lines around the corner of an eye with her forefinger. "It's a little early for the sweet talk, lover.''

"It's never too early or too late for what I want to do with you.''

Her breath caught in her throat when she recognized the

passion in his gaze. His eyes darkened as his pupils dilated. "We can't," she whispered.

"Why not?"

"Because I have to get up and eat before I'm sick."

Sweeping her off the bed, he carried her to the bathroom. Stripping off his clothes, he joined her in the shower as the warm water rained down on their naked bodies.

Jolene luxuriated in the feel of his hands when he soaped her body, lingering on her sensitive breasts.

"I can't believe you have a brother-in-law who's a governor and a first cousin who's an Oscar and Grammy winner." She had to talk, say anything to keep her mind off what his fingers were doing to her.

Michael stood behind Jolene, his hardness throbbing against her hips. "We're just average folks."

"If you guys are average, then I'd hate to meet the extraordinary ones." Her breath was coming in short pants.

Turning her around, he placed a hand over her belly. "You're carrying one of the extraordinary ones."

Looking directly at him, she gave him a gentle smile. "I pray you're right." Closing her eyes, she swallowed back a wave of nausea. "We'd better end this shower right now because this extraordinary child is draining his mama's food reserves."

Michael and Jolene walked the mile separating the Delgado property from the Lassiters. The rising sun had painted the landscape a vivid shocking pink. Emily had not put in an appearance by the time they'd left the house after eating a light breakfast of fruit, toast, and juice. There was no reason for them to rise early, because Alejandro and Esperanza had slept over with their cousins.

"Watch it!" Michael warned, tightening his grip on Jolene's hand and jerking her back. She looked down, gasping as a snake slithered away only inches from her booted foot. "Rattler."

She slumped against his side, and for the first time since meeting Michael Kirkland, she could admit to herself that she was glad he was carrying a gun.

"I don't know if I could get used to living out here."

"It takes some getting used to. As long as you respect nature it will respect you. That rattler would rather retreat than attack."

Not willing to take her gaze off the dry arid ground, she asked, "Will you be all right walking back?"

"Of course, *mi amor*. Chris and I used to camp out at night in the desert."

She shuddered visibly. "That may have been all right for you and Chris, but I'm having none of that for my son."

He gave her a sidelong look. "Your son, Jolene? Won't I get to have a say in his upbringing?"

Turning her head, she hid a smile. "A little."

"It's going to be more than a little," he grumbled in Spanish.

"What did you say?" This time she did look at him.

He met her unwavering stare. "Learn Spanish."

"Teach me," she taunted, answering his challenge.

He shifted his eyebrows. "You really want to learn?"

"Yes."

Releasing her hand, he curved an arm around her shoulders. "We'll begin with the words that pertain to love."

He whispered in her ear, translating them, and leaving her face burning with shame. They crossed the small stream dividing the two properties, coming face-to-face with Shadow. He stood like a guard, watching them as they made their way past him in the direction of the house.

"Salem still has the best silent alarm system in the Mesilla Valley," Michael remarked as the house came into view.

"Will he attack?"

"Only on command from Salem. But no one's willing to come on Lassiter property to test whether he will or won't."

"What did Salem mean last night when he mentioned something about a legacy?"

There was a pregnant silence before Michael said, "It means we dare risk everything for love."

"Everything?" The single word was filled with awe.

"Everything, Jolene. And that includes dying for you."

As casually as she could manage, she nodded her head. What was there for her to say? He loved her enough to give up his life for her, and in that instant she felt the same. She would forfeit her life and that of her unborn child to protect him.

"I would do the same for you, Michael."

In one forward motion, she was in his arms, her face buried against his warm brown throat. Relaxing, she sank into his cushioning embrace, feeding on his strength and praying the danger that had stalked her was a part of her past. That Preston James had taken it to the grave with him.

Jolene stood behind the fence, staring at the exquisite beauty of the Thoroughbreds prancing around the corral. "They're so elegant."

Salem stood next to her, his arms resting on a rail of the fence. "In my professional opinion, aside from the wolf and cheetah, they're the most perfectly formed animal."

"Sara told me that her father was a preeminent horse breeder."

"He was. He bred a Kentucky Derby and Belmont Stakes winner. Eve and Matt sold their home to Chris and Emily and Sara and I bought the horse farm. I had the stables and the paddocks moved on this side of the stream."

"Are you breeding the horses to race, too?"

Salem shook his head. "No. I've set up a registered stud

farm. You would've enjoyed seeing Joe Russell training the horses. He was Matt Sterling's trainer for almost thirty years. After Matt sold the house and he and Eve moved closer to the city, Joe married their housekeeper and bought a little place down near El Paso. I'm willing to bet Joe and Marisa will show up for your wedding. Right now they're in Chicago visiting with Marisa's son and grandchildren. Matt and Eve are visiting with Joshua and Vanessa in Ocho Rios.''

Jolene smiled, recalling the weekend she'd spent with Michael in Ocho Rios. They hadn't talked about a honeymoon, but she wanted to return to Jamaica as his wife.

"I have a confession to make," Salem said after a comfortable silence.

Staring up at him, she studied his distinctive profile with a ridge of high cheekbones under dark red-brown skin. "What is it?"

Shifting his position, he rested his back against the fence, staring directly at her. "I didn't ask you to come here alone to look at the horses. Michael or Emily could've brought you without me being here."

Her pulse accelerated. It wasn't what he'd said as much as what he hadn't said. "Why did you ask me to come alone?"

He ran a large slender hand over the mixed graying black hair pulled back off his high forehead. "Why is Michael carrying a gun?"

Her expression showed confusion. "Because of the coyotes.''

Salem shook his head. "I'm not talking about Las Cruces, but Washington, D.C."

Closing her eyes, she slumped back against the railing. When Michael introduced Salem he'd said he was the family vet and psychic. Was the man able to predict the future? Could he see the danger that had stalked her?

She opened her eyes, but would not meet Salem's intense stare. "There was a man who wanted to kill me."

"There is a man who *wants* to kill you."

This time she did look at the mysterious vet. "That's not true. He's dead."

Salem stared down into her large dark eyes, seeing things she would never be able to see. "One man is dead. But there's another one chasing you."

She swayed slightly before righting herself. "Have you told Michael?"

"No. I'm telling you because I want you to be very careful."

"Who is this man?"

"I can't see his face because he has a lot of people around him—very powerful people."

Jolene felt her heart pumping so hard she was certain Salem could see it through her blouse. "Why would he want to kill me?"

"You know something he doesn't want you to know. A young woman is going to come to you with a name, and when she does, you'll know who he is. Then you must take steps to protect yourself and your unborn child." Fear gripped her, closing off her throat as she fell against Salem's hard body, swallowing her screams of dread and horror. He held her until the trembling eased. "You must let Michael protect you. If not, then you'll never live to marry or bring your baby to term."

Silent tears stained her cheeks. Was she destined to die like her twin, with a child in her womb?

"Promise me you'll let Michael protect you." He handed her a handkerchief from a pocket in his jeans.

"I promise," she sniffled, wiping away her tears.

* * *

Michael heard the music as he knocked on the door to the cabin. He pushed the door open when he heard Gabriel's voice telling him to come in.

Gabriel sat on the floor, bare-chested and barefoot, scribbling notes on music sheets. The carpet was littered with pages bearing notes for every instrument in an orchestra.

Putting the pad and pencil aside, he stood up. He embraced Michael, kissing both cheeks. "What did I do to deserve an audience with my esteemed older cousin?" he teased, twin dimples winking with his warm smile.

"Older by two weeks, *primo*."

Taking a guitar off the sofa, he placed it on the floor, patting the cushion for Michael to sit down. "That means you'll become a senior citizen two weeks before I do."

Placing a hand over his heart, Michael rolled his eyes upward. "I'm devastated."

Gabriel sat down opposite Michael on a matching armchair. "Where's Jolene?"

"She went to see the horses."

Gabriel shook his head. "I don't know why, but I'm not feeling horses. Every time I come out here, Emily tries to get me to ride, but I turn her down. I suppose it has something to do with a fear of falling and breaking a hand or finger." He wiggled ten long brown fingers. "I need all of these bad boys for my work."

Michael studied his cousin, noting his hair was longer than he'd seen it in years, the inky black waves falling over his forehead. His face was gaunt, giving his strong features a certain sensuality that hadn't been there in the past. A lethal calmness had replaced the former glint of humor in his large gold-brown eyes.

"Are you all right, Gabe?"

"Yeah. Why?"

"You just seem out of sorts."

Running his fingers through his tousled hair, he smiled.

"I'm always out of sorts when I'm in my creative mode. How about yourself? I can't believe you're going to tie the knot and settle down."

Michael laced his fingers together, staring at the toes of his boots. "I didn't think I would until I met Jolene."

Crossing muscular arms over a broad hairy chest, Gabriel stared at Michael's bowed head. "What is it about Jolene, other than her looks, that made you fall in love with her?"

Green eyes smoldered with an unquenchable fire as they shifted upward. His gaze caught and held Gabriel's. "She makes me lose control, *primo*."

An expression of shock froze the musician's pleasant features. The family joke was that Michael and his uncle Joshua were robots, automatons, and both could take the bravest man's nerve by just glaring at him.

There was a long, penetrating silence before he whispered, shaking his head in amazement. "Unbelievable!"

Michael smiled. "Amen."

Thirty-four

Jolene returned to Washington, D.C., looking better than when she'd left. Her day of beauty at the Santa Fe spa left her coiffed, her face gleaming from a European facial, and her hands and feet pampered. She'd declined the full-body massage because of the early stage of her confinement.

She was able to conceal her apprehension from Michael whenever she replayed Salem Lassiter's warning in her head on the return flight. Just before the jet touched down, she told him she'd changed her mind about staying at her apartment and wanted to go home with him.

Michael directed the taxi driver to drop them off at Jolene's brownstone, where she picked up clothes to last her for three days, and then they walked the short distance to his house.

Jolene waited until Monday to call Claire and tell her about the million-dollar donation to complete construction of the safe house. She told Claire that Michael wanted to remain an anonymous donor and of his appeal to dedicate the facility to her deceased twin. Claire reassured her that the board would honor Michael's request.

Deborah walked into her office, noticed the ring on her finger, and squealed. She held her hand, staring at the center diamond flanked by two smaller princess-cut diamonds, gushing.

"It's fabulous, Jolene. I wish you and Michael all the best."

"Thank you, Deborah."

"Have you set a date?"

"Yes. New Year's Eve."

A soft gasp escaped her. "That's only a month away."

"I know. I'll be sending out invitations at the end of the week. Can I count on you to come—unless you have something else planned?"

"I'll be there with bells on. Where's it going to be?"

"West Palm Beach, Florida."

"Count me in."

Jolene clasped her hands. "Good. Everything's happening so quickly."

"Are you going to need help with the arrangements?"

"I don't think so. My future sister-in-law is coordinating everything. My mother spoke to Michael's mother last night and they plan to meet sometime this week in Chicago. Michael has several toddler nieces and nephews who'll become flower girls and boys. All I have to do is shop for a dress and show up on time."

What she did not tell Deborah was that the dress had to be loose enough to accommodate her thickening waist. By the time she exchanged vows with Michael, she would be into her second trimester.

"I need you to watch the office while I go to the post office to pick up my mail."

Deborah glanced at her watch. "Why don't you go now before it gets too crowded?"

"You're right about that. I'll see you in a little while."

Gathering her purse, she retrieved her car keys and left the Sanctuary. Just as she pulled the seat belt over her chest, she reached for the small pager in her purse, turning it on. Salem's warning had her so uneasy that she found herself staring at every man who passed her either on foot or in his car, wondering if he was the one.

She picked up a bundle of mail that had accumulated during her week's stay in New Mexico and returned to her office without any mishap. It was only when she was finally inside that she was able to relax completely, totally unaware that Michael had followed her.

April waited patiently, knowing this time she would escape from her prison. Stanley had left for Asia earlier that morning with a group of elected officials on a so-called fact-finding mission. They'd asked him to accompany them as a consultant. She knew he had given his housekeeper specific instructions that she was to be kept locked in her room at all times. Now all she had to do was wait.

Staring at the clock on the table next to her bed, she heard footsteps, then the key turning in the lock. It was her signal. Fingering the small disposable razor, she pressed the sharp blade over the flesh on her left wrist. She increased the pressure until a ribbon of blood flowed onto the sheets. Working quickly, she cut the right.

When the door opened, she heard the tray crash to the floor. She sat on the bed, eyes closed, blood spurting from her severed arteries. Miss Phillips screamed once, and there was silence and blackness.

Jolene got the call on her cellular phone at 4:40. The caller identified herself as a hospital social worker calling on behalf of April Stansfield. "Miss Stansfield attempted suicide this morning. She's been stabilized, but has been asking for you. Is it possible for you to come to see her?"

"Of course. I'll be there as soon as I can."

Her hands were shaking slightly when she told Sally to let Deborah know that she had a client in crisis. She wasn't certain whether she'd come back to her office.

Then she called Michael, leaving a message on his answering machine that she was going to visit a client in the hospital. Remembering Salem's warning, she left the name of the hospital.

Jolene showed the nurse sitting beside the bed her pass, asking if she and her client could have some privacy. April's pale face blended in with the white bedding. Her flaxen hair flowed over the pillowcase like gold threads. Clear fluids dripped through an IV tube taped to the back of her right hand. Tears blurred Jolene's vision when her gaze rested on the tiny, bandaged wrists.

"April, can you hear me? It's Miss Walker."

Her light gray lashes fluttered as she struggled to surface from her comforting slumber. A small smile parted her lips. She was free. She had escaped.

"Miss . . . Miss Walker?"

Jolene moved closer to the bed. She touched April's cheek with the back of her right hand. "I'm here, baby."

She smiled, not opening her eyes. "You came."

"Of course I came. I've been waiting for you to call me."

April swallowed. Her throat was dry and scratchy. "I couldn't call you, because I was locked in. He found my pager and punished me by locking me in."

Leaning over the tiny body, Jolene whispered in her ear, "Who is he?"

Turning her head, April stared directly at Jolene, her blue-gray eyes filled with courage for the first time. "Stanley Willoughby." She hesitated when Jolene's jaw dropped. "He's been raping, beating, and drugging me since I was twelve."

Jolene felt her stomach recoil. April had said the man was powerful, had ties to the Oval Office. The man *was* the Oval Office. It didn't matter what political party the president belonged to, Stanley Willoughby was always available to sell his influence.

"Why, April?"

"He wanted my mother. After she rejected him, he came after me. He'd dated my mother in college, but when she met and married his best friend, he swore revenge. Even though my mother married Brian Stansfield, she continued to sleep with Stanley. She used her body and beauty to manipulate him. Then she found herself pregnant, and she told him she didn't know whose baby she carried. Fortunately for Holly, I looked just like her. Then my father died, leaving the administration of my trust fund to Stanley.

"Holly's husband left her enough money to last her the rest of her life, but he didn't count on her newfound extravagant lifestyle. Within three years she was broke. When she turned to Stanley for money, he turned her down. That's when she offered me to him, and when I confronted her she slapped me, telling me that I was liar. But he paid her, with money from my trust fund. I heard them arguing when he told her he wouldn't give her any more money. She countered by telling him that she'd sold him his own daughter.

"After this revelation he became a little crazy. He had

nightmares where he'd wake up screaming that he was inno-cent—that he hadn't done anything. I know he's afraid that I'll tell everything.''

Jolene smoothed wisps of hair off her forehead. ''It's all right, April. I'm going to make certain Stanley Willoughby pays for what he's put you through. He won't ever hurt you again.''

She nodded. ''Please, be careful. He has someone follow-ing me at all times.''

''Don't worry about me. Just try and get well. I'm going to make arrangements for you to go some place where you'll be safe.''

Closing her eyes, she shook her head. ''That's all right, Miss Walker. I'm going to meet my mother. And when I see the whore, I'm going to spit in her eye.''

Jolene was caught off guard by the venom in April's voice. ''Where is your mother?'' April took so long to answer that Jolene thought she hadn't heard her.

''She's in hell, Miss Walker. Stanley had Holly Stansfield murdered. Someone took her sailing out on the ocean, dumped her overboard, and she has never been heard or seen since.''

''Are you certain he had her killed?''

''Yes. He told me himself.''

''I'm going to find out how soon you can be discharged.''

''Don't bother yourself, Miss Walker. It's all going to be over soon.''

She kissed the young woman's cheek, then walked out of the room and out of the hospital. Standing outside in the cool night air, she inhaled a lungful of clean air. April's confession played in her head like a broken record.

She'd heard many horror stories of rape and incest, but this one came in around the top of the list. The man had used his power and influence to manipulate and murder. He might have ties to the Oval Office, but he wasn't immune

to justice. And she doubted whether the sitting president
would risk his own position as the most powerful leader in
the free world to protect his best friend.

She went to retrieve her car from the visitor's parking
lot, unaware that she was under surveillance. Pulling out of
the lot, she drove toward Georgetown, a dark-colored sedan
following at a comfortable distance.

Michael saw the man drive out of the parking lot after
Jolene left. He noted the license plate number. Reaching for
his phone, he punched in a number, activating the speaker
feature.

"Gray," came the familiar voice.

He smiled in the dark confines of his SUV. "Kirk here.
I need you to run a plate for me." Merrick had a computer
with incredible capabilities.

"Hold on."

Michael kept his gaze on the dark car as he drummed his
fingers on the steering wheel. The automatic he usually wore
in the small of his back lay on the passenger seat.

"Kirk?"

"I'm here."

"It's leased to a company: Willoughby, Strauss, Young,
and Sutherland."

"The law firm?"

"The one and only.

"What do you know about them?"

"Not too much," Merrick Grayslake said. "I know Willoughby is close to the president."

"Is he married?"

"No. Wait for me to pull up some information on him."
There was silence, then Gray's voice. "He's the executor
of a trust fund for an April Stansfield. Her father came from
old money. I believe it was marine insurance."

"Look, buddy, I need you to tap into a hospital's computer. I want to know if they admitted a patient with that

name.'' He gave Merrick the name of the hospital Jolene had just visited.

''Bingo, Kirk. They admitted April Stansfield late this morning for an attempted suicide.''

''Thanks, man. Keep your eyes open for an invitation in the mail.''

''What for?''

''I'm getting married, and I expect you to attend.''

''You try and keep me away.''

''Later, Gray.''

''Later, Kirk.''

Pressing a button, Michael ended the call. It was apparent Jolene was going back to his place, with the man in the dark sedan in pursuit. Waiting until she drove down the street leading to his house, he sped up, cutting off the car following her off. The man slammed on his brakes, pulling over to the curb, and Michael jumped out of his vehicle, gun in hand, before the man could react.

Pointing the small automatic in his face, Michael said quietly, ''Get out with your hands in plain sight.''

The loose flesh on the man's bloated face shook like gelatin. ''Look, mister, take the car. It's not worth dying for.''

Michael experienced a rush of anger. Because he was a black man, the Pillsbury Doughboy mascot thought he was a carjacker. The driver was young, probably in his early thirties, but was grossly overweight. It was apparent he was having an ongoing affair with too many Big Macs. His thinning hair was neatly brushed; however, perspiration had pasted it to his gleaming scalp.

Snatching open the door, he motioned with the gun. ''Get out, Tiny!'' The large man fell out and would've landed on his face if Michael hadn't caught him.

''What the hell are you doing with my wife?''

"Your wife ... I ... I don't know what you're talking about."

Michael slapped him hard across the face. "Wrong answer. Now, I'm going to ask you again, why were you following my wife home?"

"I ... I don't—"

His words stopped again when Michael backhanded him, this time harder than the first time. "This is the last time I'm going to ask you—"

"He told me to follow her."

"Now we're getting somewhere. Who is *he*?"

"I can't tell you."

Michael arched an eyebrow. The man wasn't completely spineless. He hit him again, this time under his soft belly, close enough to his genitals to cause severe pain. "We're going to a love-in, and you're going to be the guest of honor."

Tucking the gun in the waistband of his jeans, Michael grabbed a thick right thumb. "The marines have a quote: 'Pain is weakness leaving the body.' How much pain can you tolerate before I break all of your fingers?" He applied enough pressure for the man to rise to his toes.

"All right," he moaned softly. "All right. I'll tell."

"Talk to me, Peewee."

"Mr. Willoughby got a call that his ward was hospitalized, so he called and told me to keep an eye on her."

"Does keeping an eye on her include following my wife?"

"No ... no."

"No?"

"Mr. Willoughby told me a lady would probably come to see his ward, and if she did, I should follow her."

"Follow her for what?"

"Just follow her."

"Did he tell you to hurt her?"

He shook his head, the loose flesh on his jowls flapping. "I wouldn't hurt her. I've never hurt anybody in my life. I'm just a law clerk."

"Where is this Mr. Willoughby?"

"He was on his way to China."

"Was?"

"He changed his plans. He's on his way back to the States."

"When do you expect him to arrive?"

"Sometime tomorrow morning."

Michael released his thumb. "Let me see your driver's license."

Reaching into the rear pocket of his trousers, he withdrew a leather case, his hand shaking uncontrollably as he gave it to Michael, who held it under the beam of a headlight.

"I know who you are and where you live. I'm going to call you at your office tomorrow, and you're going to tell me if Mr. Willoughby has returned. Jerk me around and I'm coming for you. Talk to the police and you're a dead man. Do you understand me?" He gave him back his license.

"Yes, sir."

"Get lost."

The law clerk bowed several times before he scrambled to get back into his car. He closed the door quietly, then took off, leaving tire tracks on the asphalt.

Michael walked back to his own car. He leaned against the bumper, trying to slow down his heart. It had been racing when he'd confronted the man. And he had been prepared to cause bodily harm if the man hadn't given him the answers he sought.

Now all he had to do was wait—wait for Stanley Willoughby's return to find out why he wanted to kill Jolene.

Thirty-five

Minutes after the jet carrying Stanley Willoughby touched down on the Tarmac, April Stansfield was whisked out of the hospital and taken to an undisclosed location.

"Are you telling me that you don't know who signed her out?" Jolene asked the clerk sitting in the Patient Information office.

"I'm not at liberty to give out that information. Miss Stansfield is over twenty-one, therefore if she wants to sign herself out, then there's nothing anyone at this hospital can do about it."

"This patient lost more than two units of blood. There's no way she could've walked out of here without assistance."

"I'm sorry, Miss Walker, but I have work to do."

Jolene stormed out of the office, fuming. She'd made arrangements to have April taken to a safe house in the Midwest, but someone had signed her out. But where had they taken her? Would they see that she had medical attention?

Anger and frustration warred within her as she paced the floor outside the office. She had to do something—anything—to save April. She couldn't lose her. April could not end up like Jeanine.

Knowing the clerk would not change her mind, she left the hospital and returned to the Sanctuary.

A week later, Jolene and all of Washington discovered the whereabouts of April Stansfield. Her decomposing naked body was discovered in a Dumpster in a rundown section of the city. The coroner's report listed the death as a drug overdose. She'd injected a lethal dose of pure heroin into her veins.

Jolene sat in her office, staring at a photograph of a smiling April Stansfield in a cap and gown when she'd graduated high school. How could she have smiled when she had been brutally and systemically raped and beaten for half her life?

Placing a hand over her slightly rounded belly, she thought of the child in her womb. What if it was a girl? Could she become another April? Jeanine? She buzzed Sally.

"Yes, Miss Walker."

"I'm going out. I'll leave my phone on just in case you need to reach me."

"Okay, Miss Walker."

Gathering her purse, she made her way out to the parking lot. She no longer had to concern herself with client confidentiality. April was dead, and dead people did not sue the living.

Jolene walked over to the woman sitting behind a glass partition. "I'd like to see Mr. Stanley Willoughby."

"Your name, please."

"Miss Jolene Walker."

"Do you have an appointment with Mr. Willoughby, Miss Walker?"

"No, I don't. But I believe he'd want to see me."

"Please have a seat while I contact his private secretary."

She sat down on a chair covered in maroon leather of the highest quality. It was as soft as whipped butter. Every piece in the reception area spoke of elegance and success. Willoughby, Strauss, Young, and Sutherland was the top litigating firm in D.C.

Picking up a current issue of *Town & Country,* she found herself engrossed in an article. Forty minutes later, an elderly woman greeted her.

"Mr. Willoughby knows you're here. As soon as he finishes an overseas call he'll see you. Meanwhile, is there anything I can get to make you comfortable?"

"Nothing, thank you."

What she wanted was to look Stanley Willoughby in the eye and tell him that she knew what he'd done to April.

She turned her attention back to her magazine article. Two hours after she'd walked into the law firm, she was led down a plush carpeted hallway to Willoughby's office.

He stood behind his desk, watching her approach. Her gaze never faltered as she moved close enough to see the vacant look in his cold eyes.

"Miss Walker? It is Miss Walker, isn't it?"

"Please, don't insult my intelligence."

A noticeable tic jumped under his right eye. He had to admit that his nemesis was stunning. Her face was a clear flawless dark brown that shimmered with an appearance of excellent health. Large intelligent dark eyes looked directly at him, showing no fear. And she had a right to fear him, because he'd wanted her dead. However, he'd withdrawn the contract on her life because April was dead.

"Please sit down, Miss Walker." He indicated a chair pushed under a round table in a corner of his spacious office.

She made her way over to the table, but Stanley moved quickly, pulling out a chair for her. Mumbling a polite thank-you, she sat down. He took a chair opposite her.

"May I offer you something to drink? Water? Juice?"

Dismissing her pride, she said, "Juice, please." It was close to the time when she was scheduled to have a light snack.

Stanley stood up, walking over to a wet bar. He took out a bottle of apple juice, filled a glass with ice, retrieved several napkins, and returned to the table.

Jolene took her time twisting off the cap, pouring the juice into the glass, and taking furtive sips, her gaze never leaving April's killer's face. His benign appearance did not fool her. There was something about his eyes—they were the mirrors of his soul, and his soul was cold. No, she thought, he did not possess a soul.

"I'd like to talk to you about April Stansfield."

"Have you come to offer your condolences?"

"I said a prayer for her when I read about the police finding her body. So my answer is no."

Stanley adjusted a cuff of his custom-made shirt. "Then why are you here?"

"I wanted to see what kind of monster would rape a child." He flinched as if she'd struck him. Deciding to press her attack, she said, "I wanted to look you in the eye when I told you that I know April did not die from a drug overdose because she'd injected herself. I know she was murdered."

"My ward was a junkie, Miss Walker. And you should know better than anyone that junkies are liars."

"April abused substances, but she was not a heroin user. She told me she was afraid of needles, that she would never inject herself. Pills, alcohol, and cocaine were her drugs of choice.

"But what about you? You abused her repeatedly. You

raped her, beat her, and stole from her. You sit here—the model citizen, hiding behind your fancy clothes, fancy office, and your powerful friends." Leaning forward, she squinted at him. "I know what you've done, and you know what you've done. And what you don't know is perhaps everything April told me was recorded. Which means you had your man break into the Sanctuary for nothing.

"A word of warning, Stanley." She spat out the name. "If you ever send one of your goons after me again, it will be the last time. Because if anything happens to me, then get ready to exchange your Savile Row suit for an orange jumpsuit." She put down the glass. "Thank you for the juice."

She pushed back the chair, and without a backward glance she walked out of his office, down the hallway, and out of Willoughby, Strauss, Young, and Sutherland.

Her knees were practically knocking together as she buttoned the jacket to her suit. Pressing a button on the remote, she unlocked her car and slipped behind the wheel. She turned on the engine, adjusted the heat, and sat staring out through the windshield while the stiffness in her limbs eased with the warmth.

Then, without warning, the tears fell. She cried for April and she cried for Jeanine. She had fought relentlessly for justice for her sister, and even though Lamar had to give up five years of his life, it still hadn't brought her sister back. Now, there was Stanley Willoughby. He had murdered April; he had killed her over and over during the years he raped and beat her.

The gnawing hunger in her belly reminded Jolene she had to eat. She had to nourish the life growing inside her. Putting the car in gear, she headed across town. She would stop and pick up something to eat before she returned to the Sanctuary.

* * *

Stanley Willoughby felt like smashing things. He wanted to punch holes in the walls, throw the phone through the plate-glass window.

"How dare she!" he ranted under his breath. How dare the social-worker come to his office and accuse him of things so horrible, so vile that it pained him to listen to her.

Picking up the receiver to his private phone, he dialed a number. When he heard the voice on the other end respond, he said, "I've got a job for you. The social worker just won an all-expense-paid trip for a wonderful cruise to nowhere."

He replaced the receiver on its cradle, smiling. Once he got rid of Jolene Walker, he would be able to sleep again without taking the pills.

Michael walked into the house fifteen minutes after Jolene. She sat in the teahouse, staring out at the night. He flipped a switch, flooding the space with soft golden light.

Hunkering down beside her chair, he held her hands. "How are you?"

"Not good, Michael."

He sat on the floor, pulling her down to sit on his lap. She had put on a little weight. "What's the matter, darling?"

"I read about a client in today's newspaper. The police found her in a Dumpster. They claim she died from a drug overdose."

"What do you mean, they claim?"

"They found heroin in her blood. She never abused heroin because she was afraid to inject herself."

"Maybe she swallowed it."

Jolene shook her head. "No. The article specifically said there were track marks on her arm."

Michael had also read the article when the name April

Stansfield had jumped out at him. Steven Miller aka Tiny, had followed his instructions. He'd called Mr. Miller at his office, and he'd reported that Mr. Willoughby had returned to the office after his aborted Asian trip.

Hanging up, Michael had then called the firm back and asked to speak to Mr. Willoughby. His private secretary wouldn't let him speak directly to her boss, but promised to give him his message. And Willoughby finally had called him. It was to place a hit on the woman he planned to marry in another two weeks. With Gray's help, Michael had illegally tapped Willoughby's private line in his office, intercepting the call to the hit man who had given April the lethal dose that had ended her young life.

A master of disguises, Merrick Grayslake had gained entrance to Willoughby's office by impersonating a heating and ventilation technician checking thermostats. It had taken him less than thirty seconds to place the tap and get out undetected.

They'd traced the call to a thug who had earned a reputation for making people change their minds during union contract negotiations. Merrick had surprised the man early one morning when he kicked open his door and injected him with a syringe filled with sodium amytal before he had a chance to recognize who'd stuck him. The serum had worked quickly, and within twenty minutes, Merrick had all the information on Stanley Willoughby and April Stansfield's whereabouts.

Merrick had driven the unconscious man to a remote area in West Virginia and left him, while Michael had called Detective Kevin Sutton to tell him where to find April's body.

Holding Jolene, Michael listened while she poured her heart out, telling him everything about her sessions with April. She told him of her visit to Stanley Willoughby and his pompous reaction to her accusation.

"It's going to be all right, Jolene. April did not die in vain. The man responsible for causing her so much pain will pay for his crime and his sins."

Staring up at the man she had fallen in love with, she managed a sad smile. "You sound so sure."

"Everything in this universe is balanced: black and white, good and bad, right and wrong. The man will not go unpunished."

Sighing heavily, her smile widened. "I hope you're right."

I know I'm right. What he couldn't tell Jolene was how he was going to make Willoughby pay.

"Hungry?"

"Starved," she countered.

"You know, we only have two weeks before the wedding."

"I still have to buy a dress."

"When do you plan on shopping for one?"

"Tomorrow. Will you come with me?"

"Of course."

Curving her arms around his neck, she nuzzled his cheek. "Maybe I'll only work half a day. Perhaps I can convince someone I love to take me out to lunch before I go and look at something that will fit my rapidly changing body."

Placing a hand over her belly, he smiled. "I like your belly."

"It's not only my belly. It's also my breasts and behind. I turn a corner and the rest of me still hasn't caught up."

"After dinner, I'm going to bathe you, then give you my special massage. And if you don't fall asleep on me, I'll show you how much I like your belly, breasts, and your very delectable behind."

She gave him a sassy smile. "Is that a promise?"

Kissing the tip of her nose, he said, "I'm even willing to put it in writing."

"You just made me an offer I can't refuse."

Michael stood up, cradling her to his chest. He'd missed her. Even though they'd shared a bed every night since their return from New Mexico, Jolene wouldn't let him make love to her. Whenever he asked if something was wrong, she'd tell him that she was tired. She was tired, and he resigned himself to taking cold showers. But there were nights the showers failed to ease the throbbing hardness, so he lay awake for hours, listening to her soft snores. When he finally did fall asleep it was time for her to get up.

"Are you sure you're going to give me some tonight?"

She wrinkled her nose at him. "What do you mean by giving you *some*?"

"You know what I mean."

"No, I don't, Michael Blanchard Kirkland."

"Yes, you certainly do, Miss Jolene Walker."

"No, I certainly don't," she crooned.

His hand moved up her skirt, gathering fabric. His fingers grazed her nylon-covered thigh. Anchoring his thumb in the elastic waistband to her pantyhose, he pulled down the panty and cradled her heat in his palm.

"This is *some*!"

Jolene slapped playfully at his hand, but his fingers caught in the nylon, tearing the threads.

Her eyes widened. "You ripped my pantyhose."

Moving quickly, Michael raced up the staircase, Jolene several steps behind him. He grabbed her as she raced into the bedroom, lifting her off her feet and carrying her over to the bed.

Mouths, tongues, and hands were busy as they undressed each other. Torn pantyhose, April Stansfield, Stanley Willoughby, and the clients at the Sanctuary ceased to exist as they came together in a joining that swept away all of the world's ugliness.

Michael loved her long, yet gently, mindful of the gift in

her womb. His control broke completely when she wrapped her long legs around his waist, holding him fast. Their dammed-up passion broke, sending them on a magical trip to another galaxy.

They lay side by side, holding hands. Jolene did not want to move, but she had to. "Michael?"

"Yes." His voice was still heavy from a lingering passion that continued to simmer in his groin.

"I have to get up and eat."

"Would you mind if I ordered in?"

"Not at all."

Releasing her hand, he turned over and picked up the telephone. He told the woman answering the phone that he was willing to pay extra if they rushed it.

Jolene pressed a kiss along his straight spine, inching down his back until her tongue traced the outline of the tattooed dragon. Michael jumped off the bed as if she'd burned him.

His pale gaze glittered like bits of glass. "Don't do that."

Suddenly she remembered another time when she'd kissed him in the same spot and he'd lost control. A knowing smile curved her mouth. She'd discovered the most vulnerable part of his body.

"Come, lover. Let me taste your dragon. Does it breathe fire?"

Her laughter followed him as he stalked to the bathroom and slammed the door, locking it behind him.

Jolene sat in the middle of the bed, laughing hysterically. She laughed until her side hurt, forcing her up to find a bathroom where she could relieve herself.

Thirty-six

Michael opened the passenger-side door for Jolene. His fingers gripped her waist as he swung her down to the ground. "I'll be back to pick you up at 12:30."

Smiling up at him, she said, "I'll be ready. Now, kiss me."

Needing no further prompting, he lowered his head, pulling her against his length, sampling and tasting what she so willingly offered him. His tongue slipped between her parted lips, igniting the smoldering flames that refused to go out.

Their passionate coupling of the night before had been repeated as pinpoints of light pierced the early-morning sky. This encounter had left them shaking uncontrollably, and it had been more than half an hour before either was able to leave the bed. They'd stripped one another bare, leaving each naked and vulnerable.

Jolene eased back, her gaze fusing with Michael's. There was something about his expression that was so strange that she found him vaguely disturbing.

"Are you all right?"

"Yes," he replied a little too quickly. "Go," he urged softly. "I'll wait here until you're in."

Leaning forward, she kissed his clean-shaven cheek. Then she turned and made her way to the rear entrance to the Sanctuary. The light went on in her office, and minutes later he drove in the direction of downtown D.C.

Michael found a parking space two blocks from Stanley Willoughby's office. Turning up the collar to his lined black leather jacket, he ducked his head into the wind as he walked casually along the sidewalk. There was no need to rush. He was scheduled to meet Kevin Sutton before he finally came face-to-face with the man who'd hired someone to kill Jolene and April Stansfield. And he was willing to bet that Willoughby was responsible for at least another murder—that of Preston James.

He planned for the man's reign of terror to come to a quiet end in another hour. That was, if Willoughby preferred it that way. Otherwise, it was certain to be played out in the press, and the celebrated attorney would live out the remainder of his life disgraced. Michael would offer him an option. After all, it was more than he'd offered April or Jolene. It would have to end today, because he did not intend to begin his life with Jolene with threats following her and his unborn child.

He saw the van parked across the street from the offices of Willoughby, Strauss, Young, and Sutherland. He knocked on the side door, and it opened to reveal Kevin Sutton's impassive expression.

"Get in."

Michael climbed into the van and the door quickly closed behind him. "Has he arrived?" he asked, nodding to the two other police officers in the van.

Kevin forced a smile. "He came in ten or fifteen minutes ago."

Unzipping his jacket, Michael shrugged it off. His gaze swept over the electronic surveillance equipment sitting between the front and rear seats.

Lifting the front of his black cashmere mock turtleneck sweater, he bared his chest. "I'm ready."

A police department technician opened a bag, withdrawing the wires and a minute microphone. He'd convinced Kevin to let him wear a wire when he met with Willoughby. As a licensed attorney, he was familiar with entrapment, and reassured the homicide detective he would be able to elicit a confession from Willoughby that would stand up in court.

"Sir, could you please remove your firearm?"

Michael gave the man a cold, lethal stare. "It stays."

The technician looked for support to Kevin, who said, "Let him keep it."

After being wired, followed by a sound check, Michael left the van and strolled to the entrance of the two-story building housing the offices of Stanley Willoughby and his partners.

Opening the door, he stepped into the reception area. The receptionist wasn't in her position behind the glass partition. It wasn't quite 8:30, probably too early for the woman to begin her workday.

He turned the knob on the door leading to the inner offices, finding it unlocked. A smile tilted the corners of his mouth. He was still smiling when he stopped at the door to Stanley Willoughby's office and rapped lightly on the open door.

Stanley heard the knock, his head coming up quickly while his gaze narrowed. "Who are you?" he asked in a quiet voice.

Leaning against the door, Michael folded his arms over

his chest and crossed one booted foot over the other. "I'm the cowboy you've been looking for."

Stanley rose slowly to his feet, the color draining from his face, leaving it a ghostly gray. So, he thought, this was Jolene Walker's bodyguard. He had to admit he looked formidable: tall, broad-shouldered, and dressed entirely in black. But the man had to be a fool to come to his office, on his turf. Did he really believe he could intimidate him?

"How did you get in here?"

"I walked."

"What do you want?"

Michael pushed off the door, closing it behind him. He made his way across the room, stopping on the other side of Willoughby's desk. "I want to know why you've placed a hit on Jolene Walker."

Stanley noticed his eyes for the first time. They were a pale cold green, the color incongruent with his khaki-brown face. "I don't know what you're talking about. I don't know this . . . this Jolene Walker."

"You're a liar, Willoughby. She came to see you yesterday. She spoke to you about a young woman who had been a client of hers. That client *was* your ward."

Pulling himself up to his full height of five-eight, Stanley effected an expression of innocence. "I still don't know what you're talking about, Mr.—"

"Cowboy," Michael said with a feral grin.

His flippant response shattered Stanley's composure. Reaching down, he pressed a button on a small box. "Get in here!"

Less than a minute later, Steven Miller rushed into the room. He stopped up short when he recognized the man with his boss. Fear rendered him motionless and speechless.

"Please show this gentleman out of the building."

The law clerk's face quivered as he wagged his head from side to side. "But, Mr. Willoughby . . ."

Reaching around his back, Michael pulled the small automatic from beneath his jacket. He cradled it in a two-hand grip, his gaze never leaving Willoughby's face.

"I want both of you to sit down. Over here," he ordered Steven. He motioned where the law clerk should sit. "Now!" The two men sat down in unison. He took a step and straddled a corner of the large desk.

"I wanted to conduct this interview without a witness," he began in a soft tone, "but since you wanted your subordinate to throw me out of your office, Mr. Willoughby, you'll have to suffer the ultimate humiliation of having him hear all about your sordid lifestyle."

Closing his eyes, Stanley slumped against the leather back of his executive chair. The tic tortured his right eye, sending sharp pains shooting through the orb.

"Look, Mr. Kirkland . . ." His words trailed off when he realized his faux pas.

Angling his head, Michael smiled. "So, you do know who I am."

"And it's apparent you don't know who *I am*."

"I know exactly who you are. You're a sick twisted punk who raped a twelve-year-old girl, turned her onto drugs, beat her senseless whenever the mood hit you, and then killed her when she told Miss Walker about you."

Steven Miller gasped, his eyes widening as he stared at his boss. His jaw worked spasmodically, but he wasn't able to get the words stuck in his throat out.

Smiling, Stanley waved a manicured hand. "I'm going to give you exactly one minute to walk out of here, or I'm going to call the police and have you removed for trespassing. And if you're lucky, I won't have you charged with threatening me and my law clerk with a dangerous weapon."

Michael reached into a pocket of his jacket with his right hand and withdrew a mini tape recorder. Leaning forward, he held his thumb over a button. "What's on this tape won't take a minute. It's a telephone conversation between you and a man. Listen carefully, and I think you'll recognize the voice." He pressed the button, and Stanley's voice was heard saying, "I've got a job for you. The social worker just won an all-expense-paid trip for a wonderful cruise to nowhere."

Again, Stanley's face lost its natural color. "That could be anyone's voice."

"But it's not anyone's voice. It's yours. And the man to whom you made that call is willing to testify in a court of law that you paid him to kill Jolene Walker. He'll also testify that he was paid to inject April Stansfield with enough pure heroin to kill more than half a dozen people. Do you want to hear his confession? That's the next selection on this tape."

Stanley felt his world closing in on him. How had Michael Kirkland gotten that tape? Had he tapped his telephone, and if he had, when had he done it?

"It's illegal to tap a phone without a court order."

"And what you did to April was not only illegal, but immoral."

"I did nothing to her but take care of her."

"You call raping her taking care of her?"

"I didn't rape her!" Stanley shouted.

"Are you saying she came to you willingly?"

"She seduced me."

Michael arched an eyebrow. He'd gotten Willoughby to admit that he had slept with the girl. "Seduced you, how?"

Willoughby took a furtive look at Steven Miller, who sat motionless, his mouth gaping. "I don't want him to hear this."

Michael nodded. He waved the gun in the clerk's direction. "You can go, but don't call the police. Disobey my orders and I'm going to pop your boss."

Pushing off the chair, Steve rushed from the room, saying, "I'll do as you say."

Once the door closed softly, Michael put the gun down on the desk where he could reach it quickly. He glared at the arrogant man staring back at him. "You're saying that she seduced you?"

"She told me that she was tired of being a virgin and that she wanted to know what it felt like to be a woman."

"How old was she when you first slept with her?"

Stanley shrugged a shoulder under his custom-made shirt. "I don't remember."

Reaching out, Michael caught the front of his shirt and pulled him across the desk. "This cowboy's going to put his spurs so far up your ass that it will look like you have braces on your teeth. Lie to me again, Willoughby, and I'm going to hurt you real bad."

"She was eighteen."

Michael picked him up and threw him against a wall. And before he could recover, he grabbed him again. "Wrong answer," he growled against his pale face.

"Seventeen," Stanley hissed between clenched teeth.

Michael hauled him several feet, then flung him against the opposite wall. A large painting fell to the floor, glass and wood littering the carpet.

A burning rage shook Michael as he forced himself not to put his hands around the man's neck. "How old, Stanley?"

"Fifteen."

"Wrong!" His voice bounced off the wall seconds before the trembling lawyer made contact with the last remaining wall. "One more wrong answer and you're going through the window."

Stanley Willoughby saw his own death in the near-colorless green eyes. There was no way he could defend himself against a man who was a full head taller and probably outweighed him by at least thirty pounds.

He couldn't believe it. He, Stanley Warwick Willoughby, godfather to the president's son, bullied by a renegade soldier. He had come into his office, mugging him like a crackhead on a rampage.

Michael picked Stanley up, holding him above his head as he walked toward the large plate-glass window. Tightening his grip around the back of his neck, he lifted him higher.

"Stop! Please don't. Don't kill me. I'll talk, but please don't kill me."

Michael's sigh of relief echoed his captor's. He wouldn't have thrown the man through the glass, but he was prepared to beat him senseless if he had to.

Flinging him down to a leather sofa as if he were a rag doll, he stood over him. "Talk."

Stanley told everything. From Holly Stansfield offering her daughter for money, to his raping and beating the child whenever she refused his advances. He confessed to contracting for someone to kill Jolene and April. It was when he talked about Holly Stansfield that he broke down completely, sobbing like a child.

"I loved her. I loved her when she never loved me."

Michael didn't wait to hear anymore. He had gotten enough on the tape. He knew he'd used excessive force to get the confession, but he didn't care. Even if Stanley Willoughby wasn't charged with rape and murder, it no longer mattered, because the man had been toppled from his throne by a social worker who'd risked her life to save an abused young woman.

He walked out of the building, coming face-to-face with Kevin Sutton. Pulling up his sweater, he removed the hidden microphone, handing it to the homicide detective. "I didn't play fair, but you heard what you need to arrest him."

Kevin gave Michael a level stare. "I don't know how much will hold up in court, but I'm going to try and convince the DA not to let him off because your methods were a little unorthodox.''

''I never hit him, but I'm willing to bet he's going to experience real pain in a couple of hours. And the pain will be nothing compared to what he did to that child.''

Kevin patted Michael's shoulder. ''Thanks. Now, let me go in and read this animal his rights before I haul his butt outta here. Thanks again. Paige and I will see you and Jolene on the thirtieth.''

''You bet.'' Jolene had asked Paige to be her matron of honor. Her brother, Damon, had agreed to be his best man.

Kevin walked into the law firm while Michael walked the two blocks to where he'd parked his car. As he drove back to Georgetown, he felt a sense of relief sweep over him. He didn't know if Willoughby would enlist the support of his influential friends, but instinct told him that the man was finished in Washington. He had admitted on tape to his own addiction to prescription drugs. He'd also confessed to using the money from April Stansfield's trust fund for contributions to several political campaigns. He'd broken enough laws to be charged with at least one or two crimes, but what Michael did not want was for him to walk away a free man. He had to pay for his crimes and for his sins.

Thirty-seven

Michael had admitted to Gabriel that whenever he was with Jolene he found it virtually impossible to maintain his self-control, and it was about to happen again. In less than twenty-four hours, he and Jolene would become husband and wife.

The hum of conversation and laughter floated around him, but his thoughts were not with the crowd mingling in the library at the Coles' West Palm Beach estate, but on the news program he'd viewed earlier that evening. The press had interviewed the president, eliciting his reaction to his best friend being charged with misconduct of his discretionary authority over his ward's trust fund. Stanley Willoughby had accepted a plea bargain to spend two years in jail for larceny. The man was responsible for two, and perhaps three deaths, and all he had to give up was two years of freedom. Prosecutors were disappointed because, despite the taped confession, a judge had ruled they did not have enough concrete evidence to charge him with statutory rape and manslaughter. Where was the justice? he thought. His head came up when he heard someone calling his name.

Clayborne Spencer tapped his watch. "You have exactly twenty-two hours to change your mind."

Michael smiled at Regina and Aaron's son, shaking his head. "Forget it, *primo*. I'm not backing out." Jolene had retired for bed hours ago, while he retreated to the library to celebrate what had become a mock bachelor party.

"If he backs out, I'll marry her," Jason Cole said quickly.

"She's too old for you," Michael told David Cole's youngest son.

Jason, the mirror image of his older brother, Gabriel, minus the pierced lobes, flashed a wolfish grin reminiscent of his father's. "I like older women."

"At twenty-three, what do you know about women?"

"Enough," Jason said proudly.

"Hey, David, it looks like one of your offspring is thinking about marriage," Joshua Kirkland said teasingly. "Maybe you'll get a grandchild before you're seventy-five."

It had become a topic of good-natured teasing between David and his older brothers whenever they taunted him about his children's reluctance to marry. Gabriel, Alexandra, and fraternal twins, Ana and Jason—ages thirty-two, twenty-eight, and twenty-three, respectively—had indicated, to their parents' dismay, that they weren't ready to settle down. All four thought of themselves as free spirits.

At sixty-seven, David Cole was a strikingly handsome senior citizen. His once-raven hair was now completely silver. His deeply tanned olive skin radiated good health. He glared at his half-brother. "You got something to say, brother?"

Tall, elegant, and still slender, Joshua Kirkland lounged on a silk-covered chair, a rare smile curving his strong mouth. His pure white hair shimmered under recessed lighting like newly fallen snow under dappled sunlight, and the light green eyes he'd passed along to his daughter, son, and grandson twinkled with the smile.

"Yeah, brother. What's up with your kids?"

David's mouth tightened, twin dimples deepening in his cheeks. "If that firewater you're drinking is responsible for you talking smack, then I'll excuse you, *brotha*!"

Seventy-nine-year-old Martin Cole, the family's reigning patriarch, tapped his sister-in-law's shoulder to get her attention, then whispered in her ear. Petite, sultry-looking Serena Morris-Cole walked over to David, slipping her arm through her husband's. "You got something to say about my children, Mr. Joshua *no-middle-name* Kirkland?"

The entire room erupted in laughter. Joshua was the only one in the family who did not claim a middle name.

Holding up his hand, Joshua signaled that he'd been bested. "You win," he said, laughing loudly. Rising to his feet, he extended his arms. Serena walked into his embrace, her head coming only to his shoulder.

Her clear brown eyes were smiling. "Even though you're a pompous, arrogant snob, I still love you."

"And I you," he whispered, brushing his mouth over hers.

Michael smiled at his father's antics. It wasn't often that the man allowed himself to relax completely, and it was apparent that both Kirkland men were not as controlled as they would like to believe they were.

He and Jolene were scheduled to exchange vows at exactly eleven P.M. the following evening. They'd come to Florida a week before, joining the many descendants of Samuel and Marguerite Cole who came to West Palm Beach to celebrate Christmas, the one-hundredth birthday of the family matriarch, and the nuptials between Miss Jolene Walker and Michael Blanchard Kirkland. They'd come one by one, as couples, trios, and large groups, until the twenty-four-room mansion containing four apartment suites built by Samuel

Cole for his wife and four legitimate children overflowed with five generations.

Michael met Jolene's parents, Oliver and Frances Walker, who warmly welcomed him as a son. He was equally drawn to the elegant middle-aged couple responsible for producing the exquisite woman with whom he'd fallen in love. Joshua and Vanessa had opened their Palm Beach home to the elder Walkers, the two couples bonding as if they'd known one another for years.

Leaning over, Michael whispered in his mother's ear that he was going to bed. Vanessa placed a hand alongside his jaw, kissing him.

"Good night and sleep well."

He stared down into her large dark eyes. It was only after he saw his mother and Jolene together that he realized that he had fallen in love with a woman who reminded him of his mother.

"I'll try."

Vanessa watched her son's retreating back as he walked out of the library. She and Joshua had done well. Their children had done very well. A smile lit up her face as she watched her husband hug David's wife. It had taken thirty-eight years of marriage and the promise of another grandchild to get Joshua to let go of his iron-willed control—out of bed. At seventy-six and seventy-one respectively, some of the passion had waned, but their love for each other knew no bounds, and she suspected it would be the same for her son and his bride.

Jolene felt as if all eyes were on her as her father led her down the flower-strewn carpeted path within the brightly lit Japanese garden at the Cole family estate. Her gaze was fixed on the man standing next to Damon McDonald. As she neared him, his eyes spoke to her, saying, *Come to me, my love, my darling.*

A warm breeze lifted the skirt of an overcoat of Alençon lace embroidered with pearls and beads, molding it to her ripening body before settling back around her ankles. A simple empire strapless sheath of four-ply crepe shimmered like liquid through the lacy coat. She'd opted for an off-white shade. Paige wore a similar design in a deep forest green. A circlet of tiny white roses and baby's breath took the place of a veil. Her bouquet contained a profusion of snow-white and deep pink roses held together with streamers of green velvet ribbon. Alejandro and Esperanza Delgado, along with Isaiah, Nona, and Eve Lassiter, stood motionless off to the side, their gazes filled with amazement as they watched their Aunt Jolene and her father move closer.

Michael turned around to face her, his lips twitching in a smile. Her impending motherhood made her lush, alluring. A swell of breasts rose above the modest neckline of her dress, the lower part of his body betraying his lust for the woman who was scheduled to deliver his son or daughter in another six months. He'd fallen in love with her in one garden and would marry her in another one.

The weather had cooperated, the nighttime temperature in the low sixties. The shimmering light from a full moon competed with the portable spotlights illuminating the garden and the space set aside for dining and dancing. Cushioned folding chairs, numbering one hundred and ninety, held family, friends, and business associates.

Most of the staff from the Sanctuary had come for the wedding, along with Claire and Walter McDonald. Bobby Ridgewell had come with Deborah Madison clinging to his arm. Merrick Grayslake had arrived unescorted, and was quickly surrounded by most of the single women who wanted to know who he was and what he did for a living. Michael shook his head when he overheard the man make up a story so plausible that he almost believed it himself.

Oliver Walker came beside Michael Kirkland and placed his daughter's hand on his outstretched one. The two men shared a knowing wink moments before Oliver stepped back and returned to sit beside his wife, who dabbed her eyes with a lace-edged handkerchief.

Jolene smiled up at Michael, silently admiring his close-cropped black hair on his well-shaped head. She took in the stark-white wing collar and dark green silk bowtie against his brown throat, a matching green satin waistcoat, and the meticulous tailoring of the tuxedo gracing his tall, muscular body.

She held his hand, staring deeply into his eyes as the soft sound of a guitar punctuated the silent night. Her eyes filled with tears as she listened to Gabriel's rich baritone voice singing "True Companion."

Michael sang softly under his breath as Gabriel began the third verse.

Tears blurred Michael's gaze when the song ended. He prayed he would not break down completely before he repeated his vows.

"Let's do it *quick*," he whispered to the judge waiting to begin the ceremony that would wed him to the woman at his side.

The judge nodded, and ten minutes later, after an exchange of vows and rings, he presented Mr. and Mrs. Michael Kirkland to their invited guests and the world.

Jolene wound her arms around her husband's neck, glorying in the feel of his mouth on hers. She gasped audibly when he swept her up in his arms and carried along the carpet, then spun her around and around to the sound of thunderous applause.

"Michael!"

He stopped, grinning at her. "Yes, Mrs. Kirkland?"

Tightening her grip on his strong neck, she kissed him again. "Congratulations, Mr. Kirkland. Happy New Year."

Gently lowering her satin-covered feet to the ground, he cradled her against his length. "Congratulations to you, too. I think we'd better greet our guests so they can get this party started."

They hugged and kissed their parents, then stood in a receiving line to thank everyone for coming to celebrate their very special day. They planned to spend the night at a hotel in West Palm Beach before flying down to Ocho Rios later that afternoon.

Joshua and Vanessa had given them an envelope with their names written across the front. Michael opened it, read the document, and then handed it to her. They had given them the deed to the house on Ocho Rios as a wedding gift.

She'd become a part of the legacy of which Salem Lassiter had spoken. She'd dared to risk everything for love and had won.

Epilogue

The pains came, faster and harder. Jolene gripped Michael's hand, praying. She prayed for the pain to stop and for her baby to be born. The bright light in the delivery room nearly blinded her whenever she opened her eyes.

Dr. Tyler Cole hovered between her legs. "It's coming, Jolene. I see hair—lots of dark hair."

Jolene and Michael had decided they did not want to know the sex of the baby beforehand. They'd selected names: Joshua Michael if it was a boy, and Teresa April if it was a girl.

"Don't push until I tell you to," Tyler ordered. He waited for another contraction. "Push, Jolene. That's good. The shoulders are out."

He turned the baby's head gently, and then pulled out a trembling little girl. His dark eyes crinkled above his surgical mask. "It's a girl. Welcome to the world, Mistress Teresa April Kirkland."

Working quickly, he slapped the baby's bottom. A loud

wavering cry filled the room. Leaning over his wife, Michael kissed her parched lips. Her labor had been long and difficult, but she had insisted on going through natural childbirth.

Tyler cut and clamped the umbilical cord, suctioned his tiny cousin's nose and mouth, then handed her to Dr. Aaron Spencer, who washed the perfectly formed baby, then weighed and measured and checked her reflexes before he wrapped her in a blanket and presented her to her parents.

Jolene smiled at her daughter. She was beautiful, more beautiful that she could've ever imagined. She was truly her father's daughter. In fact, she looked like her aunt, Emily Kirkland-Delgado.

Michael stared at his daughter, unable to believe she was now a reality. He stared mutely as Jolene placed her to her breast. The tiny pink mouth began sucking, but stopped when she fell asleep. She was tired and her mother was tired.

They would remain in the hospital for several days before he brought them home. He had two months before he began his new position as an instructor at a small military school in Virginia.

After he and Jolene had returned to Georgetown after a weeklong honeymoon in Ocho Rios, he'd made a monumental decision: He would end his military career. He'd been interviewed at two military schools, and he'd decided on the one in Virginia, because he would be able to come home every day. He was scheduled to teach two courses: military law and history.

Running his fingers through the damp curls on his wife's head, he smiled at her. "Thank you for making my life so complete."

Sighing, Jolene nodded. She was exhausted and very, very happy. Closing her eyes, she drifted off to sleep, holding her daughter to her breasts. It had taken less than a year for her to realize her dreams. The Jeanine Walker Retreat House was nearing completion, April's abuser had met an untimely death when he'd overdosed on pills in his prison cell, and the man she loved and married finally admitted that he'd fallen in love with her the instant he saw her.

What he didn't know was that she'd felt the same.

Maybe one day she would tell him.

Then ... maybe not until they celebrated their fiftieth wedding anniversary!

Dear Readers:

Michael and Jolene have taken their final bows in the first book of the Hideaway Sons and Brothers Trilogy, joining the others in their generation of sexy, sophisticated Kirklands, Delgados, Lassiters, and Coles who dare risk everything for love.

Dr. Tyler Cole will continue the legacy in November 2002 when he encounters a woman in the Mississippi Delta who will pull him into a daring game of deception as they struggle to trust each other to capture a love that promises forever.

I thank all of you for your ongoing support as I strive to bring you the characters and plots you have come to expect from me.

Peace,
Rochelle Alers

P.O. Box 690
Freeport, NY 11520-0690
roclers@aol.com
www.rochellealers.com

SIZZLING ROMANCE BY
ROCHELLE ALERS